The Dragon Universe

Space is vast. Earth bound humans have little perception of how big it is.

Within 50 light-years of Earth are about 64 stars similar to Earth's sun, Sol. More than 500 reside out to 100 light-years. At 500 light-years the count becomes 64,000. For all types of stars, not just stars similar to Sol, the count at 500 light-years is at least a couple of million.

Planets reside around those stars. Some of those planets are inhabitable. Some are inhabited. In Earth's northern sky is a swath of stars that are home to an old species of interstellar explorers. They refer to their region of the Milky Way as *The Dragon Universe*.

Some believe long ago those explorers visited Earth thus giving rise to dragon myths, and when they pointed to the region of the sky from whence they came, that part of the sky became associated with dragons. And thus, today, some of us call that constellation *Draco*.

There are many stories out there in *The Dragon Universe*. This story is one of them.

The Dragon Universe

Utopia Origins

**There is no friend
who is a better friend
than a dragon friend.**

The Dragon Universe

Utopia Origins

Lester D. Crawford

Dracotation

Dedication

To my mother, Doris, who did everything in her power to encourage and enable my interests in science and technology and science fiction and fantasy, and for tolerating my precocious nature and the experiments I conducted in my "lab."

Contents

The Dragon Universe

Utopia Origins

Prelude

The town was awesome. Humans and dragons everywhere, living together, working together, thriving together. The streets were wide, paved, and clean in the bustling business district and in the residential neighborhoods. Many houses had what I at first thought were excessively large attached garages. However, when I saw a dragon come out of one, I realized the garages were dragon weyrs. Some houses that didn't have room next to them had a weyr built on stilts as an additional story. Landing and takeoff pads for dragons were everywhere. Dragons flew past overhead as often as they passed by walking down the street. And, people were everywhere, coming and going, exuberant in everything they did, and often in the company of a dragon.

I said, "I've never seen a world like this. It's Utopia. How did you do it?"

A half dozen dragon hatchlings and human children ran past heading for a playground festooned with play structures, some suitable for hatchlings, some suitable for children, and some suitable for both to play together.

My tour guide laughed and said, "We're far from being a utopia — we have our problems — but I can tell you about a few of the courageous heroes, both people and dragons, who challenged their societies' beliefs and in so doing changed the world."

Part One
Paladins

Prologue

Dragon war. Generations of dragon war. Like the dragon-slayer knights who came before him, Patrick had had his share of battles with dragons, driving them away *to protect families, communities, and all people*. But, dragons had become rare. Seeking them to attack had become an expensive, resource-consuming endeavor with no benefits.

The time had come for the dragon-slayer knights to take on a new mission, a mission of defense rather than offense. Patrick had a plan; however, his plan was being thwarted. He was weary of having his efforts blocked, but he was not yet willing to give up.

Chapter 1
Quietest of Whispers

Patrick paced a circle around the room, agitated after a day of conflicts with his peers. He needed to shove it away, calm his mind, and restore his spirit.

He paused at the chessboard to study the status of the game. The chess set was a work of art fashioned from exotic wood. Two shades made the board and elegantly carved pieces. A different shade made the frame. He loved strategy games like chess, and Miyuki was a formidable opponent at such games. It was her move and she would bring that move tonight. She and he sharing the evening meal and conversation always brightened his mood.

A knock with a special, familiar pattern came at the door. That knock pattern always made Patrick feel bouncy. Opening the door revealed a smiling Miyuki dressed in shirt and trousers the same dark brown as her clever eyes with hem, sleeves, and collar trimmed in the bright yellow of honeystar flowers that matched her personality. Slung over her shoulder was the ruby red pack she always carried.

Patrick said, "Doctor Miyuki."

Miyuki said, "Colonel Patrick."

Chin held high, she strode to the chessboard, moved a piece, and gave him a fiendish grin.

He cocked his head and said, "Hmm. That will require some thinking for how to respond." He recorded the move on his score sheet. Miyuki had an identical board at her home, and a score sheet, so they could continue their game regardless of who visited whom. "In the meantime, it's mealtime." He led her into the dining room. "For tonight's meal, I acquired two hearty servings of today's special from Amala's Eatery."

Miyuki grinned. "What was today's special?"

"Roast, steamed rattidash root, buttery rolls, jancy berry pie, and to top it off, mugs of draust."

Patrick and Miyuki had practically been siblings since childhood even though they weren't related. As children growing up in the Village of Grandized, neither had felt they fit in with the other children, but in each other, they had found kindred spirits who longed for intellectual adventures and challenges.

Miyuki took her accustomed seat, putting her pack on the floor next to her. Patrick retrieved the food from the hot box, stepped around the pack, and served. The delicious aroma that filled the room made him realize how hungry he was.

Miyuki said, "How's work?"

"Horrible."

"Why's that?"

"Colonel Leena is doing everything she can to undercut me, Colonel Tyson halfheartedly sides with her, and General Nola is apathetic about doing anything about anything."

"What are you going to do?"

"Keep trying. Changing the dragon-slayer knights' mission is the right thing to do. I just need to get everyone else to follow that path with me."

Miyuki said, "Change begins with the actions of a few, and with the quietest of whispers. I bet you're yelling at them."

"I'm not yelling at them."

"They feel like you are, and yelling triggers people to stand fast against what you're saying."

Patrick sighed. "You're right, as always. But, I don't think I can whisper." He again sidestepped the pack to sit in his seat. "Why do you always bring your pack to our evening meals?"

"It's my medical pack."

"But, why here?"

"I have nightmares."

"What sort of nightmares?"

She picked up her spoon and looked at her reflection. "I dream I'm somewhere and something happens and someone calls out 'Is there a doctor in the house?' and I don't have my medical pack with me. So, I keep it with me at all times."

"Does that help with the nightmares?"

"No, I still have the nightmares."

Patrick giggled.

Miyuki put the spoon down. "It's not funny."

"I'm not laughing at your nightmares. Do you know the name of my warhorse?"

"No."

"Her name is *Knight-Mare.*"

Miyuki's smile warmed Patrick's heart.

Patrick and Miyuki had spent years apart. Patrick's path had led him to being an officer in the dragon-slayer knights while Miyuki's path had taken her to medical school and a career as a doctor.

Recently, their paths had crossed again when Miyuki accepted an opportunity at the medical clinic in the City of Imperium, the location of the Dragon-Slayer Academy and the seat of the intercounty government, the Council of Counties, of the Lurean River Valley. They had never lost contact with each other, and in their regular exchange of letters, they always included a chess move.

Miyuki had not informed Patrick she had arrived — she had wanted to settle in before contacting him. When Patrick encountered her in the market, it had been a joyful surprise. Their face-to-face relationship had continued where they had left it when they followed their separate paths upon entering adulthood.

Patrick had needed his lifelong friend. These evenings when they talked and she shared her wisdom and calm demeanor helped him cope, help he needed now more than ever. They spent the remainder of the evening before Miyuki returned to her home sharing food, drink, and conversation.

Chapter 2
Why Was I Not Included

As was his normal morning routine, Patrick sat at his desk doing paperwork. He was reviewing the budget to be discussed at an upcoming meeting when he noticed line items for food provisioning used only during a campaign against dragons. The orders had been added and executed since the last time he had reviewed the budget. That couldn't be right. He would have been involved in the meeting if a new campaign had been planned.

Patrick went to the War Room to study the huge battle map on the table that filled the center of the room. The map showed the entire Lurean River Valley and extended into the mountains on either side. The valley was detailed, but large areas of the mountain wilderness were sparse in specifics.

Aslan entered, froze, and then said, "Colonel Patrick."

"Captain Aslan. What do you have there?"

"Nothing."

Patrick stared at him.

"Colonel Leena told me to file it."

"Please, hand it over."

"Yes, Colonel Patrick."

The report contained details about knight movements.

"Why isn't the battle map up to date?"

"Colonel Leena told me not to bother with the map, just file the reports."

Patrick checked the filing cabinet, found a folder containing several reports, and said, "Thank you, Captain Aslan."

Aslan jumped out of his way as Patrick stormed past.

Without the courtesy of a knock, he barged into Leena's office, slammed the folder down on her desk, opened it, and said, "I had wondered where Colonel Tyson was."

Twirling a lock of her hair in her fingers, Leena glanced at the folder, and said, "Colonel Tyson has taken the Fourth Battalion on a campaign."

"Why was I not included in the planning for this?"

Leena leaned back in her chair. "You would have argued against it."

Jabbing a finger at the papers in the folder, Patrick said, "You also left out Captain Mahtab and Captain Lekan."

"You have contaminated their thinking and they would have sided with you."

"These actions are a transgression of proper process and undermine our rules, norms, and values. You can't sanction me, or my staff, for proposing a new mission for the dragon-slayer knights."

Leena stood. "It's not a sanction. We wanted to proceed without arguing with you."

"Why? This campaign won't find any dragons. They're gone, maybe almost extinct. They're no longer a threat."

Leena came around her desk. "There's more at stake than dragons. The economy depends on campaigns. Recruitment depends on campaigns."

Shaking his head, Patrick said, "Campaigns don't help the economy. The ones who benefit are the brokers between the producers and the Academy. In fact, those resources would be better spent enhancing infrastructure, building more business opportunities, and helping the community." He paused before adding, "The recruitment argument might be valid. Knights want action, but as it is, it's rare to find dragons anymore."

Leena pointed at him. "You have lost your way."

Nola entered the room and said, "What's going on here?"

Leena pointed again and said, "General Nola, Colonel Patrick is upset we held the campaign planning meeting without him."

Nola turned to Patrick. "We left you out because you would have argued against it. We were sending the campaign regardless, so why bother including you in the planning. The Council of Counties and I, as well as Colonel Leena and Colonel Tyson, are satisfied with how things are working. We sent this campaign and we're planning more. We're sticking with it."

"Yes, General Nola." Patrick stormed from the room.

He paced in his office, angry, disappointed, and frustrated, and then realized he was late for his midday meal with Miyuki.

Chapter 3

I've Had Enough

Miyuki already occupied their favorite booth at Amala's Eatery, her red pack in the seat next to her.

"Doctor Miyuki, sorry I'm late."

"Colonel Patrick, you're not late. I'm early."

"Thank you, but we both know that's not true." Patrick pulled a piece of paper from his pocket, handed it to Miyuki, and settled opposite her.

She read it then stared out the window before she turned to him smiling.

Patrick smiled too. "Yes, it's a good move."

"It's a bizarre move."

"Let's see you counter it."

Artisan sandwiches and draust were today's midday meal.

When they finished their sandwiches, Miyuki stared at Patrick, reading him, he knew, then said, "Is work still horrible?"

"It's worse. They dispatched a new campaign without including me, or my staff, in the planning meeting. I've had enough."

"What are you going to do?"

Patrick pushed his empty plate away. "I'm resigning."

Miyuki almost spilled her drink. "You can't. Since you were a child, you've wanted to be a dragon-slayer knight. That was all you ever talked about. You said it was the right thing to do. You'd constantly recite that mantra, or whatever it is: *To protect our families, our communities, and all people.* It's all you ever wanted."

"It's no longer the right thing to do, and I'm not sure it ever was."

She took his hand. "I'm not one to interfere with other's choices, but I think you should take this slowly and give it more thought. You're important to the dragon-slayer knights, and to the Academy. What would they do without you?"

"There are plenty of people who can do my job. They'd manage."

"You underestimate your value. There's a reason why you're the Knight Champion and Lead Strategist."

"They don't listen to me anymore. They say *I've lost my way.*" He sighed. "I need to move on."

Miyuki began to say something more but Aslan interrupted when he rushed into the eatery and to Patrick and Miyuki's booth.

Short of breath, Aslan managed to say, "Colonel Patrick, I have a message for you. It's important." He handed Patrick an envelope and ran back the way he had come.

Patrick broke the envelope's seal, read the contents, and inhaled sharply.

Miyuki said, "What?"

In a haunted whisper Patrick didn't know he had, he said, "Dragons are attacking."

Chapter 4

Dragons Are Attacking

Patrick entered the War Room where members of the command staff and support staff stood in silence around the battle map staring at it.

Leena, who was frantically twirling a lock of her hair, marched to him, and with a mocking tone, said, "They're gone, maybe almost extinct." She pointed at the map. "See what's happening with your no-longer-a-threat dragons, you fool."

The battle map showed three groups of red dragon markers. Six markers covered Grandized, the village closest to Imperium, another six marked Nykall, the second closest village, and a third set of six obscured Atra, the third closest village. A single marker with a diacritical mark indicating a dragon seen in motion and the direction of travel set near Gration Knoll outside of Grandized.

Patrick said, "Is that all that's been reported?"

"That's all that's had time to come in so far, but that's 19 of the monsters," said Leena. "Isn't that enough?"

After reviewing the reports, Patrick said, "It's not 19."

"Sure it is. Count them on your fingers and toes if you have to."

"The timestamps on the reports from Nykall and Atra show that those two thunders of six is the same thunder. When Nykall mustered their resident knights, the thunder fled moving to Atra. Captain Aslan, please, remove the markers from Nykall and make new markers to indicate locations attacked but where the dragons have left."

"Yes, Colonel Patrick." Aslan removed the markers and began fashioning new markers.

"What's the status of our defenses here?"

Nola said, "Captain Odell has the five squads currently at the Academy distributed around the Academy."

"What about Imperium?"

"We don't have any knights out there."

"Please, have Captain Odell assign two of the squads to the city. We need more information, and information from farther out."

Leena said, "That'll take a while."

He faced her nose to nose. "Well, it shouldn't, and it wouldn't, except you blocked my plan for faster communications."

"That plan was to support your foolish idea about watch towers."

To Mahtab, he said. "Captain Mahtab, please, retrieve our communications plan."

"Yes, Colonel Patrick." Mahtab rushed from the room.

"Captain Mahtab's and my communications plan would have added rapid communications, not just for the dragon-slayer knights, but for message services throughout the valley. It would have enhanced dragon-slayer, personal, and business communications everywhere. But, regardless of your opinion, we need rapid communications now."

Mahtab returned and handed Patrick a binder.

He took it and said, "General Nola, we need to implement this."

She waved her hand dismissively and said, "Go ahead."

Patrick handed the binder back to Mahtab and said, "Please, take charge of this. Requisition any resources you need and put it into effect as quickly as possible."

Mahtab took the binder, said, "Yes, Colonel Patrick," and hurried away.

Patrick turned to the battle map. "Where's the Fourth Battalion?"

Aslan said, "This morning's report was the most recent, and it was sent several days ago."

"Please, update the map with what we have. Also, place markers for off duty knights on their home villages."

"Yes, Colonel Patrick." Aslan placed blue markers deep in the eastern mountains almost on the edge of the map and then started spreading more markers across the map on many of the villages.

"Captain Lekan, please, take one of Captain Odell's squads assigned to the Academy and find the Fourth Battalion. Coordinate with Captain Mahtab to create a rapid communications relay. Get us information about what's happened to them."

"Yes, Colonel Patrick." Lekan sprinted from the room.

Leena huffed. "Do you think you're in charge?"

Patrick turned to Nola and said, "I'm sorry, General Nola."

"It's fine." Nola made another dismissive hand wave. "We were kind of stalled before you came in."

Patrick turned to Kalani. "Captain Kalani, what's the status of the infirmary?"

"We're staffed and ready for any casualties that might come in, but so far there's been none reported."

"Good. Doctor Miyuki's activating the city clinic's mass casualty plan, so we have that resource too." Patrick paused to catch his breath. "There's not much more we can do until more information comes in. I'll be in my office. Please, bring me the reports the moment they arrive."

Patrick left the room steeped in apprehension, his instincts screaming impending catastrophe.

Chapter 5
Failed To See the Truth

Patrick slumped at his desk his face buried in his hands. Leena was right: he was a fool. He had failed to see the truth: dragons weren't gone and they weren't almost extinct. Well, if the 13 seen are all of them, they might be almost extinct, but he doubted those were all of them. He assumed dragons were attacking the entirety of the Lurean River Valley. In all the recorded history Patrick knew, dragons had never done anything like that. Something had changed.

From his pocket, he pulled out his knight and stared at it, turning it in his fingers. Miyuki had given him the chess piece on his ninth birthday because all he ever talked about was becoming a dragon-slayer knight. Sculpted from fine marble, the piece had always been shiny and silky, but it was even more so now after years of him fidgeting with it, spinning it in his fingers, and rubbing his thumb on it whenever he sank into deep thought.

He needed to figure out the dragons' strategy and how to counter it. One strategy kept returning to him, a strategy so enticing he couldn't escape it, a strategy he would follow if he were leading the dragons, a strategy that scared him because every counterstrategy he imagined failed thus leading to destruction throughout the valley.

A knock at the door brought Patrick's attention back to his office. He said, "Please, enter," as he returned the knight to its pocket.

Aslan came in with reports. "Two packets arrived — one from the north, one from the south."

"Thank you, Captain Aslan. Please, wait while I review them."

The reports detailed how the villages of Eldum, Splain, and Kaxs to the north, and Delina, Runrill, and Steeckem to the south had been attacked. Adding those to Grandized, Nykall, and Atra made nine villages reporting attacks. The Nekmunnik River Bridge was damaged and unusable. Several sections of the Lurean Road, the main north-south road that ran the length of the Lurean River Valley, were damaged. Every wagon, carriage, and caravan on the road had been destroyed. Several boats navigating the Lurean River were forced onto beaches and then had their hulls stripped off. However, there were still no reports of people or animals being harmed.

The dragons always attacked in thunders of six and would flee when the local dragon-slayer knights tried to engage them. Timestamps still suggested only two thunders were involved. The knights had formed platoons and were pursuing the dragons trying to engage them but without success because, when the knights approached, the dragons would flee to strike somewhere else.

The last set of reports contained observations of a single dragon, the same dragon, who kept flying past first going north, then going south, and then north again. That was interesting, and suspicious.

Giving the reports to Aslan, Patrick said, "Thank you, Captain Aslan. Please, update the map."

After writing a note and sealing it, he went to the War Room where Nola and Leena watched as Aslan updated the map.

Patrick said, "General Nola, Colonel Leena, I'm going into the field to see what's happening first hand. I'll return as soon as I can."

Nola made her dismissive hand wave and said, "Go ahead."

Leena pasted her sneer on her face and said, "Typical."

Patrick ignored her, handed a sergeant the note he had written, and said, "Please, see to it that this is delivered to Doctor Miyuki." He then left to seek information and answers.

Chapter 6
Ride To Grandized

As Patrick rode toward the Village of Grandized, the sun ended the day by flooding the sky with orange. A crescent Mina followed the sun toward the horizon. In its waxing gibbous phase, Echna had already risen and would light the way as Patrick rode through the night.

He wore his full armor, which was remarkably comfortable. Made of Gird-metal, the armor was practically indestructible — even dragon talons, which could cut anything, couldn't cut it. More importantly, weapons made of the metal could penetrate dragon hide, which itself was practically indestructible.

His warhorse, Knight-Mare, also wore Gird-metal armor, but her armor didn't seal as Patrick's did. Clever-Cleaver, his packhorse, wearing no armor, followed behind Knight-Mare. Clever-Cleaver was not intended to be in a battle. His job was to carry supplies and equipment.

The dim moonlight prompted Patrick to adopt a slower pace after Knight-Mare almost stumbled into the first section of damaged road. He didn't want another surprise like that. Each stretch of damaged road required skirting, which would slow traffic and require repairs that would be time and resource consuming.

Part way through the night, Patrick came to a camp next to the road. One of the two people in the camp came out to greet him.

"Good evening, Knight. I'm Relay Rider Hann."

"Good evening, Relay Rider Hann. I'm Colonel Patrick."

"I've heard of you. I'm one of the riders hired by Captain Mahtab for the rapid communications relay network. I'm waiting for the relay rider from Grandized. I'll take the packets to Imperium."

"I'm glad for your help."

"You're invited to stop here for the night."

"No, thank you. I'm continuing on to Grandized."

"Safe journey, then. Watch out for road hazards. There's a significant one up ahead."

"Thank you." Patrick resumed his ride down the road.

An hour later, the remains of several wagons, like bones picked clean, loomed before him. Parts of the wagons were smashed, but most of the wood and iron showed clean cuts typical of dragon talons. There were no people, no horses, and no bodies of people or horses. Patrick hoped that supported the accuracy of the reports that said the dragons weren't harming people or animals. As he passed, he noticed, stacked to either side of the wagon debris, the cargo the wagons had carried, undamaged, as if the dragons had unloaded the wagons before destroying them. That was odd.

The sky glowed pink in the east as Echna slipped below the horizon in the west. Just after the sun had risen, Patrick entered Grandized. What he saw disturbed him.

Chapter 7
Seeking Information and Answers

Knight-Mare and Clever-Cleaver navigated around the damaged road cobbles as they made their way toward the stables. On both sides of the street, outside of houses with holes in their roofs, families with dazed expressions huddled, but they appeared to be persevering as they shared their morning meal. Stacked around them were tools and materials for temporary roof repairs.

As Patrick approached the stables, a relay rider with message packets strapped to her saddle waved as she rode past headed toward Imperium.

The wagon yard contained three demolished wagons and a smashed caravan. The stable building itself was undamaged. Leaving his horses with the hostler, Patrick hurried toward the village's administration building. Along the way, he passed more people gathered outside of damaged buildings. Some waved at him. Children circled him until their parents made them leave him alone.

He overheard a person whisper to their companions, "That's Colonel Patrick, the Knight Champion. He'll stop the dragons." Patrick became self-conscious hearing that. People could tell who he was because his rank and name were written on his armor and clearly visible, if it wasn't too dark.

He felt bad because he hadn't found a strategy to protect these people and their community. He felt bad seeing the destruction that had been inflicted upon the village in which he had grown up. And, he felt bad about things he couldn't even yet define.

The administration building's bell tower lay shattered on the street, the large bell buried in the debris, a bell used to summon villagers to meetings or to warn of dragon attacks, which had never happened before. Sections of the building's roof were gone, but the walls still stood. An armored knight greeted him.

"Colonel Patrick, I'm Sergeant Ovidia."

He smiled though she couldn't see it under his helmet. "I remember you from training. I was impressed with your skills and knowledge."

"Thank you, Colonel Patrick. Please, come inside and I'll update you and turn over command."

"I'm not here to take command."

The sergeant paused as she was turning.

Patrick said, "I've read your reports. You're doing a good job. I'm here to reconnoiter." He looked at the building. "Is this place safe?"

"The master builder assures us the building is stable. We're in a room that still has a roof." She turned, led him inside to an office that buzzed with activity and removed her helmet. "This is our command center." A man broke away from a group standing around a paper-strewn table. "That's Mayor Valent."

Patrick removed his helmet, huffed, and said, "I know Mayor Valent."

"Colonel Patrick." Valent shook Patrick's gauntleted hand. "I haven't seen you in a while."

That had been intentional. Since his parents had passed away, Patrick had had no reason to return. He didn't have fond memories of growing up in Grandized and felt no connection to the place. Valent was one of the reasons for that. Valent had been the biggest, baddest bully in Grandized and had insisted the other children not play with Miyuki and Patrick. Patrick would be happy if he never saw Valent again.

Valent said, "From here, we're coordinating our community response. Sergeant Ovidia is doing an excellent job helping us plan the distribution of food and supplies, and keeping the dragons away."

"I have nothing to do with keeping the dragons away," Ovidia said. "The dragons haven't returned since their initial attack. They went south."

To Ovidia, Patrick said, "What happened to the other two knights mentioned in your reports?"

"I'm sorry I didn't keep a squad, or the almost-a-squad, with me as is normal protocol. I understand the importance of never confronting a dragon alone, but I decided Knight Alex and Knight Kali were better used by joining a platoon to pursue the dragons south."

"That's for the best. With so many other potential targets, the dragons won't be attacking the same place twice, at least for now."

Mealtime chimes rang outside the building.

"That's our improvised warning bell. A dragon's been spotted." Ovidia put on her helmet, picked up her shield, unsheathed her long sword, and exited the building.

Patrick followed as he put on his helmet and drew his long sword. He didn't have his shield since he had left it with the supplies carried by Clever-Cleaver.

Outside, people were dashing into hiding places to cower. Patrick and Ovidia took positions in the middle of the street ready to respond to wherever the dragon landed.

Ovidia said, "I suspect it's the Dragon Paladin again."

"Dragon Paladin?" Patrick echoed.

"That's what we've been calling her. She's a single dragon who flies by, but never attacks. I expect her to be coming from the north."

The wait was short before a dragon raced past west of the village headed south toward the Gration Marshes. The dragon was magnificent, and scary. On her wings were curved streaks of yellow, the yellow indicating she was female since male dragons had no yellow highlights.

Ovidia sheathed her sword. "It's strange, but even as they did all this damage, when the dragons attacked they didn't harm a single person or animal. In fact, they didn't even touch the stables where the horses were. Why is that?"

"I'm sure it's a part of their strategy, but I haven't yet figured out that strategy; although, I have my suspicions." Patrick sheathed his sword. "Reports mention a dragon that keeps flying north and south. That's the dragon in those reports?"

"Yes, Colonel Patrick. She flies the same course several times a day."

"I'm going to check it out."

"I'm sorry I don't have a squad to send with you. Do you wish for me to accompany you?"

"No, you keep up the good work here, Sergeant Ovidia. I'll be fine by myself."

Chapter 8

Enter the Dragon

Patrick headed southwest encouraging Knight-Mare to make good time, but not so fast that Clever-Cleaver couldn't keep up. He needed a place to observe the dragon. Not far outside of Grandized, on the edge of the Gration Marshes, was Gration Knoll. Miyuki and he used to have adventures in the marshes, and the knoll was a favorite spot for a picnic when on those adventures. From there, he would be able to see the course the dragon flew.

At the edge of the knoll, he left Knight-Mare and Clever-Cleaver hidden in a copse of trees, fetched his binoculars from the supplies Clever-Cleaver carried, and climbed to the peak.

It seemed the entire world could be seen from there. To the east, the Nekmunnik River flowed from a deep valley in the Eastern Mountains down to form a delta in the Gration Marshes before spilling into the Lurean River that flowed from north to south down the center of the valley. Using the binoculars, the damage to the bridge that crossed the Nekmunnik was obvious.

Running north and south, parallel to the Lurean River, were terraces cut by the river through the valley in ages long past, each level higher than the previous, climbing like steps to the foothills that abutted the mountains to the east. The same terraced pattern could be seen in the hills on the west side of the Lurean leading to the Western Mountains. The hills were covered in a mixture of prairie grass vibrant with pink and blue flowers, forests of dark, shadowy greens and browns, and only on the east side, farm fields verdant in newly sprouted grain crops.

Carried on the southerly breeze came the sweet scent of the marsh grass that grew among the trees in the alluvial soils deposited in the delta by the Nekmunnik. Patrick had always associated that scent with the color green and lush vegetation, and paper since farms on the south side of the marshes grew the marsh grass used in papermaking, paper that always kept the aroma of its origins.

He dropped to the ground, propped himself on his elbows, and used the binoculars to scan the southern horizon.

The monster was headed straight for him and moving rapidly. Her course brought her from the villages farther south. He put on his helmet and ducked into a thick clump of jancy berry bushes. His armor sealed completely and, with his helmet filters in place, the dragon wouldn't smell him, and the Gird-metal of the armor blocked the multitude of other dragon senses. Only if she saw him would she know he was there, and that would be difficult since the green and brown armor blended well with the bushes, and she wouldn't be looking for him.

She soared past not far above the highest point of the knoll with the air rushing over her wings making a low whistle and creating a wave of wind that flattened the grass as it swept across the ground following her. Patrick stood and watched her continue north until she disappeared on a course that would take her to the villages up that way.

He returned to his horses and moved them to a place with grass and water, checked his long sword and short sword in their scabbards on his belt, took the crossbow, quiver of bolts, and shield from his supplies, reassured Knight-Mare and Clever-Cleaver he would return, and then scampered back to the peak of the knoll. Convinced the dragon — the Dragon Paladin as Ovidia had called her — coordinated the dragon attacks, Patrick was determined to take the monster down.

Chapter 9

Crossbow Cocked and Loaded

At the knoll's highest point, Patrick assembled a blind using jancy berry bushes — a technique he had used in the past to ambush dragons, although he had never tried ambushing a flying dragon. For this to work, the dragon would need to fly low enough over the peak for the crossbow bolt to hit the target.

He didn't like the new crossbow weapons. Dragon-slayer knights had always had success using melee weapons, so why did they need range weapons; except, the only way to take down a flying dragon was with a range weapon. This crossbow was the prototype. Two others had been built so far. Those had been taken by the Fourth Battalion on their campaign. Engineers were talking about building a crossbow they called a *polybolos* that would hurl crossbow bolts in rapid succession by cranking a handle.

One issue with the weapon was the Gird-metal bolts themselves. They were not aerodynamically stable and began to tumble after about 20 paces. When a sudden force was applied, such as when releasing the bolt, the Gird-metal of the bolt dampened the momentum and introduced rotation. Engineers referred to this behavior, and many other attributes of Gird-metal, as *acting weird*, which Patrick didn't think was an actual engineering term. He had insisted the bolts have cutting edges on their sides in hopes that even when tumbling, the bolts could still inflict damage.

Crossbow cocked and loaded, he nestled in the blind watching the northern horizon. As he waited, he drank from his canteen and ate a dragon-slayer knight nutrition ration from the stash on his belt. Patrick liked the nutrition rations. His mother even got them for him when he was a child. He was sitting in the spot where Miyuki and he used to have their picnics that occasionally consisted of nutrition rations. Those were joyful days. How things had changed.

After a long wait, he saw the dragon coming from the north. He readied himself. A moment before she crossed over the peak, Patrick stood, aimed by leading the target, and pulled the trigger. The crossbow released with a *thwack*.

The bolt flew true, and then began to tumble. The dragon reacted to him standing by fanning her tail wings and shifting the angles of her primary wings to turn, but her momentum meant it was too late to change her trajectory. She collided with the bolt, which caught her left wing and ripped a hole through the yellow arcs on the wing sail.

The dragon's shriek was the most chilling scream Patrick had ever heard. Not even the dragons he had lacerated with his Gird-metal sword had made such a sound. The dragon rolled left and spiraled down to crash with the sound of snapping trees in the marsh south of the knoll.

Patrick scrambled down the slope to finish the job.

Chapter 10
When We Fought, You Were Furious

Sprawled on her back, motionless, the dragon lay among broken trees at the edge of a narrow clearing. She was six times longer than Patrick was tall, with nearly half of that being tail. Her neck was the length of a person. Her jaws were large enough to snatch up a person leaving only their legs dangling out. A small tree protruded through the hole in her left wing. Scuff marks covered the ground where she had been trying to right herself. Patrick set aside the cocked and loaded crossbow and quiver of bolts, drew his long sword, and charged intending to end this the proper way.

The dragon lifted her head and used her arm to parry his sword, which sliced into her flesh. He spun and brought the sword across her neck. A good strike, but it left his shield on the wrong side to ward off the dragons next move, a mistake a Knight Champion should not have made.

With a roar, she struck with her talons causing a loud, metallic screech and a dazzling violet flash from Patrick's armor as the strike sent him flying into a tree, which caused another flash. He dropped his shield as the dragon clamped her jaws on him biting hard several times as if she were chewing, causing yet more flashes, and then threw him ten paces into another tree with another flash. He bounced off the tree and landed next to the crossbow his sword skittering out of reach.

That had hurt. He had been struck before in training and in battles with dragons, and the armor always made a violet flash, but the talon strike and crushing jaws were the worst he had ever experienced and the armor's flashes were so bright they hurt the eyes. From right shoulder to left hip, his armor was deeply scored by five parallel gashes. On his chest were multiple sets of deep dents in the pattern of the dragon's teeth. The damage was the worst he had ever seen in armor, but the armor had not been penetrated. He was amazed he was still alive, but that was the nature of the *acting weird* protection provided by Gird-metal armor.

The dragon screamed and managed to reach the small tree and sliced it away with her talons to free her wing. She righted herself and faced Patrick. Bright, orangey-red blood seeped from the wounds on her arm and neck and the tear in her wing.

The dragon said, "The humans attack dragons, and damage dragons, and murder dragons, and drive dragons from our weyrs. The humans are monsters. The Dragon Council has decreed the dragons will put an end to the humans' attacks. I will begin with you."

The dragon lunged.

Patrick picked up the crossbow and pointed it in the general direction of the dragon. *Thwack*, the crossbow released. The bolt traveled true, striking the dragon in the chest just to the left of her throat. She howled, skidded to a stop as she collapsed, reached for the bolt, and pulled it out. Blood poured from the wound.

Retrieving his sword, Patrick prepared to charge intending to drive the sword into the dragon's chest to its hilt.

Patrick hesitated.

This was not the right thing to do. In all his history studies and his knowledge of battles, he had never read or heard any mention that a dragon-slayer knight had ever killed a dragon. Wounded them, yes. Drove them from their homes, yes. But, not killed. *Dragon-slayer knight* was a misnomer.

The dragon lashed out her tail, wrapped it around him, and squeezed causing another violet flash. Patrick felt a snap vibrate through his armor. A flick of the tail sent him sailing into another tree the impact again causing a flash. He lost hold of his sword as he fell to the ground stunned. The armor's left rerebrace and pauldron separated, fell away, and bounced across the ground.

A swipe of the dragon's talons sliced his exposed shoulder and arm. He screamed, vertigo sickened him, and he clasped at his shoulder. The monster snarled and prepared to reach inside his armor with her talons to tear him apart. He fumbled for his short sword, but couldn't get it out of its scabbard.

The dragon hesitated.

Patrick panted and shook with chills and fear. Pain and tears clouded his vision, but he could see the dragon standing over him with her talons extended. Finally, the short sword came out of its scabbard, but little good it did him as he feebly waved it.

The dragon retracted her talons and said, "You are bleeding."

With sword and voice shaking, Patrick said, "So are you." His pulse raced, but from fear, shock, or blood loss he didn't know.

The dragon worked her jaws, twisting her mouth from side to side, and then she extended her neck toward him. She puckered her lips and went *ptooey*. A wad of spittle splattered on Patrick's shoulder and arm.

"Hey." He dropped his short sword and wiped at the goo with his gauntleted right hand, which smeared the slick gunk on the glove but didn't help remove it.

The smug dragon cocked her head and said, "I hit the target perfectly."

"Why did you do that?"

"You were losing copious amounts of blood. Dragon saliva stops bleeding. Dragon saliva also destroys disease-causing organisms. And, dragon saliva has pain-blocking properties."

Patrick kept wiping at the slime and said, "It won't come off."

"Do not remove the saliva. You need the saliva to stay alive. When the time comes to remove the saliva, ample quantities of water will wash the saliva away." After watching him scraping at the gunk, the dragon said, "Stop trying to remove the saliva. I will need to apply more saliva if you remove the saliva."

"No, don't spit on me again."

He had smeared the spit, but it clung to his shoulder and arm, and now his armor. He gave up trying to remove it and slumped against the tree. The bleeding did look as if it had been reduced, his pulse slowed, and his pain subsided. Freed from the mantle of that pain, clear thinking returned.

Patrick looked at the dragon and said, "You talked. Dragon's can't talk." But, the dragon really had spoken; although, she used archaic pronunciation with an uneven yet lilting accent.

"Obviously, dragons can speak."

"How?"

"Dragons have an organ in our throats that allows us to make the sounds."

"I mean, how is it you know my language?"

"Dragons learned the human language when dragons first encountered the humans, before the humans began attacking dragons."

Patrick had never read that dragons could speak, and he had never heard a dragon speak. The world felt as if it was tipping. He braced himself with his good arm to keep from falling over. Talking dragons. If this was real, he didn't know what to do with that knowledge.

The dragon spat on herself and tried to smear the saliva on her wounds.

"You're doing a horrible job of that." Patrick leaned to his right side and dragged himself toward the dragon.

The dragon pulled back. "What are you doing?"

"I'm going to help smear that goop on you."

He removed his helmet and right gauntlet and used his hand to scoop the slobber blob that was slowly oozing down the dragon's arm and spread it on the arm wound. Viscous and slimy, the translucent saliva glistened with a slight golden tint, and was odorless.

Holding out his hand, Patrick said, "Please, give me more spit." He grimaced as the dragon spat in his hand. "I'm putting this on the crossbow bolt wound. It looks bad, and it's bleeding a lot. I assume I need to get the stuff into the wound as best as I can."

"That is the proper treatment."

After poking that handful of glop into the hole in the dragon's chest, he held out his hand again and said, "Please, more spit," and again grimaced. The gunk was warm. If it had been much warmer, he wouldn't have been able to hold it.

The bleeding from the bolt wound stopped with that handful. Patrick leaned back and breathed heavily. His head felt light and swirly, but he managed not to pass out.

"I'll work on that neck wound now," he said as he held out his hand.

After the neck, he moved to smearing spit on the edges of the torn wing sail. The dragon kept him supplied with spit, but she looked as bad as he felt. He was concerned she might faint. He was concerned he might faint.

As he worked, he said, "Do you have a name?"

The dragon opened her eyes as if startled awake. "I am *<Improecley>*."

"I assume that's a dragon word. It's pretty, very musical with some growliness." He held out his hand.

She went *ptooey* again then smacked her lips before she said, "Beauty is a property of the dragon language."

"Indeed, but I can't make those sounds. May I call you *Fury*?"

"Why do you wish to call me *Fury*?"

"Because, when we fought, you were furious. I've never fought a dragon who was so furious."

"I am furious. The humans murdered dragon parents who were protecting their young-dragon as she escaped."

At a loss for words, Patrick only managed to say, "I'm sorry," which sounded inadequate.

He didn't know how to read the dragon's expression, but her eyes narrowed and he thought she scowled.

She exhaled hard, took another breath, and said, "You may call me *Fury*. What should I call you?"

"My name is *Patrick*."

"Patrick is a nice human name."

"Thank you. I'm sorry I harmed you, Fury. I'm sorry for all of this. Attacking dragons is not the right thing to do. It never was."

Fury said, "Thank you for helping me," as she laid her head on the ground.

"Thank you for spitting on me."

Her subtle expression might have been a smile that almost became a laugh. She made a cooing sound.

Patrick felt a tingle, reached to scratch it, and smeared dragon spit on the back of his neck.

"I must rest," said Fury. "I do not know how long I will be in rest." Her eyes closed and she appeared to go to sleep.

Patrick fell over, his head resting on the dragon's hand.

Chapter 11
He Couldn't Believe What He Had Done

When Patrick opened his eyes, the sun sat low in the western sky. Fury still appeared asleep. He placed his arm next to a nostril. A slight fogging on the armor showed the dragon was breathing.

Patrick pushed himself away not believing what he had done: he had treated a dragon's wounds, a dragon he had tried to kill, a dragon who had almost killed him. What was he thinking? As soon as she regained strength, she would come at him again. He had to leave.

Fury had said something about water removing the saliva. He crawled to a nearby stream that meandered between the dry spots in the marsh and stuck his slime-covered hand into the flowing water. His initial disappointment at the results subsided after he lay there for a while with his hand dangling in the water too tired to move when the saliva loosened and began coming off. He cleaned his gauntlet as well, but left the slimy mess on his shoulder and arm — it had stopped the bleeding and diminished the pain.

Over his shoulder and arm, he snapped in place the rerebrace and pauldron then sheathed his swords. Putting on his helmet and gauntlet proved difficult because he could barely move his left arm. Once his helmet and gauntlet were on, he slung his shield, crossbow, and quiver on his back and, after one last glance at the dragon, headed in the direction where he hoped to find Knight-Mare and Clever-Cleaver.

Patrick skirted Gration Knoll instead of trying to go over. The sun slipped away leaving Echna to cast eerie moonbeams and moon shadows. The shadows didn't help Patrick's mood. He told himself that feeling a forest at night was spooky was natural, but there were no threats in the forest. Miyuki and he even camped in this forest when they were young. In the mountains, there were miser cats that were fierce, especially when protecting a kit, but they rarely came into the valley and even then typically avoided people, and besides, nothing could harm him in his Gird-metal armor, except a dragon.

He had always thought himself invincible when wearing his Gird-metal armor. Now he knew that that feeling of invincibility was an illusion. A dragon could kill an armored knight if they chose to. They simply never had. Thoughts about Fury distressed him. The dragon was in no shape to come looking for him. However, thoughts of her wouldn't leave him alone and they gave him a feeling of panic and anxiety that added to his misery and discomfort.

After stopping several times to rest, and once to eat a nutrition ration and drink from his canteen, Patrick thought he was close to where he had left his horses. He searched for the meadow, but had no luck. He leaned against a tree, slid to the ground, and closed his eyes to rest.

∞∞∞∞

Bang. Patrick startled awake. Bang, bang, bang. Something was beating on him ringing his armor like a muffled bell. He grabbed the clapper that turned out to be a stick attached to a horse standing in a shaft of moonlight.

"Clever-Cleaver, what are you doing?"

The horse dropped the stick and sighed.

"I'm glad to see you too. And, you, Knight-Mare."

Knight-Mare nickered.

"Let's go home."

He loaded his gear onto Clever-Cleaver, mounted Knight-Mare, and headed straight toward Imperium cutting through prairies, grain fields, and patches of forest, still haunted by thoughts of Fury.

Chapter 12

Is There a Doctor in the House

Patrick reached the Academy soon after sunrise. He left Knight-Mare and Clever-Cleaver with the hostlers and went to his office. He wrote a note, sealed it, and then went to the War Room. Determined to hide his physical condition, he carried his helmet and right gauntlet under his left arm to have an excuse not to use the wounded arm. He pushed thoughts of Fury from his mind, steadied himself with deep breaths, entered the room, and strode straight to the map.

He said, "Please, report."

Aslan was on duty. "These are the reports that came in while you were gone. The map is up to date." He handed Patrick several folders.

Patrick spread the folders on a conference table and leafed through them. Based on timestamps, and the markers on the map, two more thunders of six had hit villages farther north and south, making 24 dragons attacking villages. They were now also striking villages farther away from the Lurean Road. The situation was getting worse.

Aslan said, "Colonel Patrick, may I ask what happened to you?"

"What do you mean?"

"Your armor, it's — well, I've never seen that kind of damage before."

"A dragon encounter. It's nothing to worry about." He handed Aslan the message he had written. "Please, see that this is delivered to Doctor Miyuki. I'm going home to clean up and get some rest. I'll return when I'm ready."

"Yes, Colonel Patrick."

Barely functioning, Patrick left. His home was near the Academy's northern entrance, but he wasn't sure he could make it.

∞∞∞∞

He closed the door behind him — he had made it home. It's amazing what sheer determination can accomplish. Avoiding touching any furniture, he lay in the middle of the hardwood floor feeling horrible and his mind dwelling on Fury. The best thing to do was keep busy.

Using his right hand, he removed most pieces of his armor except the parts on the right that his right hand couldn't grasp and he still lay on the backplate. The effort left him panting.

At the door came a knock with a special, familiar pattern.

"Please, come in." His voice came out strained.

Miyuki opened the door, peered in, and said, "Colonel Patrick?" When she saw him, she gasped.

Patrick said, "Is there a doctor in the house?"

"Patrick." Miyuki rushed in.

"Please, close the door. I don't want anyone to see me like this."

After closing the door, Miyuki came to his side, dropped her medical pack, knelt, waved her hands appearing not to know where to begin, and said, "What happened to you?"

"A bad day at work." Images of the fight with Fury flashed in his mind.

"We need to take you to Captain Kalani at the Academy's infirmary."

"No, he can't know about this. No one can know about this. They'll use it against me and things are too critical to allow that."

"I'll take you to my clinic then."

"No, that won't work either. Someone will tell the Academy. I think it's wrong to impose on you, but I don't know what else to do. Will you help me, here, and keep it secret?"

"Of course. I would do anything for you, Patrick."

"Thank you, Miyuki. You're the most wonderful person in the world."

"What happened to your armor? It has gashes and dents."

"Fury."

"Fury?"

"That's the name I gave the dragon I fought. The knights call her *Dragon Paladin*, but I thought *Fury* was a better name."

"You fought a dragon? And, you gave it a name?"

"Of course I gave her a name. I had to call her something, and I didn't want to call her *Dragon*? Who in his right mind would give a dragon the name *Dragon*? Please, help me get the rest of my armor off." He lifted his right arm.

After removing the armor — he rolled to his right side so she could pull the backplate from under him — Miyuki said, "What is this slimy stuff on your shoulder and arm?"

"Fury spat on me." The image of that moment was gross.

"The monster spat on you? How? Weren't you wearing your armor?"

"I had an armor malfunction — pieces came off."

"Where was your squad?"

"I was alone."

"Oh, Patrick. Even I know you're not supposed to take on a dragon alone."

He took her hand. "Don't tell anyone."

"I won't. I need to clean the slime off. You'll get infected."

"Fury said dragon spit kills germs, but more importantly, it stops bleeding. I would have bled out if it weren't for her spitting on me. Also, it relieves pain. I'd really be hurting if it weren't for the spit."

"That sounds bizarre. Did you get hit on the head too?"

"No, and it's not bizarre. It's just something we didn't know about dragons. Don't get the spit on your hands, or anything else. It's hard to get off."

"Wait." She narrowed her eyes. "Did you say *the dragon said*?"

"Yes, dragons can talk, which is something else we didn't know."

"Why didn't we know that?"

"We've never tried talking to them. If we ever did, it's been forgotten."

"This is getting even more bizarre. You believe the dragon?"

"Yes, Fury is honest and frank. She's beautiful too. She has awesome yellow highlights shaped like the two crescent moons nearing eclipse." He grasped Miyuki's wrist. "Oh, Miyuki, I tore a hole in her wing that shredded the crescents, and I cut her arm and neck, and I hit her in the chest with a crossbow bolt."

Miyuki laid her other hand over his and said, "Do you hear what you're saying?"

"What do you mean?"

"That dragon almost killed you and you sound like you regret fighting back."

Patrick stared at Miyuki then said, "I almost killed her first. I had my chance, but I couldn't do it. It wasn't the right thing to do. Everything I've ever believed was right is wrong."

"You're suffering delirium because of your wounds. Once you've recovered, your thoughts will clear. Let's move you to the couch so I can work on you."

"No, don't get blood and spit on my furniture. I can clean the floor, but I'd never get blood stains or the spit out of my furniture."

"You're worried about your furniture at a time like this?"

"I like my furniture."

"I think it's garish; although, I'm not surprised you chose it."

He motioned toward the back of the house. "In the store room is a cot. Please, get it and I can lie on it."

After Miyuki prepared the cot and Patrick moved onto it, she examined him thoroughly and said, "I need more supplies to deal with this."

"Don't you have what you need in your medical pack?"

She looked at the pack then pointed at him. "I don't have enough for this. You have five slices down your shoulder and arm, and I can't tell how deep they are with the spit in the way. You're looking stable, you're not bleeding, your breathing's fine, your pulse is steady, although rapid, and you're not running a fever. You'll be okay while I get supplies."

"Won't they notice you taking supplies from the clinic?"

"I don't need to go to the clinic. As I said, I have nightmares. I purchased my own supplies and keep them at home. I'll be quick. Don't go anywhere."

"I was thinking of working in the garden while I waited."

Miyuki smiled, said, "You'd better not," and then carefully closed the door behind her.

∞∞∞∞

Someone speaking his name woke Patrick. He opened his eyes to see Miyuki's brown eyes filled with worry staring at him.

She said, "I half expected to find you out in the garden just to be funny."

"I don't have a garden."

Her face froze before she said, "I knew that."

Patrick knew she didn't know that and would have laughed if he could have.

Miyuki patted the large, over stuffed pack sitting next to her that, unlike her ruby red medical pack, was storm-cloud gray. "I have everything I need. The first step is to get the gunk off you. How do we do that?"

Patrick said, "Water. Lots of water. Water running over it for a while will make it come off."

"Well then, please, get in the tub." Miyuki helped him to the washroom, removed his shredded shirt, and said, "Please, remove your trousers."

"Not in front of you."

"Oh, Patrick." She looked him straight in the eyes. "Quit being modest. I'm a doctor and deal with this all the time."

Once Patrick was in the tub, Miyuki set the water to run over the spit. While he endured that, she went to the other room to prepare the cot for the procedure she had planned.

She returned to check on the progress of the water and said, "Your home is not a sterile environment. There was a cobweb the size of a serving platter in the corner."

"I noticed that when I was lying on the floor, but I didn't feel like getting up to do anything about it."

"Well, I took care of it."

When the spit let loose and washed away, pain returned and blood began to well up. Miyuki covered the wounds with absorbent gauze then placed a pill in Patrick's mouth. "Please, swallow this. It will help with the pain. Then we'll get you back on the cot." Once he was on the cot and covered, except for his shoulder and arm, she said, "I'll put you to sleep now."

"By reciting that boring fable you liked as a child? What was it called?"

"*The Miser Cat and the Lapaki.* I still like it. How can you make jokes at a time like this?"

"It's the only way I can cope."

"This medication will put you to sleep. When you wake, I'll be done." She placed a sweet wafer on his tongue that dissolved to nothing and then he was gone.

∞∞∞∞

Patrick woke himself when he screamed.

"It's okay, Patrick. I'm here."

He looked into Miyuki's bloodshot eyes and said, "Where's Fury?"

"The dragon? She's not here."

"Is she okay?"

"I don't know."

"I'm hurting." He reached to his shoulder and felt bandages.

"I didn't want to give you more pain medication until you were awake and I could judge the effect. I'd hate to overdose you, or addict you. Please, take this." She put a pill in his mouth.

"Thank you. How did it go?"

"It went well. The cuts weren't as deep as I'd feared, but they weren't superficial. The edges were cleaner than I can do with my best scalpel. That simplified the suturing, and I hope minimizes scarring. We won't know about loss of function until you heal and we do physical therapy. For now, I need you to drink plenty of fluids and I've made some broth for you. Then I need you to rest."

"Rest. That's what Fury said. After I helped her spread spit on her wounds, she said she had to rest. She went to sleep. Oh, Miyuki, I left her there with no one to care for her."

"I'm sure she's fine. She's a dragon. Dragons are practically indestructible."

After having the broth, Patrick went back to sleep. When he next woke, it was morning. Miyuki administered more pain medication and helped him to the necessary to relieve himself.

When he came out, he said, "I'm going to the Academy."

"You can't go out in your condition."

"I must. Things are critical. Actions have to be taken. Help me dress so my shoulder and arm are hidden so no one will notice."

He feared she would refuse to let him leave, but she acquiesced, helped him dress, gave him a medication she said would help him push through his weakness and fatigue, and said, "I'm going with you."

"You don't need to do that."

"Yes, I do. While you're there, there might be a need for a doctor in the house."

Together, they headed toward the Academy so he could face whatever opposition Leena would throw at him.

Chapter 13
I'm Going Back

Miyuki wasn't allowed in the War Room, so Patrick left her in his office. She was not happy, but he assured her he would be fine, which was also what he told himself. He pushed away the haunting thoughts of Fury, each of which caused his pulse to spike, took several deep breaths, summoned a manifestation of his most confident and empowered self, and entered the room where Leena, twirling a lock of her hair, watched Aslan placing new markers on the map.

Patrick said, "Please, report."

Leena made her usual sneer and said, "The great hero has returned."

From her adjoining office, Nola came into the room.

"Colonel Patrick." Aslan came straight to Patrick even as Leena gave him a glare. He motioned toward the conference table and said, "The newest reports are here. They report strange behaviors by the dragons. The map markers are up to date."

Patrick took a seat at the table keeping his left arm tucked tight to his body, suppressed every sign of his physical discomfort, and read. The thunder of six who had been attacking along the Lurean Road north of Imperium had moved east to attack smaller villages, but now was clustered in a farm field several leagues outside of Atra doing nothing. Each time knights tried to engage them they moved several leagues to a different field.

Aslan said, "What does it mean, Colonel Patrick?"

"They're disorganized. I took out the Dragon Paladin."

Images of Fury's blood made him close his eyes and bow his head. Was Fury okay? He slumped and was glad he was sitting or he would have dropped to the floor.

Nola said, "The Dragon Paladin?"

Patrick straightened. "That's what the knights in the field were calling her. She was coordinating the dragons' attacks. I took her out, so the dragons have no one coordinating their attacks now."

"That's what happened to your armor," Aslan said.

"Your armor?" said Nola.

"Colonel Patrick's armor had —" Aslan hesitated when Patrick gave him a narrow-eyed look. Aslan then said, "Colonel Patrick's armor had minor dragon talon scratches." Aslan nodded to Patrick.

Patrick nodded then moved the conversation to a new topic. "We have a critical issue that needs to be addressed." He stood, bracing himself against the table. "The dragons have destroyed our transportation infrastructure — wagons and boats. Provisioning the populations in cities and villages has become almost impossible. Food shortages will become a crisis if we don't begin mitigation."

Nola said, "What's your suggestion?"

"According to the reports, and my own observations in the field, the dragons aren't damaging the cargoes carried by wagons and boats, and they aren't harming people or animals. That means pack animals can transport goods. Colonel Leena excels at logistics. I recommend she lead the effort."

Leena said, "Who do you think you are?"

Nola stopped Leena by making her dismissive hand wave toward her. "Colonel Patrick's right. You're skilled and experienced and have friends and contacts among the brokers, merchants, and transportation guilds. You're perfect for the job."

Leena's eyes burned as she glared at Patrick. He had been sincere that Leena was perfect for the job, but it pleased him he had interfered with whatever scheme she had planned.

Before Leena could voice any more objections, Patrick said, "I'm returning to the field for follow up. I'll return as soon as I can." He left the room.

∞∞∞∞

In his office, he collapsed into a chair, laid his head back, and breathed hard.

"Oh, Patrick." Miyuki felt his forehead, checked his pulse, and then opened his uniform jacket and shirt to check his bandages.

"I'm fine. I just used all my energy." He tried to stop her probing, but failed.

"Let's get you home and in bed."

"I can't. I have to find Fury. I have to know if she's okay."

"You can't go gallivanting off in your condition. You'll kill yourself."

"I have no choice. I'm going back to where I left her."

Chapter 14

To See Her, To Talk to Her, To Be with Her

Patrick travelled across the same prairies, grain fields, and patches of forest as before only going toward Gration Knoll. Miyuki had helped him put on his armor. Throughout the process, she had lectured him about how foolish it was to face the dragon again when he should be in bed recuperating from the previous encounter. She had wanted to go with him, but he had refused. She had wanted him to follow the rules and take a squad of knights with him. He said he would be fine alone. She had sulked as he rode away.

He rode Knight-Mare, who was in her full armor, but Clever-Cleaver wasn't with them. The equipment and supplies his packhorse carried wouldn't be needed on this mission. He was only going to see if Fury was still where he had left her. Unending swirls of anxious thoughts and worries about her well-being compelled him to go, but he didn't know what he would do if he found her there. Nor did he know what she would do.

To move his thoughts away from Fury and the edge-of-panic feeling they caused, he concentrated on the future of the dragon-slayer knights.

By attacking, when in the past they had always fled, the dragons had changed the war. The old strategy no longer worked. The entire organizational structure of the dragon-slayer knights needed to be replaced with regional command centers that could respond quicker. More knights would be needed to protect cities, villages, roads, bridges, wagons, and boats.

More range weapons would be needed, weapons with greater power, range, and accuracy. Maybe the polybolos crossbow was needed after all. Could engineers design and build such a weapon? Engineers also talked about a crossbow powerful enough to hurl a needle sharp iron bolt with sufficient force to penetrate dragon hide, a bolt that would maintain stability during flight.

Patrick didn't like how the future looked.

∞∞∞∞

Patrick left Knight-Mare in the same meadow as before and made his way to where he had last seen Fury. The sun had set and almost full Echna lay low in the sky barely penetrating the forest from that angle. Dead quiet and stone stillness permeated the darkness that hid the gloom and doom that dwelled in shadowy places. The silence overwhelmed his senses as he strained to hear any sound that would warn of the dragon's presence. Long sword drawn and held before him ready to strike if danger threatened, he entered the small clearing in which he had left the wounded dragon.

Fury wasn't there.

Patrick's disappointment caused him to sink to the ground. He leaned against a tree not understanding what was driving him, but he wanted to see her, to talk to her, to be with her. Head bowed, he let his weariness consume him.

∞∞∞∞

Echna had moved high enough to cast her rays into the clearing when Patrick sensed something coming from the southeast. Leaping to his feet and wincing at the pain in his shoulder, he brandished his sword in that direction and stared into the dark forest trying to see what was there. He had never felt such a peculiar sensation before and couldn't guess what caused it. He could see nothing, hear nothing. The feeling became less precise, more spread out, until it felt as if the something was all around him. Then, a massive dragon stepped between the closely spaced trees and into the moonlight, a dragon with crescents on her cheeks.

She and he stared at each other, assessed each other, anticipated each other, each an object immoveable, each a force irresistible.

Making tiny circular motions with the tip of his sword, Patrick said, "You're here."

"As are you," said the dragon in her strange, lilting accent.

"Now what?"

"I do not know." Fury dropped her backside, then her front, and then crossed her wrists in front of her.

Patrick sheathed his sword, removed his helmet, settled to the ground, and leaned against a tree. He said, "You have bandages."

Fury looked at herself. "A thunder applied the bandages."

"A thunder? Do you mean a group of dragons? A *thunder* is what we call a group of dragons."

"You are correct."

"What do you call a group of people?"

"We refer to a group of the humans as *the humans.*"

"That's it? Just *the humans?* You don't have a fancy term like *mob* or *crowd* or *herd of humans?*"

"*The humans* is all we need."

"How about *a press of people?*"

"*The humans* is all we need. Every dragon knows the meaning of *the humans.*"

"That sounds boring."

She shook her head. "The term needs no embellishment. *The humans* are the humans. What is the condition of your damage? I will apply more saliva." She began working her lips.

"No, don't spit on me. I don't need more spit. My wounds are well bandaged under my armor."

"You have pain."

"A little, but so do you. I feel it in my arm and neck and chest, and in a wing I don't even have. I assume it's pain empathy. What else could it be? How are your wounds?"

She said, "I am well."

"You're wounded."

"I am slightly damaged. Rest stabilized the damage. Then the thunder found me and helped me to their camp."

"More dragons came after I left?"

"A thunder arrived. The thunder was angry about you damaging me."

"I'm glad I'd left before they got here. What about your wing? Will you be able to fly again?"

Fury moved her left wing, which caused a stab of pain in Patrick's phantom wing. "The damage is extensive, but I believe my wing will heal and I will return to the sky."

"I hope so. You're an incredible sight when you fly."

She cocked her head. "Thank you. How do I look when I am not flying?"

"You're an incredible sight then too."

With jubilance in her voice, she said, "Thank you."

Patrick's feeling of impending panic was gone, his pulse had slowed, and he relaxed, the tenseness in his muscles gone. He was sitting with a dragon and feeling comfortable, even happy. How odd was that? Moreover, Fury was happy. How he knew, he did not know. The best he could describe it was feeling her happiness inside him. Was it happiness empathy? The situation was strange, but he didn't care. He liked how he felt.

∞∞∞∞

Patrick woke and looked around, confused, then remembered his situation. The sun had risen and Fury was watching him.

"I'm sorry I fell asleep." He straightened himself.

"I also slept," said Fury. "The feeling of tranquility encouraged sleep."

"I need to get back to the Academy. I have responsibilities." Patrick got to his feet.

Fury stood. "I need to return to the thunder or the thunder will come looking for me. And, I must appoint a new controller."

They stared at each other.

Patrick said, "May I meet with you again?"

Fury bobbed her head. "I would enjoy meeting with you again."

"Will you meet me here in two days?"

"I will be here." She turned, squeezed between the trees, and walked into the forest heading southeast.

After hesitating, looking at the spot where the dragon had disappeared among the trees, Patrick walked northeast.

As he walked toward Knight-Mare's meadow, Patrick's sense of something coming became a sense of something moving away. The farther away it went the more precise the direction. Then it was gone and a sense of loss fell over him. Somehow, moving away from Fury caused it. Moreover, she not being near had also caused the horrible feelings he had had after leaving the dragon the first time. He had no idea why or how, but now that he knew about it, it wasn't so bad. He would see her again in two days. He could survive the anxiety until then.

He ate a nutrition ration as he rode toward home, half dozing, his mind wondering, and lucky the saddle's stirrups helped him stay in the saddle. He thought about the dreams he had had while sleeping next to Fury and her statement that she must appoint a new controller.

He tensed and said, "Knight-Mare, go faster."

Chapter 15

Dragons Are About To Attack Again

As Patrick approached the Academy, he saw Miyuki reading a book while sitting on a park bench under a tree. When she noticed him, she shoved the book into a pocket on her medical pack and came out on the road to meet him.

Patrick removed his helmet and said, "What are you doing here?" He tried to keep his exhaustion out of his voice, but he was sure Miyuki heard it anyway.

"Waiting for you."

"Don't you have work?" Knight-Mare pawed to express her eagerness to get to the stables. Patrick said, "Please, patience, Knight-Mare," and patted the horse on her armor with his gauntleted hand making a dull *clank, clank.*

"I finished my shift. You weren't home and the people at the Academy said you hadn't returned. I was worried. I figured you'd return from the direction in which you had left. Patrick, you look horrible."

"Thank you. I can't say the same about you." Miyuki smirked, which made Patrick smile. "Please, come with me, and be quick. The dragons are about to attack again."

∞∞∞∞∞

Still in his armor, Patrick entered the War Room and said, "Please, report."

Leena said, "You've decided to grace us with your presence?"

"Colonel Patrick," said Aslan cutting off anything else Leena was about to say. "The map's up to date. No changes to villages within a day's message range, but packets have come in from farther out and with older timestamps containing the same descriptions of attacks. A packet arrived from Captain Lekan. He met knights from the Fourth Battalion who carried a report from Colonel Tyson." He handed Patrick the folders.

Nola came out of her office, but waited while Patrick read the reports.

When he finished, he acknowledged Nola then turned to Leena. "Colonel Leena, the Fourth Battalion needs food supplies. Please, make arrangements to deliver what they need for their return journey." He turned to Nola. "General Nola, we need to send messages to all knights to prepare for resumed dragon attacks."

Leena again said, "Who do you think you are?"

Nola made her dismissive hand wave toward Leena and said, "Colonel Leena, please, send the food." Then to Patrick she said, "What makes you think the dragons will resume their attacks?"

"I may have taken out the Dragon Paladin —"

Nola interrupted with, "Is that what happened to your armor?" She pointed. "That's more than minor dragon talon scratches."

Patrick ignored her and said, "If I may continue, the dragons are about to appoint a replacement controller who will resume coordinating the attacks. They're using economic activity to select targets." He pointed at the map. "They think big roads and worn roads indicate a lot of activity, so they're hitting those. They began with the Lurean Road and the villages along it, but all the new attacks will be on side roads and villages."

Leena said, "How is it you know that?"

"Field observations and intelligence gathering. We need to inform the knights in the field about what to expect."

Nola waved a hand and said, "Do it."

Patrick turned to Aslan and said, "Captain Aslan, please, commandeer anyone you need to prepare messages and dispatch the packets."

"Yes, Colonel Patrick." Aslan rushed off.

"I'm going to clean up and get some rest. I'll check back later."

Leena followed Patrick into the hallway, grabbed his bad arm, which caused a bolt of pain, and said, "I'm not letting you get away with this."

Patrick kept the pain from his face as he said, "Get away with what?"

"Getting General Nola's position. I'm getting it."

"What are you talking about?"

"General Nola is preparing to retire. I'm getting the position of Knight General of the Dragon-Slayer Academy. This organization will be mine, and then I'll deal with you." She turned and walked away.

Chapter 16

This Really Is the End of the World

With Miyuki's help, Patrick made it home displaying an air of being his normal self all the way. But, once the door closed, he collapsed to the floor.

"Oh, Patrick." Miyuki knelt beside him.

"I'm fine. I just don't have to keep acting now that I'm home."

"You're going to kill yourself, and I'll be angry if you do."

"You're already angry."

"Not as angry as I'll be if you kill yourself." She began helping him remove his armor.

Patrick said, "Colonel Leena said General Nola's preparing to retire. Have you heard anything about that?"

"No. Please, roll to your side so I can get this piece out."

After grunting and groaning, he said, "Colonel Leena says she wants General Nola's position and I'm interfering. Colonel Tyson would be a better choice. General Nola may be showing indifference to performing her duties, but at least she's letting me do mine in this crisis. If Colonel Leena was in charge ...." He shook his head. "The dragons are destroying the world. We don't need this right now."

"Please, get on the cot so I can examine your wounds and put on fresh bandages." As Miyuki worked on his shoulder and arm, she said, "Did you find that dragon?"

"She showed up soon after I arrived. She's remarkable. She has tan colored horns that angle back on top of her head. And, the pupils of her eyes are an intense red like your medical pack. And, she has red edges on her wings. And, green and blue streaks. And, of course yellow crescent moons on her wings and cheeks. But, she's mostly a beautiful brown, like your eyes."

"Thank you. I appreciate having my eyes compared to the color of a monster, but doesn't brown describe all dragons?"

"Sort of, well, at least all the ones I've seen. But, she's different. She's beautiful. And, she's not a monster. Ouch!" Patrick jumped.

Miyuki said, "Sorry. That stitch was too tight, so I cut it."

Patrick sighed and said, "Fury had bandages on her wounds. She said a thunder found her and applied the bandages. Did you know dragons call a group of dragons a *thunder* like we do?"

"I'm not surprised that since she's speaking our language, she's using the same words we use."

Patrick scrunched his brow. "I hadn't thought of that. She wanted to spit on me again, but I told her I didn't need any more spit."

As Miyuki applied ointment to Patrick's wounds, she said, "I'm sure this salve is as good as dragon spit and a lot more sanitary." She began rewrapping his shoulder and arm.

"A report arrived from the Fourth Battalion. Dragons destroyed all their wagons and the supplies the wagons carried, which is odd considering what the dragons have been doing to cargoes elsewhere. I think it's because of what else the report described.

"The knights encountered three dragons. They killed the two larger ones, but the smaller one escaped." Patrick grabbed Miyuki's hand, tears swarmed in his eyes, and he cried. "Oh, Miyuki, it was a family. They killed the parents as they protected their child so she could escape."

Miyuki froze. "How do you know that?"

"Fury told me. We hadn't killed any dragons before. We'd wounded them, but we'd never killed any. That's what changed. That's why the dragons are attacking. To save themselves, they will put an end to us."

Miyuki finished the bandaging and said, "You're getting yourself worked up. You need to relax and rest. You'll think more clearly after some rest."

"Miyuki, this really is the end of the world."

Chapter 17

Too Much Crisis, Too Much Calamity

Scenarios scampered through Patrick's mind as he stared at the corner from his prone position on the cot. Miyuki curled on the couch with her book.

She said, "Why are you staring at the corner? The cobweb's gone."

"I'm thinking."

"You're supposed to be resting. Closing your eyes might work better for that. What's that in your hand, and where did you get it? You haven't left the cot."

"I always carry it in a pocket." He handed it to her.

"It's the knight I gave you. You still have this?"

"Of course. It's the best gift I've ever received."

She examined it closer. "It's worn."

"I like holding it when I think."

"Apparently you think a lot." She handed it back. "You're supposed to be resting, not thinking."

"Too much crisis, too much calamity, too much end-of-the-world. I have to stop it."

"What you have to do is rest and heal. Please, close your eyes."

Patrick closed his eyes as commanded, but he continued thinking and running the knight through his fingers until Miyuki made him put it back in his pocket.

∞∞∞∞

He woke to the aroma of food cooking. He knew he shouldn't have closed his eyes. Now he was behind in his thinking. Miyuki let him sit at the table to eat. The food was marvelous, even better than the nutrition rations he had been living on for the past few days. She then let him lay in his own bed where he went back to sleep.

Morning came. After he convinced Miyuki that no matter how much she insisted he stay in bed he would report to the Academy, she helped him dress in his uniform while instructing him not to be moving his arm. They then went to their respective jobs.

∞∞∞∞

After reviewing the newest reports, which mentioned no new attacks, Patrick went to his office, took out his knight, and thought. After a while, he put the knight away and wrote. Late in the afternoon, new reports arrived. Dragons were again attacking villages as he had predicted. He stood, breathed deeply, and went home.

Miyuki waited on his porch.

She said, "Are you getting back into bed now?"

"No. Please, help me put on my armor."

"You're going to go see that dragon again, aren't you?"

"Fury and I agreed to meet tomorrow. I want to be early."

"Why didn't you tell me?"

"Honestly, my mind's been so out of balance, I forgot to mention it. I would have told you if I had remembered to. I never hide anything from you. In fact, you're the only person I don't hide anything from."

"I'm not happy about this."

"I know, but I must go. The future depends on it."

Chapter 18

We Can Come To an Agreement

Patrick could feel the dragon's presence as if she were all around him. He wished he understood what caused it.

He stepped into Fury's clearing, faced the dragon, and said, "You came."

"As I said I would." Her lilting accent was a pleasure to hear again.

"I missed you."

"As I did you."

"Why is that?"

Fury dropped into her loaf position and crossed her wrists. "I do not know. The sensation confuses me."

Patrick removed his helmet and made himself comfortable on the ground leaning against a tree. "Me too. How are your wounds?"

Fury said, "I am well."

"You're still wounded."

"My damage is healing. You have less pain."

Patrick nodded. "I am feeling better; although, I think a lot of that is simply being here with you."

After a long pause with them sitting in silence, Patrick said, "The most recent reports indicate dragons are attacking again."

"I appointed a new controller."

The silence between them returned.

Patrick managed to pluck up the courage to address what he knew he needed to do.

"What would it take to get the dragons to stop?"

Fury narrowed her eyes. "The Dragon Council has decreed the dragons will put an end to the humans' attacks. We will escalate our efforts until we achieve our goal. We do not intend to stop until our goal is achieved."

"Escalate your efforts? What does that mean?"

"Currently, dragons are destroying the humans' wagons and boats and damaging structures, bridges, and roads. We will progress to fully destroying structures, bridges, and roads. As a last resort, we will begin murdering the humans' animals, and the humans."

Patrick felt dread at those words, but overlaying his fear he felt revulsion, Fury's revulsion.

"You don't want to do that, do you?"

Fury dipped her head. "Dragon instincts guide us to nurture food animals. Murdering the humans conflicts with those instincts."

"Food animals?"

The dragon lifted her head, looked Patrick in the eyes, and quickly said, "The humans are not food animals. The dragons of this world do not consider sophonts to be food animals and do not consume sophonts. However, dragon instincts still insist the humans should be nurtured. Nevertheless, dragons will do what we must to protect ourselves from the humans." She laid her head on the ground.

Patrick fell silent leaving the sound of the wind in the trees to fill the void. His mind roiled with thoughts of the end of the world. He had to save his people.

"What if we surrender?"

The dragon lifted her head and shook it. "We are not interested in the humans surrendering."

"Then, what do you want?"

She stood, towering over Patrick, and with anger in her voice, she said, "The humans attack dragons, and damage dragons, and murder dragons, and drive dragons from our weyrs. The humans are monsters. We want the humans to stop attacking and murdering dragons. We want the humans to leave dragons alone." She turned and walked toward the forest.

"Don't go."

She stopped and still facing away said, "Why should I stay?"

"We can come to an agreement that says people will stop attacking and murdering dragons and will never do it again, and the dragons will stop attacking us. I'll present it to the Council of Counties."

Fury turned. "Will the humans accept the agreement?"

"They don't have a choice. It's either agree or perish." Patrick removed his gauntlets and pulled a scroll and writing implement from a compartment on his utility belt. "What needs to be in the agreement?"

∞∞∞∞∞

Patrick and Fury spent the remainder of the day negotiating the wording for the peace agreement.

When the document was finished, Patrick said, "I will present this to the Council of Counties and do my best to convince them to accept it. How will we know if the dragons accept it?"

"Dragons will stop damaging and destroying the humans' wagons, boats, structures, bridges, and roads. However, if the humans violate the agreement, the attacks will resume and escalate and will not cease again."

Patrick put the agreement in the compartment on his belt, put on his helmet and gauntlets, and said, "I'll take it back and present it."

Fury hesitated before saying, "May I see you again?"

Patrick looked at the marvel that was the dragon Fury and said, "A thunder of dragons couldn't keep me away from you."

Chapter 19

One Must Choose a Path

Someone sat in the dark in one of Patrick's porch chairs. The glow from Echna, which hung low in the western sky, revealed Miyuki, sleeping. She looked uncomfortable. Patrick settled on the top step, removed his helmet, leaned against the post, and watched her.

He had chosen the wrong path for his life. Instead of coming to Imperium and the Dragon-Slayer Academy, he should have gone with Miyuki to Moxclore where she attended the university and medical school. All those years spent apart. All those years wasted. Now it was too late. Now it was the end of the world.

Miyuki made a snort, jerked up, and saw Patrick.

"Patrick." She knelt beside him. "Are you okay?"

"I'm fine. I was watching you."

"That sounds creepy."

"No, it's not. I was thinking about the mistakes I've made in life, about the paths I've followed, and the paths I should have followed, and how everything I've done thinking it was the right thing to do was wrong."

"Are you sure you're okay?"

"I'm fine."

Miyuki huffed and said, "You always say that," which made Patrick laugh. "Why are you laughing?"

"Every time I ask Fury if she's okay, she says 'I am well' even though she's badly wounded."

"The two of you have something in common: denial. Let's go inside so I can check your condition and replace your bandages."

Patrick didn't say anything as Miyuki worked — even giving him a sponge bath so he wouldn't get his new bandages wet. She then made him go to bed. He went, but he insisted he wouldn't sleep long because he had critical work to do at the Academy.

∞∞∞∞

After the morning meal, Miyuki went to her shift at the clinic and Patrick went to the Academy where he reviewed the newest reports, updated the documents he had already written, and wrote an official version of the agreement Fury and he had negotiated. He had Aslan take the documents to the print shop in Imperium to have copies made using their colloid replication machine, enough copies for every member of the Council of Counties and every member of the Dragon-Slayer Academy command staff.

Aslan returned and said, "Colonel Patrick, the copies are ready."

"The next thing I ask of you," said Patrick, "may pose a risk to your career. Certain people will not be happy. You are allowed to decline my request."

"Colonel Patrick, one of those copies goes to me. I read it while I waited at the print shop. I'll do anything you ask of me."

Patrick smiled. Fulfilling his responsibilities had put Aslan in many difficult situations having to deal with the general, the colonels, especially the one he reported to, and the other captains, but he always did the right thing, and he always did it well. Sometimes Patrick was surprised Leena kept Aslan on her staff. Maybe she simply wanted to ensure Patrick didn't have him on his staff.

"Thank you, Captain Aslan. Please, stash the copies in the council chambers where no one will find them. Then, at tomorrow's council meeting, when I enter, distribute the copies to the council members and command staff."

"Will do, Colonel Patrick." Aslan smiled and took his leave.

∞∞∞∞

While waiting for Miyuki to arrive for the evening meal, and to poke and prod his wounds, Patrick stared at the chessboard. A move had been teasing him even taunting him from the back of his mind, a move that was risky, a move that could cause the loss of the game, a move that wouldn't let him not make it. When Miyuki arrived, he moved a knight.

"That's a move a fool would make."

Patrick nodded. "I've been a fool more than once."

"Are you sure you want to make that move?"

"When one must choose a path, the path not taken might have been the path one should have taken, but I've decided to commit to this path."

"Okay. I'll think about how to respond."

After redressing Patrick's wounds and having the evening meal, they talked and reminisced about old times and paths not taken.

Miyuki would spend another night on Patrick's couch, which she said was comfortable, even though garish, so she could help him dress as formally as he could and then go with him to the Council of Counties meeting the next morning.

Chapter 20
Council of Counties

Patrick and Miyuki arrived at the council chambers. The Sergeant at Arms of the Council of Counties blocked their access.

"I'm sorry, Colonel Patrick. I've been instructed that you and anyone associated with you are not to be allowed entry."

"By whom?"

"The Council."

"And, who instructed them?"

The Sergeant at Arms paused while suffering beneath Patrick's glare before he said, "Colonel Leena."

"You can't bar my entry."

"I'm sorry, Colonel Patrick. I have my instructions."

∞∞∞∞

After they returned to Patrick's home, Miyuki said, "I can tell you're about to do something foolish."

"They're not stopping me. This is too important. Please, help me put on my armor."

"Attending a public meeting in armor, and I assume armed, is not permitted."

"I don't care. The path before me may not be the path I wish to follow, but I have no choice but to follow it. I will perform my duty even if it's the last duty I perform. Besides, it's the right thing to do, maybe the only right thing I've ever done."

∞∞∞∞

Patrick found the Sergeant at Arms' expression as he approached the second time amusing.

65

"Colonel Patrick, you can't enter the council chamber dressed in armor."

"Do you think you can stop me? Please, stand aside."

Taking one additional step was all that was required to prompt the Sergeant at Arms to move. Patrick entered the chamber with Miyuki following. One of the council members was speaking, but that stopped at the sight of an armored knight. Aslan leaped to his feet and began distributing documents. All that disturbed the silence that clung to the air was the sound of stacks of paper landing on desks.

Leena stood and said, "You can't be here." She turned to her staff sitting behind her. "Please, get him out of here."

Patrick didn't want a confrontation, but he would not be removed from the meeting. He placed his hand on his long sword ready to draw.

None of Leena's staff moved.

Aslan nodded to Patrick. Patrick nodded and removed his hand from his sword's hilt. Aslan deserved a reward after this.

Using his most authoritative command voice to ensure he could be well heard while wearing his helmet, Patrick said, "I'm here to explain the situation with the dragons, where the conflict is headed, and what we must do to prevent disaster."

Leena said, "Don't listen to him. He's a fool. He's pushing us to economic failure and social collapse."

The Leader of the Council, who had been flipping through the papers Aslan had laid in front of him, said, "I think we will listen to what Colonel Patrick has to say. Please, sit Colonel Leena. Colonel Patrick, you have the floor. Please, continue."

During the commotion, Nola contributed nothing. She didn't even bother looking at the papers Aslan set in front of her.

When Aslan placed the papers in front of Leena, she knocked them aside scattering them. Patrick felt sorry for her. Leena was so focused on her goal of taking control of the Dragon-Slayer Academy she had removed herself from the reality of the threat civilization faced.

Patrick said, "Thank you, Leader of the Council. The first page of the document being distributed is an executive summary. The next 23 pages contain details of the dragon attacks, so far. Page 25 is my analysis of anticipated future actions by the dragons.

"To summarize, the dragons have destroyed all wagons and boats they could find and they have damaged buildings, bridges, and roads beginning along the Lurean Road then expanding east and west from there. They haven't harmed any people or animals, though. Based on reports received thus far, I assume the pattern repeats north and south throughout the Lurean River Valley."

Patrick paced to the left a couple of steps. "My analysis indicates that until the dragons achieve their goal, they will escalate their attacks to more thoroughly destroy buildings, bridges, and roads, and then to killing animals, and then to killing people."

The crowd murmured.

Leena stood again. "That's nonsense. What makes you think the dragons even have a goal? They're just monsters."

Patrick wanted to stare Leena down, but she couldn't see his expression hidden by his helmet. "My analysis is based on my field observations and intelligence gathering."

"Where did you gather the intelligence?"

"From the Dragon Paladin."

"That's absurd. How could you get information from a dragon?"

"Dragons can talk."

That statement generated more noises from the crowd.

Leena swiped her hand through the air. "That's a lie. Dragons can't talk, and we can fight them. We can stop them from doing any more damage."

Patrick shook his head. "We can't fight the dragons. In the past, when we attacked them, they fled. Sometimes they struck out while trying to escape causing minor armor damage, but they never fought back. Look at my armor." Holding his injured left arm close to not reveal its limited movement, Patrick used his right hand to tap his armor and its gashes, teeth marks, and crush dents. "This is what a dragon can do when they fight back. We may think we're invincible in our Gird-metal armor, but we're not. I might have been able to kill her, but I know that if we had not stopped our battle, the Dragon Paladin would have killed me. We stopped fighting when we realized it was the wrong thing to do. We then helped each other with our wounds. I'm alive because she helped me."

The crowd murmured a spooky sound.

Leena pointed at Patrick. "Then you betrayed us."

"I gathered information."

Leena began to say something else, but the Leader of the Council interrupted her. "What is the dragons' goal?"

Patrick made an airy wave. "It's simple. They want us to stop attacking them."

The Leader of the Council leaned forward. "After all these generations of the Dragon War, why did they decide to do this now?"

Patrick paced to the right. "The Fourth Battalion succeeded in killing two dragons. We had harmed dragons in the past, but we had never killed any. That's what changed. They intend to put an end to the threat even if that means putting an end to us."

That caused a gasp from the crowd followed by murmuring and audible whispering.

Patrick said, "The good news is they don't want to harm anyone. They just want us to leave them alone." He stepped closer to the council. "On the last page of the document you'll find the peace agreement I negotiated with the Dragon Paladin. To summarize: 1) People and dragons will not attack each other. 2) People and dragons can go anywhere they want and live anywhere they want without interference from the other. 3) A committee of people and dragons will arbitrate disputes that might arise. It's that simple."

In a loud voice, Leena said, "This can't be allowed."

Patrick pointed at the council and said, "All the information you need is in the document. Two paths lay before you. One leads to our survival. The other leads to our destruction. Choose wisely. As for me, I can do no more. I'm done." He turned and walked out of the council chamber.

Miyuki followed.

The last he heard from the chamber was Leena screaming about something.

∞∞∞∞

Patrick remained silent on the walk home. Once inside, he said, "Please, help me remove my armor and check my shoulder and arm."

"Are you okay?"

"I'm fine," then he added, "I'm in pain."

As she worked on him, Miyuki said, "Oh, Patrick. You're killing yourself."

"Well, I'm done now. No more Academy."

"What?"

"There's nothing more I can do. It's up to the council now. I'm going to visit Fury."

"I'm not surprised." Miyuki began collecting armor pieces.

"I'm not wearing my armor."

"You're confronting that dragon without your armor?"

"I don't need my armor. Fury's my friend. She won't harm me."

Chapter 21
He Went to Her and Hugged Her Snout

When Patrick arrived at the stables without his armor and prepared Knight-Mare for a ride without her armor, she became excited: time for a fun ride, not a work ride. Clever-Cleaver also became excited because he always went on the fun rides too. Patrick and his two horse friends headed off across the same prairies, grain fields, and patches of forest as before, but with more playfulness. He noticed his repeated trips were making a trail across the countryside.

After leaving Knight-Mare and Clever-Cleaver in Knight-Mare's meadow, Patrick made his way to Fury's clearing expecting to have to wait for her since he was early. As he approached, though, he felt her presence — she was early. He quickened his pace.

The dragon lay in the clearing staring at the place at the clearing's edge where Patrick emerged.

Patrick said, "You're early."

Fury sat up. "As are you."

"I was eager to see you."

"I too was eager to see you."

He went to her and hugged her snout. "How are your wounds?"

"I am well."

"And, getting better I assume."

She rubbed her head on him. "How is your damage?"

"I'm fine ... and slowly healing."

"What is the cloth loop around your neck and arm?"

Patrick lifted his left arm causing a pain spike and a groan. Fury flinched and reached to her left shoulder.

He said, "It's a sling. Miyuki insisted I use it. It supports my arm and helps keep me from moving it too much." He stepped back to better look at the dragon. "I delivered our agreement to the Council of Counties. What happens next is up to them. I can do no more."

"I hope the humans accept the agreement."

"I do too."

Fury's gaze moved to the forest behind Patrick. "Two animals the humans call *horses* are approaching."

"What?"

Knight-Mare and Clever-Cleaver came into the clearing. Knight-Mare reared. Clever-Cleaver backed into the forest. The horses' responses were interesting. The warhorse was trained to help fight and the packhorse was trained to stay out of the way but keep the equipment handy. However, they were also trained to accept novel things and situations, with a little help.

Patrick shook his hand at Fury. "Please, don't eat them."

Fury sighed. "Dragons on this world do not consume the humans' animals."

"I'm sorry. I'll remember that. They think we're on a fun ride instead of a work ride, so they must think they didn't have to stay where I left them." Patrick walked over to the horses. "Knight-Mare." He held out his hand. "Please, touch."

The warhorse calmed then touched Patrick's hand with her nose.

He held out his hand to Clever-Cleaver and said, "Clever-Cleaver, please, touch."

The packhorse came forward and touched his hand.

He motioned toward the dragon. "This is my friend, Fury. She is a good dragon. Knight-Mare, please, follow. Clever-Cleaver, please, follow." He led them around the edge of the clearing staying in what the horses would feel was their safe zone to let them get a good look at the dragon. He then walked over to the dragon, patted her on the neck, and said, "Safe."

Both horses made a snort, looked at each other, and then with Knight-Mare in the lead, they walked toward Fury. They stopped two paces away from the dragon and snorted again.

Patrick said, "This is my warhorse, *Knight-Mare*. This is my packhorse, *Clever-Cleaver*."

Fury said, "Hello warhorse Knight-Mare. Hello packhorse Clever-Cleaver."

The dragon speaking surprised the horses, but then they snorted again, turned, and walked to a promising patch of sweet smelling marsh grass to begin grazing.

"That went well. I hope it goes as well when I introduce you to Miyuki."

Patrick and Fury spent the remainder of the day talking and sharing the good feelings being together brought them. When evening came, Fury selected a place with fluffy grass, walked two circles, made little marching steps, and lay on her left side creating a crescent with her neck, body, and tail. Patrick climbed into the middle of the ring of dragon, lay beside Fury, and snuggled against her. The dragon hooked the tip of her tail over him, the tail that was so powerful it had partially crushed his armor, but which now conveyed affection, and then covered them both with her right wing to shelter them from the night. A feeling of contentment and love filled Patrick as he slipped into sleep.

In the morning, Patrick and Fury said their goodbyes and went their separate ways.

Chapter 22

It's the Path I've Chosen

Miyuki sat on the park bench.

Patrick said, "What are you doing here again?"

"I like this park. Look at the view. You can see the river and prairies and grain fields and patches of forest, and this tree makes lovely shade." She paused. "How did it go?"

"We had a wonderful visit, all three of us." He patted the horse he rode. "You've met my warhorse, *Knight-Mare*, although I don't think I actually properly introduced you. This is my packhorse, *Clever-Cleaver*." He pointed to the other horse. "They got to meet Fury."

"Don't dragons eat horses? And, Knight-Mare is a warhorse trained to fight dragons. How did she react to the dragon?"

"Dragons don't eat our animals, and Knight-Mare's trained to help me fight in general, not just dragons. Once I showed her Fury was a good dragon, she liked Fury. So did Clever-Cleaver."

"Where's your sling?"

Embarrassed, he said, "Here." He showed her the sling hanging on his saddle's horn. "I took it off before topping the hill. I don't want anyone from the Academy to see me wearing it. But, otherwise, I've been wearing it as you ordered."

Miyuki narrowed her eyes. "You'd better."

∞∞∞∞

Arriving at Patrick's home, Miyuki said, "I have a move." At the chessboard, she moved a piece.

Patrick cocked his head. "Hmm."

Miyuki went through her process of examination, cleaning, and rebandaging Patrick's shoulder and arm. Then she rummaged through

73

Patrick's cold box for prepackaged ingredients from Amala's Eatery to make sandwiches.

After they ate, she said, "What are you going to do with yourself now?"

"I have no idea. Does your clinic need a down-and-out unemployed knight? I'm good at waving around pointy things without poking myself."

"I don't think so, especially that particular skill, but I don't handle hiring, except for my work-team, and you're not qualified for that."

"I'm not qualified for anything."

"You have many skills."

Patrick strolled over to the chessboard and moved a piece.

Miyuki said, "What are you trying to do?"

"I'm trying to win, of course."

"Like that?"

"It's the path I've chosen."

The knock at the door did not use Miyuki's special pattern — Miyuki was standing next to the chessboard. Patrick wasn't used to any other knock at his door. He opened it.

"Colonel Patrick," said Aslan. "I have a message for you." He handed Patrick an envelope.

"Thank you, Captain Aslan. How are things at the Academy?"

"In disarray."

"Why's that?"

"There was a disagreement with the Council of Counties, so General Nola and Colonel Leena both resigned and left."

Wide-eyed, Patrick said, "Where'd they go?"

"General Nola headed off to Riverfork to be with her grandchildren and rumor has it Colonel Leena headed to Luremkel to run her sibling's fish market business."

"Has Colonel Tyson returned?"

"No."

"Who's in charge?"

"No one, but I'm trying to hold things together."

"You're quite capable, Captain Aslan. I have faith in you. Good luck with it." Patrick closed the door.

Miyuki said, "That didn't sound good."

"Captain Aslan will do fine. It's a great opportunity for him."

Patrick broke the envelope's seal, read the contents, and inhaled sharply.

Miyuki said, "What?"

In a weak whisper, Patrick said, "The Council of Counties wants to make me Knight General of the Dragon-Slayer Academy."

Chapter 23
The Right Path to Follow

The next day, Patrick — dressed in his best uniform, the one he never wore because he wanted to keep it at its best — met with the Council of Counties. Having already decided to walk away from the Academy and life as a dragon-slayer knight made Patrick feel empowered. With no shortage of skilled and talented knights ready for opportunities, he didn't have to take the job, and he wouldn't unless he had it his way. The negotiations were brief — they only required half the day. In the end, Patrick had what he wanted, and he felt good that it was the right thing to do, the right path to follow.

∞∞∞∞

Miyuki waited in their favorite booth at Amala's Eatery, her red pack in the seat next to her.

As he approached, he said, "Doctor Miyuki."

She said, "Colonel Patrick."

Patrick dipped his head and said, "Actually, it's General Patrick."

"You accepted the position?"

"They gave me all I wanted, which gives me the ability to do what needs to be done. How could I turn it down?" He settled into the booth doing his best not to jostle his arm.

"Now what?"

"A lot of work to plan and implement that change, and there's no guarantee of success. One concession I made to alleviate the council's fears, and my own, was to turn the dragon-slayer knights into a force that could actually do battle with dragons if the dragons were to renege on the peace agreement. If it comes to that, we won't be able to simply chase the dragons away as we have for generations. If we're not ready to fight them in real battles, things will get really bad for us really fast."

Miyuki placed her fingers on his left wrist feeling the pulse. "Are you worried about that?"

"I fear for our survival if we aren't ready, but I trust Fury. I don't believe there will be a problem." Then he smiled. "Guess what the council decided to call the peace agreement?"

Appearing satisfied with Patrick's pulse, she released his wrist. "How could I guess that?"

"They're calling it the *Paladins' Peace*."

"Paladin, as in the Dragon Paladin?"

"It's the plural possessive — Paladins'. They said I'm also a paladin." He laughed. "Isn't that a lark? I'm no paladin."

"Apparently some people disagree with you."

After eating, Miyuki departed and Patrick returned to his office to begin the work required by his new job.

∞∞∞∞

Over the next few weeks, there were no dragon attacks. Patrick wrote plans and began implementing those plans. The Fourth Battalion returned looking as if they had endured great emotional and physical suffering. New assignments and promotions were made, the first two being Aslan and Mahtab being made Knight Colonels with more to follow as reorganization plans were implemented. At Mahtab's recommendation, Hann became Manager of the Rapid Communications Network and the Council of Counties split that organization off as its own service separate from the Academy. Patrick made multiple visits to Fury's clearing. And, Miyuki's and his chess game progressed. With every task completed, Patrick felt more enthusiasm about the future.

∞∞∞∞

A knock with a special, familiar pattern came at the door. After checking himself to ensure he wore his sling properly, Patrick opened the door.

Patrick said, "Doctor Miyuki."

Miyuki said, "General Patrick." She marched to the chessboard, moved a piece, and grinned.

Patrick ran his fingers across his chin and said, "Hmm."

Miyuki interrupted his pondering by saying, "Do you have news?"

After staring at the chessboard, he said, "I do. I'll share it while we eat. I've cooked an evening meal fit for you."

"Fit for me? Does that mean the food is good, or bad?"

Patrick led her into the dining room. "You'll have to tell me. Since you came to town, you haven't had an opportunity to sample my cooking."

"I didn't know you could cook."

"There's a reason I ran into you at the market."

Miyuki set her pack down and took her seat. "I thought the only thing you ate that didn't come from Amala's Eatery were those dragon-slayer knight nutrition rations."

"These are good." He pulled a nutrition ration out of a pocket.

"You carry one of those with you?"

"Yes, at all times." Patrick returned the nutrition ration to its pocket to eat later and said, "I prepared cottage pie. It's my mother's recipe with meat, gravy, potatoes, vegetables, and cheese."

"It sounds challenging."

"It was, especially with the limited use of my left arm."

Judging from Miyuki's hearty appetite, and request for seconds, the food was good. Another success in a string of successes.

Between bites, Miyuki said, "Tell me the news?"

"Regarding the idea of touring the Lurean River Valley visiting villages and cities to explain and promote the Paladins' Peace —"

"Go on."

"We've decided to do it."

"I'm going with you."

"I was hoping you would."

She patted his hand. "Someone has to take care of you and make you do your physical therapy."

"Thank you, Miyuki. You're the most wonderful person in the world."

A few days later, and after Patrick had met with Fury again, everything was ready. Harbingers had been sent ahead to reserve speaking venues, to secure lodging, and to arrange for supplies. The squad of knights accompanying them was ready to ride as were a work-team of bureaucrats and technocrats. Since there were no wagons or carriages, all of them having been destroyed and new ones not yet available, they would ride horses and carry supplies on packhorses. Patrick would ride Knight-Mare and be accompanied by Clever-Cleaver. For Miyuki he had secured the third best horse in the county: an experienced, intelligent, and beautiful golden mare named Honeystar.

∞∞∞∞

Patrick and Miyuki stood at the chessboard.

Patrick moved his last bishop.

Miyuki said, "Ha." She captured the bishop with a rook. "Check."

"Hmm," said Patrick. He captured her rook with his last knight. "Checkmate."

"Huh? Why did you do that?" She snatched her king off the board and cuddled it.

Patrick spread his right hand and said, "I was trying to win."

Miyuki placed the king on the board on its side. "The way you were playing, you shouldn't have won."

"I admit that with all that's been happening I was chaotic with my moves."

"You were foolish with your moves. Well, that evens our win/loss ratio, but I'll win next time."

"I'm willing to let you try. Clever-Cleaver carries a portable chessboard that uses magnets to hold the pieces. We can play while we travel."

Miyuki's delighted grin added to Patrick's joy.

Then Patrick said, "Oh, by the way, to let you know, Fury will be meeting with us occasionally while we travel. It'll be an opportunity for you to meet her."

Miyuki's eyes widened. "I'll get to meet a dragon?"

"Not just any dragon. You'll meet the dragon Fury, the most wonderful dragon in the world."

Epilogue

Patrick had had a plan for the future. However, Patrick's plan had been thwarted, which didn't bother him now. His new plan was better, if he could make it work. It was a plan for a future in which people and dragons would be friends, a plan that would change the world.

Part Two
Heroes

Chapter 1

Will We Grow Up To Be Heroes

When Jake entered the village inn, a gruff man with unkempt hair and rumpled clothing sitting at a table by the door, drink in hand, confronted him. The man said, "Hey, you. You'll never be a hero."

"You're wrong. Someday, I will be a hero."

The man sloshed his drink. "Your mother and father were once thought of as heroes for being dragon-slayer knights. But, the Paladins' Peace turned them soft. All the dragon-slayer knights have gone soft."

"My parents fought dragons — I've seen the damage on their armor — and they train so they're ready to fight dragons again when needed." Jake took a breath and then emphasized, "And, they *are* heroes."

"Dragon-slayer knights don't fight dragons anymore. They just go to their little school and play like they do."

Jake lifted his chin and said, "What do you know? You've never been a dragon-slayer knight, never had armor, or shield, or dragon-slaying sword, and you've never fought a dragon."

Luke came over and said, "Jake, please, ignore Mister Travis."

"He's saying bad things about dragon-slayer knights and my parents."

"He's always saying those things."

Luke dragged Jake toward the far side of the room.

As they walked away, Travis said, "Mark my words: Dragons are coming back and we're all doomed."

Luke picked up his broom. "No one pays attention to him and you shouldn't either. Why are you here?"

"I finished my chores and came to help you finish yours so we can go practice dragon-slayer knight."

"Your parents *practice*. We *play* dragon-slayer knight." Jake pointed. "There's another broom behind the counter. Help me finish sweeping."

∞∞∞∞

As they walked toward their clubhouse in the riparian forest on Jake's farm, Jake said, "We will be heroes."

Luke kicked a stone off the trail. "We're only nine. We have plenty of time to become heroes."

"We're close enough to being ten that we can say we're ten."

Luke shook his head. "That's not how age works. We're not ten until our birthdays."

Jake loved his cousin Luke. Their fathers were siblings, and Jake and Luke had grown up together almost as if they were twins. Jake imagined them finding their heroic futures together, fighting dragons side by side, even though Luke was less enthusiastic about that future than was Jake.

At their clubhouse, they pulled out their huge straw dragons, made multiple trips into the forest to hide the dragons among the shadows of the trees and bushes, and then donned their pretend armor, shields, and stick swords.

Luke said, "Ready to slay dragons?"

Jake had never seen an actual dragon or dragon battle, but his imagination filled in the blanks. "Let's do it." He charged into the forest.

After a successful afternoon of slaying dragons — resetting the battlefield and dragon menagerie several times to try different scenarios — Jake sighed and said, "I have to go. Livestock don't like their evening meals to be late."

As they put away the dragons, armor, shields, and swords, Luke said, "Dad's making his stew again, so we'll have a crowd at the inn tonight."

Jake closed the clubhouse door. "Will we grow up to be heroes? Or, will I just be a farmer and you an inn keeper?"

Luke put his hand on Jake's shoulder. "You have a better chance of being a hero than I do. You're bold, ambitious, and determined. Nothing can stop you. But, I'll probably never leave the inn. See you tomorrow."

Chapter 2

I Want To Be a Dragon-slayer Knight

As Jake entered the house, the aroma of fresh buttery rolls and simmering vegetables filled his senses and made his stomach growl.

Mom peaked out from the kitchen and said, "Jake, you're done with your chores? Good. Go wash. Dad's almost finished with his concoction."

She ducked into the kitchen. Dad said something about it not being a concoction.

After washing and dressing for the evening, Jake returned and took his seat at the table. Dad placed his favorite bronze stewpot on the trivet in the center of the table, steam wafting from it.

Jake said, "Stew? Luke said Uncle Ryan was making stew tonight."

"He gave me the idea. He calls his *Famous Fantasy Stew*. I call mine *Regular Reality Stew*." Dad chuckled, said, "Mine's better," and filled their bowls.

Mom smiled and nudged Dad with an elbow. "Uncle Ryan's stew fills the inn, which might tell you something."

Jake selected one of Mom's buttery rolls, dipped it in his stew, and took a bite. After swallowing, he said, "Do you think I'll grow up to be a hero?"

Dad took a roll, set it on his plate, and said, "Why do you ask that?"

"Mister Travis said I'll never be a hero."

"Don't listen to Mister Travis." Mom patted his arm and put a roll on her plate. "He's just an old agitator with nothing left to agitate. Besides, you're only nine years old. You have plenty of time to become a hero."

"I'm close enough to being ten that I can say I'm ten."

Mom shook her head. "That's not how age works. You're not ten until your birthday."

Mom and Dad scooped spoonfuls of stew.

Jake said, "I want to be a dragon-slayer knight."

Mom and Dad froze their stew-filled spoons in midair.

Mom put her spoon in her bowl and said in a quiet voice, "No, you don't. Being a dragon-slayer knight is brutal duty."

Dad set his spoon in his bowl. "Besides, General Patrick and the Dragon Paladin made peace, and we will not break the Paladins' Peace."

Mom picked up her spoon and began poking at the stew in her bowl. "Dragons are filthy, smelly, disgusting, and dangerous monsters. You don't want to meet one."

Dad nodded toward Jake and said, "There are other ways to be a hero. Being a farmer is heroic."

Jake scrunched an eyebrow.

"Look at this food." Dad waved a hand at the concoction in the stewpot causing the rising steam to swirl. "Feeding people is heroic. Uncle Ryan even makes his stew using our produce and meats."

Jake sighed. "It's not the same."

Dad began stirring his stew and said, "You'll find your calling, but dragon-slaying won't be it." He stopped stirring, stared into his bowl, then glanced at Mom. "Dragons —" he took a breath, "might even return to the caves in the hills. The Paladins' Peace gives them that right."

Mom sighed and said, "We'll ignore them."

Jake looked at Dad then at Mom. "But, you're still training to fight."

"We are ready and will stay ready," said Mom. "General Patrick has been training us to do what we would need to do, in case something goes wrong."

"But, it won't," Dad added. "We're doing our part to help General Patrick keep the peace."

Mom stared at Dad. "If we have to, we'll fight."

Dad nodded. "We will, if we have to. Our job is still *to protect our families, our communities, and all people.*"

The rest of the meal was uncharacteristically quiet as Mom and Dad kept glancing at each other.

∞∞∞∞∞

In the morning, after Jake filled the feed and water troughs for Mom's and Dad's dragon-slayer knight warhorses and packhorses, finished feeding the livestock, and hoed a few weeds sprouting in the cotton, he went to meet Luke at their clubhouse so they could do what they did after chores on most non-school days: play dragon-slayer knight. Luke was weaving straw patches onto a dragon that had been slain a few too many times. Jake helped.

Jake said, "Mom and Dad said dragons might return to the caves."

He and Luke were familiar with the caves, and had heard stories about one particularly large cave called *Dragons' Cave* in which dragons had lived before dragon-slayer knights drove them away long ago. That cave was up the hill from Jake's farm. They had explored it but found no signs dragons had ever lived there.

Patching finished, Luke sorted through their collection of straw dragons. "Why would dragons want to live in those caves?"

Jake selected his favorite dragon. "It would be a good place to live if they wanted to eat our animals, and people."

They began distributing the dragons in the forest. So it could surprise him later, Jake hid his favorite dragon behind a large bush speckled with dragon-eye flowers, called that because the flowers were fire red with black centers. He thought people wouldn't notice a dragon peering out because the dragon's eyes would blend in, if a dragon's eyes really were the color people told him they were.

Luke selected his favorite dragon, the one with the biggest teeth. "Your parents wouldn't let them do that, would they?"

"I don't think so, but they say they won't break the Paladins' Peace."

Luke put his dragon behind the largest tree, a tree big enough that occasionally he hid two dragons behind it. "Wouldn't eating our animals and people break the Paladins' Peace?"

Jake shrugged. "You'd think so."

After hiding the remaining half dozen straw dragons, they returned to the clubhouse, suited up, and began searching and slaying.

Midway through their dragon-slaying mission, the village's great bell tolled. The bell rang in a repeating three rings and a pause pattern — a call for everyone to gather that usually meant something bad had happened.

Chapter 3

Dragons Have Been Seen

Jake and Luke dropped their play armor, shields, and swords and ran to the village administration building where people were gathering in front of the steps. Murmurs spread through the crowd like waves with each crest louder than the previous. Jake and Luke climbed to the top of the steps on which Ryan, the mayor, Eveeta, and a few of the village council members stood watching the crowd grow.

Luke said, "What's going on, Dad?"

"Dragons in the hills."

"Dragons?" Jake scanned the crowd and saw his parents.

Eveeta raised and waggled her hands. As she waited for the crowd to quiet, she said, "Innkeeper Ryan, who rang the bell?"

Ryan furrowed his brow, made a nod toward a man at the front of the crowd, and said, "Mister Travis."

Eveeta snorted. "He's always trying to cause trouble."

"What will you say?"

"I won't deny the report, but what's important is to calm everyone."

When the crowd had quieted enough for her to speak, Eveeta used her public address voice to say, "It's true. Dragons have been seen up by Dragons' Cave." After the collective gasp at the report's confirmation and the renewed murmurs had died down, she said, "There's nothing to worry about, and we're not in danger. The Paladins' Peace is in place. Please, ignore the dragons and go about your business."

Addressing the crowd rather than those at the top of the steps, Travis blurted out, "Mark my words: We're all in danger. Something has to be done about those dragons."

Eveeta said, "There's no danger, Mister Travis."

"Where are the dragon-slayer knights?" Travis looked around. "They need to rid us of the monsters."

The crowd grumbled an echo of Travis's statement.

Jake's mom and dad climbed the steps to stand next to Eveeta, Mom on the left, Dad on the right. "Please, silence," they commanded in unison.

Jake knew the community held his parents in high regard; nevertheless, he was impressed when the crowd instantly went quiet. The people in front even cowered back a step causing movement to pulse through the crowd as that back step propagated.

Dad said, "We are aware of the dragons. They are not a threat. Since the Paladins negotiated peace, there have been no transgressions. The dragons will not break the Paladins' Peace. As Mayor Eveeta said, we are not in danger."

Mom said, "If the dragons become a threat, we will deal with them."

Dad looked at Mom with pinched brow before turning to the crowd. "The Paladins' Peace allows people and dragons to go anywhere they want and to live anywhere they want without interference from the other, so the dragons have the right to be there. They will not harm anyone. They won't even compete for resources. We can live side by side, neither of us disturbing the other. Please, ignore them."

Travis huffed and opened his mouth.

Eveeta said, "Please, enough from you, Mister Travis," which caused Travis to close his mouth and sneer. "We may have been at war with the dragons forever it seems, but the world has changed. The Paladins made peace. And, Knight Krista and Knight Dylan say we're safe."

Jake noticed his parents glance at each other, expressions unreadable.

Eveeta made shooing motions with her hands. "There's nothing to worry about. Please, everyone go about your business and ignore the dragons."

Roiling with mumbles, the crowd dispersed, everyone returning to his or her work, including Ryan, Eveeta, the council members, and Mom and Dad who held hands and talked as they walked away. Travis waited, though, his arms crossed, his face in a scowl, and silent.

When only Jake and Luke remained, Travis came to them, looked down his nose at them, and said, "This is your chance. Be heroes. Get rid of those dragons. Mark my words: If you don't, they'll destroy the village and eat everyone." He turned and stormed off.

∞∞∞∞

Jake and Luke returned to their training mission, but Jake's mind was elsewhere.

"What's wrong, Jake? You're not slaying dragons."

"I think we could do it."

"Do what?"

"Get rid of the dragons."

"Are you kidding?"

"We've been practicing." Jake waved his stick sword at the straw dragons.

Luke pointed his stick at one. "This isn't *practice*. It's *play*."

"We can do it." Jake performed a full thrust jab with his stick into the straw dragon Luke had pointed to.

"Leave me out of it. Anyway, I have to go. Tonight will be busy again." Luke put away his gear and dragons. "See you tomorrow."

Jake was lost in thoughts about slaying dragons as he watched Luke leave.

Chapter 4

You're Being Foolish

At the evening meal, Jake's parents bustled as usual; however, they were strangely quiet and gloomy.

Jake said, "What do you think about the dragons?"

"Dragons?" Mom and Dad said it simultaneously with high-pitched voices and looked at each other as if each had surprised the other.

Dad said, "Nothing's wrong. Everything's fine. The Paladins' Peace is in place."

Mom nodded. "That's right. No problems, yet. We'll ignore them."

Dad forced a smile that didn't reach his eyes. "There won't be any problems."

After one more, "Everything's fine, so far." from Mom, they returned to being quiet and gloomy.

Everything Jake knew about dragons he had heard from others. As it had been with Mom's and Dad's parents and grandparents, they had been dragon-slayer knights all of their adult lives, but they never talked about dragons or the Dragon War.

Mom and Dad ran their farm and regularly went to dragon-slayer knight training, but there hadn't been any campaigns against dragons since the Paladins' Peace was forged six years ago. Before that, Mom and Dad had occasionally gone on campaigns to force dragons away from lands occupied by people. If both Mom and Dad went, Jake stayed with Luke and Uncle Ryan.

Jake's only memory of Mom and Dad returning from a campaign had been the last campaign six years ago. He had been told they were part of the Fourth Battalion. Jake remembered when Mom and Dad returned, their armor was damaged, and they were in a gloomy mood for weeks.

He feared that gloom was returning and believed that to prevent it, something had to be done about the dragons.

∞∞∞∞

Determined to leave early, Jake rushed to finish his morning chores, but instead of meeting Luke at their clubhouse, he headed into the hills above the farm to where he could see Dragons' Cave. Hiding behind a cluster of boulders, he watched the cave hoping to see the dragons. None showed themselves. As he waited, he thought and planned and convinced himself even more that he could do it.

When he at last went to the clubhouse, Luke was waiting.

Luke stood with hands on hips. "Where have you been?"

"I was trying to see the dragons."

"Did you?"

"No, but I did come up with a plan."

"A plan for what?"

"For how to get rid of the dragons."

"You're still talking about that? We're supposed to ignore them."

"Mom and Dad are upset. And, you heard what Mister Travis said. Will you help me?"

Luke waved Jake off with his hands. "No. What makes you think you can fight dragons anyway? Only dragon-slayer knights in Gird-metal armor can fight dragons."

"Mom and Dad have armor, shields, crossbows, and swords."

"So?"

"I'll use their armor, shields, crossbows, and swords."

"That's the most ridiculous thing I've ever heard."

"I'm being a hero." Jake headed toward home.

"You're being foolish." Luke followed.

Chapter 5

I'll Be a Hero

"What are you doing?" Luke kept glancing out the window. "Your parents will catch you."

"No, they won't. They'll be gone all day. They're delivering produce."

Jake had gone into his parents' room and now stood before the armory closet. He took a deep breath and opened the doors to reveal two suits of Gird-metal armor in mottled colors of mud and grass both well maintained but scarred by long gashes Jake assumed were from dragon talons. The damage proved the armor worked since Mom and Dad were still in one piece. Mounted on a display rack, and dappled in the same brown and green colors as the armor, were Gird-metal shields, Gird-metal dragon-slaying long and short swords, and crossbows and quivers of Gird-metal bolts.

"Those are too big for you."

Luke was right. Jake couldn't wear either suit of armor. The suits were identical except for size, damage, and the names inscribed on them: *Knight Krista* and *Knight Dylan*. He took the breastplate and plackart of the smaller one and put them on. They were lighter than he expected and came down over the tops of his hips.

From the lookout position he had taken at the window, Luke whispered, "Someone's coming."

Jake picked up the helmet for the smaller suit, put it on his head where it wobbled, and then took one of the dragon-slaying short swords because it was his size.

"It's your parents. They're almost here."

Closing the armory doors and hoping his parents wouldn't look inside, he said, "Let's go."

"They're about to come in the front door."

"We'll go out the back."

Jake let Luke out the back and carefully closed the door to keep it from slamming. They ducked behind the copse of trees at the edge of the yard hoping his parents hadn't glanced out the window.

Luke said, "Now what?"

"We go to Dragons' Cave."

"You're going to be in a lot of trouble."

"No, I won't. I'll be a hero."

Chapter 6
Dragon Egg

Jake climbed the hill with Luke following.

Luke said, "You can't do this."

"Yes I can. If you're not helping, stay quiet."

"I won't stay quiet. I don't want you to get hurt. And, the only way to keep from getting in trouble is for you to sneak that stuff back before your parents notice it's gone."

"I'm doing it."

When the cave came into view, Luke said, "I'm not going in there."

"You don't have to. There's a pile of boulders near the cave where you can wait."

"I'm not going any closer. I'm staying here."

Jake left Luke hiding behind a boulder that was itself concealed behind a jancy berry bush, which were common among the boulders on the sunny slope. He continued climbing the hill stealing from bush to bush and boulder to boulder in the manner he had used many times when practicing dragon-slayer knight until he was at the closest pile of boulders. After seeing no signs of the dragons, he dashed the final distance to the cave.

At the entrance, he paused to prepare himself for what he expected to find inside a cave occupied by filthy, smelly, disgusting, and dangerous monsters: muck, refuse, a horrible stench, and dangerous monsters. He adjusted his helmet, held his dragon-slaying sword in front of him as he always did when practicing dragon-slayer knight, and stepped inside.

Shadow hid everything. He moved to a wall, adjusted his helmet, and waited for his eyes to adapt while he listened for sounds. All was quiet. When he couldn't hold his breath any longer, he inhaled expecting to choke on the smell. To his surprise, the scent prompted a memory of the lodging rooms at his uncle's inn. Ryan decorated the rooms with honeystar flowers. The air here smelled of those flowers as well as evergreens and sweet-moss.

As his eyes adapted, he moved forward and found the debris he had expected, except it was well organized with a base of evergreen boughs turned up around the edge as a rim holding a layer of sweet-moss and fresh grass sprinkled with five-petaled, golden honeystar flowers. Snug in the middle lay a piece of wood, like a post, as long as but bigger around than Jake's torso, and with rounded ends. Its color was that of fresh cut lumber with a dark brown wood grain pattern that weaved and waved lengthwise.

To the left was another debris pile made of the same materials as the first, only larger, much larger. Jake peered over its rim. It was a nest. The insides encompassed almost as much space as his farmhouse. Something, or two somethings, had flattened the moss and grass. The straw dragons Luke and he made stood taller than a person, but were still small enough to pick up and hide behind trees and bushes. Judging by the depressions in the nest, real dragons were bigger than the rooms in his house. Holding forth the dragon-slaying sword, he spun around, helmet rattling, wondering where the dragons were.

His gaze returned to the object in the smaller nest. An epiphany came to him: It was a dragon egg. He touched it feeling its not quite smooth texture, its warmth, and the motion of something stirring within. A tingle tickled the nape of his neck causing him to shudder and scratch at it. A feeling of curiosity and wonder washed over him before he reminded himself of his mission. If the dragons weren't here, he couldn't strike at them, but he could destroy the dragon egg so there would be one less dragon in the future.

He raised the dragon-slaying sword.

Friend?

Jake jumped and looked around. "Who said that?"

No one had spoken. It wasn't a sound. It was something he felt inside himself.

Friend.

Again, not a word, but a feeling, inside, all over.

He called out, "Who's there?"

My friend.

His breath catching in his throat, Jake backed away from the dragon egg until he was at the cave entrance where he turned and ran.

He made a panicked dash down the slope, helmet bouncing on his head, loose armor jangling, and the dragon-slaying sword throwing him off balance. Glare blinded his shadow-adapted eyes causing him to almost collide with bushes and boulders. Luke stepped out from his hiding place, grabbed Jake by the arms, and stopped him.

"What happened? Did you slay a dragon?"

Between gasps, Jake said, "No. They weren't there."

"Why are you so scared?"

"There's something —"

Jake glanced toward the cave, broke loose of Luke's grip, and continued running down the slope.

His headlong charge down the hill left Luke behind. His parents were working in the large vegetable garden. He ran straight toward them, crying out, "Mom. Dad." He ignored their expressions when they saw what he wore and glanced behind him in the direction of Dragons' Cave.

Mom cried out in horror, "Jake, what did you do?" She seized the dragon-slaying sword from his hand.

Dad pulled the helmet off Jake's head and said, "Did you harm a dragon? Did you break the Paladins' Peace?"

"No. They weren't there."

"You could've brought the dragons' wrath down on us."

"I didn't do anything. The dragons weren't there."

Mom glared at him. "Please, go to your room."

"But, something —"

Dad said, "Please, do as your mother says, and don't come out until we say you can."

"But —"

Mom handed the dragon-slaying sword to Dad, lifted the breastplate and plackart off Jake, said, "Please, go," and sent him scurrying toward the house.

Chapter 7
I'm Sorry I Wanted To Harm You

His mind muddled, Jake sat on his bed, his arms wrapped around his knees, and rocked. The evidence proved dragons lived in the cave, even though he hadn't seen them. Where could they have gone? The cave was clean, smelled nice, and the nests were well made. That was not what he had expected, not how dragons had been described. If dragons being filthy, smelly, and disgusting was a lie, what about the stories that said they were dangerous monsters?

Why was the dragon egg alone? Stories said dragons were practically indestructible, that nothing could harm a dragon except a dragon-slayer knight with a Gird-metal dragon-slaying sword. Did those stories also apply to dragon eggs? Dragon parents wouldn't worry about a dragon egg because only a dragon-slayer knight with a dragon-slaying sword could harm it, and the Paladins' Peace said no one would.

The dragon egg was the most beautiful thing Jake had ever seen. Its image filled his mind's eye. He still felt the curiosity and wonder that had washed over him when he touched it.

Jake began writing in his journal to help him sort through his thoughts and to document his experience in the cave. He wrote about his feelings of desire, hope, and confusion, feelings that seemed to come from somewhere else, from someone else. He cried as he wrote the last line of the journal entry: *I'm sorry I wanted to harm you.*

A feeling of forgiveness, empathy, and love absolved him of his guilt. He smiled through his tears and looked out the window toward Dragons' Cave.

∞∞∞

That night, he was only allowed to leave his room to attend the necessary and eat his evening meal. When he fell asleep, he dreamed of being with the dragon egg, of holding it and protecting it. He also dreamed of being inside the dragon egg, snug, warm, almost ready to break out, and of longing for his friend. In those parts of the dream, he was someone else.

When he woke the next morning, he paced around his room, the dragon egg dominating his thoughts, until he was interrupted.

"Jake," Luke called from outside the window. Jake had no idea how long Luke had been there. "Where are your parents?"

"They went to the village."

"I'm sorry I ran off yesterday."

"That's okay, Luke. There's no reason for you to get in trouble for something I did."

"You didn't tell me what happened. You only said the dragons weren't there."

Jake sat on the edge of his bed, propping himself with his hands on either side. "It wasn't what I expected. Dragons keep a clean home, have nests instead of beds, and I think they're a lot bigger than we thought."

"Is that all? You were scared out of your wits."

"There was a voice. No, not a voice. I don't know what it was. It was a feeling. It scared me." Jake stood, walked to the window, and sharing a secret, whispered, "There was a dragon egg."

"A dragon egg?"

"It was the most beautiful thing I've ever seen. Tan with dark brown lines, and this big." He held out his hands as if telling a fish tale. "I almost broke it, but I didn't." He cried a few sobs. "I need to see it again. I need to go back."

"You can't."

"I have to." He began climbing out the window.

"Why don't you go out the door?"

As if it were obvious, Jake said, "This is faster. The cave is just up there." He lifted his arm to point and fell out of the window into Luke's arms.

Luke helped him stand and said, "You're being foolish again, and you'll be in even more trouble."

"I have to go back."

"I'm not going."

"It's just me that needs to go." He squeezed Luke's hand and said, "Thank you for being a good friend."

Luke gripped Jake's hand with both of his. "Don't say that like you're not coming back."

"I'll be back, probably." He broke Luke's grip and took off at a run up the hill.

Chapter 8

May I See the Dragon Egg Again

Jake stepped into the cave and stopped to catch his breath while his eyes adapted. A large shape that hadn't been there before loomed ahead of him. Something, possibly it, made melodic mumbles and growls. Similar sounds came from another shape farther inside. The first shape came toward him. Jake backed away and hit the wall.

His improving sight revealed a huge creature, a monster, a dragon, its head above him at several times his height, almost touching the ceiling.

In an indomitable voice, it said, "You have violated the Paladins' Peace. You shall suffer for the transgression. All the humans shall suffer for the transgression." The creature's wings partially opened, its jaws gaped, and it reached toward Jake.

Pressing himself tighter against the jagged wall, Jake said, "I didn't do anything."

The dragon paused. "You were here. Your scent betrays you. Furthermore, even as difficult as Gird-metal is to detect, there is evidence of a murder weapon. You violated the Paladins' Peace."

"No. I didn't do anything. I'm sorry. May I see the dragon egg again, please?"

"You tried to murder our egg."

"No. Well, I was going to, but I didn't. I'm sorry. May I see it?"

Curled around the dragon egg's small nest was a second dragon, its ears pinned back, and its spiky teeth bared. With its wings, it hid the dragon egg from Jake's view and it exhaled a low-pitched growl that rattled Jake's insides and made his sinuses ache.

The first dragon lunged. Jake ran out the exit. On his back, he felt the wind from a swipe of dragon talons.

A thunderous roar followed Jake out of the cave, but he didn't look back. He sprinted to the nearest cluster of boulders and crawled into a depression under them expecting the dragon to be on top of him.

Nothing happened. After he caught his breath, slowed his pulse, and stanched his tears, he peaked around the edge of the boulders. The dragon stood in a threatening stance in the cave's entrance glaring at him. It growled and settled to the ground with its feet tucked under it, eyes still on him.

Jake didn't get to see the dragon egg, but it still beckoned him. He had to see it, had to be close to it, absolutely had to. If he didn't, his heart would burst.

How could he get past the dragon blocking the entrance? And, what about the other dragon? He had to get in there. He had to get to the dragon egg. He wiped another wave of tears from his eyes, and steeled himself. This was no time for crying. He had to get to the dragon egg.

The dragon's color was slightly darker than Dad's favorite bronze stewpot and not too different from Jake's own color. It was at least seven times longer from tip of nose to tip of tail than Jake was tall. It held its wings tightly folded to its body. Crimson highlighted the wings' edges and deep blue traced the spars. Green patches the color of newly sprouted wheat decorated its jaws and cheeks. The horns that jutted back from the top of its head were the color of the caramel candy Mom made. Its eyes held glints of fire red.

If he was going to get to the dragon egg, be with the dragon egg, he had one option. He stood tall to display confidence and dignity, and approached the dragon.

Chapter 9
Getting To See the Dragon Egg

As Jake approached, the dragon went into its threat stance again standing on its hind legs, partially opening its wings, holding its hands out in front, and baring its gleaming white teeth. Talons the same color as the teeth slid out from the tips of its fingers. Up close, its eyes were a match for dragon-eye flowers and were narrowed in anger.

The dragon huffed, said, "Leave," and began a steady, low growl.

Jake squeaked out, "I've never met a dragon before. You're amazing."

The dragon's eyes widened, the growling stopped, its jaws closed, and its arms and wings slightly relaxed.

Jake added, "You're beautiful, or handsome. Are you a female dragon or male dragon?"

With a lilting accent, the dragon said, "You do not recognize my gender?"

"I see nothing that gives me a clue."

It relaxed even more. "I have no yellow."

"No yellow?"

"No yellow is a male trait."

"You're a male dragon, then."

The dragon's wings closed and his talons withdrew into his fingertips as he dropped out of his threat stance onto all fours. "Are you a human child?"

Jake caught himself scuffing the grass with his toe and resumed his dignified pose. "I'm ten years old. Well, technically, I'm nine, but I'm close enough to ten to say I'm ten."

The dragon shook his head. "That is not how age works. You are nine years old. A human child or a dragonet is not ten years old until the human child's or the dragonet's ten year hatching day. I thought you looked strange. The humans all look alike, but you are small." The dragon settled to the ground and crossed his wrists.

Jake sat and said, "People don't look alike. Some people are darker than I am and others are lighter. We have different hair. Mine makes big curls, but for some people, their hair is wavy, or tightly curled, or straight. Some people don't have much hair at all. And, people's hair can be different shades of black, brown, blond, gray, and even red like your eyes. Some people are tall, some are short, some are fat, some are skinny. People are all sorts of combinations of those things. And, our faces are all different. Have you ever seen a person up close?"

The dragon sounded defensive when he said, "I have seen the humans — from a distance. Dragons have high resolution vision so I can see well at a distance."

"Then you need to pay closer attention to what people look like because we're all different. You're the only dragon I've ever seen. Do all dragons look like you?"

The dragon held out his arm to show off a blue stripe. "Dragons' red, green, blue, and yellow highlights differ making each of us unique. However, even without taking into consideration our highlights, dragons simply look different from each other."

"Are you all the same bronzy-brown?"

"Some dragons' color is slightly darker and some dragons' color is slightly lighter, but with rare exceptions, all dragons are dragon colored."

Melodic and growly sounds came from the cave. The dragon turned his head and made similar sounds in return.

Jake said, "What's that about?"

"My life-mate says I am supposed to be driving the human away, not having a pleasant conversation with the human."

"I'm enjoying our pleasant conversation. Besides, doesn't the Paladin's Peace say people and dragons can go anywhere they want?"

"I do not believe the Paladin's Peace is meant to allow humans to enter a dragon's weyr without permission. Regardless, my life-mate is correct that I am supposed to be driving the human away. Before I do that, explain why you came to my life-mate and my weyr to violate the Paladins' Peace."

Jake said, "I didn't do anything."

The dragon looked down his nose at Jake. "You came with the intention of violating the Paladins' Peace even though your mission failed. Explain why."

Jake rubbed his hands together. "All my life I've been told dragons are monsters and a threat. Then you moved into the cave. My parents wouldn't do anything about it. They said they won't break the Paladins' Peace, but I thought something had to be done to protect the village. I thought you might eat our animals and people. So, I wanted to make you leave."

"The humans are sophonts and the dragons of this world do not consume sophonts, and the dragons of this world do not consume the humans' animals." The dragon stood and glared at Jake, which prompted Jake to stand. "The humans attack dragons, and damage dragons, and murder dragons, and drive dragons from our weyrs. The humans are monsters. Dragons have never damaged the humans, with one exception: <Improecley> damaged the Human Paladin, but that was the only time a dragon damaged a human."

Jake said, "Why do people attack dragons?"

"We do not know. You will have to ask the humans why the humans attack dragons. After <Improecley> fought and damaged the Human Paladin, <Improecley> and the Human Paladin forged the Paladins' Peace. Now she works with the Human Paladin to maintain the Paladins' Peace. Since the Paladins' Peace was agreed upon, the humans have not attacked dragons. Now, you have violated the Paladins' Peace."

Jake bowed his head, scuffed his toe in the grass again, and said, "I didn't do anything."

"You came here intending to violate the Paladins' Peace."

"I'm sorry. I was wrong. You're not a monster. And, you have the right to be here."

Another round of sounds came from the cave.

The dragon signed, responded to the cave, and then said, "It is time for you to leave."

Jake clasped his hands in front of his chest and said, "May I see the dragon egg again before I leave, please?"

"Why do you want to see our egg?"

"I don't know. I ... feel the need. It's the most wonderful thing I've ever seen. I need to see it again, please."

The dragon stared at Jake for so long Jake felt he had failed.

Finally, the dragon said, "Wait here. I will ask," and he went inside the cave.

From the cave came musical noises and growls that sounded like an argument in the form of a song.

When the dragon returned, he said, "You may see our egg. If you attempt to damage our egg, I will consume you."

The dragon's jaws were as big as Jake, and Jake knew what the dragon threatened to do the dragon could do.

"But, you said dragons don't eat people. And, wouldn't eating me break the Paladins' Peace?"

"If you attempt to damage our egg, I can do to you anything I want to do to you."

Jake held up his hands and said, "I won't do anything wrong. I promise."

"Then, follow me." The dragon led Jake inside.

Chapter 10
Dancing All the Way Home

Entering the cave, Jake moved slowly as his eyes adjusted to the dim light. The mother dragon stood behind the dragon egg's nest with her wings mantled over it. She watched him with narrowed eyes and furrowed brow. Her colors were similar to the father dragon's colors with the addition of yellow bars across the bridge of her snout, on her wings, and a few more streaks farther back.

The mother dragon bared her teeth, said, "If you attempt to damage our egg, I will consume you," then she snapped her jaws.

Jake said, "The father dragon said he would do that, so you two would have to fight over who gets to eat me." He raised his hands. "But, that won't be a problem because I promise not to harm the dragon egg."

After a huff, the mother dragon moved her wings to reveal the dragon egg.

It was as marvelous as before, tan and brown, and long and oval. Jake took a deep breath and reached out. The mother dragon growled. Jake jerked his hand away.

"May I touch it, please? I won't harm it. I promise."

The mother dragon made a small nod.

Jake leaned forward and laid his hand on the dragon egg. It was warm, he felt movement inside it, and he felt *my friend* inside himself, which made him smile and giggle.

"You did an amazing job making the dragon egg." Jake turned his smile to the mother dragon. "It's the most beautiful thing I've ever seen."

The mother dragon cocked her head and said, "Thank you."

"It must have really been hard to do."

The mother dragon looked at the father dragon. "I told my life-mate his participation in the task was easy. I performed the burdensome and difficult process involved in the task."

The father dragon said, "I have never denied that your contribution was more difficult and more significant than mine. There was nothing I could do about that, except to say, 'You performed the task well.'"

The mother dragon made a snort then rubbed her head on the father dragon and entwined her tail with his.

The father dragon said to Jake, "Enough of seeing our egg. Now, leave."

When Jake didn't move, the father dragon growled, and used his snout to push Jake toward the exit. Jake stayed calm even with the huge jaws at his back as he was escorted out.

Staying in the cave's entrance, the father dragon said, "Do not return."

The dragons were nice, Jake liked them, and he knew they would let him see his dragon egg again tomorrow. Jake danced all the way home.

Chapter 11

Protecting the Dragon Egg

Jake celebrated his success by eating the piece of caramel candy he had been saving for a special occasion. He wondered when his parents would be home. He wanted to tell them what had happened, but then thought better of it. His dragon egg should remain his secret. However, he could tell Luke.

A frantic knocking came at the door and he heard Luke call out, "Jake."

Jake opened the door and said, "Guess what I did."

Wide-eyed and panting, Luke said, "Mister Travis has a mob he's leading to Dragons' Cave to drive away the dragons."

"They can't do that. We have to stop them."

Jake's first thought turned him toward his parents' room, but the dragons wouldn't be happy if he showed up with a dragon-slaying sword. He turned toward the kitchen, but a kitchen knife wouldn't work either.

He turned back to face Luke, who said, "Why are you running in circles?"

"I don't know." He pushed Luke out the door ahead of him and said, "Please, find my parents. Tell them what's happening."

"What are you going to do?"

"I'm going to protect my dragon egg." He ran toward the barn.

Hoe. Shovel. Rake. None of the garden tools would do. The only thing he had ever practiced using as a weapon was a stick. He selected a spare tool handle and ran toward Dragons' Cave to protect his dragon egg.

The mob from the village could be seen climbing the hill — men and women waving garden tools, and axes, and pitchforks. Jake rushed to beat them to the cave. When he arrived, the father dragon met him.

"I said do not return."

"People are coming to drive you away."

The dragon said, "I told you the humans are monsters."

"They're confused and misguided. I'll stop them. Please, go inside."

He pushed on the dragon, as if he could move a dragon. When the dragon finally retreated inside, Jake faced the approaching mob, holding his stick as if it were a two-handed sword.

Travis said, "Please, get out of the way."

Jake waved his stick and said, "Please, Go home."

Travis stepped aside and motioned for a few larger individuals to step forward.

Jake backed into the cave. "I said go home."

"I said get out of the way." Travis let the mob be a wall between him and Jake's stick.

Jake backed farther into the cave as the mob kept advancing. He had backed well into the cave — his dragon egg and the dragon parents were right behind him — before he resolved to stand his ground. "I won't let you harm the dragons."

Travis sneered. "We're here to make them leave, but mark my words: If you don't get out of the way, we'll hurt you."

Jake placed his feet in a fighting stance and swung his stick causing the closest people to step back. "Who wants to be the first to try?"

Luke, Ryan, and Eveeta came in, slipped around the mob, and moved to the side away from the mob.

Eveeta commanded, "Please, stop this, Mister Travis."

Travis said, "You stay out of this, or mark my words: We'll hurt you too."

Mom and Dad entered standing on either side of the mob in full armor that blended into the environment with dragon-slaying swords on their hips, shields on their arms, and crossbows and quivers on their backs. At the sight of Jake's parents, the dragon parents made an alarmed sound.

Jake said, "It's okay, mother and father dragon. The dragon-slayer knights are my parents. They won't break the Paladins' Peace."

Seeming to expect Jake to back off when challenged, a man with a pitchfork stepped toward him. Jake brought his stick sword down above the tines forcing the tool's points into the floor then swung the stick at an angle catching the man on the chin. The man screamed, dropped the pitchfork, and reached for his face. Jake's full thrust jab with his stick into the man's paunch caused the man to *oof* loudly and double over. A hard whack across the man's back sent him to the ground where he moaned.

As the man crawled to the protection of the mob, he said, "Watch out. He's dangerous."

Jake lifted his stick sword in preparation for the next assailant and said, "Who's next?"

Dad said, "Jake, what are you doing?"

"I'm protecting my dragon egg." He glanced back and added, "And, my dragon egg's parents."

"Why?" said Mom.

"Because you're wrong about dragons. They're not monsters. Dragons are decent and peaceful, and they deserve our respect, and our protection."

The murmurs Jake's words triggered from the mob were interrupted by a loud crack. Everyone went silent and looked past Jake. Jake turned to look. In the small nest, his dragon egg jiggled and sticking out of it were two caramel colored spikes. The spikes pulled back inside. Another loud crack and the spikes reappeared sending shell fragments flying. A dragon's wet, glistening bronze head then poked out and went, "Squawk."

Jake moved quicker to the dragon egg than did the dragon parents, who watched in dismay, but didn't interfere, as he dropped his stick sword and began helping the dragon hatchling break out of its shell. The shell fractured into large shards revealing a perfect dragon with short wings flapping and short tail flopping, comically large hands and feet, an oversized head, large eyes with irises the color of glowing embers, and when freed of the dragon egg and stretched out, from the tip of its nose to the tip of its tail it was almost as long as Jake's dad was tall. Accenting its dark bronze color were red, green, and blue, but no yellow.

The dragon hatchling looked at the dragon parents, but turned his attention to Jake and again went, "Squawk."

He stepped off the edge of the nest into Jake's arms, which sent Jake sitting hard to the floor. The dragon hatchling rubbed his head on Jake's cheek. Jake hugged him and inside himself he felt shared joy and love and *my friend.* They were one — one heart, one soul, one life.

Tears swarmed in Jake's eyes and he said to the dragon hatchling, "I feel as if I've always known you." He turned to the mob and in his public address voice said, "Meet my friend. His name is *Squawk*."

Squawk turned toward the mob and said, "Squawk."

A grumble spread through the mob and everyone with anything that could be used as a weapon raised it.

Subtle hand signals flashed between Mom and Dad with each signal becoming more emphatic yet still subtle. Finally, Mom's shoulders slumped and she made one more sign. In unison, Mom and Dad moved forward away from the mob and turned to face them, Mom on the left, Dad on the right.

Jake said, "What are you doing?"

Mom said, "Your father and I are protecting your friend, and his parents, and the Paladins' Peace, but after this is over, young man, you have a lot of explaining to do."

Squawk looked at Mom and said, "Squawk."

Jake said, "Yes, Mom."

Casually resting his hand on the hilt of his long sword, Dad addressed the mob. "Dragons are practically indestructible, as are dragon-slayer knights in Gird-metal armor. You don't want to trifle with either. The Paladins' Peace will not be broken. Please, go home, and accept that dragons are here to stay."

In unison, the dragon-slayer knights stepped forward. The mob broke and fled the cave. Travis cowered without his mob wall to stand behind and shouted, "Mark my words: This ain't over." Then he too ran. Only Luke, Jake's parents and uncle, and the mayor, along with the dragon parents, remained, staring in astonishment at Jake and Squawk.

Hanging over the edges of Jake's lap, Squawk curled up, wrapped his tail around Jake's waist, nestled, and continued rubbing his head on Jake's cheek. A scratch behind Squawk's ear caused the hatchling dragon to make a rumbling purr.

Jake said, "The world is changing. In that new world, you and I will be heroes."

Part Three
Changing the World

Chapter 1

I Want a Dragon of My Own

"The world's changing, Dad."

"No, it's not."

"Yes, it is." Luke continued scrubbing the serving counter but glanced at Dad out of the corner of his eye.

Dad heaved a sigh, wrinkled his brow, and said, "The Paladins' Peace may have ended the Dragon War and says we have to tolerate dragons, but regardless of what happened with Jake and that dragon of his, it doesn't say we have to be friends with them."

Evenings featuring Dad's *Famous Fantasy Stew* always drew a crowd to the inn. In the kitchen, the savory aroma of the stew's simmering vegetables, meat, and spices merged with the scent of freshly baked buttery rolls and jancy berry pie. The smells wafted into the common room where the staff made preparations and then out the door to entice customers.

"Squawk isn't Jake's dragon; they're friends because people and dragons can be friends. And, you've met Squawk's parents. You know how nice dragons are."

"I met them once, over a year ago, when you made me help stop the mob that went to drive them away."

"The dragons were nice, weren't they?"

Dad began lighting heaters that would keep the serving pans hot. "I didn't notice. I was too busy being astonished when that dragon hatched and jumped into Jake's lap."

"Don't call him *that dragon*. His name is *Squawk*."

"It's not natural for a child and a dragon to do that."

"It's natural for them. It's as if they're linked." Luke put out napkins. "Squawk is learning to walk on two legs."

Dad lit the last heater. "Dragons do that?"

"Sometimes." Luke set serving trays on the end of the counter. "Squawk's talking is improving too. When I arrive, he still runs circles around me saying, 'Luke, Luke,' and then rubs his head on me and says, 'Like Luke,' but he can speak in full sentences now instead of just baby talk. He's also getting better at speaking the dragon language. It sounds musical, and growly."

"How is it dragons can speak our language? They don't have the mouths for it. And, where did they learn it?"

"I don't know. Did I mention playing hide-and-seek with Squawk?"

"Maybe."

"You don't listen when I talk about Jake and Squawk."

Dad handed Luke silverware caddies that jingled with shiny spoons, forks, and knives.

"I listen. I just don't retain. You're constantly talking about them and I lose track."

Luke rolled his eyes and said, "Jake and I used to play hide-and-seek with Squawk. He would cover his eyes with his hands while we hid. When we were ready, he'd walk around looking for us. When he found us, he'd jump up and down and squeal. When it was his turn to hide, he'd crouch and cover his head with his wings not understanding his wings don't hide him. We'd walk around him saying, 'Where's Squawk? Where's Squawk?' He'd giggle under his wings. Then, Jake would part Squawk's wings, peek in, say, 'There he is,' and Squawk would jump up and down and squeal. It was so much fun. But, we can't play hide-and-seek with him anymore. At least not the part when *we* hide."

"What happened?"

"Squawk's father said dragons have many senses, more than people do, but it takes a while for a dragon hatchling to learn how to use them. Squawk figured out how to use his dragon sense of smell. Now, when we hide, he sniffs, comes straight to our hiding place, and jumps up and down and squeals."

The staff finished the last preparation step — setting out vases of sweet scented, golden honeystar flowers. It was time to put out the *Now Serving* sign, bring out the food, and begin serving.

Luke said, "Dad, I want a dragon of my own."

"NO!" The room froze. All eyes turned. "Sorry. Let me rephrase that using my inside voice. No."

∞∞∞∞

After last year's events, Jake thought he and Squawk would be heroes because his relationship with dragons would change the world. That hadn't happened. At first, Luke and Jake talked a lot with everyone about Squawk and his dragon parents. The village children were enthusiastic. The adults wanted nothing to do with dragons. The adults made rules prohibiting talking about dragons or bringing them to the village.

Regardless of the rules, Luke obsessively talked to Dad about dragons. And, while Jake didn't bring Squawk to the village — being a dragon hatchling, he was too rambunctious for that — Luke and he did spend their free time at Dragon's Cave where Squawk and his parents lived.

Luke liked Squawk, but their relationship wasn't the same as what Jake had with the dragon hatchling. Jake and Squawk understood one another without words. When they were together, they glowed with happiness. Luke wanted to experience that happiness too. However, he would never feel the connection Jake and Squawk felt. Luke needed his own dragon hatchling and no one was going to help him find one. He would have to find and hatch a dragon egg on his own.

Dad had taught him how to care for himself in the wilderness and how to forage for food. That knowledge was his means for achieving his goal. To his pack of camping gear, he added enough food to supplement what he'd forage to last long enough to find a dragon egg. Now he stood ready to begin his quest.

He had never gone against Dad's wishes before, but he couldn't continue living this way. He had to have a dragon hatchling of his own. He had to find a dragon egg. As dawn lit the sky, Luke left the inn.

Chapter 2

The Dragon's Rock

Luke believed more dragons with dragon eggs lived in the foothills, but after four days systematically searching, checking eight caves marked on his map and ten smaller ones not on the map, all he had found were empty caves.

His food was dwindling. He'd expected to find fruits and roots, but only dry grass covered this stretch of slope. Earlier, he'd found a berry bush that turned out to be spike berries. The angry red berries were inedible and they had spikes that stuck in your skin. If he didn't find forage soon, he might have to return home with his quest unfulfilled. Despite his growing despair, he remained determined to continue his quest sure that today would bring success. The next cave would contain a dragon egg.

The cave was empty. As was the next. And, the next.

Not all of the caves looked suitable for dragons, but the larger ones looked much like Dragon's Cave. What if Squawk's family was the only dragon family in the foothills? He refused to believe that. Surely more dragons lived in the foothills.

A small stream, banks covered with honeystar flowers, provided a refill for his canteen and a slab shaped boulder provided a resting place with a view of the Lurean River Valley with its mixture of golden, late-season prairie grass, patches of shadowy green and brown forests, and farm fields where people were harvesting grain. Moving away from the river, the land made a series of steps each rising higher until meeting the foothills bordering the mountains. The Village of Darmok where Luke lived was on the highest step before the foothills took over. He was higher in the foothills than he'd ever been. The idea of going farther into the mountains was daunting. He worried his quest for a dragon egg was hopeless.

A shadow drew Luke's attention skyward to a hawk's silhouette circling, spiraling downward, coming closer. Then he realized it wasn't a hawk; it was a dragon. Instincts brought primal fear: A monster was coming. He jumped down and ducked behind the boulder. Around him, a dusty gust stirred the grass and from the other side of the boulder came the crunch of dry grass crushed.

A lilting voice said, "What were you doing on *my* rock?"

Taking deep breaths, Luke calmed himself. It was only a dragon. A dragon wouldn't harm a person. The Paladins' Peace said so. He would not let the dragon frighten or intimidate him. He stood and faced the dragon. She stood on all fours, her tail held high, her head held low, her wings spread wide, and appearing ready to pounce.

Luke struck his confidence pose — feet apart, fists on hips with elbows akimbo, chin held high — and said, "This isn't *your* rock. It's a *public* rock." He sat on his end of the boulder and faced the valley.

The dragon closed her wings, climbed on the other end of the boulder, sat on her haunches supporting herself with her arms, and wrapped her tail around her hands and feet. After a glance at Luke, she bent her ears back, and with the chin on the end of her wedge-shaped snout held high as Luke had his, she stared out at the valley in the same manner as Luke.

Yellow highlights indicated the dragon was female, but she was not as large as Squawk's parents who were seven times longer than Luke was tall. This dragon was only five times longer.

After listening a while to the wind whispering through the grass, a wind that carried the scent of honeystar flowers that made him long for home, Luke felt compelled to speak, but didn't. Dragons were patient, but he was determined to outwait the dragon. It was a matter of pride, and stubbornness.

After a long wait, the dragon said, "This rock is my rock."

Luke responded, "It is not."

After a while, the dragon spoke again. "I have seen the humans at a distance, but I have never met a human."

"I've met dragons, three of them."

The dragon glanced at Luke. "You are smaller than I expected a human to be."

"You're smaller than what I expect a dragon to be. Well, you're larger than Squawk, but he's a dragon hatchling. You're smaller than his parents, though."

The dragon wiggled. "I am ten years old. I will grow larger."

"Ten? So am I. But, I'm almost eleven."

The dragon spoke a short, musical "Oh," and said, "You are a human child. Now I understand why you are small."

"You too are a child. That's why you're small."

"I am not a child." She sounded offended.

"You're ten. We're not much different from each other."

The dragon looked at her hands, extending her talons to examine them, looked over her shoulder at her wings, which she fluttered; and flicked the end of her tail where it was wrapped around her feet. Then she turned to Luke and tilted her head as she examined him before she said, "We are significantly different."

"That's not what I mean. You're ten and I'm ten. We're both ten-year-old children."

"Ten years old is old enough to begin my Emancipation Cycle and live on my own. And, I too am almost eleven years old."

Jake said, "Dragons move away from home when they're ten?"

The dragon dipped her head. "Normally, a dragonet does not become a young-dragon and begin their Emancipation Cycle before they are twelve years old, if the dragonet is mature enough." Then she lifted her head. "I am mature enough now, but my parents say I am still a dragonet. I come to my rock to be angry."

"Angry?"

"I am angry with my parents. I am not angry with you, even though you are sitting on my rock."

"It's not your rock."

"My parents say dragonets are to be in the weyr at night."

The dragon snapped open her wings, and with a mighty wing stroke and a powerful push of her legs, launched herself into the air, veered south, and sped away.

Her sudden departure had surprised Luke, but he was glad she'd left. He was encouraged by the meeting, though. The world really was changing if he could talk to a strange dragon, and it was proof other dragons did live in the foothills. Donning his pack, he continued his quest by seeking a dragon egg in the next cave.

Chapter 3
On a Quest To Find a Dragon Egg

The next cave was empty, although it was a good place to spend the night. Luke made an entry in his journal to document his quest then slept. In the morning, he again fretted over his food. If he were home, he'd be having one of Dad's wonderful morning meals, and he'd not need to wait with everyone else because Dad would serve him first. He missed Dad, and home.

His search could continue, if he ate less. When he ran out of food, he could head downhill. Days meandering from cave to cave had not taken him far — he could reach home in a day. However, he had to have a dragon egg, so he put aside the idea of going home. He would continue his quest. Eventually, he'd find something to eat.

He hadn't gone far toward a promising rocky outcrop that would surely have a cave when he saw a dragon's silhouette. It was the same dragon as the previous day. He shielded his face from the dust she kicked up backwinging to land in front of him.

The dragon said, "You have returned from your weyr."

"I don't have a weyr; I have a house. And, I didn't go home."

Frozen with her wings partially closed, she said, "You are a human child. Are you not required to go to your house at night?"

"I'm on a quest."

"Oh. What is a quest?"

"A search."

"Oh. For what do you search?" Her wings resumed closing.

"A dragon egg."

Her wings stopped closing, her eyes went wide, and her jaws fell open showing her needle sharp teeth. She said, "Why are you searching for a dragon egg?"

"My cousin Jake has a dragon hatchling. I want one too."

The dragon said, "A dragon cannot be possessed."

Luke hesitated then rephrased, "Jake has a dragon hatchling *friend*. I want one too. Why did you come back?"

"I am curious about you." Then the dragon preened. "And, I am a dragon. You must want to be amazed by my magnificence."

Luke's belly rumbled.

The dragon cocked her head. "What is the sound you are making?"

"It's my stomach. It's telling me I'm hungry."

"Oh." The dragon's partially closed wings snapped open, she leaped into the air, and she flew away.

Luke said, "I hope she doesn't come back," and went to the rocky outcrop, which had an empty cave.

After he'd hiked farther, a strong gust of wind from behind startled him. He spun around to face the dragon.

"I brought food for you." She handed him green stalks.

He said, "It's ... grass."

The dragon nodded.

Luke waved the grass at the dry grass around him. "Just like this grass."

"The grass I brought for you is fresh. The grass is green, and soft, and moist."

"People don't eat grass."

The dragon's shoulders slumped and she cocked her head. "Oh. Are you certain the humans do not consume grass? My parents taught me the humans consume grass."

"I'm certain. Cows and horses eat grass, not people."

"Oh. What do the humans consume?"

"In school they said we're omnivores. That means we eat meat and vegetables and fruits and grains and roots and nuts. We eat lots of things, but not grass."

"Oh." The dragon's wings snapped open and, in a gust of wind, she was off again.

Bringing food was nice of her, even though she was wrong about what people ate, but Luke wished she'd stay away. He dropped the grass and continued his quest.

When the sun was high, the dragon returned. She landed and held out a bush, the whole bush: tan limbs, deep green leaves, bright blue berries, and white roots with dark brown dirt clods attached.

She said, "I brought food for you."

"That's a jancy berry bush."

"Do the humans consume this kind of fruit?"

"Jancy berries are very good, both to eat and for making pies. But, you're supposed to pick the berries off the bush and leave the bush growing in the ground so it can make more berries."

"Oh." She set the bush down and launched herself skyward again.

Luke said, "Now what's she doing?" and began picking the juicy berries.

He'd finished packing the berries he hadn't eaten into food containers when the dragon returned. She held her folded hands before her.

"I brought food for you. I picked the fruits off the plant." She opened her hands.

"No. Those are spike berries. Those can't be eaten, and the spikes stick in your skin and are hard to get out, and they hurt. Let me get my first aid kit. It has forceps to pull them out and a salve that stops pain."

"Oh." The dragon laid the berries to the side.

Luke stopped digging in his pack. "Didn't those stick in your skin? Please, let me see." He took her hands, which were more than twice as wide has his, and examined her palms.

"The fruits tried to penetrate my hide, but dragon hide is strong."

"Are you sure you're not hurt?"

"I am well. Dragons are *totally* indestructible."

"I've always heard that as *practically* indestructible."

"Everything about dragons is strong and powerful." She picked up a stone the size of Luke's fist, extended a talon from the tip of a finger, and began carving.

"That's granite, and you're cutting it."

"I enjoy making rock sculptures." She finished and handed him the stone. "This rock sculpture is for you."

"It's my face. Thank you. What's your name?"

She said, "I am <*Emidonley*>."

"That's the kind of noise Squawk and his parents make. It's pretty, but I can only make a few of those sounds. May I call you *Ladyhawk* instead?"

"Why do you wish to call me *Ladyhawk*?"

"You're a lady. And, the first time I saw you, your fanned out tail wings and wide spread primary wings made you look like a hawk. Together, those make *Ladyhawk*."

"What is a *lady* and what is a *hawk*?"

"A *lady* is a female. A *hawk* is a bird." When, in silence, the dragon stared at him, Luke added, "I know you're not a bird, but your silhouette in the sky is hawk-like."

"Oh. You may call me *Ladyhawk*."

"My name is *Luke*."

"Luke is a nice human name."

Luke put the rock sculpture in his pack and put the pack on. "Will you walk with me, please?"

"Where are we going?"

"I'm on a quest to find a dragon egg. My map shows another cave up there. Help me look inside, please."

Chapter 4

Song and Dance

The cave was empty. They headed toward the next cave on the map, a cave a long way away. Luke kept looking for rocky outcrops in which unmapped caves might hide.

Ladyhawk said, "I do not often walk places. Dragons are creatures of the sky."

"You don't know what you're missing. There are many surprises on the ground. You should walk more often."

Beyond the next rise lay a slight depression holding scattered boulders that had fallen from an escarpment above.

Ladyhawk's eyes widened. She crouched, lowered her head, wiggled her backend, twitched her tail, and said, "Those rocks are my rocks."

"They're not your rocks."

She spread her wings, leaped, glided to the nearest boulder, struck a regal pose, and said, "This rock is my rock." She leaped to the next boulder and posed again. "This rock is my rock." Then, to the next, passing over Luke as he weaved his way between the boulders. "This rock is my rock."

Before she could claim another boulder, Luke said, "How is it you know my language?"

She paused, perching on the boulder. "My parents taught me the human language."

"Why do they know it?"

Another leap. "All dragons know the human language."

"I mean why? I assume dragons haven't always known it."

"Oh. When the humans were first encountered, dragons learned to speak with the humans." She leaped to the next boulder. "Dragons have taught their offspring the human language ever since."

"How do you make the sounds? Your mouth moves as if you're talking, but your mouth isn't made right for talking."

"A structure in my throat makes the sounds. Dragons can make any sound."

"Can you show me?"

She hopped again before pausing to make sounds. A lapaki's *cheep-cheep-chow*, which sounded funny coming from a dragon. The *snarl* of a miser cat, which sounded scary coming from a dragon. *Thunder*, which prompted Luke to look for storm clouds. Then she said, *"I am on a quest to find a dragon egg."*

Luke said, "What was that last one?"

"The last sound was an imitation of you."

"I don't sound like that."

"My imitation of you was accurate." She hopped to the last boulder as Luke continued toward the edge of the boulder field. "The human language is terrible." She hopped off the boulder and walked beside Luke out of the boulder field making one last wistful glance at the boulders as they left them behind. "I do not understand how the humans communicate without confusion. As with everything about dragons, the dragon language is precise and perfect."

"I think the dragon language sounds musical."

"If you think the sound of the dragon language is musical, you should hear a dragon song."

"Dragons sing? Can you show me?"

She stopped, stood on her hind legs, and sang a pure note that became multiple harmonizing tones. The melody turned brisk and bouncy as she sang dragon words.

In rhythm with the song, she swayed, swooped, and twirled. She stretched her arms one direction then the other as she leaped from foot to foot. Her wings unfurled and she played peek-a-boo by flourishing them in front and behind her body. She floated and glided, her movements appearing to defy gravity. Beginning at her head, she made a sinuous wave that traveled down her neck, through her chest, abdomen, and hips, and down her tail to its tip. With her back to Luke, she fanned her tail wings wide and shook her hips to rattle them. As the song ended, she spun around to face him with her arms and wings spread wide, her head held high.

Her muscular physique's bronze color shimmered in the sunlight. Streaks of sunshine yellow bounded by royal blue traced the spars of her primary and tail wings. The same yellow and blue outlined where angled back, caramel colored horns grew on her head. Green bands the color of newly sprouted wheat ran from her eyes, down the sides of her neck, above her primary wings, below her tail wings, and down the sides of her tail to its tip. On her chest, at the base of her neck, was a serving tray sized, ruby red oval.

She opened her eyes, looked around, closed her eyes, crouched, wrapped her tail around her feet, and concealed herself by mantling her wings over her head and body.

Luke parted her wings. A shaft of sunlight lit her face. She opened her eyes revealing irises the color of embers glowing in a campfire.

Luke said, "That. Was. Awesome."

The dragon's ears pricked and she relaxed her wings. "You liked my song and dance?"

"That was the most incredible thing I've ever heard or seen. You're amazing."

Ladyhawk made a cooing sound and rubbed her head on Luke. He wrapped his arms around her snout, but then a tingle tickled the nape of his neck causing him to shudder and reach back to scratch it.

Luke said, "It makes me want a dragon hatchling of my own even more."

Ladyhawk stood, closed her wings, and said, "A dragon cannot be possessed."

Luke took off walking. "Let's go. It's still a ways to the next cave and a dragon egg."

Ladyhawk followed.

Chapter 5

Then the Dragons Were Gone

As evening approached, clouds gathered.

Luke said, "Rain's coming. I need to set up my shelter."

"I can shelter you."

"You need to go home for the night."

"I will stay with you."

"Don't your parents expect you to come home?"

"I could ask you the same question."

Luke removed his pack and set it down. "Dad's probably mad I ran off. I really miss him. Won't you miss your parents? Won't they be mad if you don't come home?"

Ladyhawk lifted her chin. "I am mature enough to be on my own."

"Are you sure? I know I'm not." When Ladyhawk paused, her mouth open but her words not coming out, Luke said, "How can you shelter me?"

"I will show you."

The dragon walked two circles, made little marching steps, lay down, wiggled, and smiled at Luke. He had never before noticed that dragons smiled. The gesture was subtle, but genuine. Inside himself, he felt Ladyhawk's joy, which brought a flutter to his chest.

"Join me," she said, leaning on her side and bending her neck and tail into a curve.

He picked up his pack and sat inside the dragon crescent. Raindrops began to fall.

Luke said, "How is this sheltering me?"

The dragon's wings snapped open and folded over her head and over him covering them both.

Luke laughed and said, "Wings are for more than hiding under. But, you're getting rained on."

"Rain cannot damage a dragon. However, rain on my head is annoying. Sheltering keeps the rain off my head."

"This is cozy. Thank you." He spread his sleeping roll and climbed in.

Ladyhawk snuggled her head close and hooked the tip of her tail across him.

∞∞∞∞

"Luke, the rain has stopped and morning has arrived."

Luke grumbled then said, "It's still dark."

The dragon lifted her wings.

Luke covered his eyes. "Bright light. Bright light."

"I told you morning had arrived."

"I needed to get up anyway. Please, wait here."

When he returned, he put his sleeping roll away, ate berries, and donned his pack. "Let's go find a dragon egg."

"Are you continuing that silly quest?"

"It's not silly. And, you're supposed to be helping me find a dragon egg."

"Why do you think I am supposed to help you find a dragon egg?"

"Because you came with me on my quest."

"I came with you because you asked me to walk with you."

He nodded. "So you could help me find a dragon egg."

She shook her head. "I never said I would help you find a dragon egg."

"I need a dragon egg."

"There are no dragon eggs here. No dragon families live here except the family to the north," she pointed north, "and my family," she pointed south.

"How do you know?"

She made a sweeping motion with her hand. "I would sense the dragons with my dragon senses."

"If you're not going to help me, what good are you?"

"If that is your attitude, maybe I should leave."

"Maybe you should."

"Maybe I will."

130

"Go ahead, leave. Please, go away and don't come back." Luke scowled.

Ladyhawk's ears folded flat, her pupils constricted, and a subtle scowl settled on her face.

Luke forced down the corners of his lips, pressed the middle of his upper lip to his nose, and furrowed his brow until his eyebrows met.

Ladyhawk narrowed her eyes and furrowed her brow. The tip of her tail twitched.

Her gaze shifted to look past Luke. Her eyes went wide, her ears sprang up, her jaws parted, and inside himself, Luke felt impending catastrophe. From the south, two silhouettes approached.

Shadows raced across the ground then, with a gust of wind, the dragons landed facing Ladyhawk. The dragons, a male and a female, were as large as Squawk's parents were. The three dragons engaged in an intense dragon language discussion that ended when Ladyhawk dipped her head. The two large dragons leaped into the sky heading in the direction from which they had come. Ladyhawk glanced at Luke then followed them.

The abruptness of the dragons arriving and leaving left Luke feeling frustrated. As Ladyhawk retreated into the distance, he found it difficult to catch his breath. Weakness in his legs caused him to sink to the ground. His pulse raced. His stomach ached.

Ladyhawk stopped, turned to face him, and hovered. The other dragons looped around behind her and encouraged her to continue with them.

Then the dragons were gone.

Chapter 6

No One Else Was Like Her

Luke sat in the grass with his arms wrapped around his middle. He'd never felt an illness like this. After a while, the ill feeling diminished, but he still felt desperation verging on panic. He got to his feet. He still had his quest to do.

If Ladyhawk was correct, the foothills were a lost cause. He needed to go into the mountains to find a dragon egg. Looking south toward where the dragons had flown, he said, "I'll find a dragon egg without your help." He walked east toward the mountains.

A slab shaped boulder reminded him of where he had met Ladyhawk. He'd been scared at first, but she had turned out not to be scary. She was kind and curious, and the way she kept claiming ownership of boulders was endearing. And, she was caring. When she learned he was hungry, she'd brought him food.

Luke stumbled and fell, his arms landing in a pool of cold water. If he hadn't stumbled, he would have stepped into the spring. He wiped his face, scolded himself for letting his mind wander instead of paying attention to where he was going, and topped off his canteen.

Lining the banks of the stream that flowed from the spring were honeystar flowers. Proudly peeking out from among the golden flowers were the sky blue flowers of rattidash. He pulled one out of the ground, washed the long, fat, purple root, and began eating. It was sweet and tender. If Ladyhawk were here, he could show her another food he could eat. The thought of how she'd say *Oh* and fly away to find some for him made him smile. He collected more of the roots to take with him.

The top of the next hill revealed glorious mountains spanning the entirety of the eastern horizon; mountains with flanks dappled in multiple shades of green forest and peaks white with snow and ice. Luke wasn't impressed. Ladyhawk's song and dance had been more magnificent than any mundane mountain view. She could make any sound, but she spoke and sang with a soothing, smooth cadenced voice. Her movements were graceful and precise. Her hide had the appearance of scales, but it was soft and supple belying the strength beneath. She smelled floral. Sheltering under her wings had made Luke feel more serene than he had ever felt before. She was friendly, kind, caring, smart, talented, funny, and beautiful. No one else was like her. And, he had told her to go away.

He took a shaky breath and said, "I need Ladyhawk."

He turned away from the mountains and walked south.

Chapter 7
Rescued and Reunited

Luke walked. The fear of never seeing Ladyhawk again drove him onward. He didn't know how, but he'd find her or his heart would burst.

He had walked for hours when something touched him, but not on the outside. The feeling was inside. Energy and excitement replaced his desperation and panic. A direction pulled at him as if he were a compass needle. He followed it.

The hills gave way to rugged gullies. Luke continued in the direction that drew him. The farther he went, the stronger the feeling became, but the direction became less precise. He somehow knew that meant he was getting close. He quickened his pace.

When he came to a path on a ledge, he followed it around a corner, and around another, and another. The path wasn't straight, but it tended in the correct direction. Around the last corner, though, he stood on a narrow, rocky shelf with the steep slope reaching above and dropping below with no way forward. He turned to backtrack, but the ledge behind him collapsed leaving a gap too wide to cross. More pieces of rock chipped off further reducing the ledge he stood on. He found handholds, held himself against the cliff face, held back his tears, and took a breath to call out for help.

The feeling that drew him went from being imprecise to surrounding him. Then the wind began to gust. Behind him, beating her wings in a figure eight to hover, an exquisite dragon gleamed in the afternoon light.

"Luke, what are you doing?"

"I'm trying to find you."

"This is not the correct place to find me."

"You're here, aren't you? Can you help me, please?"

"I cannot fly close to the cliff without hitting my wings, but I have an idea. I will land next to you."

"You what?"

Ladyhawk threw herself into the wall of rock at Luke's right. The cliff had no handholds suitable for a dragon. Instead, she drove her talons into the cliff. The stone her right hand talons dug into cracked and sloughed off causing her to lose her grip. The slab of rock hit her right foot knocking it loose from the cliff. Luke felt pain in his right foot. He also felt as if he were losing his balance. He gripped his handholds tighter. Ladyhawk fluttered her wings and again drove her right hand and foot talons into the cliff. Once she had a firm hold, she folded her wings.

She said, "I will take you in my arm."

"You what?"

She pulled her left hand's talons from the cliff, wrapped her arm around him, and pulled him to her. The dragon's grip was more on his pack than on him, though. He grasped the pack's straps.

"I'm slipping."

The dragon pulled her right hand's talons from the cliff, wrapped her arm around his legs, and hugged him tightly with both her arms.

"I have a secure hold on you."

She pushed off pulling her foot talons out of the cliff as she did. Luke felt weightless as they fell backward. Ladyhawk rotated to right herself and snapped open her wings to arrest their fall. Luke felt strain in parts of his body he didn't even have. At the bottom of the ravine, the dragon canted her wings, landed next to the stream, and released him.

He shed his pack, ducked under her still open wing, and knelt at her right foot, which she was holding off the ground. "You hurt your foot." He pulled her foot into his lap causing her to tip over and lay on her left side.

"My foot is not damaged. After rest, my foot will be fine." She flexed it. "My foot is already better and I have not even used rest yet."

He released her foot, raced under her wing and around to her back to examine her wings' shoulder joints. "You hurt your wings."

"My wings are not damaged."

"I felt the hurt."

"A small amount of strain is not uncommon. After rest, my wings will be fine." She flexed her wings up and down, forwards and backwards, and in circles making Luke duck. "My wings are already better. I may not need to use rest after all for either my foot or my wings."

With a gust of wind, the two large dragons arrived. They landed far enough apart to not tangle their wings then converged as they approached.

Together, Luke and Ladyhawk faced them.

Chapter 8

Love and Contentment

The dragon adults spoke in the dragon language. Ladyhawk dipped her head. Luke felt shame wash over him. As the dragons continued to speak, Luke felt a rush of pride, and Ladyhawk raised her head.

"What'd they say?"

"My parents are disappointed in me for leaving the weyr when I was not allowed to leave. However, my parents are impressed with my quick thinking and actions to rescue you."

When her parents spoke again, Ladyhawk pulled Luke to her and brought her wings around to conceal him.

"What'd they say?"

"My parents say you must return to your house."

"Please, uncover me. If they're talking about me, I want to be a part of the conversation."

Ladyhawk parted her wings, slightly.

"Please, all the way. And, don't squeeze."

She put her wings away and let him stand on his own.

To the dragon parents, Luke said, "If you're talking about me, please, speak my language."

The father dragon narrowed his eyes, moved closer to loom over Luke, and said in a menacing voice, "A stray human child does not belong with dragons."

Ladyhawk again gathered Luke in her arms, drew him close, and flung her wings around him. "Luke is my human."

The mother dragon said, "A human cannot be possessed."

Ladyhawk hesitated then rephrased, "Luke is my human *friend*."

"Ladyhawk." Luke pushed against her arms.

"I am sorry." She unwrapped him and let him go.

Luke faced the dragon parents, struck his confidence pose, and said, "I'm not a stray. I was on a quest searching for — well, I found Ladyhawk. I know now she's what I sought. Now that I've found her, I'm not leaving her ever again."

The father dragon slammed down his talons. The mother dragon roared. The scowls on the faces of the two huge dragons made Luke wish Ladyhawk would hide him under her wings again, but she didn't. Instead, she crouched to his level and huddle close to him.

Luke lifted his chin, stared at the adult dragons, and said, "You won't harm me."

The dragons deepened the furrows of their brows and bared more of their teeth. The father dragon said, "What makes you think we will not damage you?"

"Because, Ladyhawk's kind." He laid his hand on her neck. "She learned that from you. Besides, I don't think you'd break the Paladins' Peace."

The dragons' scowls broke into stymied dismay.

The mother dragon said to Ladyhawk, "You do not know how to care for the human child."

"Luke cares for himself."

"The human child became stuck on a cliff."

Luke scuffed his toe in the gravel and said, "I thought it was a trail that would lead me to Ladyhawk. And, it did, sort of, although not in quite the way I had intended."

The father dragon said, "You do not know what kind of human food grass to feed the human child."

Ladyhawk took a sharp breath. "That reminds me. What you taught me about the humans consuming grass is not correct. The humans do not consume grass. Cows and houses consume grass."

Luke said, "It's horses, not houses. Cows and horses eat grass."

"Oh." Ladyhawk turned to her parents. "Cows and horses consume grass. Luke is teaching me about human foods the humans actually consume. Luke taught me about a human food fruit he can consume and a fruit he cannot consume."

"I found another food I can eat. It's a plant root. I brought some to show you."

"Oh. Show me the human food plant root."

Luke glanced at the dragon parents. "Maybe we should do that later."

The father dragon said, "The humans will say we violated the Paladins' Peace by stealing the human child."

"No, they won't." Luke paused before continuing. "Well, Mister Travis would have — he didn't like the Paladins' Peace — but he left after Jake and Squawk got together."

The mother dragon brought her head to Luke's level and, in a sweet voice, said, "Do you not miss your parents?"

"I miss Dad a lot. I've never been away from him for so long."

"Do you think Dad is sad?"

"Dad's worried about me, I'm sure. I shouldn't have run away. But, I had to find a —" He looked at Ladyhawk. "I found Ladyhawk. I can't leave her."

"You will let Dad stay sad?"

"I don't want to do that."

"What is the solution to the problem?"

"I don't know. I can't leave Ladyhawk, though."

Ladyhawk said, "I will accompany you to your house."

The dragon parents reacted, in unison, with, "NO!"

The father dragon said, "You cannot go to the human town. The humans are monsters."

"People aren't monsters." Luke's words echoed off the ravine's walls.

The mother dragon said, "The humans attack dragons, and damage dragons, and murder dragons, and drive dragons from our weyrs. The humans are monsters."

"I admit people used to do that, but the world is changing. We now have the Paladins' Peace." Luke wrapped his arms around Ladyhawk's neck. "Now we can be friends. If Ladyhawk goes with me, I'll go home. Otherwise, I'll stay here with her, and with you."

The two dragon adults stared then moved away, held their heads close, and whispered.

Luke said, "Your parents don't like me, do they?"

"My parents do like you."

"How do you know?"

"I can hear them talking. My parents forget how well my ears function."

"What are they saying?"

"They do not understand what has happened to me and why I am attached to a stray human child." She raised her voice drawing her parents' attention. "Luke is friendly and kind and caring and sophisticated and talented and funny and cute —"

Luke interrupted with, "Cute?"

She turned to him and said, "You are very cute," before continuing to address her parents. "I do not want to be separated from Luke again. Separation causes pain."

The stream's murmur covered the silence that lasted so long Luke felt he'd lost the argument for staying with Ladyhawk. What would he do if he were forced to leave her?

The mother dragon said, "You may accompany the human child to the human child's weyr."

Ladyhawk said, "The human child's name is *Luke*, and Luke lives in a *house*."

"You may accompany Luke to Luke's house. Your father and I will accompany you. When Luke arrives at his house, you will return with us to our weyr."

After several subtle expressions shifted across Ladyhawk's face, she said, "We will deal with the returning to our weyr issue later. Let us begin our journey."

Luke said, "It's almost dark. Morning would be better."

"Oh." To her parents, Ladyhawk said, "I am taking Luke to our weyr. In the morning, we will begin our journey."

With her parents following, Ladyhawk led Luke to the most splendid cave he had ever seen. Her well-made nest was spacious, lined with soft sweet-moss, and it had a floral scent. To the left of the nest, proudly displayed on a ledge in the cave wall, were dozens of rock carvings of animals. To the right of the nest was a substantial assortment of flat, round river rocks in a pile half as tall as Luke.

Ladyhawk scampered onto the small mountain of rocks triggering avalanches that sent stones skittering across the floor in every direction. She reached out with her arms, tail, and wings to scoop the escaping cobbles back onto the pile, the remarkable dexterity of her wings allowing her to capture even the most wayward. Once the heap stabilized, she said, "These rocks are my rocks."

"That's a nice hoard," said Luke.

"My rocks collection is not a *hoard*. My rocks collection is a *collection*."

"Okay. That's a nice collection."

She lifted her chin and smiled her subtle smile. "Thank you." She climbed off the pile causing a new series of avalanches. Using her arms, tail, and wings again, she pushed the rocks back onto the mound. Once satisfied the rocks would stay put, she climbed into the nest, and said, "This is where I sleep." After walking two circles, making little marching steps, lying down, and curling up, she said, "Join me."

Luke placed his sleeping roll in the middle of her sleeping knot and climbed in.

Ladyhawk rubbed her head on him and hooked the tip of her tail across him. A feeling of love and contentment filled Luke as he slipped into sleep.

Chapter 9

You and I Are Changing the World

After hiking for two days with Ladyhawk perching on every boulder along the way to claim ownership, they topped the last hill overlooking the Village of Darmok. The dragon parents stopped.

Ladyhawk said, "My parents do not trust the humans and want nothing to do with the humans, but I will go with you into the human town."

"The adults won't break the Paladins' Peace, but they don't trust dragons and won't approach. However, the children are excited about dragons." Luke said to the parent dragons, "When the children surround Ladyhawk, don't worry." He patted Ladyhawk on the shoulder. "They won't harm her."

∞∞∞∞∞

Shocked by what they saw as Luke and Ladyhawk approached, people moved out of the way and then gathered behind them to follow them to the inn. When they stopped, the adults and children gathered in a circle around them but stayed back a dozen or more paces.

Dad pushed through the crowd, swept his son up in his arms, and hugged him. "Luke, where have you been? I've been searching everywhere."

Luke returned Dad's hug. "I'm sorry I ran off. Forgive me, please. I have someone for you, and everyone else, to meet."

Dad set Luke down and wrinkled his brow at the dragon.

Using his public address voice, Luke said, "Meet my friend. Her name is *Ladyhawk*."

Despite attempts by the adults to keep their wide-eyed children at their sides, the children broke free and rushed forward making *oohing* and *aahing* sounds.

The throng stopped. One child said, "May we touch her, please?"

Luke said, "Politely ask her."

The child turned to Ladyhawk. "May we touch you, please?"

"You may touch me."

The children mobbed her.

Luke yelled at the children, "Please, be gentle with her." Then he moved to stand by Ladyhawk's head and said to her, "See how the adults stand back, but the children are excited. This is the future." He hugged his dragon friend. "You and I are changing the world."

Part Four
Tipping Point

Chapter 1
Seeking Evidence

Eradicate the humans. That was <Arizesyley's> desire. But, no, the Dragon Council wouldn't let her. The Paladins' Peace had ended the war with the humans, and the Council insisted dragons would not violate that peace. With evidence, though, she believed she could convince the Council to change its mind. Yet, another morning soaring over the borderlands seeking evidence of the humans preparing to attack had again revealed nothing. Frustrated, she returned to her weyr.

When she entered, <Kedekitley> jumped up from his drafting table, bounded to her, pulled her into his arms, twined his tail tightly around hers in a tail hug, mantled his wings over her, rubbed his head on hers, and said in the dragon language, "<I love you and missed you. What did you find?>"

"<I also love you and missed you. I found nothing.>"

"<The humans are not preparing to attack.>"

"<Give the humans the opportunity and the humans will attack.>" She expressed her frustration with a huff. "<What are you working on?>"

She followed him to his drafting table where he said, "<This is the design my human friend created for the bridge he wants me to help construct. The design is excellent, and sophisticated. The humans appear to be more sophisticated than we believe them to be. I am analyzing the design to ensure there are no mathematical calculation errors.>"

"<The Council said dragons are not to interact with the humans, and now you are validating the humans' mathematical calculations?>"

"<The Council is wrong. Dragons convinced the humans to end the war by damaging the humans' infrastructure. If we help repair the damage, we demonstrate we can be the humans' friends. Being the humans' friends will sustain the Paladins' Peace.>"

<Arizesyley> said, "<I agree the Council is wrong. However, if we eradicate the humans, the humans will never again murder dragons and we no longer need the Paladins' Peace.>"

"<Attacking the humans would violate the Paladins' Peace. Helping the humans does not violate the Paladins' Peace. Besides, dragons do not eradicate food animals.>"

"<The humans are sophonts, not food animals.>"

"<Even though we do not consider the humans to be food animals,>" said <Kedekitley>, "<instincts tell us the humans are food animals, and dragons do not eradicate food animals. Dragons nurture food animals. Have you lost your instincts?>"

"<My instincts are intact, but my common sense takes precedence. I will continue seeking evidence the humans are preparing to attack.>"

"<I wish you would give up your notion of eradicating the humans and join me in making friends with the humans.>"

Shaking her head, she said, "<Never. We have discussed this before. I will not change my mind. You do what you must, but the humans are monsters. I will not be friends with the humans.>"

"<You could stop petitioning the Council to eradicate the humans.>"

She furrowed her brow and made her most stern frown. "<Are you here because the Council told you to encourage me to change my attitude about the humans?>"

He tightened the twining of his tail with hers and rubbed his head on hers again. "<I am here because you are my life-mate and I love you, but I admit the Council told me to keep you under observation.>"

"<Tell the Council I will not violate the Paladins' Peace, but I will find evidence to justify eradicating the humans. In fact, the Conclave is in five days. I will tell the Council myself.>" She untwined her tail and walked toward the weyr entrance. "<I am flying another patrol.>" As she passed through the foyer, she glanced back and said, "<I love you. You are the best dragon. I am glad you are my life-mate.>"

Chapter 2
The Human Child

Her primary wings outstretched in their soaring configuration, the fan of her tail wings steering her, <Arizesyley> rode the updrafts over the borderland foothills. She could ride the wind all day without a single flap, scanning the ground with her dragon senses, searching, seeking, hoping to find evidence of the humans' treachery. The humans were always rushing from place to place on foot, on horseback, in their wagons, and in their boats on the Great River, but she never saw anything suspicious, and at the altitude where she flew, the humans never noticed her.

She went far to the south and far to the north, but in the middle, near her weyr, was from where she thought the attack would come. The Lesser River flowed out of the mountains and made easy access to where most dragons lived. The worst attacks had come from here, attacks that had resulted in the murders of dragons, attacks that had convinced the Council to strike back.

When the Council had ordered the attacks on the humans' roads, bridges, structures, wagons, and boats while not damaging the humans or the humans' animals, she had been furious. She had wanted to argue for eradicating the humans, but she had been too young to have a voice in the deliberations. Before she was old enough, <Improecley> and the Human Paladin, after an epic confrontation, had made peace.

On the mental map her dragon senses created of her surroundings, an anomaly appeared. She came about and swept the area again. Two humans lay on the ground. Flying lower to bring more of her senses within range, she detected no signs of life. Dead humans lying about was not normal.

She wanted to investigate, but stopped herself from spiraling down to land. She was safe at altitude, and because she always stayed in the sky, she never risked an encounter with the humans. If she landed, she would be vulnerable to human attack. Except, her senses would warn her of nearby humans, unless they wore the armor the humans acquired from the Gird creatures. The Gird creatures' green and brown metal provided the humans a shell as strong as dragon hide, and it somehow interfered with dragon senses making the humans difficult to detect. The Gird-metal was also used to construct murder weapons that could penetrate dragon hide. Nevertheless, she wanted to know why the humans were here, and dead. If she was vigilant, and brave, she could land and investigate. She spiraled down.

Scents indicated other humans had been there. She kept her wings ready to launch herself into the sky and concentrated on her surroundings, searching, seeking, fearful the humans were still near.

One scent indicated a human was near. To have been as strong as it was, the human did not wear Gird-metal armor, but the human must have been shielded in a place that tempered her other dragon senses. If the human came out of that place, she would know. As long as the human stayed put, she would have an opportunity to investigate the dead humans.

The humans' bodies had damage sufficient to cause death. Scuffs on the ground indicated a struggle. The scent of most of the spilled blood matched the two dead humans, but several patches were from other humans. None of the blood matched the scent of the human hiding nearby.

She still didn't have the answer as to what had happened to cause the deaths of the two humans. Maybe the hiding human could tell her. She would need to risk an encounter with the human to ask the question. Be vigilant. Be brave. She could do this. She turned to the task of locating the human.

Following the human's scent up the gully led to a massive slide of dirt and boulders. The scent came from a small gap under a large boulder wedged against smaller boulders. She lowered her head to gaze underneath. From far in the back, human eyes returned her gaze.

Steeling herself, and preparing her wings for a quick escape, she said in the human language, "Come out from under the rock."

A quiet whimper came out.

<Arizesyley> said, "I will not violate the Paladins' Peace. Come out."

"No, no, no."

"Come out."

After a spell of silence, a shuffling sound came out of the hole followed by a dirty human child only three-quarters the size of a human adult. Even though the human child had no Gird-metal murder weapon and looked incapable of damaging a dragon, <Arizesyley's> fear of the humans caused her to step back and tense her wings.

The human child said, "Are the Cultists gone? Where are Mommy and Daddy?" The human child ran down the gully its tangle of dark hair bouncing as it called out "Mommy, Daddy."

Maintaining her readiness for flight, <Arizesyley> followed the human child.

The human child knelt at the first body and said, "Daddy, Daddy, Daddy." Moving to the second body, the human child shook the body, and said, "Mommy, Mommy, Mommy." The human child then sat on their heels and began a keening cry.

<Arizesyley> said, "What happened to the humans?"

Between ragged sobs, the human child said, "The Cultists ... killed ... Mommy and Daddy."

<Arizesyley> tilted her head at an inquisitive angle and said, "All right then. Are Cultists humans?"

"Yes, yes, yes."

"The humans are dead because of human on human violence? I am not surprised. The humans are monsters." She prepared to take flight.

The human child said, "No, no, no, where are you going?"

"I am returning to flying my patrol."

"No, no, no. Please, don't leave me." The human child glanced toward the road.

<Arizesyley's> pulse jumped when she realized she had lowered her guard. She scolded herself, resumed her vigilance, and again prepared to take flight. "This situation is none of my concern."

"Please, don't leave me. The Cultists will return."

"What do you expect me to do?"

"Please, take me with you."

"Why would I take a human child with me?"

"Because ... you don't want me to die."

<Arizesyley> didn't care what happened to the humans. Yet, the human child looked so helpless. Tears from their intense green eyes flowed down their face. The human child's skin was almost the same color as the dust that covered it. The human child's tears turned the dust to mud. Her nurturing instincts made her decision for her. She said, "I will take you with me."

"Please, wait, wait, wait." After removing a silver object from the body called *Mommy* and hanging it around their own neck, the human child took a trembling breath, and said, "Please, help me bury them."

<Arizesyley> hesitated until the human child's pleading eyes prompted her to move to a suitable place to dig. As they worked, the human child kept glancing toward the road. So did <Arizesyley>.

For the last step, the human child insisted <Arizesyley> use her dragon strength to force a rockslide to cover the spot. The human child clutched the object around their neck and said, "I don't want the Cultists to find them." With the task finished, the human child said, "We need to leave. How will you take me with you?"

"Climb into my pouch." <Arizesyley> lifted a wing and stretched open a flap of skin on her side.

Even through their tears, the human child's eyes lit up. "Dragons have pockets?"

"Dragons have pouches, one on each side, that allow us to carry our eggs until they are close to hatching and to carry our hatchlings until they become dragonets and are large enough to fly on their own. The pouches are also useful for carrying other items. You will fit inside. Climb into my pouch."

"No, no, no, it's not a pouch. It's a pocket." The human child climbed in and said, "Please, go, go, go."

<Arizesyley> took flight.

Chapter 3

Trying to Return the Human Child

When <Arizesyley> entered the weyr, <Kedekitley> rushed to her, embraced her as he always did, and said in the dragon language, "<I love you and missed you. What did you find?>" Then he sniffed. "<Why are you emitting the scent of the humans?>"

She pulled what she had found out of her pouch and gently set them down.

<Kedekitley> staggered back, his eyes wide. With shock in his voice, he said, "<Where did you acquire a human child?>"

The human child hid behind <Arizesyley's> leg and peeked out to look at <Kedekitley>.

"<The human child was orphaned.>" In the human language, she said to the human child, "Do not be afraid. This dragon is my life-mate. He is a good dragon. Sometimes, he is too good. He helps the humans by validating their mathematical calculations." She gave him a stern look.

<Kedekitley> continued in the dragon language, "<Why did you bring her to our weyr?>"

"<Her? How do you know the human child's gender?>" She moved to look at the human child, but the human child kept moving to stay behind her.

"<I was taught to identify a human's gender using ultrasound and scent signatures that contain gender specific data points. If you are not correct, the human will correct you. Regardless, you should not have brought the human child to our weyr.>"

She shook her head. "<The human child's parents were murdered by the humans. I could not leave the human child alone and in danger of not surviving. Dragons nurture food animals, although, the human child is not a food animal. The human child is a sophont.>"

<Kedekitley> craned his neck to the side trying to get another look at the human child where she hid behind <Arizesyley>. "<Your instincts activated; so, even though you want to eradicate the humans, you brought the human child to our weyr? You need to return the human child to the nearest human town to where you found the human child. I will go with you.>"

She contemplated the situation. She had not considered what to do with the human child when she agreed to take the human child with her. She said, "<You are correct. It is best that I return the human child to the humans. I can do the task on my own. I am brave, and I will be vigilant. You stay here.>" She put the human child back into her pouch. As she left, she said, "<That the humans murder other humans as well as dragons is more evidence the humans are monsters and need to be eradicated.>"

∞∞∞∞

<Arizesyley> spiraled down and backwinged to make a gentle landing in the human town's small central open space. The humans cried out and scattered. From high altitude, she hadn't noticed, but up close, it was obvious the human town's structures were in poor repair. In the mix of many human scents, she recognized a few from the human child's parents' murder location.

Be vigilant. Be brave. She could do this. She only needed to deliver the human child and leave. She kept her wings ready for a quick departure.

The humans who had run away returned carrying bows and arrows and sharp pointed tools, spears, and sword weapons. She felt a spasm of fear, but let out the breath she'd been holding when the weapons she could visually examine did not leave the disturbing fuzzy void of Gird-metal in her other dragon senses. The weapons the humans used to threaten her would do little more than gouge her ablative hide.

She said, "I will not violate the Paladins' Peace. I am here to return a human child I found." She pulled the human child out of her pouch and set her down.

One of the humans cried out, "It's the beast child. Kill it."

The human child screamed, "No, no, no."

A spear flew at the human child. <Arizesyley's> dragon reflexes allowed her to knock the spear aside.

More humans in the crowd shouted, "Kill the beast child."

<Arizesyley> drew the human child to her, wrapped her wings around her as a shield, and said, "You are violating the Paladins' Peace."

A volley of arrows and thrown weapons hit her followed by humans with swords running up to slash and stab. The humans continued to cry out, "Kill the beast child."

The human child said, "The Cultists want to kill me."

She clutched the human child to her chest, spun around using her tail to knock the humans away, spread her wings, leaped straight up, and raced to her weyr.

∞∞∞∞

As she entered the weyr, <Kedekitley> stood preparing to sprint to her but stopped when she set down the human child she had been clutching to her chest.

He said, "<You did not return the human child.>"

The human child crawled into a corner, curled up by wrapping her arms around her knees, and cried.

"<You are damaged.>" <Kedekitley> rushed to <Arizesyley>.

"<I am not damaged.>"

"<You have gashes.>" He examined the cuts, scrapes, and gouges in her hide.

"<I am well. The gashes are superficial.>"

"<Did the humans do this to you?>" He wrapped his arms and tail around her and laid his head against her neck. "<I am sorry I told you to go to the human town. I should have accompanied you. I should have gone in your place. You being damaged is my fault. I did not expect the humans to attack you.>"

She hugged him back. "<The incident is not your fault. I was being brave and doing what we thought was best for the human child.>"

He turned toward the human child. "<Is the human child damaged?>"

"<I scanned the human child with my ultrasound. I detected no damage.>"

The human child cried out, "Why, why, why did you take me there?"

<Arizesyley> said, "I was returning you to the humans."

"The Cultists want to kill me."

<Kedekitley> said, "<What happened?>"

"<The humans attempted to murder the human child. I told you the humans are monsters and must be eradicated.>" To the human child she said, "I am sorry, human child. I did not understand the humans wanted to damage you." She pulled away from <Kedekitley>, lay next to the human child, wrapped an arm around her, and said, "I promise to never let the humans damage you, ever."

<Kedekitley> came to crouch next to her and the human child and said, "<What will you do?>"

"<I will keep the human child.>"

Chapter 4

We Should Not Blame Ourselves

<Kedekitley> said, "<You know nothing about the humans. How do you think we can care for the human child?>"

"<Did you say *we*?>"

"<If you keep the human child, I too keep the human child.>"

<Arizesyley> smiled and said, "<You are the best dragon, but me choosing to keep my human child makes my human child my responsibility.>" She brushed pieces of plant out of her human child's hair.

"<I accept you wanting to be responsible for your human child, but I will assist you.>"

"<Thank you. Since you know about the humans, you can tell me what to do.>" Then, she took hold of <Kedekitley's> hands and, in an anxious voice, said, "<What should I do?>"

"<Based on what I have observed, you must first show your human child where to make a toilet for when she needs to reduce her mass and where to find clean water for drinking.>"

"<That is a beginning. While I do that, construct a nest for my human child.>"

∞∞∞∞

She led her human child out of the weyr and to a safe place in the forest suitable for her human child to use as a toilet. Trying to be polite, <Arizesyley> turned away, but stole a peak and was pleased that her human child knew proper hygiene procedures. She then took her human child to the rapidly flowing stream from which she and <Kedekitley> occasionally drank water.

When she and her human child returned, <Kedekitley> said, "<I did not have the materials for constructing another nest. Instead, I removed

some of the materials from our nest to construct a place for your human child to sleep.>" He indicated the corner where he had placed the temporary nest. "<Tomorrow, I will gather the materials needed to construct a proper nest.>"

She said, "<Thank you.>" Then to her human child, she said, "You will sleep here."

Once her human child was settled in the temporary nest, <Arizesyley> joined <Kedekitley> in their nest.

She said, "<Did you notice the red highlight on my human child's cheek, neck, and arm? I did not know the humans had highlights as dragons do.>"

"<I had noticed the highlight. No other human I have seen has had dragon-like highlights.>"

"<The highlight means my human child is special.>"

In the night, she heard her human child moving about and crying. With her infrared vision, she could see her human child trying to cover herself with the nest bed plants, and her human child's infrared color was wrong.

To <Kedekitley> she said, "<My human child's body temperature is below what I thought was the normal body temperature for my human child.>"

"<Your human child must be cold.>"

"<You did not tell me the humans become cold.>"

"<The clothing the humans wear is supposed to keep the humans warm. That is what Xenkerdecley told me. Why else would the humans wear clothing?>"

She nudged him. "<You do not know much about the humans, do you?>"

"<I know some things about the humans.>"

To her human child, she said, "I am sorry, human child. I did not know you would become cold. Come to our nest. I will keep you warm."

Her human child whimpered and said, "I can't see you."

"<That is something else I should mention,>" <Kedekitley> said. "<Besides having limited visual acuity, the humans see poorly when light intensity is low.>"

"<That information is useful to know. Is there more information I need to know?>"

"<There is probably more information. I will tell you when I think of more information.>"

She said to her human child, "Come toward my voice. You will encounter nothing between where you are and where I am." Her human child shuffled across the floor. "You are progressing well." A moment later <Arizesyley> said, "One more step and you will touch the nest. Climb in."

Her human child climbed into the nest. <Arizesyley> wrapped an arm around her and drew her close. Her human child laid her cheek against her, clutched the object she wore around her neck, and continued crying.

<Arizesyley> said, "Why are you still crying?"

"Mommy and Daddy are dead." Her human child took a few shaky breaths and said, "They told me to run and hide. They said they would stop the Cultists." She paused. "The Cultists killed them. My fault, my fault, my fault."

After listening to her human child's sobs, <Arizesyley> said, "I know how you feel."

"How can you know how I feel?"

"Because ... my parents were also murdered by the humans."

Her human child's breath caught, which stopped her crying. "What happened?"

"The humans with Gird-metal armor and Gird-metal murder weapon swords attacked the weyr where my parents and I lived. The humans had new murder weapon crossbows that shot Gird-metal bolts." <Arizesyley> paused to catch a breath, tears welling up in her eyes. "My parents told me to run and hide. They said they would stop the humans. The humans murdered my parents." <Arizesyley> began crying. Between her sobs, she said, "It is not your fault the humans murdered your parents anymore than it is my fault the humans murdered my parents. It is not our fault. We should not blame ourselves."

Together she and her human child cried.

As happened every time when she cried in the night, she felt <Kedekitley> comfort her by covering her with his wing. This night, he also covered her human child.

Chapter 5

We Must Ask the Humans

At first light, <Arizesyley's> human child said, "I'm hungry."

"<That is something else I should mention,>" <Kedekitley> said. "<The humans consume human food several times per day. I will acquire human food for your human child.>" He gave <Arizesyley> a rub with his head then trotted out of the weyr.

"My life-mate is acquiring human food for you."

Her human child said, "Thank you, thank you, thank you," and then tugged on <Arizesyley's> hand to make her accompany her into the forest to take care of her morning needs.

When <Kedekitley> returned, <Arizesyley> accepted the human food, scrunched her face, and said, "<Thank you. This looks ... delicious.>" She forced a smile, turned toward her human child, handed her human child the human food, and said, "This human food is for you."

Her human child took the human food, stared at the stalks, and said, "It's ... grass."

<Arizesyley> nodded.

"People don't eat grass."

<Arizesyley's> shoulders slumped and she tilted her head. "All right then. Are you certain the humans do not consume grass? My parents taught me the humans consume grass."

"I'm sure people don't eat grass."

<Arizesyley> turned to <Kedekitley> and said, "<If the humans do not consume grass, what human food do the humans consume?>"

"<I did not pay attention to the human food my human friend consumed,>" said <Kedekitley>. "<I assumed the human food was grass.>"

"<That is not helpful.>"

<Kedekitley> tilted his head and thought before saying, "<We must ask the humans what human food to feed your human child.>"

"<The humans want to murder my human child. The humans are monsters and must be eradicated.>"

"<What else can we do besides ask the humans? We can visit my human friend's human town. The humans in my human friend's human town have been good to me. Although, the first time I visited, the humans appeared frightened, but the humans did not attack me. I believe the humans will help us. I will accompany you and stand by your side to protect you, but I do not believe the humans in my human friend's human town will attack us.>"

<Arizesyley> prepared to respond, but hesitated when she noticed her human child staring at her, feet apart, fists on hips with elbows akimbo, brow pinched, and the corners of her lips turned down. Having no experience with the humans, she had no idea how to interpret the posture or exaggerated expression. She would have to analyze it later. She turned back to <Kedekitley> and said, "<How many of the humans do you know?>"

"<I only interact with my human friend. My human friend interacts with the other humans.>"

She huffed and said, "<You know one human you believe is a good human, and based on that you believe the other humans are also good humans? I do not trust the humans and I do not want to go to the human town.>"

He pointed toward her human child, who still stared at them, and said, "<Your human child needs to consume human food. We need information about human food and how to care for your human child. I cannot design a another solution to the problem.>"

"Please, stop, stop, stop. Don't talk about me when I can't understand you." Into the silence her outburst caused, her human child said, "What were you saying about me?"

<Arizesyley> said, "My life-mate and I will go to the human town to ask the humans what human food to feed you."

"No, no, no. Please, don't leave me."

"I will take you with me."

Her human child shuffled backward into the corner. "No, no, no, they'll kill me."

"We will go to the human town where my life-mate's human friend lives. My life-mate says the humans in his human friend's human town are good humans."

"No, no, no."

She went to her human child, crouched, and lowered her head. "I trust my life-mate's judgment that the humans in his human friend's human town are good humans. We need information the humans can provide."

Her human child remained silent, but crossed her arms, shook her head, and made the same exaggerated expression as earlier by creasing her brow and forcing down the corners of her lips. Based on how her human child behaved that time, the expression meant her human child was not happy with the situation.

"Come with me. I promise to protect you. I will not allow you to be damaged."

Her human child's glare softened and she said, "Okay, okay, okay, I'll go. But, I'll be angry with you if they try to kill me again."

"I will keep you safe." <Arizesyley> stretched open one of her pouches and said, "Climb into my pouch."

Before climbing in, her human child said, "It's a pocket."

Chapter 6

How Do We Care For the Human Child

A bell tolled and the humans fled. <Arizesyley> followed <Kedekitley> as he glided to a landing in the circular open space in the human town's center. <Kedekitley> closed his wings, but she kept her wings open and ready for a quick escape.

She said, "Human child, stay hidden until I know the situation."

"I will, I will, I will," came a muffled reply from inside her pouch.

<Arizesyley> tilted her head toward <Kedekitley>. "<The humans running away is not a good sign.>"

From her pouch her human child said, "Are you talking about me again?"

"I am not talking about you, human child."

<Kedekitley> said, "<The first few times I visited the human town, the bell tolled and the humans also ran away. Later, the human that became my human friend told me to meet him in the open space on the east side of the human town away from the other humans. That prevented this reaction.>"

"<Then why did we not land where your human friend said to land? Are we in danger?>" She flexed her wings.

"<We are not in danger. Dragons landing in the middle of the human town might frighten the humans, but the humans will not attack us. We needed to land in the middle of the human town to attract the humans' attention since my human friend was not expecting to meet with me today.>" Then he looked north and added, "<I am not surprised the humans in Gird-metal armor are coming to ask us why we are here.>"

"<You did not warn me the humans in Gird-metal armor would confront us. Will the humans have Gird-metal murder weapons?>"

A lone human came running into the open space. The human wore parts of a Gird-metal armor suit and carried other parts. They also held a

Gird-metal shield. Two Gird-metal murder weapon swords in scabbards were attached at their waist. On their back was a crossbow and quiver of Gird-metal bolts. The human struggled to hold the shield while putting on the remaining pieces of armor.

<Arizesyley> laid back her ears, bared her teeth, growled, and moved closer to <Kedekitley> as he stood proud and brave and announced, "We will not violate the Paladins' Peace."

From her pouch, her human child said, "Your life-mate can talk?"

<Arizesyley> said, "Quiet, human child. And, yes my life-mate can talk."

The bell quit ringing as two more humans rushed into the open space wearing full Gird-metal armor with shields, murder weapon swords, and crossbows and bolts. As the fully armored human in the lead passed the struggling to dress human, the armored human said, "Knight Ned, it's nice of you to respond quickly, but not being in full armor is the same as not having armor at all. Please, finish armoring up and get into position."

The struggling to dress human's head bobbed and they said, "Yes, Sergeant Asa."

The fully armored human assumed a fighting stance with shield and sword at the ready. The second fully armored human assumed a fighting stance a human-length behind and to the right of the lead armored human.

<Kedekitley> repeated, "We will not violate the Paladins' Peace."

<Arizesyley> said to <Kedekitley>, "<I told you the humans cannot be trusted. The humans must be eradicated. We need to leave.>"

Before she could take flight, another human ran into the open space panting and yelling, "Please, stop."

<Kedekitley> said, "<My human friend has arrived.>"

She paused, but kept her wings ready for flight.

<Kedekitley's> human friend reached the lead armored human, stopped, took a few deep breaths, and said, "I'll handle this."

Finally armored, the first to arrive armored human drew their sword and assumed a fighting stance a human-length behind and to the left of the lead armored human.

The lead armored human said, "Please, stand down, but stay here and stay ready." The three armored humans, in unison, sheathed their

Gird-metal murder weapon swords. The first to arrive armored human began fidgeting with their armor.

<Arizesyley> realized that when the first to arrive armored human had approached without wearing all of their Gird-metal armor, her senses had detected extensive amounts of information, but she had been too distracted to pay attention. Now, a comparison of the armored humans' scent signature she had acquired to her human child's scent signature revealed the gender indicating data points <Kedekitley> had mentioned. If her human child's signature indicated female, the now armored human's signature indicated male. Furthermore, <Kedekitley's> human friend was male. She felt pride in her accomplishment of learning to use her dragon senses data points to identify the humans' genders.

<Kedekitley's> human friend approached <Kedekitley> and said, "Dragon, it's good to see you, but ... what's going on? We're not scheduled to meet again for four more days, and you're not supposed to land in the plaza."

<Kedekitley> said, "Human, I am pleased to see you. My life-mate and I need information."

<Arizesyley> did not know how to interpret <Kedekitley's> human friend's brow creased expression as he stared at her. The expression had similarities to her human child's not happy expression, but it was slightly different.

Then he said, "Information? About what?"

Maybe the expression was a request for details. In response, she said, "We need information about how to care for my human child." She removed her human child from her pouch and set her down. Her human child ducked behind <Arizesyley's> leg and peeked out at <Kedekitley's> human friend.

<Kedekitley's> human friend took a sudden breath and his eyes widened. "Where did you get her?"

Two human adults, a female and a male, followed by a human female child about the same size as her human child came from a nearby structure. More of the humans approached and gathered in a circle around <Kedekitley> and her. She tensed her wings and took another step closer to <Kedekitley>. Her human child stayed close to her.

The human female adult from the structure said, "Please, come here child, we'll help you."

From behind her, her human child said, "No, no, no."

<Arizesyley> picked up her human child, brought her wings around to conceal her, and said, "I am responsible for my human child. I will not allow my human child to be damaged."

<Kedekitley> said, "I too will not allow my life-mate's human child to be damaged."

The human male from the structure said, "We won't harm her."

"No, no, no. Please, don't give me to them. They'll kill me," said her human child from under <Arizesyley's> mantled wings.

<Arizesyley> said, "We need information about how to care for my human child."

The human female said, "What kind of information?"

"What human food should I feed my human child?"

"I'm hungry," said her human child still under her wings.

The human male turned to the human child who had followed him and said, "Anitra, please, fetch a box of cinnamon breadsticks."

"Yes, Grandpa." The human child ran to the structure.

The human female said, "Why does she think we'll kill her?"

"The humans attempted to murder my human child. The humans are monsters. I now keep my human child safe, but we need information about how to care for my human child."

The human male said, "Who tried to kill her?"

Her human child said, "Cultists."

The other human child returned from the structure carrying a small box and handed it to the human male.

"Thank you, Anitra. Here child, we have food for you."

Her human child said, "No, no, no."

The human male stepped forward. <Arizesyley> stepped back, tightened the mantling of her wings, laid back her ears, bared her teeth, and growled.

The human male stepped back, held up a hand, and said, "It's okay. I won't harm her."

The human's words did not calm her. She glanced at <Kedekitley> whose slow blink and his sitting down told her to stay calm.

"Anitra, you're less threatening. Please, take them to her." The human male handed the box to the human child.

The lead armored human said, "No," and moved toward <Arizesyley>.

She tensed again, ready to leap into the sky.

<Kedekitley's> human friend restrained the lead armored human and said, "It's okay. They won't harm Anitra."

The lead armored human stopped, but shifted their weight from one foot to the other and back.

The other human child came halfway and sat on the grass. "Please, let me give her one of these. They're good."

<Arizesyley> made a stuttering motion, indecision flickering. She glanced at <Kedekitley> again. He continued to display calm. She opened her wings and set her human child down. Her human child tried to hide behind her again, but she pushed her human child out in front. "Let the human child give you the human food."

The other human child waved the box and said, "These are cinnamon breadsticks. They're good." She removed a human food item from the box and took a bite of it. "Yum."

Looking up at <Arizesyley>, her human child said, "Please, come with me."

Her human child sat opposite the other human child with the box between them. <Arizesyley> sat on her haunches, tail wrapped around her feet, supporting herself with her arms. She kept her wings partially spread to be ready for protection or flight.

The other human child said, "They're made of a special kind of bread that's rolled up with butter and sugar and cinnamon inside." She held up the human food item she'd bitten to show the layers. "And, they're covered with sugar and cinnamon. See, the white stuff is sugar and the brown stuff is cinnamon." She took another bite, picked up a second human food item from the box, and held it out.

Her human child accepted the human food item and took a bite.

The other human child said, "What's your name?"

Between bites, her human child said, "*Naia.*"

<Arizesyley> said, "You have a human name?"

"Yes. It's *Naia.*"

"Why did you not tell me you have a human name?"

"You never asked."

"My name is *Anitra,*" said the other human child. Motioning toward the humans behind her, she said, "That's my grandma, *Sasha,* and grandpa, *Sochi.* They're bakers. That dragon-slayer knight," she indicated the lead armored human, "is my mom. Her name is *Asa.* When she's not being a Knight Sergeant, she's a tailor."

Mom? <Arizesyley> couldn't sense anything about the lead armored human called *Asa* because of the Gird-metal armor, but she assumed Asa must have been female.

Naia motioned toward <Kedekitley's> human friend. "That's my dad. He's Grandma and Grandpa's child. His name is *Sten.* He builds things."

<Kedekitley> looked at Sten and said, "You have a human name?"

"Yes. It's *Sten.*"

"I always call you *Human.* You never corrected me."

"*Human* works."

"A *sten* is the human measurement for mass."

Sten made an odd sound and said, "It's a different sten. A *sten* is the measurement for mass, but *Sten* is also my name."

After a sigh, <Kedekitley> said, "The human language is terrible. I do not understand how the humans communicate without confusion."

"We manage ... most of the time."

To Sten, Asa said, "I've heard you call this one *Dragon.* What do you call the other one?"

"Calling Dragon *Dragon* works well with him calling me *Human,* but I don't know her." Sten pointed at <Arizesyley>.

"You don't know that dragon and you let Anitra approach her?"

"She's a good dragon."

"How do you know?"

Sten said, "First off, dragons don't harm people. Furthermore, she's Dragon's mate. Dragon wouldn't have a mate that wasn't as good as he is. So, I know she'd never want to harm anyone."

The human's words made <Arizesyley> feel guilty for wanting to eradicate the humans. <Kedekitley> gave her a wink and a smile. She wondered if that was his way of reiterating his belief that *his* solution to the humans-murdering-dragons problem was the *correct* solution.

Sasha motioned toward her and said, "What's your name?"

She said, "I am *<Arizesyley>*," a name she was proud of because it contained some of the most beautiful and melodic dragon language sounds.

Sten said, "People can't make some of the music-like and growly noises of the dragon language, so we can't say their actual names. That's why you have to give them a name."

Naia said, "Her name is *Cinnamon*."

Sochi said, "Why *Cinnamon*?"

Naia picked up another human food item from the box and held it up to <Arizesyley's> arm. "Because — well, except for her beautiful red, green, blue, and yellow colors — she's the color of cinnamon; therefore, her name is *Cinnamon*." She pointed at <Kedekitley>. "His name is *Spice*."

Sten said, "His name is *Dragon*."

In a stern voice, Naia said, "No, no, no, his name is *Spice*. Cinnamon and Spice and Naia are nice." Naia made an odd sound then consumed the human food item.

"Maybe we should ask them if it's okay to call them *Cinnamon* and *Spice*," said Sten. "I think that would be the polite thing to do."

<Arizesyley> nodded to <Kedekitley>, who tipped his head in return, and then she said, "Calling me *Cinnamon* and calling <Kedekitley> *Spice* is acceptable."

Sten stepped closer to <Kedekitley> and, in a whisper he apparently didn't know was loud enough for <Arizesyley> to hear with her dragon sense of hearing, said, "I'll keep calling you *Dragon* because it's more awe-inspiring." She agreed that the name *Dragon* was as awe-inspiring as was <Kedekitley> himself.

When <Kedekitley> said to Sten, "I will keep calling you *Human* because the name is descriptive," She almost laughed because *Human* was a ridiculous name and inspired no awe.

<Arizesyley> turned to Sasha and Sochi and said, "May we have more of the human food to take with us?"

Sasha held out her hands. "You can leave Naia with Sochi and me. We'll care for her."

"No, no, no." Naia tried to hide behind her again.

She picked up Naia and said, "I promised my human child — Naia — that I will keep Naia safe from the humans. I will care for Naia. May we have more of the human food?"

Sasha said, "She needs more than cinnamon breadsticks. In fact, the breadsticks should only be an occasional treat. She needs a balanced diet with fruits and vegetables, and meat and fish, dairy products, beans and nuts, and things like bread and noodles and cereal made with grain. And, she's filthy and needs to be washed. And, she needs new clothes; what she's wearing are in tatters. And, she needs boots."

<Arizesyley> stirred her wings and twitched her tail.

Sasha made up and down motions with her hands. "Please, don't leave. I understand you won't give her up, and apparently, she doesn't want to leave you. We'll gather supplies you can take with you."

Sasha waved her hands at the surrounding crowd of the humans. Three of the humans from the crowd and Sten went to Sasha where she stood next to Sochi. The lead armored human, Asa, after waving her hands and fingers at the other two armored humans, also went to Sasha. Asa removed her head cover, which exposed her to <Arizesyley's> senses, confirmed her gender, and provided a sensory signature for future reference.

The group spoke so quietly she could not make out the words even with her dragon sense of hearing, except for something Sten said: *They want to care for her.* She felt satisfaction that at least Sten understood their intentions.

As the group talked, Anitra said, "Yes, Grandma," pulled away from the group and ran off.

When the group separated, the three humans from the crowd, and a fourth human Sten talked to, ran off in different directions taking a few other of the humans with them.

Sasha turned to <Arizesyley> and said, "We're gathering supplies. Please, be patient."

<Arizesyley> glanced at <Kedekitley> who had stood and partially opened his wings when the humans began whispering. He closed his wings, sat, and gave her a slow-blink nod to tell her he was calm and she too should be calm. She set Naia on the ground.

"What's wrong with Naia's skin?" said Sasha. "I thought it was dirt, but it's not all dirt."

"No, no, no." Naia grasped at <Arizesyley>. "They want to kill me."

She picked up Naia, cradled her in her arms, and again mantled her wings. "I will not allow Naia to be damaged."

From under her wings, Naia said, "My splotch is why the Cultists want to kill me."

"It's only a birthmark," said Sasha.

"The Cultists say it makes me a beast child."

"It doesn't make you a beast. Many people have birthmarks. I have one, although it's not as awesome as yours. It's on my — well, it's located where I can't show it off."

Sten said to <Kedekitley>, "Dragon, we really are willing to take Naia and care for her."

Naia said, "No, no, no. Please, don't give me to them."

<Kedekitley> said, "<Arizesyley> — Cinnamon — promised to care for Naia and to protect Naia. I will assist Cinnamon. The humans do not need to worry about Naia. Naia will be safe and well cared for."

"I know, and I trust you, but still —"

Three humans returned: two carrying boxes and one with a tangle of rope.

Sasha showed <Arizesyley> the contents of the two boxes. "These boxes contain all sorts of things like a blanket and pillow, teeth cleaner, hair brush, pails, towels, soap, cooking pots, plates, bowls, cups, eating utensils, fire starters, and canteens." She looked to the side and said, "And, here comes the washing tub."

A human carrying a large, shiny metal container approached. He placed the container next to the boxes. Behind him came Anitra pulling a small, dark blue wagon whose wheels squeaked with every turn.

"Are you hiding Naia again?" said Anitra. "Please, put her down so I can show her what I brought."

She set Naia down, but Naia held on to her hand.

Anitra opened the box that rode in the wagon and said, "I brought all sorts of clothes, and a coat, and boots and socks, and books."

"Books?" Naia tugged <Arizesyley> along as she went to the wagon and picked up one of the books.

Anitra said, "Do you know how to read?"

"Of course I know how to read. Mommy and Daddy —" Naia stopped, clutched the object hanging around her neck, then said, "Mommy and Daddy taught me well."

"I have something special for you."

"All of these things are special."

"This is even more special."

From under a clothing item, Anitra pulled out a tube shaped piece of cloth with a long narrow appendage sticking out each end, four shorter appendages hanging off the bottom, and wide flaps thrusting out on the sides. She handed the cloth object to Naia. The object was as long as Naia's arm.

Naia said, "It's a dragon."

<Arizesyley> almost jumped when Asa flailed her arms and cried out, "A dragon? I told you not to make a dragon."

"Oh, Mom." To Naia, Anitra said, "Mom taught me how to make stuffed animals. She's shaped like Dad's dragon. When I made her, he had been the only dragon I'd seen."

<Arizesyley> said, "No dragon is that color."

"I only had cotton fabric and no dyes to color it."

Naia tried to hand the cloth dragon back to Anitra. "No, no, no, I can't take your dragon."

Anitra pushed the cloth dragon back to Naia. "It's okay. I made two of them."

"You made two of them?" said Asa as Sten held onto her. <Arizesyley> was sure that if Sten had not wrapped his arms around the armored human, the armored human would have charged.

"Oh, Mom." Anitra turned up her eyes and shook her head before pulling a second, identical cloth dragon from under the clothing item. "They're siblings. You keep one and I'll keep one."

Naia hugged the cloth dragon and said, "Thank you, thank you, thank you. I'll call her *Sugar*."

<Arizesyley> still struggled with interpreting expressions made by the human's, but she decided the exaggerated expression on Naia's face was a smile that meant she was happy.

Another human returned with an additional box.

Sasha said, "Here's the food." She opened the box. "This one has fruits and vegetables, dried meat and fish, peas, corn, cheese, and bread. It's not a lot, but it'll last a few days. You'll have to return when you need more."

<Arizesyley> tilted her head and said, "All right then." After a pause, she continued, "I am overwhelmed. I did not know caring for Naia would be complicated. I do not know where to begin. What is the purpose of that container?" She pointed.

Sasha said, "It's a washing tub. You use it to wash laundry and to wash Naia."

<Arizesyley> tilted her head again. "All right then." She took a breath. "I do not know how to wash Naia."

"I'm not a baby." Naia's outburst froze everyone. "I can wash myself. I can dress myself. I can prepare food. I can read and write. I'm almost grown-up. I know how to use all these things. Mommy and Daddy taught me well." She clutched the object hanging around her neck.

<Kedekitley> said, "With so many containers, multiple trips will be required to transport the supplies."

"I have a solution to that problem," said Sten as he and Sochi spread the tangle of rope. "This is a *cargo net*. We can load everything into it for you to carry in one trip."

The humans placed the boxes and washing tub into the net.

<Arizesyley> said, "I am responsible for Naia. I will carry the supplies."

<Kedekitley> stepped between her and the net. "I will carry the supplies while you carry Naia."

She stared at him with her obstinate determination face before she relented and said, "You carry the supplies."

"Please, put the wagon in too." Anitra pulled the squeaking wagon to the net.

Naia said, "You're giving me your wagon?"

"I think you'll need it."

"Thank you, thank you, thank you."

Anitra grasped Naia's hand. "Dad has his dragon friend, but I've never met anyone who lives with dragons. Please, visit and tell me what it's like."

"That's a good point," said Sasha. "You need to return with Naia occasionally, and not just to fetch more supplies. You can't raise her to be a dragon. She needs to socialize with people so she knows how to be a person. She needs people friends. She needs to attend school."

Sochi said, "Please, remember, we're always here, ready and willing to help with anything you need."

Sten said to <Kedekitley>, "Dragon, we're still scheduled to meet in four days. You can tell me then how things are going."

"I told Cinnamon the humans in this human town are good humans," said <Kedekitley>. "Thank you for your help. I have enjoyed seeing you again, Human." He grabbed the closed end of the cargo net and prepared to take flight.

<Arizesyley> helped Naia, who still held the cloth dragon, into her pouch and said, "I am tempted to believe what — Spice — said about the humans in this human town being good humans. Thank you for your help."

She took to the sky with <Kedekitley> following close behind.

Chapter 7

Caring for the Human Child

Naia insisted on using the little blue wagon to move the supply boxes into the weyr all by herself. <Arizesyley>, with <Kedekitley> at her side, watched and cringed with every agonizing squeak of the wagon's wheels.

<Kedekitley> scrunched his shoulders at a particularly loud squeak and said, "<After what happened to you when you attempted to return your human child to the humans, I had worried I was wrong about good humans.>"

<Arizesyley> rubbed her ear and said, "<I still believe the humans are monsters.>"

"<Some of the humans are good humans and some of the humans are bad humans. I am reassured the humans in my human friend's human town are good humans as good as my human friend.>"

"<The humans in your human friend's human town acted as if they were good humans, but I still believe the humans must be eradicated.>"

Naia said, "Done, done, done. Now I want to try out the tub."

<Arizesyley> tilted her head. "All right then." She blew out her breath and took another. "I do not know what to do with the washing tub."

"We fill it with hot water."

She tilted her head to the other side. "All right then."

"I can make a fire to heat water."

"We could use water from the hot spring. The hot spring water is already hot."

"You have a hot spring?"

"I will take you to the hot spring."

"We should take the tub, a pail, a towel, soap, brush, new clothes, and socks, and the boots." Naia put the washing tub and other items in the wagon, picked up the wagon's handle, and said, "Please, show me, show me, show me."

"Wait." <Kedekitley> retrieved a container from the alcove that held his tools collection and applied some of its contents to the wagon's wheels where they connected to the body of the wagon. "Now move the wagon." When Naia rolled the wagon, the wheels didn't squeak. <Kedekitley> preened and said, "The problem is solved."

<Arizesyley> wrapped her tail around him and rubbed her head on him. "You are the best dragon."

He lifted his chin and said, "Thank you. While you learn how to use the washing tub, I will solve the problem of constructing a proper nest for Naia."

∞∞∞∞

<Arizesyley> led Naia along a wide path bordered by tall trees whose leaves cast shadows that made light and dark dappled patches on the ground. The path led to a pool large enough for two dragons to lounge in. Steaming water flowed from a fissure in the rocks to fill the pool. On the far side, a cascading creek sang a song of burbles.

Naia said, "That looks hot, hot, hot."

"The temperature of the water coming from the hot spring is perfect." <Arizesyley> slipped into the pool causing a surge of water to overflow into the creek.

Naia made a quick poke at the water. "No, no, no. Hot, hot, hot."

"If Spice were here, Spice would say, 'That is something else I should mention.'" She wobbled her head and mocked <Kedekitley's> voice. "'The humans do not like perfect temperature hot spring water.'"

Naia made an odd sound then said, "It might be perfect for dragons, but it will scald a person. I'll add water from the creek to make the temperature perfect for me."

<Arizesyley> submerged in the pool before surfacing enough to watch Naia set the washing tub in a grass-covered area. She used the pail to haul water first from the spring and then from the creek.

"Now it's perfect, perfect, perfect." She removed the object hanging around her neck and said, "Mommy and Daddy would be proud of me."

She placed the object in the wagon, removed the tattered clothing she wore, climbed into the washing tub, submerged, brought her head out of the water, and soaked, occasionally dipping her head under the water again. "This is nice, nice, nice."

"Do the humans enjoy soaking in warm water?"

"It's hot, it's just not scalding, and I enjoy it. I think most people do."

After they listened a while to the singing creek, the singing birds in the trees, and enjoyed the aroma of the golden flowers that grew along the creek's banks, Naia said, "The water's cooling. I should finish washing before it gets cold."

"Do the humans not enjoy soaking in cold water?"

"A cold bath's no fun, but sometimes people play in the river or in the creek. That water's cold."

She scrubbed, rinsed, climbed out of the washing tub, dried herself, dressed in the new clothes, socks, and boots, and hung the object around her neck again. After dumping the water from the washing tub into the grass, she loaded the wagon and then pulled a brush through her hair. <Arizesyley> knew of many uses for various types of brushes — <Kedekitley> had several in his tools collection — but she never imagined the humans used a brush to remove hair tangles.

When Naia finished, she said, "Done, done, done. I want to go look at the food now."

<Arizesyley> climbed out of the pool, spread her primary wings and tail wings, and gave a shake.

"Hey, hey, hey."

"Oops. I am sorry, Naia."

"Okay, okay, okay. I'll dry."

∞∞∞∞

The first thing <Arizesyley> saw as she and Naia entered the weyr was <Kedekitley> standing by his newest creation, his head held high.

He said, "The problem is solved. Look at what I constructed."

Naia climbed in and bounced. "It's a nest, and it's my size, and it's soft, and it smells like honeystar flowers and fresh grass."

<Kedekitley> patted the edge of the nest. "The nest is larger than you are. I constructed the nest to still fit when you become an adult-sized human."

<Arizesyley> smiled and said, "Do not consume the grass."

Naia furrowed her brow and said, "I told you, people don't eat grass."

<Arizesyley> decided Naia's expression meant exasperation.

"That is why I decided to add grass." <Kedekitley> grinned and waved a few stalks of grass. "Grass is a nice nest bed material and I now know Naia will not consume the grass."

Naia furrowed her brow again.

<Arizesyley> wrapped her tail around <Kedekitley>, rubbed her head on him, and said, "You are the best dragon."

He puffed out his chest and said, "Thank you."

Naia climbed out, gathered the blanket and pillow, and put them in the nest.

<Kedekitley> said, "I placed your nest next to Cinnamon's and my nest. If you wish, the nest can be moved."

"This spot is perfect, perfect, perfect." Naia placed the cloth dragon on the pillow, the dragon's tail draping onto the blanket. "Thank you, thank you, thank you."

<Arizesyley> ran her fingers through the grass in <Kedekitley's> and her nest. "<You added grass to our nest.>"

"<The grass reminds me of my nests while growing up. I wanted to try grass again, and to find out how you like grass.>"

"<The grass has a nice aroma. I am willing to learn how well grass works for sleeping.>"

"<You will like the grass, I am sure.>" He rubbed his head on her.

She said, "<Fly a patrol for me. Because of today's activities, I have not had an opportunity to fly a patrol. I am concerned I will miss signs the humans are preparing to attack. I need evidence to present to the Council, but I must stay with my human child to keep my human child safe.>" She met Naia's glare and said, "I am not talking about you."

"<I will fly a patrol.>" <Kedekitley> waggled his wings and wiggled his tail.

"<Thank you. Do you know where to patrol and what to look for?>"

"<Of course I know where to patrol and what to look for. I have flown patrols with you before.>" He cantered out of the weyr.

"What was that about?"

<Arizesyley> looked toward the weyr's entrance, sighed, and lay down. "Spice is doing a task for me."

Naia sat next to her. "You love him, don't you?"

"I do love Spice. Do you want to know a secret? Spice is the best dragon."

"That's not a well kept secret. I've heard you say it to him more than once. When you say it, he puffs up." Naia wiggled her shoulders. "He loves you too. I see a glimmer in his eyes every time he looks at you."

<Arizesyley> dipped her head. "I know Spice loves me. I am not the best dragon. Spice loves me anyway. That is another reason Spice is the best dragon. Spice is strong and an amazing genius. Spice is an exceptional hunter. Spice is creative. Spice is caring and affectionate. Have you noticed how wonderful Spice's horns are?"

"They look like yours, light brown and pointy."

"Spice's horns are better, and Spice's color is also wonderful." The tip of her tail wagged.

"He's the same color as you: brown, like rich garden soil. And, you both have red, green, and blue streaks, except you also have yellow. Why is that?" Naia ran her fingers along the zigzag yellow streak on <Arizesyley's> arm.

"No yellow is a male trait. I like the green on Spice's cheeks, and the blue on Spice's ventral surface, and especially the wavy red on Spice's neck, chest, shoulders, and wings."

"You mean the red marks that look like flames?"

"You think Spice's red highlights look like flames?"

"Pretty much."

Naia sorted through the human food stopping when she found several long, fat, purple pieces of plant root. "Look, look, look, rattidash root." She almost bit into one. "No, no, no, I can't eat it now. I must make a meal plan."

<Arizesyley> tilted her head. "All right then. What is a *meal plan*?"

"On our farm, Mommy and Daddy —" Naia stopped to clutch the object hanging around her neck and took a deep breath. "Mommy and Daddy and I had a large garden, an orchard, a couple of fields of grain, and a few animals. We grew enough food that we were never hungry, but we planned when and what to eat so we wouldn't run out before the next harvest. I'll make a plan for when I'll eat this food. Do you want to share the food?"

"All of the human food is for you."

"What do dragons eat?"

"Dragons consume food animals. When Spice and I need to feed, Spice and I hunt in the mountains. There are many food animals in the mountains. Spice and I never go hungry."

Naia sorted the human food containers into separate collections. "Mommy and Daddy would be proud of me. The peas and corn and potatoes will require cooking, but don't worry; I know how to do that. We'll need to ask for more food in a few days."

"When you tell me we need to return to the human town to ask the humans for more human food, I will take you to the human town."

"They were nice, weren't they?"

She hesitated before saying, "The humans in Spice's human friend's human town acted as if they were good humans, but my experience with the humans has not left me believing there are good humans."

Naia inhaled then said, "I know what you mean. When the Cultists came, they started taking our food and supplies. Then they burned our home and called me a beast child and tried to kill me. That's when Mommy and Daddy and I ran."

"You are safe with me. I will not allow the humans to damage you."

Naia hugged <Arizesyley's> snout, which was as large as Naia, and said, "Thank you, thank you, thank you," and then she consumed the purple plant root.

∞∞∞∞∞

<Arizesyley> sensed <Kedekitley> had returned, stood, held out her arms, and waited for him to enter the weyr to give her a hug. He did not disappoint her.

In the midst of his hug, he said, "<I love you and missed you.>"

She lingered in the hug before she said, "<I also love you and missed you. What did you find?>"

"<I found nothing. However, the humans in my human friend's human town were gathering in their meeting structure. That activity is not suspicious. The humans are not preparing to attack.>"

"<Give the humans the opportunity and the humans will attack.>"

Naia came running. "Anitra gave me pajamas. I haven't had real pajamas since I outgrew my old ones. Anitra was so nice. I want to see her again."

<Arizesyley> said, "When I take you to the human town for more human food, you will see the human child Anitra. Now, you, Spice, and I must sleep."

"I'll get ready for bed." Naia paused before saying, "Please, come with me."

"Why do I need to come with you?"

"I don't want to go outside alone. Please, come with me to visit the necessary, wash my hands, and clean my teeth."

<Arizesyley> looked at <Kedekitley> who smiled and said, "<You keep saying you are responsible for your human child.>"

With a sigh, she followed Naia outside.

When they returned to the weyr, Naia went to her supplies. <Arizesyley> climbed into her and <Kedekitley's> nest, walked two circles, made little marching steps, and lay down to cuddle against him.

<Kedekitley> said, "<Did you learn how to use the washing tub to wash your human child?>"

"<My human child washed herself.>"

"<Why is the human food divided into collections?>"

"<My human child divided the human food into the collections. She called it a *meal plan*.>"

"<Did you help your human child?>"

"<My human child did not require my help. My human child is sophisticated.>"

Naia, dressed in the clothing she had called *pajamas*, sat on one of her supply boxes clutching the object she wore around her neck.

<Arizesyley> said, "Naia, are you well?"

"I'm fine." She came to the nest and said, "May I sleep with you again?"

"You have your own nest now."

"I know, I know, I know, but I want to be with you. Please."

<Arizesyley> hesitated before Naia's pleading eyes prompted her to say, "You may sleep with me."

"Thank you, thank you, thank you."

Naia used the blanket and pillow to prepare a sleeping place, climbed in, snuggled with the cloth dragon, and nestled against <Arizesyley>.

Naia said, "I love you, Mother."

"I am not your mother."

"You're not *Mommy*, but you take care of me. That makes you *Mother*. Spice is *Father*. You and Father are all I have. Thank you, thank you, thank you for taking care of me." Naia scratched the back of her neck and said, "Goodnight, Mother."

<Arizesyley> felt a surge of warmth in her heart. She cooed and said, "Goodnight, Naia."

For the first night in many nights, she didn't cry.

Chapter 8

I Like This New Life

At Naia's insistence, <Arizesyley> accompanied her to deal with her morning needs. Upon returning to the weyr, Naia sat on a supply box clutching the object hanging around her neck. <Arizesyley> felt despair, an emotion she often felt when she thought about her parents; although, the feeling this time was different because she hadn't been thinking about her parents. She soothed herself by thinking about <Kedekitley> who was flying a patrol for her.

She said, "Naia, are you well?"

"I'm fine. I was just thinking."

"Will you consume human food? Father says the humans consume human food several times per day."

"I'll have my morning meal."

When Naia finished consuming the human food, she said, "What chores should I do?"

<Arizesyley> tilted her head. "All right then. What are *chores*?"

"Jobs that need to be done. Back home I helped keep our home and farm clean, and fixed things I could fix, and tended the garden, orchard, and grain fields, and the animals."

"All right then."

"You don't have chores for me, do you? I'll clean the cave."

<Arizesyley> didn't consider the weyr to be any dirtier than one might expect a cave to be, and dragons did keep their weyrs clean, but Naia found loose stones to pick up then straightened the contents of her supply boxes.

"After chores, Mommy and Daddy would teach me things."

"What kinds of things?"

"Reading, writing, math, science, those kinds of things."

"The humans have reading, writing, mathematics, and science?"

"Of course we do."

"I thought those were things Father did for the humans because the humans are not sophisticated."

Naia made an exaggerated sigh. "I'll read one of Anitra's books."

"That idea is a good idea. I will have sun-time."

<Arizesyley> went out into the meadow where the open sky let the sun shine on the grass. Her senses told her Naia was following so she wasn't surprised to find Naia standing behind her holding a book. After she settled and tucked her feet under her, she spread her wings wide, draped them across the grass, laid her head down, and inhaled the fresh air.

Naia sat in the shady nook under her wing, leaned against her, opened the book, and said, "Do dragons enjoy lying in the sun?"

"Sun-time is important for dragons. Sun light on our hide allows our bodies to manufacture a nutrient we do not acquire from food animals."

"That's nice," said Naia already lost in her book.

<Arizesyley> closed her eyes and contemplated the source of her unexpected emotions. The disruption of the predictable nature of her life could have been the cause. Maybe a new normal would settle in and ease the feelings. She hoped <Kedekitley> would return soon. His presence always soothed her fears and sorrows, and made her happy.

She sensed his approach before he dropped from the sky, backwinged, and landed next to her. The gust of wind he made caused a flutter from several pages of Naia's book eliciting a *hey, hey, hey* from Naia.

<Kedekitley> said, "Oops. I am sorry, Naia."

Because she lay on the ground and <Kedekitley> couldn't hug her as he normally did, he settled on the ground, spread his wings wide across the grass, laid his head near hers, and said, "<I love you and missed you.>"

"<I also love you and missed you. What did you find?>"

"<I found nothing. The humans are behaving as the humans normally behave. What have you been doing?>"

"<I have been watching over my human child. She reduced her mass, washed her hands, and consumed human food. Next, she picked up rocks on the weyr floor, and straightened the contents of the supply boxes. She called the activity *chores*. Now she is reading. Did you know the humans teach the human children reading, writing, mathematics, and science?>"

"<My human friend is sophisticated enough to know those subjects. I am not surprised to learn the humans teach the subjects to the human children.>"

Silence, disturbed only by the wind rustling leaves in the trees, and Naia turning pages in her book, settled on them.

<Arizesyley> kept staring into <Kedekitley's> eyes. Then she said, "<My human child said she can tell you love me because she sees a glimmer in your eyes when you look at me. My human child is correct. When you look at me, your eyes sparkle.>"

<Kedekitley's> bewildered look was entertaining, but then he turned serious and said, "<I understand statistics and probability. Science and mathematics guide me in my endeavors. I consider myself rational. Therefore, I do not believe in luck. However, that *you* love *me* is the luckiest thing that has ever happened to me.>" Then he smiled.

"<That is the most outlandishly sweet and sentimental thing you have ever said to me. You are the best dragon.>"

The mood was broken when Naia closed her book and said, "I'm hungry."

<Kedekitley> laughed and said, "<I told you the humans consume human food several times per day.>"

<Arizesyley> lifted her head, motioned with her snout toward the weyr, said, "Retrieve human food from a human food collection," and then felt a surge of fear. Naia looked at the weyr and back to her. The feeling confused her. She had no reason to feel fear.

Naia said, "Please, go with me."

"You and I are not in danger. We are safe. The weyr is safe. Be brave. Go inside, retrieve human food, and consume the human food here."

Naia looked at the weyr, took a deep breath, and said, "Okay, okay, okay, but, please, don't go away."

A sense of determination came to <Arizesyley>. She said, "I will be here. I will watch for danger. I will keep you safe, and Father will keep me safe."

Naia dashed to the weyr.

<Kedekitley> said, "<Are you troubled?>"

"<I am experiencing unexplained emotions.>"

"<What emotions?>"

"<Fear, anxiety, sadness, happiness, excitement. I am familiar with and often experience those emotions, but today the emotions occur when I know of no reason to be experiencing the emotions.>"

Naia came running from the weyr with the folded blanket cradled in her arms. <Arizesyley> felt relief and pride.

"I was brave, brave, brave. Mommy and Daddy would be proud of me."

In the shade of a tree close to <Arizesyley>, Naia spread the blanket revealing human food containers and the cloth dragon. On one side of the blanket, she placed the cloth dragon, opening and spreading its wings wide. Between the cloth dragon and her, she set the human food containers.

She said, "I'll have a picnic. I have meat, cheese, bread, jancy berries, and a canteen of water."

<Arizesyley> folded her wings.

"No, no, no, where are you going?"

"I am going nowhere." She rolled over onto her back and spread her wings again.

Naia made an odd sound and <Arizesyley> felt amusement that almost made her laugh.

To <Kedekitley>, she said, "<I have heard my human child make that sound before. What does the sound mean?>"

"<That sound is how the humans laugh.>"

"<The humans laugh?>"

"<Your human child must think something is humorous.>"

"Naia, what is it you think is humorous?"

"You."

"Why do you think I am humorous?"

"Your feet are sticking up in the air." Naia laughed again.

"My ventral surface needs sun-time."

"That idea is a good idea," said <Kedekitley> as he too rolled over.

Naia laughed more and said, "Now both of you look funny." She rolled the cloth dragon over so its feet stuck up in the air.

<Arizesyley> huffed and said, "Consume your human food."

When Naia finished consuming the human food, she bundled the containers and cloth dragon in the blanket, took a deep breath, and ran to the weyr. It wasn't long before she dashed back.

Naia said, "See? I was brave, brave, brave."

"You performed the task well." <Arizesyley> righted herself.

"No, no, no, where are you going?"

"I have had enough sun-time. I will sit in the shade now."

"I will join you." <Kedekitley> righted himself.

Naia stayed close to her as she settled with <Kedekitley> in the shade, side-by-side. She pressed against him and entwined her tail with his seeking the contentment that always came with being with him.

She said to Naia, "What will you do now?"

"I don't know. I'll think of something. Please, don't go away."

"Father and I will stay here."

Naia, always staying within sight of her, explored the meadow's open space and examined the cliff face that held the weyr.

<Kedekitley> said, "<Your human child appears fearful of being away from you.>"

"<I am my human child's protector; although, I am also feeling fear.>"

"<What do you fear?>"

"<I fear the humans surprising us, I think. If the humans were eradicated, we would no longer need to fear the humans surprising us and murdering us.>"

"<The journey would be long and difficult for the humans to come here.>"

"<That knowledge does not mitigate the feeling. I am paying attention to my senses. I will detect the humans approaching, unless the humans are wearing Gird-metal armor.>"

<Kedekitley> cocked his head as he did when he was proud of himself and said, "<I have a solution to that problem. I noticed when the humans are around, other creatures move away. I focus my senses on those other creatures. If the creatures move away, I seek the cause of the creatures' departure. The problem is solved.>"

"<That idea is a good idea.>" She rubbed her head on him. "<You are the best dragon.>"

"<Thank you.>"

Naia returned and said, "I want to build a hearth."

"All right then," said <Arizesyley> as she tilted her head. "What is a *hearth*?"

"A place where I can build a fire so I can cook. I picked the perfect spot." Naia pointed to the far right side of the cliff face where the ground was bare stone. "There. It'll be out of the way, yet easy to use. May I?"

"You may construct a hearth. I will provide assistance."

"I don't need help, but thank you, thank you, thank you for offering to help."

Naia went to the weyr.

<Arizesyley> said, "<My human child moved out of sight of me without appearing to fret.>"

"<Maybe having something on which to focus her attention keeps your human child from thinking about her fears. Or, maybe your human child is feeling more confident.>"

"<Those are possible explanations. I am also feeling less fearful and more confident.>"

Naia retrieved the wagon from the weyr and pulled it to an outcrop of gray slate that had broken into blocks each about a dragon-hand wide. She loaded the wagon, pulled the wagon to where she intended to construct her hearth, and began constructing, returning to the slate pile when she needed more stone.

With <Kedekitley> at her side, and Naia busy working on her hearth, <Arizesyley> felt safe, contented, and happy. She watched Naia for a while then closed her eyes and drowsed.

∞∞∞∞

<Arizesyley> leaped to her feet. "<Where is my human child? Wait.>" She focused on her mental map. One human was on the map, a human with her human child's sensory signature. "<My human child is there.>" She galloped toward the forest edge with <Kedekitley> following.

Naia burst from the forest to meet her.

She swept Naia up in her arms, mantled her wings around her, and said, "You are safe. Did you see the humans?"

Naia said, "I saw no one. I suddenly felt afraid, so I ran."

<Kedekitley> said, "<I will find the intruders.>"

"<Be vigilant. I cannot detect the humans. The humans must be wearing Gird-metal armor.>"

<Kedekitley> slipped into the forest.

To Naia, she said, "What were you doing?"

"I was looking for sticks to make a cooking crane. I didn't go far. I was being brave, but I stayed where I could see you."

"Why did you not ask me to accompany you?"

"You looked so cute snuggling with Father. And, I could feel how happy you were. I didn't want to disturb you."

<Kedekitley> returned and said, "<I found no evidence of the humans. I believe your human child going among the trees is what caused the creatures to move away.>"

<Arizesyley> set Naia down and said, "<That is a reasonable explanation.>"

Naia cleared her throat and said, "Language, language, language."

"I am sorry, Naia. Father and I were monitoring the creatures in the forest. The creatures moving away would indicate the humans were approaching. You going among the trees caused the creatures to move away. That means there was no danger. I will provide assistance to search for sticks, if you tell me what *sticks* are."

"No, no, no, I don't need help, but you can come with me."

With <Kedekitley> following, she followed Naia as she wandered among the trees examining downed tree pieces, which must have been what she meant by *sticks*, until she had collected three sticks as long as two human child steps and one stick three times longer. She also collected two segments of vine before carrying everything to the hearth.

<Arizesyley> said, "You constructed an impressive structure."

Naia had constructed a ring of stones as wide as she was tall and as tall as she was wide.

<Kedekitley> walked around the circle. "I agree with Mother, the structure is impressive. The stone blocks are fitted together well."

Naia grasped the object hanging around her neck. "Mommy and Daddy would be proud of me. It's perfect, perfect, perfect for all the kinds of fires I plan to make, from big to small. Now, I'll make a cooking crane."

With a tilt of her head, <Arizesyley> said, "All right then."

Naia said, "I'll show you."

She used a vine to tie the three same-sized sticks together at one end, set them with the not-tied ends spread apart on the ground, braced those ends with rocks, and placed the longer stick horizontally across the top.

"This is a *cooking crane*. I hook the cooking pot on the end of this stick and swing it over the fire to cook the food."

"All right then."

"When I start cooking, you'll understand. Now I need firewood. Please, come with me."

<Arizesyley>, with <Kedekitley> close behind, again followed as Naia left the wagon at the edge of the trees, walked among the trees gathering sticks of all sizes — long, short, thick, thin — and loaded each armful into the wagon. When the wagon was full, she unloaded it next to the hearth and returned to the forest to collect more sticks.

When Naia caught <Kedekitley> adding his own sticks to the wagon, she said, "No, no, no." She removed the sticks and held them in her arms.

<Kedekitley> said, "I am sorry, Naia. I wanted to help."

"I can do it myself. I'm almost grown-up and don't need help, but thank you, thank you, thank you for offering to help." She put the sticks back in the wagon and clutched the object hanging around her neck. "Mommy and Daddy would be proud of me."

<Arizesyley> said, "Father and I are also proud of you."

"Yes, Mother and I are proud of you," <Kedekitley> said. "You are remarkable."

"Thank you, thank you, thank you, Mother and Father."

<Arizesyley> decided Naia's exaggerated expression at being complemented was definitely a human smile, which was like a dragon smile, except for the odd exaggeration. The exaggeration explained the difficulty in interpreting the expressions the humans made. This insight should make the humans' expressions easer for her to understand.

After creating a significant collection of sticks, Naia panted and said, "That's enough firewood for now. I'll rest before moving to the next step." She sat and leaned against <Arizesyley>. "Daddy liked to say a fire warms you twice."

Once rested, Naia constructed a small structure of sticks in the middle of the hearth. Using one of the fire starters the humans had provided, she set the structure on fire and added more sticks.

"While that burns down into a good cooking fire, I'll prepare what I'll cook."

Into a container with a wire loop on top, Naia placed various animal flesh pieces and plant pieces. To that, she added water and powders whose aromas indicated they were also made from plants. She hooked the container's wire loop over the end of the cooking crane's horizontal stick, swung the container over the fire, and used a rock to hold a length of vine tied to the other end of the stick to keep the container suspended.

"That needs to cook for a while. Do dragons cook?"

"Dragons never cook."

"Do dragons build fires?"

"Father and I have not needed to construct a fire, but the Conclave always has a fire. The fire provides a warm, welcoming place to gather and talk with other dragons."

"What's the *Conclave*?"

"The *Conclave* is a gathering where dragons socialize, teach special subjects to hatchlings, dragonets, young-dragons, and sometimes older dragons, and have discussions and make decisions about policies and plans." She turned to <Kedekitley>. "<With the disruption caused by caring for my human child, I forgot about the Conclave in two days. I want to speak to the Council about my eradicate-the-humans solution to the humans-murdering-dragons problem. I cannot leave my human child. I cannot take my human child with me. What will I do?>"

<Kedekitley> said, "<I want to speak to the Council about my make-friends-with-the-humans solution to the humans-murdering-dragons problem, but I should stay with you.>" After a pause as he looked off in the distance, he continued, "<I am not able to design a solution to the problem. You and I may not be able to attend the Conclave.>"

Naia said, "Language, language, language."

"I am sorry, Naia. Father and I were talking about the Conclave. How is the human food cooking progressing?"

Naia used the cooking crane's horizontal stick to move the human food cooking container away from the fire and prepared to use a tool.

<Arizesyley> said, "What is that tool called?"

"This is a *spoon*. And, this is a *bowl*. I'll use the bowl after the food is cooked."

She used the spoon to dip a small amount of the human food, blew on it, and sipped. "Not bad, but it needs to cook longer." She moved the human food cooking container back over the fire.

After sitting awhile, watching the fire and watching the human food in the human food cooking container bubble, Naia sampled the human food again. "Now it's done, done, done." She used the spoon to fill the bowl with the human food, dipped a small amount of the human food out of the bowl with the spoon, blew on it, and consumed it. "That's good, good, good. Mommy and Daddy would be proud of me." She held a spoonful of the human food out toward her and <Kedekitley>. "Would you like some?"

<Arizesyley> said, "Thank you for offering, but we only consume food animals."

"You'll never know what you're missing." Naia continued consuming the human food.

<Arizesyley> said to <Kedekitley>, "<I thought caring for my human child would be complicated, but my human child cares for herself. My human child does not need me for anything.>" A narrowed-eye look from Naia prompted <Arizesyley> to say, "Consume your human food and ignore us talking."

<Kedekitley> said, "<Your human child's knowledge and skills are impressive. I did not know the human children were sophisticated.>"

"<You believe you know everything about the humans.>"

"<I never said I know *everything* about the humans.>"

Naia emptied the remaining human food from the human food cooking container into the bowl, finished consuming it, and said, "I'll do the dishes now. Please, come with me."

She loaded the wagon with a pail, a towel, and soap, and led <Arizesyley>, with <Kedekitley> following, to the hot spring to use hot water to clean what she'd used to cook and consume her human food. After returning to the weyr, she put everything away, and led <Arizesyley> and <Kedekitley> back to the fire.

"After our evening meal, Mommy and Daddy and I would sit and watch the fire." She held the object hanging around her neck. "Sometimes we'd talk. Sometimes we'd tell stories. Sometimes we sat quietly. I feel like sitting quietly tonight."

Naia sat between <Arizesyley's> arms and leaned against her. As the fire burned out, Naia fell asleep.

<Arizesyley> said, "<My human child has disrupted and changed my life.>" She paused as she smoothed Naia's hair. "<I like this new life.>"

She carried Naia into the weyr where she and <Kedekitley> climbed into their nest. Next to her, she laid Naia and the cloth dragon, and then she covered them with the blanket. "Goodnight, Naia."

Chapter 9
Emotional Damage Realized

"I don't need more food yet, but may I go see Anitra today anyway?" Naia had finished consuming her morning human food and was performing the chore of tidying her supply boxes.

"I cannot commit to going to the human town until Father returns, but I do not know of any reason we cannot go to the human town."

"I'll get ready."

When <Kedekitley> returned, hugged her, and said, "<I love you and missed you,>" <Arizesyley> said, "<I also love you and missed you. What did you find?>"

"<I found nothing.>"

Naia said, "Are you asking Father if we can go visit Anitra?"

"Naia wants to visit the human child Anitra in the human town."

<Kedekitley> bounced on his toes. "We can visit the human town. I can visit Human again."

Naia ran to <Arizesyley>, lifted her wing, grabbed the edge of her pouch, rolled in, poked her head out, and said, "Please, go, go, go."

∞∞∞∞

<Arizesyley> glided into the human town's central open space with <Kedekitley> following. The humans scurried away, but only far enough to give her and <Kedekitley> room to land.

She closed her wings and said, "<The humans moved out of the way, but the humans did not run away.>" She removed Naia from her pouch and set her down.

"<The human behavior indicates the humans do not fear us.>" <Kedekitley> closed his wings and moved closer to her as more of the humans gathered around staying a couple of dragon lengths away.

"<Nevertheless, the humans are still reluctant to come close. Also, the bell did not ring, which is another indication that the humans do not fear us.>"

"<Do you think the armored humans will confront us?>"

"<I assume the armored humans will respond. The armored humans always respond.>"

"<I do not like the armored humans.>"

Sasha and Sochi came out of the structure and didn't hesitate to come close after working their way through the circle of the humans. What drew <Arizesyley's> attention, though, was a hoard of the human children rushing past the human adults. The human adults reached out to stop the human children, but failed. The human children charged toward <Kedekitley>, Naia, and her.

<Kedekitley> said, "<The human adults may be reluctant to come close, but the same does not apply to the human children.>"

<Arizesyley> picked up Naia, brought her wings around to cover her, and said, "I will protect you."

When the human children stopped in front of her, Anitra said, "Please, stop hiding Naia."

Naia said, "It's all right, Mother. You may put me down."

Worried for Naia's safety, <Arizesyley> delayed before she uncovered Naia and set her down.

A human child in the hoard pointed at <Arizesyley> and said, "She has yellow lightning bolts on her wings."

Another human child said, "I like the green and blue stripes on her neck and tail, and the red edges on her wings."

Yet another human child pointed at <Kedekitley> and said, "That dragon has red marks that look like flames. May we touch you?"

<Arizesyley> looked to <Kedekitley>, who wiggled and straightened his shoulders before nodding to her, then she said, "The human children may touch us."

The human adults gasped as the human children mobbed <Kedekitley> and her while making *oohing* and *aahing* sounds, which she interpreted as showing how amazed the human children were with <Kedekitley> and her.

Sten and Asa joined Sasha and Sochi.

<Arizesyley> leaned toward <Kedekitley> and said, "<That human female is the lead armored human without her Gird-metal armor. I recognize her sensory signature from when she removed her head cover during our previous encounter.>"

<Kedekitley> nodded. "<That is more evidence the humans do not fear us.>"

"<All right then. The human behavior is not expected.>"

Sten said, "Dragon, it's good to see you, but ... what's going on?"

"Human, I am pleased to see you. The human children are touching Cinnamon and me."

"I see that." To Naia, he said, "Do you need more food?"

"No, no, no, I don't need more food yet. I just wanted to visit Anitra."

Sasha waved her hands at the surrounding human adults and said, "Please, go back to whatever you were doing." She made the same hand motions at the human children. "Please, that's enough touching. Anitra, please, take Naia and the children to the playfield and continue your game."

"Yes, Grandma. Please, everyone come with me." Anitra motioned for the human children to move. "Please, you too, Naia."

<Arizesyley> felt trepidation as Naia looked up at her. She calmed herself and said, "Be brave. Go with the human child Anitra, but stay where I can see you."

Naia followed Anitra and the other human children.

Sasha said, "Please, come sit in the shade of the plantus tree and we'll talk while we watch the children."

<Arizesyley> followed Sasha as she led Sochi, Sten, Asa, and <Kedekitley> to a tall, wide-spreading tree growing next to the structure. Under the tree, the humans sat on benches. She and <Kedekitley> lay in the grass. She nestled against <Kedekitley>, tucked her feet under her, and entwined her tail with his. She kept looking to see what the human children and Naia were doing. The human children were running around kicking a ball.

<Arizesyley> said, "What is the game the human children play?"

Sochi said, "It's called *calcephera*."

She tilted her head. "All right then." She took a breath and said, "What is *calcephera?*"

"The children are split into two teams. That's why half of the children wear blue vests and the other half wear red. Anitra gave Naia a blue vest like hers. There's a net at each end of the field. One team defends one net. The other team defends the other net. The objective of the game is to kick the ball into the other team's net while keeping the other team from kicking the ball into your net. Anitra's explaining the rules to Naia."

<Kedekitley> said, "Dragons have a similar game, except dragons do not kick the ball with our feet. Dragons use our tails to hit the ball."

<Arizesyley> felt him try to demonstrate, but having her tail entwined with his stifled the attempt.

"That sounds like a fun game," said Sten. "I'd like to see it someday."

Sasha leaned forward. "Did I hear Naia call you *Mother?*"

<Arizesyley> nodded. "Naia calls me *Mother* and Spice she calls *Father*, but Naia says we are not *Mommy* and *Daddy*. *Mommy* and *Daddy* were Naia's human parents."

"What can you tell us about Naia?"

"Naia is wonderful." She tingled, her wings vibrated oddly, and her tail tried to flick even though it was entwined with <Kedekitley's> tail. She again glanced toward the human children. "I expected caring for Naia would be complicated, but Naia cares for herself. I did not know the humans could be skilled, talented, and sophisticated."

Sasha made the human laughing sound and said, "Well, in my experience, most people aren't."

Sten said, "Naia strikes me as being precocious."

Asa bumped her shoulder into his. "You say that about all the children."

"I do not. I only say it about Anitra, and now Naia."

"It sounds like Naia's one of the exceptions, not the rule," said Sasha. "But, what I mean is where did you find her?"

"I found Naia under a rock."

"Under a rock?"

Sasha creased her brow in a manner similar to how Sten had creased his brow when <Kedekitley> had said they needed information the first time they visited the human town. The expression had meant Sten was confused then and that Sasha was confused now. The expressions made by the humans were indeed similar to dragon expressions and her skill at interpreting the expressions was improving.

To alleviate Sasha's confusion, <Arizesyley> provided more information. "Naia was hiding."

"Hiding from what?"

"Naia was hiding from the humans she calls *Cultists*."

Sasha shook her head. "That still doesn't tell me what happened."

The headshake must have meant even more information was required to alleviate Sasha's confusion. <Arizesyley> drew a breath and said, "Naia said the human Cultists stole human food and supplies from Naia's home. Then the human Cultists burned Naia's home, called Naia a beast child, and attempted to murder Naia. Naia and her parents ran. Naia's parents told Naia to hide. The human Cultists murdered Naia's parents, but the human Cultists could not find Naia. Naia was hiding under a rock. I found Naia hiding under a rock."

"That's horrible."

"Me finding Naia hiding under a rock is not horrible."

"Not that." Sasha sighed — another exaggerated emotional expression <Arizesyley> had to learn to interpret — and said, "The Cultists murdering her parents is horrible."

"I returned Naia to the nearest human town to where I found Naia," <Arizesyley> said. "The human town turned out to be where the human Cultists lived. The human Cultists attempted to murder Naia. In response, I took Naia to our weyr. I told Naia I would protect her from the humans. Now, I care for Naia."

"When did this happen?"

"Today is the fourth day since I found Naia."

"It's only been four days?" Sasha glanced toward the playfield. "She must still be terribly traumatized."

Naia was running around on the field amidst the other human children. She occasionally kicked the ball. <Arizesyley's> acute hearing allowed her to hear Naia's laughter. The sound was soothing and she could feel Naia's joy.

<Arizesyley> said, "I can feel that playing the calcephera game with the human children is making Naia happy. Feeling Naia is happy also makes me happy. Is feeling that a human child is happy normal?"

Sasha said, "It's obvious she's happy right now, but I'm concerned about her trauma. The murder of her parents surely caused emotional damage. Does she have outbursts of anger?"

<Arizesyley> shook her head. "Naia has had moments of frustration, but Naia is never angry."

Everyone became quiet as they watched Naia running and laughing and acting joyful.

Then Sasha took a breath and said, "I'm worried she's suppressing her anger inside her, and the hatred of those people who murdered her parents, and the fear of those people. Occasionally, she probably feels overcome by despair. And, she feels vulnerable. That's why she's latched onto you as her protector; what better protector can she have than the dragon who rescued her? That's why she's anxious when she's separated from you. Hypervigilance is something else I've noticed; she's always looking for signs of danger and betrayal. Her self-esteem has been damaged too; that's why she keeps trying to prove her abilities and worth. And, she probably blames herself for what happened. It's good she has you. You provide her security and comfort."

"Naia does not need me," said <Arizesyley>. "Naia does everything for herself and wants no help. Naia says she is almost grown-up."

"She may think she's almost grown-up, but she has a long way to go. Children need a loving and nurturing environment and caregivers who provide affection and guidance. She needs you, and it's obvious you want what's best for her. That's what it means to be a mother."

<Arizesyley> shifted her position to see Naia better and said, "How do I repair Naia's emotional damage?"

"We don't want her dwelling on her loss and becoming depressed and withdrawn. Being preoccupied with painful memories can turn one's own mind into one's worst enemy. I'm glad to see her playing with the other children. She needs to stay engaged. Socializing with family and friends is good for her. You and Spice are her family. We and the children are her friends."

Naia kicked the ball, which rolled into one of the nets. The human children's screams brought <Arizesyley> to her feet. She extended her wings, bunched her legs to leap, and said, "The human children are attacking Naia."

"Please, wait." Sasha leaped to her feet and waved her hands up and down. "It's okay. The children are celebrating. Naia kicked the winning goal."

Both Sasha and the human children were making exaggerated emotional expressions? She still had much to learn. <Arizesyley> sighed, which wasn't as exaggerated as the sighs the humans made.

The hoard of human children with Naia and Anitra in the lead came running. Naia said, "Mother, Father, did you see? I won the game."

"Father and I saw you win the game." <Arizesyley> picked up Naia and rubbed her head on her. "You performed the task well."

Anitra said, "Dad, may we have cake to celebrate?"

"It's meal time." Sten stood. "If it's okay with Grandma and Grandpa, after eating, you and the children may have cake."

Asa examined Anitra's hands, looked at the other human children, and said, "If all of you wash your hands first."

"Please, come on everyone." Anitra led the human children around the side of the structure.

Asa said, "Please, you too, Naia."

Naia looked at <Arizesyley> with her exaggerated human smile filling her face. <Arizesyley> felt joy and calm.

"Go with the human children. I will be near. Call out if you need me. My dragon hearing enables me to hear you." She set Naia down.

Naia ran after the human children.

"Dragons are too large to fit through the door, but you should be able to stick your heads in to watch." Sochi waved in the direction the human children had gone. "The banquet room's backdoor is around back. Please, follow the children."

ococoo

<Arizesyley> stuck her head in the door. Some of the human children were already sitting on benches at a long table. The other human children

were washing their hands. Naia sat next to Anitra. Every human child was talking. The human adults entered through a door on the far side of the room. Aromas of animal and plant origins filled the air.

<Kedekitley> nudged her and said. "<Your horns are wonderful, but I want to see the human children and your horns are in my way.>"

She poked him with her tail. "<Wait your turn.>"

Sasha said, "Spice, please, come to the window. I'll open it for you."

<Kedekitley> stuck his head in the open window, which <Arizesyley> decided had a better view, and wrinkled his nose at her. She wrinkled her nose at him.

Sochi said, "Please, everyone calm down. Food's being served."

The human children stilled and quieted.

The human adults placed bowls containing pieces of animal flesh and plants and a container of liquid in front of each of the human children, but no human child touched the human food until the last human child had his human food and Sochi said, "Everyone's served. You may eat now."

The human children attacked the human food and the talking resumed.

Sasha said, "Please, no talking with your mouths full."

To <Kedekitley>, <Arizesyley> said, "<Have you seen this human behavior before?>"

He shook his head. "<This human behavior is new to me. I have always been told the humans are not sophisticated. Yet, consider the things the humans accomplish. Our belief that the humans are not sophisticated is wrong. We must accept how sophisticated the humans are so their future actions do not surprise us.>"

Sasha approached <Arizesyley> and said, "Anitra asked her mother and father if Naia can do a sleepover. Asa and Sten said yes, if you're okay with it."

<Arizesyley> tried to tilt her head, but her horns caught on the doorframe. "All right then. What is a *sleepover?*"

"Naia would spend the night here with Anitra."

Naia tensed, stopped talking with the human children, and turned toward her. <Arizesyley> cleared her confused thoughts and concentrated on feeling happy. Naia relaxed and resumed talking with the human children.

"I know what you're thinking." Sasha glanced toward Naia. "But, it would be good for her to spend time with Anitra. They'd play games, and talk, and eat, and sleep, if Naia is willing to be away from you for the night."

"Would a sleepover with the human child Anitra help repair Naia's emotional damage?"

"I believe it would help. You'd bring her back tomorrow morning. She'd spend the day and night. Late on the next day, you'd return to take her home."

<Arizesyley> turned to <Kedekitley>. "<What course of action should I take?>"

He said, "<You are responsible for your human child. You must decide on the course of action you should take.>"

Naia and Anitra approached.

Naia said, "Mother, Anitra asked me to do a sleepover tomorrow night."

<Arizesyley> felt a mix of anxiety, excitement, and indecision, which didn't help her decide what course of action to take. "Come outside, Naia, and we will discuss the sleepover invitation."

She led Naia away from the structure, settled in the grass, wrapped her tail around herself, and mantled her wings over Naia and her to give them privacy. Around the edges of her wings, light leaked in. A sweet grass aroma collected under her wings. Naia sat and stared at her. She stared at Naia. <Kedekitley> poked his head in where her wings met.

<Arizesyley> said, "You look well, Naia."

Naia said, "Your eyes are the color of embers glowing in a fire."

<Kedekitley> said, "This activity is not solving the problem. The situation needs to be analyzed and summarized, the problem defined, and a solution designed."

Naia smiled and said, "Father is smart."

<Arizesyley> smiled and said, "Father is a genius and the best dragon."

<Kedekitley> huffed and said, "May I continue? The situation is Naia has been invited to do a sleepover with the human child Anitra. That will require returning with Naia tomorrow morning and leaving Naia with the humans while Mother and I leave. Naia will stay here all day, sleep here that night, and stay here until Mother and I return to retrieve her late the next day. The problem is Naia and Mother fear the humans and neither Naia nor Mother want to be separated from the other. What is the solution to the problem?"

Before <Arizesyley> could speak, Naia said, "I like the people of Splain."

"All right then," said <Arizesyley>. "What is *Splain*?"

"Anitra told me the village is called *Splain*. I fear Cultists. I don't think any Cultists live in Splain. The people here are nice."

When <Arizesyley> said nothing, <Kedekitley> said to her, "Do you trust the humans in the human town Splain?"

She hesitated, looking at her hands as she wrung them, before saying, "The humans have acted as good humans. The humans have provided help. I thought I would always fear the humans, but the humans in the human town Splain make me feel comfortable."

<Kedekitley> said to Naia, "Would you be comfortable being separated from Mother while participating in the sleepover with the human child Anitra?"

<Arizesyley> felt distress, but it changed into anticipation.

Naia said, "Yes, but I don't want to live here. I want to live with you."

"You will always be a part of our family." <Arizesyley> hooked the tip of her tail over Naia's hand. <Kedekitley> added his tail's tip to the handholding. <Arizesyley> continued, "You will always live with us. Nevertheless, there is no reason you cannot visit with your human friends. Participating in the sleepover with the human child Anitra will be good for you."

A flood of enthusiasm washed over <Arizesyley> as Naia said, "I'd like to do the sleepover."

<Arizesyley> said to <Kedekitley>, "<Will the humans protect my human child?>"

"<You know how I feel about my human friend. That feeling also applies to my human friend's family. I believe the humans will protect your human child. Nevertheless, you must make your own choice.>"

Naia said, "Language, language, language."

<Arizesyley> rubbed her head on Naia. "I accept the choice for you to do the sleepover with the human child Anitra."

"Thank you, thank you, thank you."

<Kedekitley> said, "The problem is solved," and pulled his head out from under <Arizesyley's> wings.

<Arizesyley> said, "I will miss being with you, but you and I will be brave."

"Yes, yes, yes, Mother. We'll both be brave, brave, brave."

Light poured down on her and Naia as she separated her wings and put them away.

Naia ran to Anitra where she stood with the human adults and said, "Mother and Father said I can do the sleepover."

<Arizesyley> said to the human adults, "You humans will protect Naia using the same diligence I use to protect Naia."

"We will," said Sasha. "I'll give her a pack to carry what she wants to bring with her tomorrow. And, please, give me a moment to make a sandwich for her to take with her for her evening meal tonight."

∞∞∞

At their weyr, <Arizesyley> and <Kedekitley> watched over Naia as she spent the remainder of the day preparing for the sleepover by washing her clothes and herself, and placing into the pack clean clothes and her personal care tools. When evening approached, Naia opened the box Sasha had given her filling the air with the aroma of scorched animal flesh, plants, and fermentation.

"Wow. Look at this. It's the fanciest sandwich I've ever seen." She took a bite. "Umgoof."

<Arizesyley> said, "No talking with your mouth full."

Naia swallowed and said, "It's good."

As Naia continued consuming the human food, <Arizesyley> laid her head down.

204

<Kedekitley> said, "<Are you troubled?>"

"<After what I learned about my human child's emotional damage, I realized I have the same emotional damage. Did you know I have emotional damage?>"

"<I have always known about your experience with the humans and how that experience influences your beliefs and actions, but I have never thought of you as having emotional damage.>"

"<You have always been good to me, and good for me. You are the best dragon.>"

<Kedekitley> entwined his tail with hers and rubbed his head on her. "<Will you be all right?>"

"<I am well. My human child's excitement about the sleepover is making me feel better.>"

Naia's eagerness to prepare for the sleepover had prompted her to place her teeth cleaning tool, pajamas, and the cloth dragon in the pack. She retrieved them.

After preparing herself for the night, Naia said, "I'll sleep in my nest tonight." She climbed into her nest with her blanket, pillow, and the cloth dragon.

<Arizesyley> said, "Goodnight, Naia."

As darkness deepened, <Arizesyley> felt angst that spiked with every night sound.

"Mother?"

"Yes, Naia?"

"May I sleep with you?"

"Climb into our nest."

The angst dissolved into relief.

Naia climbed into the nest, spread her blanket, placed her pillow, hugged the cloth dragon, and nestled against <Arizesyley>. "Thank you, thank you, thank you, Mother."

"I will always be here for you, Naia."

<Kedekitley> added, "I too will always be here for you, Naia."

"Thank you, thank you, thank you, Father. I love you both."

Chapter 10

Leaving the Child for a Sleepover

After having her morning meal and making herself ready, Naia placed the repacked pack in <Arizesyley's> right side pouch, climbed into her left side pouch, and said, "Please, go, go, go."

Upon landing, Anitra and the human adults came to greet them. Naia climbed out of <Arizesyley's> pouch and retrieved the pack.

<Arizesyley> brought her head close to Naia and said, "Behave appropriately, be brave, and have fun."

Naia hugged her snout. "I know this is hard for you, Mother. Please, you be brave too. We will both be brave until you and Father return tomorrow."

To Sasha, <Arizesyley> said, "For me to trust the humans is difficult, but I trust you humans to care for Naia until Spice and I return."

"We'll take good care of her," said Sasha. "We won't let you down."

Sten said, "We'll see you tomorrow." He then moved the humans, and Naia, toward the structure.

Naia appeared happy, yet <Arizesyley> could feel anxiety. However, the anxiety was being defeated by determination. The emotions were confusing and she still didn't understand why she kept having them. But, given how sophisticated and capable Naia was, <Arizesyley> knew she would be fine. And, the sleepover would be good for Naia. With her own determination set, and convinced she was doing the right thing for Naia, she flew away with <Kedekitley> at her side.

∞∞∞∞

They hadn't gone far when <Arizesyley> spiraled down and landed on a treeless knoll. <Kedekitley> landed beside her. She began walking in circles, her tail flicking.

<Kedekitley> moved out of her way and said, "<Are you not well?>"

"<I do not know what is wrong. I am feeling anxious.>" She reversed her circling. "<I often feel anxious, but not like this.>" She stopped pacing, fidgeted in place, and looked in the direction of the human town, which was out of sight behind the tree-covered hills. "<I need my human child.>"

"<Should we return to the human town?>"

She said, "<Yes,>" and then shook her head. "<No, I do not want to return to the human town. My presence would disrupt my human child's sleepover. The sleepover is good for my human child. We should continue to our weyr.>"

"<We can attend the Conclave.>"

"<You are correct. The Conclave begins today. I keep forgetting about the Conclave. I must speak to the Council about my eradicate-the-humans solution.>"

<Kedekitley> stepped closer. "<You promised your human child that you would protect her. How can you still want to eradicate the humans?>"

"<Eradicating the humans is the only solution that ensures the humans never again murder dragons.>"

"<What will you do about your human child and the good humans who are helping you?>"

She stopped her fidgeting and stared at <Kedekitley> for a long moment. "<I do not have a solution to that problem. Let us go to the Conclave.>"

She took flight with <Kedekitley> following heading deep into the mountains toward the Conclave Grounds.

Along the way, they made stops to reduce their mass, to drink their fill from a tumbling creek, and to hunt food animals. <Kedekitley> reinforced <Arizesyley's> opinion that he was an exceptional hunter when he immediately caught his food animal. She required numerous attempts because she kept spooking the food animals before she was close enough to capture one.

When they arrived at the Conclave Grounds, <Arizesyley> hopped from foot to foot.

<Kedekitley> said, "<Are you still troubled?>"

"<I must return to my human child. I will not disrupt my human child's sleepover. I will hide where the humans will not see me.>"

"<What about speaking to the Council?>"

"<Will you speak for me? You know everything I want to say.>"

<Kedekitley> sounded startled when he said, "<I have my own solution to propose, and it is the opposite of your solution.>"

"<You are a genius. You will find a way to speak for both of us.>" She pleaded with her eyes.

<Kedekitley> gazed into her eyes then said, "<I will speak for both of us. I have no idea how, but I will design a solution to the problem of presenting both of our solutions.>"

"<Thank you. I will see you when you return tomorrow.>" She prepared to take flight.

<Kedekitley> said, "<I love you and will miss you. Stay safe.>"

"<I will stay safe. I love you and will miss you too. You are the best dragon.>"

She took flight dodging left and right flying upstream against the flow of arriving dragons.

Chapter 11

You Humans Betrayed Me

When <Arizesyley> landed in front of the structure where she'd left Naia, she expected relief from the emotions twisting her insides. The relief didn't come, and none of the humans came from the structure. "Naia, where are you?"

She went to the banquet room's backdoor and found the door broken into pieces. Inside, the long table lay on its side. The benches were scattered about as if tossed. Containers and other items were scattered, many shattered. Asa and another human were engaged in frantic conversation, which stopped when the humans saw her.

"Cinnamon, you're back."

"Where is Naia?"

Asa looked at the other human before saying, "I don't know. I was about to make Miss Nyxie tell me." She pointed to the other human who cowered.

"I detect the humans Naia calls Cultists have been here. You let the human Cultists take Naia. The human Cultists want to murder Naia." <Arizesyley> pulled her head out of the door, lifted it to the sky, and released her anguish in a keening cry that became a rattling roar.

Coming to the door, Asa said, "Anitra's gone too. So are Sten, Sochi, and Sasha."

<Arizesyley> lunged causing the humans to retreat to the far side of the room. "I trusted you humans to protect Naia. You humans betrayed me." She extended the talons on her hand and swiped at the structure slicing through the roof and wall causing a section to collapse. "All of the humans must be eradicated." She turned to leave.

Asa climbed over the debris and through the dust cloud. "Please, wait. We didn't betray you."

<Arizesyley> took flight skimming the ground following the scent trail and wagon wheel scuffs.

Soon the road she followed entered a thick forest through which she couldn't fly. She landed and galloped along the road as it twisted left and right around clusters of trees and up hills. She knew this road. It was on the maps in her maps collection. The road led to the human town where she had tried to return Naia after she had found her, the human town where the Cultist had tried to murder Naia.

She had come to the edge of the trees when her senses detected five of the humans spaced in a line across her path. Diving into a thicket of trees and bushes before the humans could see her, she paused to allow her senses and mental map to accumulate details.

The five humans formed an arc. As she moved, more of the humans came into range allowing her to assume the human Cultists' human town had a ring of human sentries around it. She hoped there weren't more of the humans who wore Gird-metal armor she couldn't detect without visually seeing the armor.

Moving to a position where she could see one of the humans revealed that the human was hiding and watching the sky. None of the humans on her map moved. They must all have been hiding, watching, waiting to sound an alarm. As she moved closer, she detected more of the humans clustered beyond the sentries.

Then, she felt Naia.

Naia was alive. Naia was afraid. Naia was angry. She'd never before felt such anger from Naia. Feeling Naia's emotions was different from her dragon senses — it didn't contribute to her mental map — but she'd felt it for a couple of days and hadn't known how to interpret it. Now she understood even though she could not imagine how it worked: she had a connection to Naia, and Naia had a connection to her.

A new sensation came from Naia: excitement. Naia knew she was near. She concentrated on thoughts of calm, quiet, bravery. Don't let the Cultists know. The excitement moderated and determination grew.

Her mental map revealed corridors between hills where the sentries wouldn't see her, as long as the sentries didn't move. She made her way through an obscured gully, entered the human town, and settled between two structures where she wouldn't be seen yet she could observe.

In the open space in the middle of the human town, the place where she had landed when she had tried to return Naia to the humans, sat Naia, bound, chained, and a cloth cover over her head. She was not alone. Anitra, Sten, Sochi, and Sasha were with her, also bound, chained, and with cloth covers over their heads. Around them stood the humans armed with bows, spears, and swords, but none of the metal she could see made the disturbing fuzzy void caused by seeing Gird-metal armor or murder weapons.

She could leap to Naia, cut her chains with a talon, and take flight with Naia before the humans could attack. She prepared to take the leap but stopped when a human dressed in clothing decorated with colorful stones spoke.

"Still no sign?"

"Nothing yet," said another human who approached the human wearing the colorful stones. "Your followers aren't very smart, are they?"

"No need to be rude, Mister Travis."

"They were only supposed to snatch the dragon's pet, but we can still make this work."

"I'm expecting you to make my followers look like heroes."

"Mark my words: My people have the weapon needed to make it look like your followers killed a dragon that was breaking the Paladins' Peace. That'll bring you more followers."

"And, we'll finally kill the beast child, and you'll get your Dragon War back."

"Don't just kill the child. Please, kill the others too. Make sure it looks like the dragon did it." The human called *Mister Travis* walked away.

Some of the humans are good humans and some of the humans are bad humans was what <Kedekitley> had said. She had to rescue Naia, but she couldn't let the good humans be damaged.

The two human children would fit in her pouches. She could pick up the three human adults with her hands and feet, but the mass would be too great to take flight without a long run to get airflow over her wings. Holding one human adult with her tail would free her feet to run. Except, there wasn't enough room to run to take flight.

She could murder the bad humans who held weapons. Except, she wouldn't be able to protect Naia and the good humans and fight the bad humans at the same time because there were too many bad humans.

What should she do?

At the edge of her senses' range, she detected more of the humans approaching from outside the ring of sentries. The situation was becoming worse. Stay calm. There had to be a solution to the problem, but she didn't know what it could be.

Horns sounded.

The human wearing the colorful stones said, "That's not the signal for the dragon's coming. What's happening?"

Another human came and said, "It's the people from Splain, a lot of them, on horseback and in wagons. The three dragon-slayer knights are with them on their warhorses. The mob looks angry."

The colorful human said, "Please, kill the hostages. Then you might want to run." The colorful human ran in the opposite direction from the approaching humans.

The bad humans set arrows to their bowstrings.

<Arizesyley> roared, leaped, landed straddling Naia and the good humans, and mantled her wings over them.

"Mmm," came from Naia as she wiggled.

"Stay down and under my wings." Using precise motions of her talons, she cut everyone's chains and bindings. Arrows struck her but bounced off her hide.

Naia pulled the cloth cover off her head, uncovered her mouth, and said, "Now what, Mother?"

"I do not know."

"Don't you have a plan?"

"I could not design a solution to the problem."

<Arizesyley> heard a *thwack* and something ripped through her wing and lodged in her hip. She gasped.

Naia yelped as if in pain and clutched her own hip. "Mother, Mother, Mother."

<Arizesyley> took a stuttering breath and said, "I am well."

"No, no, no, you're not."

Sten said, "It's a crossbow bolt."

Another *thwack* and a second Gird-metal bolt tore through her wing and penetrated into her ribs below her wing shoulder joint. She gasped again.

Naia screamed and clutched her own ribs. An instant later, <Arizesyley> felt a surge of anger so intense it made her forget her pain. Naia forced her way out from under the protection of her mantled wings.

Anitra followed.

<Arizesyley> pulled her head from under her wings. Many of the humans armed with bows, spears, and swords were running away. She yelled, "Naia, stop."

Sten said, "Oh, bother," climbed out from under her wing, shouted, "Naia, Anitra, please, stop," and chased after the human children. Sochi followed him.

<Arizesyley> moved to rise.

"Please, don't move." Sasha grasped at <Arizesyley's> neck. "Those bolts might cause more damage if you move. Sten and Sochi will protect the children."

Naia ran at the human holding the murder weapon crossbow. Another human was handing the human a Gird-metal bolt. Naia made a high-pitched, piercing human child roar and hurled herself into the legs of the human holding the murder weapon crossbow knocking him off his feet. The human fell into the other human who dropped the Gird-metal bolt as he too fell. When the empty murder weapon crossbow hit the ground, it released with a *thwack*.

Naia picked up the Gird-metal bolt and beat the human that had been holding the murder weapon crossbow on the head and body. With each blow, she screamed a word. "Please. Stop. Hurting. Mother. Stop. Stop. Stop."

The other human stood and came at Naia. She swung the Gird-metal bolt. The bolt's point sliced across the human's abdomen causing the human to cry out, curl into a ball, and fall to the ground.

<Arizesyley> wanted to get to her feet and run to Naia to keep her safe, but Sasha clung to her neck — as if that could stop her getting up to run after Naia — and said, "Please, stay put."

A human attacked Sten. Sten kicked the human in the head. The human landed on the ground and didn't get up.

A human with a sword charged Naia. <Arizesyley> almost stood, but Sasha pulled down with her full weight and said, "Please, stay put. Sten will handle it." However, it wasn't Sten who came to Naia's rescue. Anitra picked up a spear and swung the not-sharp end of it at the sword-wielding human catching the human in the face. Teeth and sword flew and the human flipped upside down before landing on the ground.

Another human charged. Anitra jabbed the sharp end of the spear at the human. The human jumped back as blood appeared on the human's clothing. With hand on chest and a scream, the human turned and ran.

Sten and Sochi caught up with Naia and Anitra and prepared to fight, but the other bad humans had run away.

The wave of humans from the human town Splain washed over everything. An armored human riding an armored horse approached Naia, Anitra, Sten, and Sochi.

To the armored human, Sten said, "How did you find us?"

"Miss Nyxie came and got me, but you were already gone. I convinced her to tell me where they took you. Then she ran off. I have no idea where she went." The armored human yelled at the other humans from the human town Splain, "Please, round up the hooligans. Don't let them get away."

Naia said, "Mother saved us, but now she's hurt," and ran toward her. The others followed.

When the armored human approached, <Arizesyley> laid back her ears, bared her teeth, and growled.

The armored human jumped off the armored horse and removed their head cover revealing Asa. "It's all right. It's me. I'm here to help you." Then she turned, pointed, and yelled at another of the humans, "You, please, fetch Doctor Dan."

A second horse that wore no armor but carried supplies stayed next to the armored horse. A third horse that wore no armor came to <Arizesyley> and nuzzled her. She had never before experienced such a thing from a food animal, although, she reminded herself, the human's animals were not food animals.

"It's okay, Abaccus." Sten patted the horse. "Someone, please, take care of Abaccus, Maximus, and Sayneigh."

Another human came and took the small ropes tied to each of the horses. "Sorry, Master Sten. We brought a string of extra horses. Abaccus untied himself. I'll take care of them."

Another human ran up and looked at her with wide eyes. "I doctor people and animals. I don't know anything about dragons."

Asa pushed him forward. "They can't be that different."

"They're a lot different."

<Arizesyley> turned her head and spat on herself where the Gird-metal bolt protruded from her ribs.

When she turned back to Naia, Naia stroked her snout. "It's okay, it's okay, it's okay, Mother."

<Arizesyley> said, "I must rest."

"Yes, yes, yes, Mother. Please, rest."

"You do not understand. Rest is a special state dragons enter that concentrates our metabolic energy on damage repair. Rest is similar to sleep, but different. I might look dead, but I will be fine. I do not know how long I will be in rest. Do not worry about me."

"Okay, okay, okay, Mother. I'll watch over you. I'll keep you safe."

"I know you will. I trust you, and the good humans." She nuzzled Naia and said, "I love you, Naia."

The last thing she heard as her perceptions slipped beneath a veil of white was Naia crying.

Chapter 12
Waking Up Bandaged

<Arizesyley's> first awareness was concern coming from Naia.

When her senses resumed, she heard, "Mother, Mother, Mother, are you awake? I can feel you're waking up."

<Arizesyley> opened her eyes. Her left eye saw a fuzzy blur that resolved into Naia's nose and eyes.

Naia sat back and said, "Doctor Dan, Doctor Dan, Doctor Dan, Mother's awake."

The humans came to gather around her.

The sun's position and the positions of the stars detected by her dragon senses indicated it was the morning of the next day. She'd only been in rest overnight.

She said, "Naia, are you well?"

"I'm fine, Mother."

"Have you consumed human food? The humans consume human food several times per day."

"I've had plenty to eat."

The human that had said he doctors people and animals pushed past the other humans and said, "Please, stand back. Give her room to breathe." When she lifted her head and wiggled, the human doctor waved his hands and said, "Please, don't be moving about. We managed to remove the crossbow bolts and control the bleeding, but we don't want your wounds to start bleeding again."

When she moved her wing to look at the bandages, she felt a spike of pain and noticed Naia flinch. Two of the bandages were large — one on her ribs below her wing shoulder and the other on her hip. A scan using her ultrasonic senses confirmed the seriousness of the wounds. Bandages also covered the holes in her wing and smaller, unnecessary bandages covered the slight gouges in her hide giving her a speckled look. The humans treating her wounds must be why she had been able to wake from rest earlier then she had expected she would.

The human doctor said, "Please, don't be moving."

Naia said, "Doctor Dan has been taking good care of you."

"I did my best, but I have no experience doctoring dragons."

"Thank you for helping me." To Naia, she said, "Naia, have you slept?"

Sasha and Sten stepped out of the crowd. Sasha said, "We've been caring for Naia. She fell asleep with her arms wrapped around you and slept all night."

"I kept having dreams I was floating in a white emptiness," said Naia. "It was strange, and lonely."

The human doctor checked her bandages and said, "I want to move you to Splain. It'll be easier to care for you there."

<Arizesyley> tilted her head. "All right then." She nodded toward the human doctor and said to Sasha, "Is this human one of the humans you said are not sophisticated?"

Sasha said, "Why do you ask that?"

"The human told me not to move about, but now the human says I am to move. The contradiction does not sound sophisticated."

"When you first woke," the human doctor said, "I didn't want you to make any drastic movements. We'll be careful when we move you to Splain."

Sten said, "We brought our strongest wagon." At the edge of the human crowd set a large, flat wagon. "It'll hold your weight. We have a double team of horses to pull it. Can you climb onto the wagon?"

She stood. "I can climb onto the wagon."

When she attempted to close her damaged wing, Naia said, "It hurts, it hurts, it hurts."

"I am well."

"No, no, no. You're not well. Your wing, chest, and hip hurt. I can feel it."

The human doctor said, "Moving your wing is flexing muscles we don't want flexed. With your permission, I will bind your wings to hold them in place so you don't accidently flex them."

<Arizesyley> froze, staring at the human doctor.

Sten said, "Please, do what Doctor Dan says."

"Yes, yes, yes, Mother. Doctor Dan is helping you." Naia made the human version of a stern expression.

"Yes, Naia." <Arizesyley> turned to the human doctor and said, "You may bind my wings."

The human doctor pointed at a human in the crowd. "Apprentice Serath, please, fetch a long rope." To <Arizesyley> he said, "You may close your right wing on your own, but let us do all the work of closing your left wing. Please, do not tense any muscles as we do it." He made a motion and a group of the humans came forward. The humans positioned themselves around her wing. "As we fold her wing closed, I'll check on how it's pulling on the wounds and bandages."

The wing folding went well. The rope arrived and was looped under her body and wrapped around her five times before the rope was tied off leaving both of her wings securely bound.

"That should work for now," the human doctor said. "Let's try the wagon again."

As she moved toward the wagon, Naia flinched, wrapped her arms around herself, and said, "Mother, Mother, Mother."

<Arizesyley> turned to her and said, "Yes, Naia. My damage still hurts a small amount. I am sorry you feel the pain too."

Her body fit on the wagon, but she had to wrap her tail around her and bend her neck so she curled into a knot as she did when she slept.

Sten said, "You're not as heavy as I thought. The springs barely compressed."

"Dragon anatomy has minimal mass," she said. "Too much mass makes flight difficult."

Naia climbed onto the wagon.

"Naia," Sten said. "It's not safe to ride up there."

<Arizesyley> wrapped her arms around Naia as Naia said, "You're making Mother ride up here, and other people are riding in wagons."

"The other wagons have sideboards. This one doesn't. That's why we're strapping Cinnamon down."

"You are strapping me down?" Her tone sounded more severe than she intended.

"With your permission. The straps will keep you from bouncing off if we hit a bump."

"Please, let them strap you down, Mother. Cargo is always strapped down."

"I am cargo am I?"

Sten said, "You're a passenger, but we don't want you to fall off."

The human wanted her safe, which gave her a better understanding of what <Kedekitley> saw in this human, what he saw in all of the good humans. "You may strap me down."

When the cargo straps were in place, Sten said, "Naia, time to get down."

"No, no, no. I'll ride here. I'm snug in Mother's arms."

<Arizesyley> tightened her grip on Naia and made her version of a stern expression at Sten. "Naia is safe with me."

After a pause, Sten said, "Okay, but keep a secure hold on her."

The horse that had nuzzled her approached followed by three other horses — the one clad in Gird-metal armor, the one carrying supplies, and a new one with no armor. Sten laughed and patted the lead horse. "I see you're raring to go. Thank you for fetching the others." Asa took hold of the ropes tied to the armored horse and supply horse. Sten handed Anitra the rope tied to the new horse. "I told you. Abaccus is remarkable."

<Arizesyley> and Naia rode the wagon to the human town Splain with Sten, Asa, and Anitra riding their horses beside them.

Chapter 13

I Will Keep the Humans

The wagon stopped at the structure where the previous day <Arizesyley> had left Naia for her sleepover. Many of the humans went in different directions. Others led the horses away.

Sten said, "We'll put you here in the plaza while we prepare a shelter for you to stay in while you heal."

Naia climbed down from the wagon, the cargo straps were removed, <Arizesyley> stepped off the wagon, and the wagon was taken away. The humans removed the ropes holding her wings, held her left wing as the human doctor and his helper examined and replaced the bandages, and then placed her wing on the ground in a relaxed position as she lay down.

"Things are looking good," said the human doctor. "We'll leave your wing open like this for now. Please, don't be moving about."

She said, "I will not move about."

"I need to check on my other patients, but I'll check on you again later," then he and all of the remaining humans except for Sten and Naia left.

Another human approached carrying a large, shiny container.

Sten said, "Do you wish for water to drink?"

"Yes, I would appreciate water to drink."

"I didn't have an opportunity to ask you about it before; so, when I sent word ahead, I guessed about how to give you water. I hope this method isn't offensive."

The human set the container in front of her.

She examined it and said, "The container is a washing tub."

"It's not a washing tub. It's a watering trough. I'll fill it with water for you to drink."

"That idea is a good idea. You are a genius like Spice."

Sten shook his head. "I doubt that."

A small wagon with a closed container on it that her dragon senses told her was full of water stopped next to the watering trough.

Sten said, "This is *potable water*." He removed a small container from the box on the side of the wagon, filled it with water, drank it, and said, "See? It's good for drinking. I'll fill the watering trough for you."

When the watering trough was full, <Arizesyley> lowered her head, puckered her lips, and drank.

Naia made laughing sounds.

<Arizesyley> lifted her head and said, "Naia, what is it you think is humorous?"

"You."

"Why do you think I am humorous this time?"

"You make slurping noises when you drink."

"You often think ordinary things are humorous."

She continued drinking.

Naia continued making laughing sounds.

When she finished, Sten moved the watering trough and said, "How about food? Do you need food? We can fetch food for you."

"I do not need food."

"That's good. I have no idea what or how to feed a dragon. If there's nothing else you need for now, I'm going home for a short while, but I'll be back."

"I am comfortable and satisfied. Thank you, and all of the good humans, for helping me."

Sten walked away. Naia followed him. She stopped Sten far enough away and whispered softly enough that even though <Arizesyley> had dragon hearing, she could not hear what Naia said. Then Sten walked away and Naia returned. Behind Naia came a group of the human adults and the human children carrying flowers.

One of the humans with the flowers said, "We didn't know how to express our appreciation for what you did rescuing our friends, but we hope you like flowers."

"I do like flowers. They are beautiful and have a nice aroma. Thank you."

Another group of the humans brought more flowers. Then another group and another group came with flowers. A crowd of the humans who didn't bring flowers also gathered with the human children in front. The humans who had left upon arriving at the human town returned bringing more of the human children. The humans looked at her with smiles and awed expressions. She was pleased the humans were sophisticated enough to recognize her magnificence, and she was pleased she was becoming skilled at interpreting the expressions the humans made.

Naia said, "I know what to do with these." She separated the flowers and weaved them into ropes that looped into rings. "Please, lower your head, Mother."

Naia slipped the ring of flowers over <Arizesyley's> head and down her neck so the flowers settled on her shoulders. The second ring of flowers was smaller. Naia placed that one over her horns.

Naia smiled her exaggerated human smile and said, "Pretty, pretty, pretty."

The gathered humans slapped their hands together, which <Arizesyley> interpreted as expressing approval.

Then, motion in the sky caught her attention and her senses told her <Kedekitley> was coming. She was excited. She missed him and had much to tell him.

He circled before descending and landing with a thump she felt through the ground. The wind gust from his landing shook leaves out of the tree near the structure. The humans scattered when he roared and lunged at them.

She said, "<Kedekitley, what are you doing?>"

"<The humans have damaged you.>" He lunged at the humans again.

"<Stop that behavior.>"

Naia stood, stepped out from <Arizesyley's> arms to face him, and said, "Please, stop, stop, stop, Father. Stop scaring people."

He looked at Naia then at <Arizesyley> his face showing confusion.

"<I agree with my human child. Stop trying to scare the humans,>" she said. "<Do not make me have to get up to reprimand you. My wing, chest, and hip hurt, and the human doctor told me not to move about.>"

"<You are damaged.>"

"<The good humans of the human town Splain did not damage me. The good humans of the human town Splain treated my damage and are caring for me.>"

"<How were you damaged?>"

"<The human Cultists damaged me. The human Cultists are some of the bad humans.>"

He examined her.

She squirmed. "<Stop scanning me with your ultrasound. You put a strange modulation on the sound that makes the sound tickle.>"

"<I must determine the extent of the damage. The modulation improves resolution and precision. You should learn how to make the modulation.>"

She pushed him with her snout. "<I am well.>"

"<You are damaged.>"

"<I am ... slightly damaged.>"

"<The damage to your hip is severe enough, but the damage to your chest is serious. The damage to your chest was almost fatal.>" He lay next to her, placed his neck and head against hers, and entwined his tail with hers.

She said, "<I will be well soon.>"

Naia said, "Language, language, language. Mother, Father, what are you saying?"

<Arizesyley> reached out to pull Naia closer. "Father is upset I am damaged."

"It's okay, it's okay, it's okay, Father. Doctor Dan is taking good care of Mother."

He said, "What happened?"

"The Cultists abducted us. Mother was brave. She saved us, but she got hurt doing it."

<Arizesyley> nuzzled Naia and said, "Naia was brave and performed the task well. Naia stopped the human Cultists who were using a murder weapon crossbow and Gird-metal bolts to damage me. Naia damaged the human Cultists."

Sochi, Sasha, Asa, and Anitra approached.

Sochi said, "It was more than the Cultists. There were others, led by a man called *Mister Travis*, who want to restart the Dragon War. Naia took down two and Anitra took down another and wounded another all by themselves."

Anitra held up her chin, made a human smile, and said, "You should see my new spear."

Naia said, "We were protecting Mother. Mommy and Daddy would be proud of me."

"I am also proud of you." <Arizesyley> rubbed her head on Naia.

The humans <Kedekitley> had caused to scatter regrouped and gathered close again.

<Kedekitley> said, "You said *the Cultists abducted us*. Who are *us*?"

"Me, and Anitra, and Grandpa Sochi, and Grandma Sasha, and Uncle Sten."

"The human Cultists took Human? Was Human damaged? Where is Human?" He stood, looked around, and called out, "Human, where are you?"

"Dragon, I'm here." Sten was running toward them.

<Kedekitley> ran to meet Sten, scooped him up in his arms, spun him around to examine him, and said, "Human, are you damaged?" He then hooked his tail around Sten and rubbed his head on him.

Sten wrapped his arms around <Kedekitley> and said, "I'm fine. I'm glad you're back." Sten reached behind himself to scratch the back of his neck. "I missed you, Dragon. When I was in the thick of the fight, I needed you and I was afraid I'd never see you again." Sten then resumed hugging <Kedekitley> who made a cooing sound.

<Kedekitley> and Sten clutched each other for several moments before Sten said, "I need to give this to Naia." In his hand, Sten held the object Naia normally wore around her neck. "Please, put me down, and come with me."

<Kedekitley> set Sten down.

"Here's your locket, Naia. The picture you wanted turned out well."

Naia opened the locket, smiled her beautiful human smile, and said, "It's perfect. Thank you, thank you, thank you, Uncle Sten."

<Arizesyley> said, "All right then. What is a *locket*?"

The humans came closer to see what Naia held.

"A *locket* is a small case for holding a keepsake." Naia held up the open locket with her hand covering the left side and showed it around. "See, this picture is of Mommy and Daddy. The other side had a picture of me when I was a baby, but I'm almost grown-up now. Uncle Sten made a new picture to put there." She uncovered the left side. "It's a picture of you, Mother, and you, Father."

Tears came to <Arizesyley's> eyes and she sighed. She gathered Naia in her arms, wrapped the tip of her tail around her, rubbed her head on her, and said, "Naia, I love you." To <Kedekitley>, <Arizesyley> said, "<The world has changed. I will keep the humans.>"

Part Five
Fear Fallacy Friend

Chapter 1

<Kedekitley>

Announce Intentions

Fourteen days before *Tipping Point.*

∞∞∞∞

A bell tolled and the humans fled as <Kedekitley> landed in the human town's central open space. The humans were a threat to dragons, but he had a solution to that problem even though the Dragon Council had said no to that solution. He planned to implement the solution regardless of what the Council had said and hoped that by so doing the world would change. He furled his wings, stood tall and dignified, and prepared to announce his intentions to the humans present.

None of the humans were present.

Structures arranged in concentric circles surrounded the circular, grass-covered open space. His dragon senses told him the humans were in and behind those structures, but none of the humans were in view. When a human peeked around the corner of a structure, <Kedekitley> took a breath to speak, but the human ducked behind the structure before he could. He hadn't anticipated this problem. How could he announce his intentions when none of the humans would listen?

The bell went quiet as three of the humans in Gird-metal armor and holding Gird-metal shields approached. Another problem he hadn't anticipated. The humans acquired the green and brown armor from the Gird creatures by trading plants and metal ores. It provided the humans a shell as strong as dragon hide, and it somehow interfered with dragon senses making the humans difficult to detect. While other weapons could not penetrate dragon hide, murder weapons made of the Gird-metal could. Proving the humans were monsters, the three armored humans each brandished a Gird-metal murder weapon sword, had a shorter Gird-metal murder weapon sword hanging at their waist, and had strapped on their back a crossbow murder weapon and quiver of Gird-metal bolts.

He unfurled his wings in preparation for a quick escape if necessary and, using his best human language skills, said, "I will not violate the Paladins' Peace."

The closest armored human said, "Why are you here, dragon?"

The human made the word *dragon* sound vulgar.

"I want to help the humans."

"Help us? We don't need help from a dragon. Please, leave."

The three armored humans advanced.

<Kedekitley> stumbled back, leaped into the air, and flew to his weyr, his heart racing.

That encounter had not gone as planned. All it had done was frighten him more than he had ever been frightened. He had never interacted with the humans before, so what had he expected? He hadn't expected the humans to hide. And, he hadn't expected a confrontation with the humans in Gird-metal armor, wielding Gird-metal murder weapon swords, and ready to violate the Paladins' Peace, an agreement that gave him the right to be there. He had not thought this endeavor through well enough. Regardless, he still thought his solution was correct. He would try again tomorrow. All he needed was courage.

Chapter 2

Sten

That Dragon Won't Be Coming Back

Sten came into the foyer, hung his hat, and put down his pack.

Asa called out from her studio, "Anitra, is that you? You're supposed to be at school."

"It's me. I'm back."

Sten stepped into the family room as Asa rushed out of her studio and charged at him. She hit him hard enough to cause him to stagger a couple of steps, wrapped her arms around him, kissed him, laid her head on his chest, and squeezed the breath out of him, which reminded him how strong her training made her. They had learned early in their relationship to let Asa do the charging after being apart; when they both did it, the resulting collision had been disastrous. However, something was different. Normally, Asa didn't collide hard enough to knock him back two steps, nor did she squeeze the breath out of him.

Sten caught his breath and said, "Are you okay?"

"I'm fine."

"I heard about the dragon."

"Oh, that. Come into my studio and I'll tell you about it."

Sten followed Asa into her studio where she sat at her worktable. She said nothing. Her hands shook as she pulled stitching out of a jacket sleeve.

Sten sat on the couch reserved for clients and waited, but finally, and gently, said, "Well?"

"I messed up the stitching. I have to start over."

Messing up anything she tailored was not normal for Asa. She was the world's best tailor, at least in Sten's mind, and based upon the demand for her work.

Sten said, "What about the dragon?"

"Oh, that." Asa set the jacket aside, went to the storefront window, and looked out at the street where people rushed past going about their day as if nothing had happened. She closed the blinds and faced him. Her voice quavered as she said, "I was so afraid."

Sten had experienced a dragon once, seven years ago. It happened the day the dragons turned and fought. They had never done that before; they had always retreated when dragon-slayer knights went after them. That day was different. That day, the Dragon War changed.

Sten had been in the north when word of the attacks came. He boarded the first southbound carriage. Along the way, a thunder of six dragons passed overhead. One separated from the group and attacked the carriage. The monster forced everyone out of the carriage, released the team pulling it, removed and set aside the luggage, and then, with aggressive glee, destroyed the carriage before taking flight again to rejoin the other dragons. Dragons were large, powerful, and deadly, except, for a reason no one understood, when the dragons went on their offensive, they didn't harm any people or animals or even the cargo carried by wagons and boats. The dragons only destroyed conveyances and damaged buildings, bridges, and roads.

Sten said, "Dragons are monsters."

Asa sighed and shook her head. "I'm a trained dragon-slayer knight like my father, and his mother, and her mother and father before that. I'm not supposed to be afraid of dragons. But, the monster stood there, on his hind legs, towering over us. Then he spread his wings. That was terrifying. Do you know how large dragon wings are? He was trying to intimidate us."

Asa, and Ned and Ted, had become dragon-slayer knights shortly before the dragons went on their offensive. They had undergone extensive training, and Asa's performance had earned her the rank of Knight Sergeant leading a squad; however, the day the dragons attacked, her squad, which included Ned and Ted, hadn't yet been called to a campaign and they had not yet confronted a real-life dragon. She had been informed of the date for her first campaign only a few days before the dragons attacked. She had looked forward to fighting alongside experienced knights and having their support and guidance when she confronted her first dragon. Instead, she had to plunge into chaos.

The day the dragons attacked, all knights activated. Asa's squad, alongside other squads experienced and new, pursued the dragons trying to engage them. However, when the dragon-slayer knights approached, the dragons flew away to attack elsewhere leaving the knights behind and leaving Asa, and Ned and Ted, with no chance to confront a dragon. Then the Paladins' Peace was forged. While Asa, and Ned and Ted, had continued attending training to keep their skills sharp in case dragon-slayer knights were needed again, today had been the first time the three knights had actually faced a dragon.

"There's nothing wrong with feeling afraid," Sten said. "What matters is what you do in the face of that fear. People say you, and Knight Ned and Knight Ted, were brave when you confronted the dragon. They say you're heroes."

Asa shrugged. "People see what they want to see."

"Did you attack the dragon like they say?"

Asa's eyes went wide. "Of course not. That would break the Paladins' Peace. We're sworn to uphold the Paladins' Peace. We just asked him to leave."

"Apparently quite aggressively."

She shrugged again. "People see what they want to see."

"They say you drove him away. The Paladins' Peace says people and dragons can go anywhere, freely, and without interference."

"Technically it says that, but we didn't break the Paladins' Peace." She paused then added, "But, I will send a report to Colonel Aslan incase a complaint is sent to the Arbitration Committee. Regardless, that dragon won't be coming back any time soon."

Chapter 3

<Kedekitley>

Friendships Could Arise

<Kedekitley> sat with his life-mate, their tails entwined, as <Arizesyley> reviewed her map and updated it with a couple of marks. He loved these moments when he could sit with her, lay his head against her, and indulge in the contentment her company brought him.

In the dragon language, <Arizesyley> said, "<Not much has changed.>"

<Kedekitley> cocked his head. "<I told you the humans are not preparing to attack.>"

"<And, I told you the humans are monsters and will attack, and I will detect the humans' preparations. That will convince the Council to eradicate the humans. I will fly another patrol.>"

He occasionally went with her on her patrols, but whether or not he went with her, every day, she soared over the borderlands seeking evidence of the humans preparing to attack. Every day she returned having found nothing. Nevertheless, she persisted. Seven years ago, humans murdered her parents. Ever since, she had been paranoid about the humans attacking again, and compulsive about finding evidence to justify the humans' eradication.

<Kedekitley> had grown up on the eastern side of the mountain range where the humans were not a problem. He knew the stories, but he had never worried about the humans. Then he met <Arizesyley> and became her life-mate. In the years since, her paranoia had infected him. However, he was a problem solver, and his solution to the problem was not to eradicate the humans, which went against dragon instincts and against the Council's edicts, but to make friends with the humans so they

234

would never again want to murder dragons. That solution would sustain the Paladins' Peace.

Precedent existed for pursuing this solution. To the consternation of the Council who declared dragons were not to interact with the humans, seven dragons that <Kedekitley> knew about already had.

<Improecley>, after a great battle with the Human Paladin, had forged the Paladins' Peace with the humans. Acting as the dragons' representative on the Arbitration Committee, she continued meeting with the Human Paladin. <Kedekitley> believed <Improecley> had actually become friends with the human and the Arbitration Committee meetings were simply an excuse to visit the human.

Two dragonets, <Emidonley> and <Mettagovley>, had somehow made friends with human children, and each had dragged their parents into interacting with the humans.

Even though those seven dragons' interactions with the humans were the result of unique circumstances, <Kedekitley> believed similar friendships could arise under normal circumstances. He was determined to prove that, and in so doing change the Council's mind about interacting with the humans.

He watched <Arizesyley> fly away and immediately missed her. He would have liked to have patrolled with her, but he needed this opportunity to continue pursuing his solution. Her patrol route would not take her near the human town anytime soon. Now was the best time to return to the human town and try again to offer the humans his help in hopes of making friends with the humans. When <Arizesyley> was out of dragon senses range, <Kedekitley> took flight.

Chapter 4

Sten

The Dragon Visits Again

The village bell tolled the rapid, panicked dragon attack pattern. Asa rushed past Sten's office.

Sten said, "Oh, bother," and followed.

At her armory, Asa snapped on her armor, strapped on her short sword, crossbow, and quiver, picked up her shield and long sword, said, "Please, stay here," and then ran out of the house.

Ned and Ted, with Ned still snapping on the last pieces of his armor, were coming from their print shop. They fell in behind Asa as frantic people motioned them toward the plaza.

"As if I'd stay here," Sten said to no one in particular as he grabbed his hat and followed.

When Sten reached the last building before the plaza, he peeked around the corner. Asa, with Ned and Ted behind and to her left and right, faced the dragon.

The first thing Sten noticed about the dragon were jaws big enough to snatch up a person leaving only their legs dangling out. The dragon was six times longer than Sten was tall, with nearly half of that being tail and another pace's worth being the neck. Standing on his hind legs, the dragon towered over the knights by three times their height. A pair of tan colored horns angled back on the top of his head. Green and blue marks highlighted his predominantly brown color. However, the most remarkable highlights were red streaks that resembled flames swept back by the wind spreading across his neck, chest, shoulders, and wide spread wings, wings that stretched wider than the dragon was long. He had no yellow, though. The dragon who had destroyed the carriage had had yellow marks, which had indicated she was female. This dragon was male, magnificent, and intimidating.

The dragon said, "I will not violate the Paladins' Peace."

He spoke well, but with an archaic accent that made some words sound odd.

Asa said, "Why have you returned, dragon?"

"I want to help the humans."

"We don't need help from a dragon."

The dragon held out his hands. "I have many skills that can help the humans."

"Like what?"

The dragon's eyes widened, his ears pricked, and he drew in his wings by half. "I can design, construct, and repair machines and structures. What do you need designed, constructed, or repaired?"

"I told you we don't need help from a dragon. Please, leave, and this time don't return."

The three knights moved forward with shields and swords at the ready. The dragon's ears drooped. He stepped back, re-extended his primary wings, fanned out his tail wings, and launched himself into the sky heading east toward the mountains.

Sten joined Asa as she removed her helmet.

She said, "I know what you're thinking. No, we didn't break the Paladins' Peace."

"I was thinking that dragon was odd. He was nothing like the dragon that destroyed the carriage."

"A dragon's a dragon. Dragons are monsters. Don't be deceived. I need to go send an update to Colonel Aslan."

The three knights headed home, but Sten remained in the plaza staring in the direction the dragon had flown pondering the dragon's bewildering behavior.

Chapter 5

<Kedekitley>

Another Attempt To Offer Help

Morning found <Kedekitley> hiding in a grove of trees on a hill overlooking the human town. He watched the humans bustling about performing mysterious activities. His courage needed bolstering for another attempt at making friends with the humans. The previous day had gone better than the first day — the armored human had at least let him say he had many skills — but this time he was determined to say more.

The Paladins' Peace had ended the human attacks, but <Arizesyley> had taught him to fear the humans would return to the humans' murderous ways. Before choosing to pursue his solution to the humans-murdering-dragons problem, <Kedekitley> had spoken with <Xenkerdecley>, his beloved mentor, teacher, and advisor. He was an elder-dragon, and because he had been a dragonet when the humans were first encountered, he was knowledgeable about those days.

At the time, the humans were barely surviving. <Xenkerdecley> and other dragons had learned the human language, had provided the humans material resources to help them survive, and had helped the humans construct shelters. He told <Kedekitley> everything he'd learned about the humans, and reminisced fondly about how he had enjoyed observing the humans growing and cutting grass for human food.

Then, the humans met the Gird creatures, acquired Gird-metal armor and murder weapons, and began attacking dragons. No one knew why.

<Kedekitley> believed the humans' discomfort was because dragons were the superior species and the ultimate predators in the universe. The humans must have had an innate fear of being food animals. However, the humans were sophonts and the dragons on this world did not consider sophonts to be food animals even though dragon instincts said they were.

With the exception of <Improecley> damaging the Human Paladin, no dragon on this world had ever damaged, much less consumed, a human.

When interactions with the humans ended, knowledge about the humans, including their language, was passed to new generations in anticipation of dragons needing to interact with the humans in the future. <Kedekitley> believed that time had come. The Paladins' Peace had stopped the humans from attacking and murdering dragons, but he believed the peace would not hold if action was not taken.

His determination renewed and his courage set, <Kedekitley> took flight.

∞∞∞∞

The bell tolled earlier than it had on the previous two visits and the armored humans entered the human town's central open space as <Kedekitley> landed.

In a show of confidence, he closed his wings almost all the way before saying, "I will not violate the Paladins' Peace."

The lead armored human said, "I told you not to return, dragon."

"I want to —"

"I know, I know. You want to *help people*."

<Kedekitley> thought the armored human's exaggerated inflection was meant to mock him, but he ignored it and said, "I am skilled and experienced. I designed the Pavilion at the Conclave Grounds and helped construct the structure. The structure is impressive and functional. I can perform the same kinds of services for the humans."

"Why do you think we need help from a dragon?"

The armored human slid the murder weapon sword into its scabbard. The other two armored humans still held murder weapons, but the lead armored human's actions made <Kedekitley> less afraid.

With added enthusiasm, he said, "Many of the humans' structures need repairing and new structures need to be designed and constructed. I am the dragon to help the humans do what needs to be done."

"We have our own designers and builders, so we don't need help from a dragon. And, landing in the middle of the plaza is disrupting people's lives and businesses. Please, leave and don't return."

After staring at the armored human, <Kedekitley> said, "Consider my offer. I will return tomorrow." He threw open his wings, leaped into the air, and flew away.

Chapter 6

Sten

What To Do About the Dragon Problem

Sten approached Asa and said, "Did I hear him say he'll be back tomorrow?"

Asa removed her helmet and nodded. "That's what he said."

"Sergeant Asa." Marita approached. "We need to discuss that dragon at this evening's community meeting. Please, be there. We need your advice."

"I'll be there, Mayor Marita."

Marita went toward the village administration building as Ned and Ted and everyone else returned to what they had been doing before the morning's dragon excitement.

Sten held Asa's gauntleted hand as they walked toward home. "What can you do about the dragon?"

"Knight Ned and Knight Ted and I can't do anything more than what we've already done. We've been bending the Paladins' Peace as it is, but we can't bend it any further without breaking it, and we're sworn to uphold the Paladins' Peace."

Once home, Asa returned to working in her studio. Sten went to his office. Spread on his desk, an unfinished design for a bridge called to him, but he couldn't concentrate.

Sten was a problem solver. He believed that for any problem, he only needed to analyze and summarize the situation to define the problem, and then design a solution. All he needed was information, thought, and logic to solve problems. That's how he handled every problem he confronted.

He could find no solution to the dragon problem.

When Anitra arrived home from school, Sten and Asa discussed with her what had happened with the dragon as they had each evening. Anitra was ten, smart, sweet, and bossy. She hated rumors and always demanded accurate information.

Generations of Dragon War had left the adults fearful and suspicious of dragons; however, the new generation hadn't learned those fears and suspicions. The village children, and especially Anitra, were excited a dragon kept visiting even though each time the dragon came the children had been in school and were not allowed out no matter how much they pleaded to go see the dragon.

∞∞∞∞

The village bell on the administration building rang the gentle, community meeting pattern as a capacity crowd filled the meeting hall. Sten sat in the front, Anitra on his right with Sten's father, Sochi, next to her. To his left sat Asa with Ned and Ted next to her. A cacophony of conversations clogged the air making it impossible to understand what anyone was saying. When Marita and the Village Council, which included Sten's mother, Sasha, came onto the stage, a polite quiet settled on the gathering.

Marita banged her gavel and said, "I call this community meeting for the Village of Splain to order. We're postponing the normal agenda until next meeting. This evening, we'll discuss our dragon problem."

Someone in the back yelled, "Kill the monster."

"Oh, bother." Sten recognized Viren's voice. He was a troublemaker who felt entitled to the benefits of living in the community, yet even though he was capable of contributing to helping the community succeed, he did the least he could get away with doing. Sten had tried employing him on several work-teams. Viren never earned what he was paid and his attitude always caused conflict with the other work-team members. A crew of three sycophants followed Viren around.

Asa, and Ned and Ted, leaped to their feet as Asa said, "We will not kill the monster. We will not break the Paladins' Peace."

"Sergeant Asa." Marita motioned toward her. "You have the floor."

Ned and Ted sat as Asa hesitated while looking around the room. Sten knew how she felt. He too was uncomfortable with being the center of attention in meetings such as this.

Asa said, "Thank you, Mayor Marita. If Knight Ned and Knight Ted and I push the dragon any more than we already have, we'll break the Paladins' Peace. We will not do that, nor will we allow anyone else to break the Paladins' Peace. There has to be another way to deal with the dragon."

"Do you have any suggestions?" said Marita.

Asa glanced at Ned and Ted before saying, "We're trained to fight dragons, not negotiate with them. We don't have any ideas. But, dragons are stubborn, persistent, and patient. He'll keep coming back until he gets what he wants."

Marita said, "He wants to help us?"

"That's what he said."

"By designing, constructing, and repairing things?"

"That's what he said."

Another person in the back said, "Managing the designing, constructing, and repairing of things is the Master Builder's responsibility. Have him deal with the dragon."

Asa said, "No. Master Sten has no training in handling dragons, and he has no armor. He'd be in danger."

That was the end of hearing what Asa had to say, even as she tried to continue. The din of discussion drowned out the ability to understand what anyone was saying. Sten looked around and considered how to reduce the room's echoing to keep the place from being so loud, but that was a problem to solve another day.

As for the dragon, he had an idea. He could give the dragon chores to do that might satisfy the dragon's desire to help. If he gave the dragon the right chores, he could keep the dragon away from the plaza, and the village. His handling of the dragon was logical, but frightening. He had heard stories of two children in a village to the south who played with a couple of young dragons. If that was true, maybe it was doable.

He faced Asa.

Her eyes widened, she shook her head, and she spoke, but Sten only saw her lips mouthing the word *No*.

Sten leaned close to her ear and said, "I can think of no other solution to the problem."

It was time for Sten to become the center of attention. Asa didn't reach quickly enough to grab him before he stepped onto the stage. The crowd did not notice him. When Marita banged her gavel several times, people quieted, and noticed Sten.

When everyone was paying attention, Sten said, "I'll do it."

The clamor began again.

Anitra wore a big smile.

Asa's brow creased and she made the worst frown Sten had ever seen her make.

Chapter 7

<Kedekitley>

Fourth Attempt Sees Results

The bell didn't toll and the three armored humans already stood in the human town's central open space. In front of the armored humans was a human without armor. <Kedekitley> circled, maintaining a safe altitude, his thoughts filled with the stories <Arizesyley> had told him about the humans attacking dragons.

Was it a trap?

<Kedekitley> detected the humans in and behind the structures as always, but there were more of the humans than on previous visits. He didn't like that the humans' behavior had changed.

Was there danger?

The armored humans were not holding murder weapon swords, which must have been concealed in the Gird-metal scabbards. The human without armor also wore a Gird-metal scabbard that surely concealed a murder weapon sword. <Kedekitley> saw no places where humans with murder weapon crossbows could hide and yet still shoot at him.

He continued circling. The humans turned as they watched him.

If he landed in the exact center of the open space, he would be farthest from any potential range weapon and would detect any spear or arrow that might come at him. Spears and arrows would only make minor gouges in his ablative hide and weren't of concern. However, the Gird-metal bolts shot from murder weapon crossbows did worry him. The Gird-metal bolts were almost impossible to detect except visually.

Using only Gird-metal murder weapon swords humans had never succeeded in murdering a dragon. Usually, an attack only resulted in a damaged dragon. Murder weapon crossbows and their Gird-metal bolts enabled the humans to murder dragons. Seven years ago, when the humans intensified their attacks on dragons by using the murder weapon crossbows to murder dragons for the first time was when the Council ordered the destruction of the humans' roads, bridges, structures, wagons, and boats.

<Kedekitley> wanted to try again to offer his help to the humans. Other than fleeing, the only solution he could design to the problem of keeping himself safe was to stay vigilant and ready to flee at the slightest provocation. The reward would be worth the risk. If he was brave, he could do this.

He spiraled down, landed, crouched on all fours for maximum power to leap into the air, kept his wings ready for a down stroke, paid attention to his dragon senses, kept his head and eyes moving as he watched for Gird-metal bolts, and said, "I will not violate the Paladins' Peace."

Everything was still and quiet as none of the humans moved or said anything for a long moment before the human without armor stepped closer.

The human stood within pouncing distance. <Kedekitley> had seen the humans from a distance many times, and dragon vision at a distance was excellent, but he had never before been so close to a human, except for the three armored humans. He couldn't perceive the physical details about the armored humans because, while he could see the Gird-metal armor, the Gird-metal left a disturbing fuzzy void in the mental map made by his other dragon senses.

The human without armor was open to him. The human was male. The humans came in a broad range of colors. This one was on the bright end of that spectrum his skin being sand colored. Sand colored hair stuck out from under the hat the human wore. His eyes were sky colored. The clothes the human wore, which <Xenkerdecley> had said kept the humans warm, were the color of forest soil. The human looked harmless, but looks were not going to deceive <Kedekitley> especially since the human was rubbing his fingers over the hilt of the murder weapon sword he wore at his waist.

The human almost spoke, but made choking noises instead. After swallowing, taking a deep breath, and standing straighter, the human tried again. "We will not break the Paladins' Peace."

That was the first time the humans had made that statement. <Arizesyley> had insisted the humans could not be trusted, but <Kedekitley> wanted to believe the cute little creature.

"I want to help the humans."

"I'm here to arrange for that."

"You will let me help the humans?" <Kedekitley's> hopes soared, but he calmed that excitement by reminding himself to remain vigilant. The offer could be a deception. "What task do you wish for me to perform to help the humans?"

"First, I need you to stop landing in the plaza. It scares people and disrupts normal activities."

<Kedekitley> felt his ears droop. The human did not intend to give him a task. The human only wanted to make him stop coming to the human town.

When the human pointed toward him, <Kedekitley> flinched. The human jerked his hand back, clutched it to his chest, and wrapped his other hand around it as if something had damaged it.

After a moment with neither of them moving, the human pointed again and continued speaking. "On the eastside of the village, there's a large yard where visiting wagons and caravans park. The far side is empty. Meet me there tomorrow morning and we'll talk about a job for you to do."

Excitement surged through <Kedekitley> and he felt his ears prick. "You will let me help the humans?"

"That's the plan."

Using it as an excuse to get away from the threat he felt, <Kedekitley> said, "Thank you, Human. Tomorrow, I will be at the location you specified."

He pushed off with his legs, made a powerful down stroke with his wings to launch himself skyward, and raced away with a sigh of relief.

Chapter 8

Sten

What Have I Gotten Myself Into

The wind gust from the dragon's departure blew Sten's hat off and almost knocked him over. He sat in the grass and watched the dragon disappear over the trees. The three knights rushed to his side.

Asa retrieved Sten's hat, handed it to him, removed her helmet, and said, "Are you okay? You look rattled."

Sten put on his hat. "I was so afraid. He was ready to pounce on me. His eyes were the color of fire. And, he has teeth. Did you see his teeth?"

"I've seen his teeth. I've also seen the dents dragon teeth can put in Gird-metal armor. You should see General Patrick's armor."

"Please, don't say that."

"You didn't get to see his talons. They're the same white color as his teeth and they slide out of the tips of his fingers and toes. They can cut anything except Gird-metal, but even that they score deeply. You should see General Patrick's armor. His battle with the Dragon Paladin before they made the Paladins' Peace did a lot of damage."

"Please, don't say that either."

"Dragons also have a prehensile tail that can wrap around things and crush them. You should see —"

"Please, stop telling me those things. I still have to meet with that dragon tomorrow."

Motioning toward Ned and Ted, Asa said, "We'll go with you."

Sten returned to staring in the direction the dragon had gone. Asa dismissed Ned and Ted then sat next to Sten putting her arm around him.

Sten said, "He was as afraid as I was. More afraid than when he talked to you. Why was he so afraid? I couldn't have harmed him, even with this short sword you loaned me."

"He was afraid we had figured out his deception."

"He's not trying to deceive us. I don't understand his motives, but he's sincere. He's odd. Not what I expected of a dragon."

"I don't trust the monster."

Sten paused still staring at the sky before saying, "Knight Ned and Knight Ted and you shouldn't go with me tomorrow."

"What? We have to, *I have to, to protect our families, our communities, and all people,* and to protect *you.*"

He turned to her. "I should meet with him alone. No dragon-slayer knights. No crowd of people peering out of windows and around corners of buildings. It needs to be just him and me."

Asa's brow creased and she made her newly found worst frown.

Chapter 9

<Kedekitley>

He Had To Do This

That encounter had left <Kedekitley> feeling vulnerable and afraid. To give himself a chance to calm and catch his breath, he hid in the grove of trees overlooking the human town.

Human was sitting on the ground. Two of the armored humans walked away. The other armored human sat with Human and appeared to be comforting him.

Had Human been afraid? Why would Human have been afraid? He had told Human he wouldn't violate the Paladins' Peace. Regardless, a dragon would never damage a human. Human had no reason to be afraid. The humans were a greater threat to him than he was to the humans.

He shouldn't be doing this. The human monsters will murder him. What would that do to <Arizesyley>, having lost her parents and then her life-mate to the murderous humans. She might go into a rage, defy the Council, and begin eradicating the humans on her own. He couldn't let that happen. The Council was correct. Regardless of those other dragons interacting with the humans, dragons should not interact with the humans. The risk was too great.

When he arrived at the weyr, he lay in the meadow outside, giving himself some sun-time and thinking time, while he waited for <Arizesyley> to return.

When she arrived, he bounded to her, pulled her into his arms, hooked his tail around hers in a tail hug, mantled his wings over her, rubbed his head on hers, and said, "<I love you and missed you. What did you find?>"

<Arizesyley> said, "<I also love you and missed you,>" and nestled tighter against him. "<A few of the armored humans have gathered at the

armored humans' training place. That is not remarkable since groups of the armored humans periodically gather. I believe the human behavior indicates the humans are keeping themselves ready to attack even though the humans appear to be making no other preparations. Everything else was unchanged.>" She tried to move, but <Kedekitley> didn't release his hold. "<I would like to add the information to my documentation, if you will allow me.>"

"<I am sorry.>" He released her.

"<Are you not well?>"

"<I am well.>"

She tilted her head and said, "<All right then.>"

Inside the weyr, she sat at her drafting table and made an entry in her documentation book. <Kedekitley> cuddled up to her and twined his tail with hers as he always did.

He said, "<Tell me again about the strategies humans use to attack dragons.>"

"<Why do you want to hear that information again?>"

"<I have no reason except to be reminded how to keep safe.>"

"<Do you still insist you are well?>"

<Kedekitley> nodded and said, "<Yes, because I am well.>"

After a sigh, <Arizesyley> said, "<The human monsters are not sophisticated. Using the Gird-metal armor to the humans' advantage, the humans stay out of sight as the humans approach a dragon, or the humans hide while waiting for a dragon to come close, and then the humans attack. The humans' strategy is that simple.>"

"<How close do the humans need to be to attack?>"

"<Using Gird-metal murder weapon swords, the humans must be closer than a dragon-span before the humans reveal themselves with an attack. Even then, the dragon might react quickly enough to escape damage.>"

"<What about murder weapon crossbows?>"

She took a deep breath. "<The humans must be closer than three dragon-spans to be effective with a murder weapon crossbow. The closer the humans are, the more effective the murder weapon crossbow. The Gird-metal bolts do not travel well because the Gird-metal bolts are not

aerodynamically stable, thus, with distance, a Gird-metal bolt will begin to tumble. Also, the sound of the murder weapon crossbow releasing travels faster than the Gird-metal bolt, which means, if the distance is sufficient, the dragon can hear the sound and react to avoid the Gird-metal bolt.>" Her voice softened. "<Nevertheless, if the humans are close enough, murder weapon crossbows are effective at murdering dragons.>"

"<You never mentioned the sound of the murder weapon crossbow releasing before. What sound does the crossbow make?>"

He regretted asking the question as despair flooded <Arizesyley's> face and her ears drooped. The information about the strategies the humans used to attack dragons she had learned from discussions with other dragons. The information about murder weapon crossbows, Gird-metal bolts, and their sound she had learned firsthand when the humans murdered her parents as her parents protected her so she could escape.

She dipped her head, took a breath, and used her dragon skill at replicating any sound to make the sound: *Thwack.* Lifting her head and grabbing <Kedekitley's> hands, she stared into his eyes and said, "<If you ever hear that sound, leap and fly away.>"

"<I will.>"

She untwined her tail from his, pulled him into her arms, hooked her tail around him, rubbed her head on his, and said, "<You are the best dragon.>"

"<Are you not well?>"

"<I am well.>"

That night, as <Kedekitley> lay side by side with <Arizesyley> in their cozy nest, she cried as she often did in the night. He comforted her by covering her with his wing.

For her sake, he had to make friends with the humans and teach the humans to trust dragons so the humans would never return to their dragon murdering ways. If <Arizesyley> could see that the humans were no longer a threat, maybe she would stop having nightmares of her parents dying.

Chapter 10

Sten

We Can Start Tomorrow

Dragon dreams filled Sten's sleep. In some dreams, the dragon who had destroyed the carriage used her talons to slice through fabric, wood, and iron. In other dreams, the new dragon, with wings spread, eyes red, and teeth bared, pounced on him. Dragons were filthy, smelly, disgusting, and dangerous monsters. All his life he had been told that. All his dreams also told him that.

As he dressed in preparation for facing the dragon, he wondered if male and female dragons behaved differently, had different dispositions. Maybe that difference was why the new dragon was odd when compared to the carriage-destroying dragon. However, when he asked, Asa said, "All dragons are the same. They're all monsters."

A knock came at the door. "Master Sten. Sergeant Asa. The dragon's here."

Sten opened the door and said, "Where?"

"He's in the wagon yard."

"He's early. What's he doing?"

"He's sitting, looking around, and slowly waving his tail."

"I'd better get out there."

Sten strapped on the short sword Asa had insisted he carry and turned to find her standing behind him fully armored, holding her shield, crossbow and quiver on her back, and her long sword in its scabbard.

Asa said, "As if I'd stay here."

"I admit I'll feel safer if you're with me, but don't spook him. If this is going to work, I'll need him to trust me." He picked up his pack, put on his hat, and took off at a brisk walk with Asa at his side.

When Sten stepped past the last wagon on the western margin of the yard, he felt a moment of spookiness — the dragon was staring at him as if the dragon had known where he would emerge.

The dragon wasn't at the easternmost edge of the yard as Sten had intended. Instead, he sat in the middle of the empty space. Sten walked across the space to stand before, but not too close to, the dragon. Asa followed, but kept her distance.

"Hello, Human. I will not violate the Paladins' Peace. What task do you wish for me to perform to help the humans?"

"What I have in mind is helping repair a section of the Lurean Road that dragons damaged at the end of the Dragon War."

"Dragons do not have much use for roads — dragons are creatures of the sky — however, I am sure I can design and construct a road."

"Not design and construct. Repair an existing road."

"I am also sure I can repair an existing road. Tell me the location of the road and I will begin."

"We can start tomorrow."

The dragon creased his brow. Sten hadn't realized dragons had facial expressions. The expression was subtle, but it was real.

The dragon said, "Why do we not begin now?"

"I have to make arrangements."

"I wish to begin now. Why did you not plan in advance?"

"I did plan, but I needed to know if you'd be satisfied doing the job before I set the plan in motion. I've never managed a dragon before and don't know what to expect. Besides, I was told dragons are patient."

"Dragons can be patient, but that does not mean we enjoy having to be patient."

Sten pulled a folded paper from his pack. "Can you read a map?"

"Of course I can read a map. I am a dragon. In fact, <Arizesyley> creates and collects maps."

The dragon word in the middle of the dragon's sentence caused Sten to pause before he spread the map on the graveled ground. He looked at the looming dragon, suppressed his desire to check the sword at his waist, and said, "Come closer and I'll show you where the road is."

The dragon looked at Asa.

Sten said, "Don't worry. She won't harm you. She's here because she's concerned for my safety. I do feel better with her watching over me."

The dragon's ears twitched. "I will not violate the Paladins' Peace."

"I believe you. And, we won't either."

The dragon nodded his head to Sten's left. "Another armored human is trying to hide behind a tree north of this open space." He nodded his head to Sten's right. "And, another armored human is trying to hide behind a tree south of this open space. The armored humans keep peeking out thus revealing themselves."

"Oh, bother. I'm not surprised Knight Ned and Knight Ted are also here. But, they won't break the Paladins' Peace."

The dragon looked around and fidgeted. "Many of the humans are watching from behind the trees and wagons."

"I told people to stay away, but they're curious. It's okay, though. No one's going to harm you."

"You are wearing a Gird-metal murder weapon sword."

Sten almost put his hand on the hilt, but again stopped himself. "Asa insisted I carry it, and I agreed to, but I won't harm you."

The dragon stared at him for a long moment, took one more look around, and dropped to all fours and moved closer.

Suppressing a shudder as jaws nearly as large as he was came close, Sten pointed at the map and said, "The damaged section of road is here, a little ways north of the village."

"I know the place. I have seen the road from the air, and <Arizesyley> has it marked on her map."

Twice now, the dragon had spoken a melodic yet growly dragon word. From context, Sten decided the sound was the name of another dragon.

"Will you meet me there tomorrow morning?"

The dragon sat up, looked around again, spread his wings wide, and said, "Tomorrow, I will be at the location you specified."

With a powerful push of legs and a mighty stroke of wings, the dragon took flight. With the gust of wind, Sten's hat and the map also took flight.

Asa caught the map, picked up the hat, came to Sten, and said, "I'm going with you tomorrow."

"Do come with me, please."

Chapter 11

\<Kedekitley\>

Designs for Paving

That meeting had gone well. \<Kedekitley\> had had a buffer of space around him wider than three dragons stretched out nose to tail. The one armored human and Human had stood in the space, but both murder weapon swords were in their scabbards and the armored human never removed the crossbow murder weapon from their back. The armored human had been the greater threat, but the armored human had remained more than a dragon-span away even as he came close to Human. Moreover, even though he was disappointed he had not been given a task to do immediately, Human did agree to give him a task to do tomorrow. All he had to do now was solve the problem of how to repair a human road.

When \<Arizesyley\> entered the weyr, he trotted to her, gave her his normal greeting hug, and said, "\<I love you and missed you. What did you find?\>"

She hugged him and said, "\<I also love you and missed you. I found nothing. What are you working on?\>"

"\<Join me and I will show you.\>"

She snuggled up to him at his drafting table, laid a wing across him, and twined her tail with his.

He gave her a rub with his head then said, "\<These are designs for paving high-traffic areas.\>"

"\<Why are you looking at those designs?\>"

"\<I was considering the techniques used to pave high-traffic areas because the ground becomes churned into mud if we do not pave high-traffic areas. This design shows gravel paving like we have on the trail to our hot spring pool. This design shows stone paving like the flight

deck outside our weyr and the flight deck and gathering areas at the Conclave Grounds.>"

She nudged him with her snout. "<That is not the answer to my question.>"

"<I am wondering if the humans are sophisticated enough to construct the humans' roads using techniques similar to how dragons construct high-traffic areas. Or, are the humans not sophisticated enough to understand such concepts.>"

<Arizesyley> tilted her head. "<All right then. Why do you wonder about the humans' roads?>"

"<I am curious.>"

"<There is no reason to be curious about the humans. The humans are not sophisticated. We only need to watch for the humans preparing to attack so we can justify my eradicate-the-humans solution.>"

"<You are correct about the humans being not sophisticated; otherwise, the humans would have solved the problem of the murder weapon crossbows' Gird-metal bolts being not aerodynamically stable. I am sure I could solve the aerodynamic stability problem.>"

<Arizesyley> smacked <Kedekitley> with her horns. "<Do not improve the human monsters' murder weapons. Sometimes, Kedekitley, you with your busy thoughts think too much about solving problems.>"

Chapter 12

Sten

Coping One Day at a Time

"I want to go see the dragon."

"Anitra," Sten patted her hand, "You can't. You have to go to school. And, it would be too dangerous for you to go see the dragon."

"The dragon hasn't harmed you."

"I always have your mother with me to protect me."

"Mom will be there tomorrow."

"She has to concentrate on protecting me. If you were there, she'd have to split her attention between you and me. That would make it harder for her to protect either of us."

"When can I see the dragon?"

He paused before saying, "I don't know. I have no idea where the problem with the dragon will lead. I'm coping one day at a time."

∞∞∞∞

That evening, Asa, Anitra, and Sten worked on their sewing craft projects together. Asa had been teaching Anitra and Sten how to make stuffed animals. Sten was proud of his.

Anitra set her horse on the table. "Done."

Asa said, "That's impressive. It looks familiar."

Anitra preened, "It's Maximus."

"It is Maximus. That's well made. I'm proud of you. It's better than your father's pig."

Sten displayed his stuffed animal. "It's not a pig. It's a miser cat, of sorts."

Anitra said, "I want to make a dragon."

Asa's icy expression chilled the room. When she finally took a breath, she said, "You are not to make a dragon."

"But, Mom."

"Definitely not." Asa tapped the table with a finger. "Dragons are not allowed in this house. Besides, you've never seen a dragon. You wouldn't know how to shape it."

"I've seen pictures of them."

"Those pictures don't show what dragons really look like. Why don't you make your father's horse?"

"Abaccus isn't a warhorse."

Sten said, "Abaccus is a good horse. He's friendly, smart, loyal, and reliable. Did I say smart? He's remarkable. I'm glad I met him when I was traveling during my training."

Anitra shook her head.

"Make Sayneigh," said Asa.

"Sayneigh's just a packhorse."

"A knight's packhorse is as important as a knight's warhorse. They just have different jobs. If you don't want to make Abaccus or Sayneigh, make Sunshine. You like riding Sunshine."

Anitra gathered fabric scraps from the table. "I'll make Maximus's armor. He's not finished until he has his armor."

∞∞∞∞∞

After tucking Anitra into bed, Asa and Sten discussed tomorrow's plan.

"Site preparation was finished today, so everything's ready," said Sten as he prepared for bed. "We'll billet the horses out of sight of the dragon."

Asa said, "Dragons aren't known to eat horses."

"It's not that. I'm concerned about how the horses will react to the dragon."

"Maximus is a warhorse. He's trained to help me fight and he's not afraid of dragons. And, Sayneigh's trained to keep out of the way but to stay handy with my equipment."

"Abaccus isn't a knight's warhorse or packhorse. I'm concerned he'll be skittish. Although, maybe not. He is quite remarkable and often surprises me."

Chapter 13

<Kedekitley>

Road Repair

In the morning, after <Arizesyley> had left to fly her patrol, <Kedekitley> flew to the location Human had specified. Human was waiting, along with an armored human. Hidden deep among nearby trees were three horses, one of which was clad in Gird-metal armor that did not seal thus allowing <Kedekitley's> dragon senses to detect the animal.

After circling a few times, looking for threats, he landed and said, "I will not violate the Paladins' Peace."

The armored human was armed as usual. Human wore the murder weapon sword he had worn the previous day and the day before that. Both murder weapons were in their scabbards. Around <Kedekitley> was the required three dragon-spans of empty space except for the two humans both of whom stood less than a dragon-span away.

Human said, "I'm glad you came."

<Kedekitley> stared at the armored human.

"She's still worried about my safety, but she's sworn to uphold the Paladins' Peace." Human waved a hand toward the armored human. "She won't harm you."

The armored human made an aggrieved sighing sound and moved to be more than a dragon-span away.

Human continued, "I convinced everyone else to stay away. I even had traffic on the road detoured while we're here."

<Kedekitley> said, "What task do you wish for me to perform to help the humans?"

Human pointed to a stretch of gravel two dragon-spans long that abutted a stone-paved road at each end. On one side was a wagon with a large, enclosed container that <Kedekitley's> senses told him held water. On the other side was a wide gravel path.

Human said, "Dragons damaged about 13 paces of road and dug a huge pit. We filled the pit and laid and compacted the first layer of substrate. We need to do the next layer. The stone workers' work-team can then lay the paving stones and we'll have our nice, straight road back in service."

"Why have the humans not repaired the road before now?"

"Priorities. Dragons did a lot of damage." Human pointed toward the gravel path. "The bypass has worked well enough, but traffic volumes are increasing and it's starting to fall apart. So, finishing the road repair has moved to the top of the priorities list. A work-team poured a gravel mix down the center yesterday. We need to spread it, dampen it, and tamp it."

<Kedekitley> preened and said, "Very simple. Very easy," and began pushing the gravel off the pile in the center to spread it to the sides shaping it so it maintained a high point in the middle that matched the existing paved road's drainage profile.

Human said, "You seem to know how to do this."

"Of course I know how to do this. I am a dragon."

"So, dragons know everything?"

"Dragons do know everything."

Human made a face distorting expression and an odd sound before saying, "If you say so."

<Kedekitley> pondered the expression and sound then decided they were the human versions of a smile and laugh. He narrowed his eyes and said, "Do you think I am humorous?"

Human's expression vanished as he said, "No, I think you and this situation are very serious."

He stared at Human as Human stood motionless. He had not known the humans had expressions that revealed their emotions. He would need to watch for those expressions and learn to interpret them.

<Kedekitley> turned his attention back to working his way down the line of gravel, spreading and shaping. Human used a tool to do the same from the other direction. Tools <Kedekitley> had in his tools collection would increase the efficiency of the task, but he could

complete the task by hand quicker than the time required to retrieve his tools. So, he continued working.

When they met, <Kedekitley> had completed a dragon-span and a half while Human had completed half a dragon-span.

Stepping back, Human said, "Well done. I'll dampen it and then we'll tamp it."

After using a hose connected to the container on the wagon to spray water on the gravel, Human handed <Kedekitley> one of two tools with a handle and a flat bottom and said, "Please, tamp the gravel to compact it."

Human begin pounding on the gravel at his end of the road. <Kedekitley> did the same from his end. He did his best, but thought the tool was rather small — it was scaled for the humans.

After a while, he looked to the sky and said, "I must leave for a short amount of time. I will return soon."

Human said, "It's a good time for a break. I'll eat my midday meal while I wait for you to return."

<Kedekitley> flew into the hills east of where Human and he had been working. He landed amongst a tumble of boulders and a grove of trees on a ridge, hid, and watched the cerulean sky over the verdant valley. He was sure he was out of dragon senses range, but <Arizesyley> might see him if he didn't hide well.

<Arizesyley> appeared, heading north on her normal patrol route.

<Xenkerdecley> had said the humans have limited visual acuity and poor low light sensitivity. While this was not a low light situation, <Arizesyley's> altitude meant the humans probably saw her as a high-flying bird. With his dragon vision, though, he could see her clearly even at this distance. Alluring yellow streaks in a jagged pattern adorned her snout, arms, and legs with larger versions on her wings. She was beautiful. He was tempted not to return to the road repair task but to fly away with her instead. But, he couldn't do that. He had to continue trying to make friends with the humans. A safe and stable future was at stake. Besides, she would be suspicious why he was here. When she was out of sight and dragon senses range, he returned to the road.

Human had finished his human food, which <Kedekitley> assumed had been grass.

Human said, "I'm glad you're back. Let me relieve myself and we'll get back to work."

Human went to a small structure that stood off to the side of the road. As Human approached the structure, <Kedekitley's> senses noticed the nearby small creatures darted away.

When Human returned, <Kedekitley> said, "What is that structure?"

"It's a toilet for bodily waste. People need to have a toilet where we work, and where we live. Some people prefer to call it a *necessary* because it's necessary."

<Kedekitley> pondered that then snorted, which caused him to think about his own emotional expressions, and said, "That is humorous."

Human made his exaggerated smile expression again and said, "I agree." He then drank from a container <Kedekitley> could sense contained water. Human put the top on the container, noticed how <Kedekitley> was staring at him, and said, "This is *water*. People need clean water to drink. I thought dragons knew everything."

"Dragons do know everything."

Human made his laughing sound again and said, "If you say so."

After finishing tamping the gravel, <Kedekitley> stood back as Human and he admired their work.

Human said, "You did well."

"Thank you."

"Do you have a name?"

"I am *<Kedekitley>*."

Human's mouth gaped, which <Kedekitley> decided was an expression of awe, before he said, "That's a nice name, very melodic, and growly, but I can't make most of those noises. May I call you *Dragon?*"

"You may call me *Dragon*. When you say *dragon*, the word sounds nice." He looked at the armored human and scrunched his brow. "When the armored human says *dragon*, the word sounds vulgar."

Human glanced over his shoulder. "Forgive her. It's a part of her job. She doesn't mean it."

The armored human called out, "I do too mean it."

<Kedekitley> huffed, turned to Human, and said, "What task do you wish for me to perform next to help the humans?"

"Tomorrow, I'll be helping with the framing of a house about an hour's ride up the road." He pointed north. "Come to that and we'll see if you can help."

"What is an *hour's ride?*"

"You said dragons know everything."

"Dragons do know everything."

"If you say so. An hour's ride is an expression of distance. It's how far you can go riding a horse for an hour."

"What is an *hour?*"

"It's a unit of time. It's one twenty-fourth of a day."

<Kedekitley> cocked his head. "Why the strange number of divisions for a day?"

Human shrugged his shoulders, which <Kedekitley> decided from context meant uncertainty. "It's the way we've always done it since the First Days as far as I know."

"Horses can move at different velocities, which would make the distance measurement imprecise."

"You're persnickety, aren't you? Let's try this. The house is about a league and a third north of here."

"What is a *league?*"

"It's how far a person can walk in an hour."

<Kedekitley's> shoulders sagged and he wondered if Human knew that meant he was exasperated. "How do the humans accomplish anything if the humans are not sophisticated enough to have precise units of measurement?"

"We have precise measurements for when we need them."

After heaving a heavy huff, which <Kedekitley> again wondered if Human understood, he said, "Tomorrow, I will find the place you specified." He unfurled his wings and prepared to leap into the air.

"Will you be able to find it?"

<Kedekitley> paused and said, "I understand the range of possible values in the distance measurement you described. And, your scent will lead me to you." He launched himself into the sky and headed to his weyr annoyed by how much the humans were not sophisticated.

Chapter 14
Sten
That Went Well

"My scent? I don't smell that much do I?" Sten loosened the chinstrap of his hat, which had kept the dragon's departing wind gust from knocking it off his head.

"Not anymore than you normally do," said Asa as she came to his side and removed her helmet.

"Can he really find me using my scent?"

"Probably. Dragons have extraordinary senses beyond anything we can imagine. I wouldn't be surprised to learn they can track the shadow of a thought through the Gration Marshes. But, they do have a weakness: Gird-metal interferes with those extraordinary senses."

"You mean he can't sense you?"

"He can see and hear me, and probably feel my armor if he touched me, but I have no idea what he might taste if he bit my armor. However, as long as I'm in full armor and my helmet filters are in place, he can't smell me, nor can he detect me with any of the multitude of other senses dragons have that we don't."

Sten stared in the direction Dragon had flown and considered Asa's words. Extraordinary dragon senses explained the spookiness he felt the previous day when Dragon seemed to know where he would appear from behind the wagons — Dragon knew where he was even though Dragon couldn't see him directly.

Asa said, "What do you think of the dragon's work performance?"

As Sten put the tools into the wagon he said, "Dragon performed well. I was impressed and the stone workers' work-team will be able to lay the paving stones ahead of schedule. I wonder what other tasks I can train him to do. He could do the work of an entire work-team, thus freeing a work-team to work on other high priority projects. If we made tools in his size, he would be even more productive."

"Don't have a careless attitude. He's still a dragon, and a monster."

Sten picked up his pack. "I'll keep that in mind, but I admit he makes it easy to forget to worry. I appreciate you being here to remind me. I'm sorry for making you stand around in that heavy armor."

"Gird-metal armor isn't heavy. In fact, it's comfortable. Although, I did appreciate the break when he left at midday so I could visit the necessary and eat something."

As they walked to the horses, Sten said, "Weren't you bored?"

"I wasn't bored. I find it interesting to watch the dragon, learning how he moves, looking for vulnerabilities."

"That sounds sinister."

"This is an opportunity few dragon-slayer knights have had: studying a dragon up close without being in actual combat. Whether or not dragons are intelligent, they are crafty. The more we learn the better prepared we'll be if we have to fight them again."

Sten mounted Abaccus. "Do you believe that'll happen?"

"I don't know what to expect and we still don't know the dragon's motives. That's why we must stay vigilant." Asa fastened her shield to Sayneigh's pack, patted the horse affectionately and spoke loving words to her, and then spoke the same loving words to Maximus and mounted. "I can't imagine any scenario where the dragon's actions are not a deception and distraction that leads to some sort of malevolent act."

Sten considered this as Asa and he rode to Splain.

Chapter 15

<Kedekitley>

Designs for Structures

<Kedekitley> sky danced as he flew to his weyr. Implementing his solution was progressing well. Repairing the road had been enjoyable. Human was a pleasure to work with. And, tomorrow, he would perform another task.

Next, he needed to solve the problem of how to construct human style structures. He landed, rushed into the weyr, activated the illumination in the chamber that held his design documents collection, searched for the ones he needed, and returned to his drafting table to study the designs.

When <Arizesyley> arrived, he rushed to her with a spring in his step, hugged her, and said, "<I love you and missed you. What did you find?>"

"<I also love you and missed you. I found nothing. You are even happier than you normally are. What are you working on?>"

He led her to his drafting table. "<These are designs for structures. I grew up living in a weyr structure because the rock of the mountains in the east is not good for natural or talon made weyr caves like ours. I do not see many weyr structures here in the west, but the humans construct many structures. I am wondering if the humans are sophisticated enough to construct structures using techniques similar to how dragons construct structures. Or, are the humans not sophisticated enough to understand such concepts.>"

<Arizesyley> nudged him with her snout. "<You spend too much effort pondering the humans.>"

"<I do not ponder the humans anymore than you do.>"

"<I'm gathering information to justify my eradicate-the-humans solution.>" She tilted her head before saying, "<I do not know why you spend time pondering the humans.>"

"<I am curious.>"

"<Curiosity has uses, but you are misusing curiosity.>"

Chapter 16

Sten

Ready to Work with Dragon Again

That evening, Anitra again expressed her dissatisfaction about not being given the opportunity to see the dragon the next day, but she was excited about doing a sleepover at Sten's parents' home and bakery. Anitra always enjoyed spending the night with Grandma and Grandpa because she was allowed to bake things. This meant Sten and Asa could leave early enough the next morning to make it to the construction site before Dragon arrived.

In the morning, as Asa and he prepared to leave, Sten said, "I appreciate you going with me and being there to keep me safe, but it's not a long-term solution. You have your own work to do."

"It's okay for now; I don't have any work that can't wait. And, if it keeps going, Knight Ned and Knight Ted are willing to take turns. It would be good for them to watch and learn about the dragon as I've been doing."

The sky promised a new day as Sten headed north riding Abaccus. Accompanying him, Asa, in full Gird-metal dragon-slayer armor, rode Maximus, who also wore Gird-metal armor. Sayneigh followed performing her packhorse duties.

Chapter 17

<Kedekitley>

Confrontation

After <Arizesyley> left to fly her patrol, <Kedekitley> left to meet with Human. Human's not sophisticated, imprecise distance measurement created a slight challenge. <Kedekitley> estimated the distance as being between 500 and 700 dragon-spans. The margin of error was significant, but he was sure if he followed the road, he would detect Human's scent, which was all he needed to find Human.

When he detected Human's scent and confirmed Human's sensory signature, he approached the location and allowed his other senses to fill in his mental map.

Human wore the hat he always wore. From the strap he wore around his waist hung the murder weapon sword. When <Kedekitley> saw the armored human standing next to Human, the armored human's image populated the map but the missing dragon senses data created a disturbing fuzzy void in that image.

Two dragon-spans away from Human, next to a construction site, stood six other hat-wearing humans. A structure five dragon-spans to the west contained the same three horses he had seen the previous day. Six dragon-spans to the north, behind a grove of trees, set a wagon and two horses.

<Kedekitley> circled and studied the tableau below, searching for dangers. He saw no weapons except for what the armored human and Human had. The open space surrounding the site was sufficient to leave no place for other humans to hide.

When he had assured himself he was safe, he landed and said, "I will not violate the Paladins' Peace."

Human approached and said, "Dragon, I'm glad you came."

"Hello, Human. What task do you wish for me to perform to help the humans?"

"We'll be putting up the house's walls. The subfloor is ready and the work-team has already framed the walls. We need you to tilt them up and hold them in place as we anchor and square the sections, brace them, and fasten them together. Your help should speed the process. I already talked to the work-team. While they were reluctant, I got them to say they'd try. Are you ready?"

"I am ready."

<Kedekitley> followed Human toward the construction site. The armored human followed but kept a dragon-span of space between them. As he came closer, the humans standing next to the construction site backed away.

One of the humans said, "We're sorry, Master Sten. We can't do it."

Human said, "Come on, people. You said you'd give it a try."

"Now that we've seen the monster, we can't. No way. We're out of here."

The humans walked toward the hidden wagon. As they made furtive glances toward <Kedekitley>, the humans' pace quickened until they disappeared behind the trees. A moment later, the wagon, with the humans inside, came out from behind the trees and headed north with the horses at a gallop.

"Oh, bother." Human kicked at the ground then threw down his hat. "Bother, bother!"

<Kedekitley> said, "Why did the humans leave?"

"Because they're afraid. Because dragons are filthy, smelly, disgusting, and dangerous monsters. That's why!"

"Dragons are not those things."

Practically yelling, Human said, "Yes, they are. Dragons are monsters that kill and destroy. That's why we've fought them for generations."

<Kedekitley> growled and said, "Dragons are not monsters."

The armored human pulled the crossbow murder weapon from their back, cocked it, loaded a Gird-metal bolt, and approached with the weapon aimed.

As <Kedekitley> backed away, he said, "The humans attack dragons, and damage dragons, and murder dragons, and drive dragons from our weyrs. The humans are monsters. Dragons have never damaged the humans, with one exception: <Improecley> damaged the Human Paladin, but that was the only time a dragon damaged a human."

With a roar of frustration and tears in his eyes, he threw open his wings, leaped into the sky, and flew away as fast as he could.

Chapter 18

Sten

What Did I Just Do

Sten watched Dragon disappear over the trees and said, "What did I just do?"

Asa said, "You solved our dragon problem. I don't think that dragon is going to return."

"Is it true dragons have never harmed anyone?"

"Don't believe what the monster said."

He turned to Asa and demanded, "Is it true?"

"Of course not." She unloaded her crossbow and returned it to her back.

Sten picked up his hat and headed toward the barn. "All I know is what I've been told to believe. I've never seen any primary or authoritative sources that explain any of it. Let's go. I need to do research."

Chapter 19

<Kedekitley>

I Saw You with the Humans

<Kedekitley> landed hard in front of the weyr.

<Arizesyley> stood in the weyr's foyer, her tail looped over her feet, its tip flicking chaotically. Her brow furrowed and she said, "<I changed my patrol route today.>"

<Kedekitley> said nothing.

"<I saw you with the humans.>"

He had been so distracted he had missed sensing her coming near the site where he had met with Human. That she had seen him with Human didn't matter. He squeezed past her, went to the nest, climbed in, curled up, and mantled his wings over himself.

She followed him to the nest. "<The Council said dragons are not to interact with the humans. You have been violating the Council's edict.>"

He stayed silent.

"<Are you not well? Did the humans damage you?>"

His words tinged with irritation, <Kedekitley> said, "<I am well and I am not damaged.>" After a pause, he added, "<The Council's edict that dragons are not to interact with the humans is correct.>"

"<What happened?>"

"<I do not want to talk about it.>"

Chapter 20

Sten

Conducting Research

Seven years ago, when the dragons attacked, they damaged most of the buildings in the village, especially roofs. A building with a hole in its roof was a building that soon rotted. In the aftermath of the attacks, the first priority had been roof repairs. However, several roofs had been left untouched, including the roofs of the library and the school. Sten had always wondered why.

For several days, Sten spent as much time as he could in the library seeking answers to his questions about dragons.

On the fourth day, Anitra set out the evening meal's place settings, Sten set out the entrée, and Asa set out the side dishes. Sten worked on his courage. His conclusion about dragons would be controversial and he needed to find the right moment to make the announcement.

He provided Anitra a serving of the roast he had prepared and said, "How have things been going for you, Anitra?"

"In math class we began working on logarithms."

"I like logarithms. Logarithmic scales are how my math stick works. It does multiplication and division by adding and subtracting logarithms."

Anitra sighed and rolled her eyes. "Dad, it's called a *slide rule*."

"You always called it my *math stick*."

"That was when I was little. I'm bigger now."

"Actually, you're not that much bigger. It wasn't that long ago."

Asa added the required servings of peas and rattidash root to Anitra's plate and said, "Sten, don't forget who you're talking to."

"I'm sorry." He patted Anitra's hand. "Even though you're precocious and growing up fast, you're still my precious child. It's hard for me to change."

"Oh, Dad." From the breadbasket, Anitra took one of her fastidious mother's perfectly shaped buttery rolls and put it on her plate.

"I'm proud you're in the math class with the older children."

"They're not that much older than me."

"Actually, they're a lot older than you." He turned to Asa. "How about you? What's been going on?"

Asa said, "Since the foolishness with the dragon is over, I'm getting caught up on my work. I'm glad things are back to normal."

For dessert, the family enjoyed jancy berry pie. After eating, Sten washed, Anitra rinsed, and Asa dried and put the dishes into the cupboards.

When all was done, Sten knew he couldn't procrastinate any longer. His conclusion would be world changing, even if it caused controversy in the short-term, and it had to be shared. His determination renewed and his courage set, he said, "Please, sit. I have something to share."

They returned to the family room to sit again at the table. Sten nodded to Anitra, and then he held Asa's hand and focused on her.

Sten said, "I have reached a conclusion about the dragons."

Asa said, "And, what is that conclusion?"

"Dragons are not the monsters we've been led to believe they are."

From the corner of his eye, Sten saw Anitra smile. However, Asa jerked her hand free from his and she made her worst frown again.

Chapter 21

<Kedekitley>

What Did the Humans Do

<Kedekitley's> senses told him <Arizesyley> stood by the nest probably scowling at him. He didn't want to talk to her. He tightened the mantling of his wings.

<Arizesyley> said, "<You interacting with the humans is why you were curious about how the humans construct the humans' roads and structures. I am angry you interacted with the humans after you were told dragons are not to interact with the humans. Now you are damaged.>"

<Kedekitley> huffed. "<I am not damaged.>"

"<You may not be physically damaged, but you are damaged. I have never seen you like this. Tell me what the humans did to you.>"

He didn't want to talk about it, but he knew she would keep asking, keep pestering. She had always been stubborn and persistent. He loved that about her, but it meant she would keep asking until she received an answer that satisfied her.

Throwing open his wings, <Kedekitley> blurted out, "<My human friend said dragons are monsters. Does that satisfy you?>"

<Arizesyley's> silence lingered before she said, "<That response is not the complete answer. What were you doing interacting with the humans?>"

<Kedekitley> sighed, plopped his head down, and dropped his wings so they drooped over the edges of the nest. "<I was trying to make friends with the humans.>"

"<Why would you want to make friends with the humans? The humans are monsters.>"

"<I believed making friends with the humans was the solution that would keep the humans from returning to their murderous ways,

that being friends with the humans would sustain the Paladins' Peace. Implementing my solution was progressing well. My human friend was working with me. Even though my human friend always had an armored human with him, and my human friend wore a Gird-metal murder weapon sword, my human friend was friendly. I enjoyed working with my human friend. Then my human friend said dragons are filthy, smelly, disgusting, and dangerous monsters, and that is why the humans have been attacking dragons for multiple human generations. My human friend is no different from the other humans. The humans are monsters and will never change.>"

<Arizesyley> slammed her fist on the ground. "<We need to eradicate the humans.>"

"<The Council said no to eradicating the humans.>"

"<And, the Council said dragons are not to interact with the humans.>"

<Kedekitley> mantled his wings again and went silent.

Chapter 22

Sten

Dragons Being Monsters Is a Fallacy

Asa jumped to her feet and leaned on the table. "You're wrong. Dragons are monsters. That's why we've fought them for generations."

Sten also stood. "That's what we've always been told, but it's not true." He too leaned on the table to face Asa eye to eye. "It's a myth passed down through the generations from parent to child. It's a fallacy."

"No, it's not. I fight dragons. My father, and his mother, and her mother and father, back to the First Days my family have fought dragons *to protect our families, our communities, and all people* because dragons are monsters."

"They're not monsters."

"Mom! Dad!"

Anitra's abrupt interruption stunned Sten into silence. Asa also went silent, staring at Anitra. While Anitra hadn't yelled, one felt compelled to pay attention to her. Sten could understand why the other children treated her as their leader.

In a commanding tone, Anitra said, "Please, calm down, and sit down, and we'll discuss this like adults."

Sten smiled and sat. Those words echoed words Asa used on Anitra when Anitra became angry about something. Asa appeared shocked, but she sat.

Anitra turned to Sten and said, "Dad, please, explain how you came to your conclusion."

After a deep breath, Sten said, "What Dragon said about dragons having never harmed people bothered me. It's contrary to everything I've been told my entire life, but it made me think. It made me curious about dragons and I wanted facts, not myths."

Asa said, "You have too much curiosity about dragons, and you know what they say about too much curiosity. Besides, it's not a myth. Dragons are monsters."

"Mom, please, silence." Anitra scowled at her mother. "It's Dad's turn to talk."

Asa clasped her hands. "Please, continue, Sten."

"I spent most of four days reading the journals in the library. Many people keep journals, and have since shortly after the First Days. Printed copies are in all the libraries. I figured that would be the best place to look. The language in the older ones is cumbersome and hard to understand, but a few enthusiasts annotated the writings. Most of the authors, even the more recent ones, had no idea how to write well. It's no wonder no one ever reads them. I also noted references to the dragons learning to speak and how that helped simplify the diversity of languages used in the First Days."

Asa said, "What's your point?"

Anitra scowled again.

"I'm sorry. I'll be quiet."

Anitra turned to her father. "Mom's right. You're off topic."

Sten said, "I'll be more concise. I compared the journals. There is remarkable consistency between them. People described the same events from different perspectives, but the descriptions were similar enough to be consistent. I take that to mean they are reliable historical documents. I could find no mention of dragons ever harming anyone."

Asa almost said something, but Anitra's glare stopped her.

"The oldest journals mention dragons helping. Then they begin to talk about driving dragons away. From that point on there are occasional references to campaigns against dragons, and a few stories about those campaigns, but still no mentions of dragons harming people." He paused and frowned. "My conclusion is that dragons have never harmed people, and the belief they have is a fallacy. Dragons are not monsters."

Asa couldn't restrain herself anymore. She leaned back in her chair and looked away. "I won't accept that. I trained for years to become a dragon-slayer knight so I could *protect our families, our communities, and all people* from dragons because dragons are monsters."

"Okay, Mom," said Anitra. "You should do your own research to find evidence to refute Dad's conclusion."

"I'll do that." Asa stood and walked out of the room.

Chapter 23

<Kedekitley>

She Left Him to His Mood

<Arizesyley> snuggled up to <Kedekitley>. He was torn between wanting to be alone and wanting to be with her. Being with her won the night. Morning would give him the opportunity to be alone; however, when morning came, she stayed in the nest with him.

From under his mantled wings, he said, "<You need to fly a patrol.>"

"<I will stay here with you.>"

"<You need to fly a patrol.>"

"<Why do I need to fly a patrol?>"

"<The Council wants the observation data.>"

He felt <Arizesyley> lift her head. "<I periodically deliver the observation data to the Council, but the Council ignores the observation data.>"

"<The observation data you leave with the Council, the Council reviews.>"

"<The Council reviews the observation data? I did not know. Why has no one told me?>"

"<The Council does not want to encourage your desire to eradicate the humans, but the Council does appreciate the observation data.>"

The weyr went silent. <Kedekitley> lifted his head from underneath his wings to find <Arizesyley> staring at nothing in particular.

She said, "<All right then.>"

"<You need to fly a patrol.>"

"<I will fly a patrol.>"

"<I will be here when you return.>"

∞∞∞∞

After <Arizesyley> left, <Kedekitley> went to his collections chambers. Unlike most dragons who had a single collection, like <Arizesyley's> maps collection, <Kedekitley> had two collections: a design documents collection and a tools collection. He loved his collections, but he did not feel like basking in the joy of either even though normally he did. Returning to the nest, he climbed in and went to sleep.

Several more days passed with <Arizesyley> flying her patrols as <Kedekitley> remained in the nest. He did not feel like moving or doing anything. <Arizesyley> checked on him and ensured he remembered she loved him and that he knew she was available to do anything he needed to have done, but otherwise she left him to his mood. He appreciated that.

Chapter 24

Sten

Hoping the Dragon Returns

The next morning, after hugs and kisses all around, Sten and Anitra watched as Asa, wearing her travel cloak and hat, rode away on Maximus with Sayneigh carrying her pack and equipment to visit the Dragon-Slayer Academy to do research. She intended to gather evidence to refute Sten's conclusion. Sten had wished her luck, but he was convinced she would not find that evidence because no evidence existed that would counter his conclusion that dragons were not monsters.

After sending Anitra to school, he went to the wagon yard where he sat in the middle of the yard until well after the time Dragon had typically come. When he accepted that Dragon wasn't coming, he went home to work on his bridge design.

For three more days, after sending Anitra to school, Sten went to the wagon yard, waited, and hoped. Every day he was disappointed. He had no idea how to get Dragon to return, but he was unwilling to give up hope. On the fifth day, it rained.

Chapter 25

<Kedekitley>

Human Sitting in the Rain

<Kedekitley> peeked from under his wings. The day was dark and dreary and a heavy rain fell. Flying in such weather was not comfortable, but <Arizesyley> believed it important to patrol, especially on a day with weather like today's. She thought the humans might use the weather to conceal their move to attack dragons because the humans were not sophisticated enough to know the weather would not give them cover. The Gird-metal armor of the horses the armored humans rode did not seal thus revealing the horses to dragon senses. Even though <Arizesyley> wanted to go, he nevertheless felt sorry for her as she flew away in the rain.

Her early return to stand in the foyer, water streaming off her in rivulets, surprised him.

He said, "<What happened? Did you find something? Are the humans attacking?>"

<Arizesyley> shook water off herself and said, "<For the past four mornings, when I passed near the human town on my new patrol route, the human with whom you interacted has been sitting in the open space on the east side of the human town watching the sky.>"

"<Why do you mention this information?>"

"<The human is sitting in the open space this morning as well even though a significant amount of rain is falling. The humans are not sophisticated, but are the humans so not sophisticated the humans do not have the sense to go under cover when it rains?>"

He thought about the information then climbed out of the nest and said, "<The human behavior sounds strange. The humans are more sophisticated than that. You have piqued my curiosity. I will go to the human town to observe the human behavior for myself.>"

Chapter 26

Sten

The Dragon Returns

"Oh, bother."

The rain poured. Regardless, Sten sat and waited. Surely, a dragon wouldn't want to fly in this weather, but he didn't know. Dragons might like flying in the rain, or didn't care that it was raining. That meant he had to wait here just in case.

Unlike the cold, wet season, during the warm, dry season, these swirling storms only occasionally rolled in from the Sorsell Sea in the south and up the valley of the Lurean River, bringing rain to the lowlands and snow to the mountains. The storm was more intense than most dry season storms. The rain fell in waves of heavy deluges with brief moments of lighter rain between. Strong, sporadic wind gusts turned the rain horizontal. These storms passed quickly, but this storm wasn't passing quickly enough.

His orange colored jacket, trousers, boots, gloves, and hood repelled the rain well, but it was uncomfortable because the suit didn't breathe making the inside humid. In addition to that, every time he looked skyward, he received a face full of rain that ran down his neck and dampened his shirt making the humidity inside the suit worse. He was lucky the wind gusts were hitting him in the back. Sensible people stayed indoors on days like this. Maybe he should go home.

Then, under the trees at the eastern edge of the wagon yard, he saw movement. The curtain of rain made the apparition indistinct, but Sten knew because of its size it was a dragon. He hoped it was Dragon himself. He stood and walked toward the phantom. As he came closer, he saw distinct red marks that caused him to catch his breath. It was Dragon.

The figure moved deeper into the trees. Sten quickened his pace fearing Dragon might leave before he could speak to him.

Under the trees, it was dark and smelled of decaying leaves. The only sounds were the hissing of the rain on the forest canopy, the sizzle-like sound of drops hitting the ground, and the squishing of his boots in the waterlogged forest floor detritus. Dragon wasn't there.

"Dragon, where are you? You didn't leave, did you?"

Dragon stepped out from behind a clump of trees and said, "I will not violate the Paladins' Peace." He stood on all fours, his head held at Sten's level. He glistened from the water streaming off him.

Sten said, "Dragon, I'm sorry I called you a monster, that I called dragons monsters. I was wrong. Forgive me, please."

Dragon lifted his head higher and said, "Why do you now know you were wrong?"

Sten looked up, shielded his face from the rain with his hand, and said, "I read the old journals, the histories people have written. None of them mention dragons harming people. They would have if it were true."

"I told you dragons have never damaged the humans, with one exception: <Improecley> damaged the Human Paladin. That was the only time a dragon damaged a human."

"I believe you. Everything I've been taught my entire life is a fallacy. The truth is dragons don't harm people."

Dragon tilted his head. "You are not wearing a murder weapon sword."

"I don't need it."

"The armored human is not with you."

"I don't need Asa's protection either. Dragons don't harm people."

"Why were you sitting in the rain? Are the humans so not sophisticated the humans do not have the sense to go under cover when it rains?"

Sten looked at his wet form, which looked like a piece of freshly washed fruit. "I'm wearing my best rain suit." He shook his finger at Dragon. "Why are you out in the rain?"

Dragon dipped his chin. "<Arizesyley> manipulated me."

"What?"

"<Arizesyley> manipulated me. She told me you were sitting in the rain. She knew my curiosity about why you were acting not sophisticated would stimulate me into leaving the weyr. She once told me I misuse curiosity. This time, it was she who misused my curiosity."

Sten laughed and said, "Curiosity must be something we have in common. Asa told me I have too much curiosity. Why are you hiding in the trees?"

Dragon glanced toward the village obscured by the rain. "I did not want the bell to toll, and I did not want to be confronted by the armored humans. I only wanted to see if you were not sophisticated enough not to go under cover when it rains."

"We're both out in the rain; so, if I'm not sophisticated, you aren't either."

After a huff, Dragon said, "My curiosity justifies my actions." He then opened his wings, and extended them forward to provide a cover over their heads shielding them from the large drops that fell from the overhead leaves.

"My hope that you would return justifies mine."

Dragon stared at Sten before he said, "You hoped I would return?"

"Yes. I wanted you to return so I could apologize, and maybe arrange for us to work together again? I liked working with you."

When Dragon hesitated, Sten worried he would say no. A gust of wind shook loose a swarm of huge drops that drummed on Dragon's wings punctuating Sten's feeling of failure.

Dragon said, "I accept your apology, and I would enjoy working with you again."

Sten stood straighter and said, "Wonderful. Asa's not going to be happy about this. She's already upset I've concluded dragons aren't monsters."

"<Arizesyley> will not be pleased either. She is upset I interacted with the humans. What task do you wish for me to perform to help the humans?"

"In two days, could you meet me at the house where we last met? And, by two days, I mean the day after tomorrow."

"I understand the two days reference."

"The house is ready to be roofed. You and I working together can do it quickly, and I'll try again to get the others to help, which would get the job done even faster."

Dragon nodded. "In two days I will be at the location you specified."

He moved his wings to spread them, which released a pool of water into Sten's upturned face.

"Oh, bother."

The subtle look on Dragon's face was precious as he said, "Oops. I am sorry, Human."

Sten wiped his face as the water soaked him on its way to fill his boots. "It's okay. A lot of water has already gone down my neck anyway." He reached out to forestall Dragon's leaving. "I apologize again for calling you a monster. And, thank you for returning. And, for being willing to work with me again."

As Dragon walked a short distance away, he said, "I am happy I came to see how not sophisticated you are. I am happy we will work together again. I will forgive <Arizesyley> for manipulating me." He leaped straight through an opening in the forest canopy and flew into the rain-shrouded sky.

All the way home, boots sloshing, Sten danced in the rain.

Chapter 27

<Kedekitley>

Will Again Work with Human

<Kedekitley> stopped in the weyr's foyer long enough to shake the water off himself and went inside. He already knew <Arizesyley> wasn't in the weyr, but he was eager to tell her what had happened. He settled facing the foyer, his feet tucked under him, and patiently waited.

When he sensed her approaching, he stood and prepared himself. She stopped in the foyer to shake herself off then stepped inside. He bounded to her, pulled her into his arms, hooked his tail around her, mantled his wings over her, rubbed his head on hers, and said, "<I love you and missed you. What did you find?>"

"<I found nothing. You are acting as if you are feeling better. Is your damage repaired?>"

"<I was not damaged, but thanks to your ruse to get me out of the nest and out of the weyr, I am feeling better.>"

She threaded her tail around him and said, "<I knew seeing how not sophisticated the humans are would help you.>"

"<My human friend and I will be working together again.>"

Breaking the hug, <Arizesyley> stepped back. "<You said you now agree with the Council that dragons are not to interact with the humans.>"

"<I changed my mind. I still believe making friends with the humans is the solution that will keep the humans from returning to their murderous ways.>"

"<If you do this, I will never stop reminding you the Council said dragons are not to interact with the humans.>"

"<And, I will keep reminding you the Council said no to eradicating the humans.>"

<Arizesyley's> brow furrowed, she huffed, and resumed their hug. "<I am not happy with you, but you are still the best dragon. Keep yourself safe. The humans are dangerous.>"

"<I am keeping myself safe. That is why I asked you to remind me about the strategies humans use to attack dragons.>"

Chapter 28

Sten

Now You've Done It

Sten needed to work on his bridge design, but he was too wound up, so he wrote in his journal instead. When he heard Anitra come in, he went to the family room to meet her. She was still in the foyer removing her boots. Her rain suit already hung from its hook, dripping.

Sten said, "How's the rain?"

After Anitra removed the rain cover from her pack, she came into the room. "It's slacking off and the southern sky is brightening."

"How was school today?"

She set her pack on the table, pulled out several sheets of paper, and handed them to him. "I was the only one in class to get a perfect score. I used the technique you taught me to keep track of the decimal points when doing logarithmic math. Why don't they teach that at school?"

"I don't know. No one else understands it when I explain it. It must work for us because we're special. I use the same technique to keep track of decimal points when I do calculations on my slide rule."

"Thank you for teaching it to me."

"You're welcome. Do you want to know what happened to me today? Dragon returned."

"He did? In the storm?"

"Someone told him I was sitting in the rain. He came to see for himself. He said I was acting *not sophisticated*." Sten made quotation marks in the air with his fingers as he spoke with a silly voice.

"What happened?"

"I apologized for calling him a monster. He accepted my apology and said he would work with me again."

Anitra smiled.

∞∞∞∞

The afternoon of the next day, as he was making progress on his bridge design, he heard the front door open. He assumed it was Anitra coming home from school.

From the family room, Anitra called out, "Dad, Mom's home."

Sten's spirits spiked. He put aside his slide rule and headed to the family room. Asa had already set down her pack and had hung her travel cloak and hat. When she saw him, she came at him in the accustomed fashion. Sten extended his arms to accept her embrace.

He said, "I'm glad you're home. I missed you. How was the trip?"

"The storm yesterday delayed my return. Only a fool would spend time out in weather like that."

Anitra giggled and said, "Dad did."

"What?"

Sten said, "After you left, I sat in the wagon yard every morning hoping Dragon would return."

Asa pulled away to look at him. "You sat out in the rain yesterday, hoping that dragon would return?"

He nodded. "Yes, and he did."

"Did Knight Ned and Knight Ted respond?"

"No."

"Why not?"

"They didn't know he was here. Dragon stayed hidden in the trees."

"Why did he return?"

"Someone told him I was sitting in the rain. He wanted to see for himself." Sten smiled. "He said I was acting *not sophisticated*."

"You were. Wait. Someone told him?"

"Apparently there are other dragons around even though we've only seen Dragon."

She sighed and said, "Wonderful, more dragons."

"Mom, Dad," Anitra waved toward the table. "Please, let's sit and listen to Mom's report about her research and conclusion."

Sten smiled at his remarkable child as the three of them took their seats.

"Mom, please, begin."

Asa took a breath. "The Dragon-Slayer Academy has many records. I went through as many as I could; they're not fun to read. They record campaigns and strategies, some of which we had covered in training. Many have details about battles, if you want to call them that — the dragons always fled. When they didn't flee, it was because they were trapped and had to fight their way out, or they were protecting other dragons as they fled."

She stopped and stared at her hands.

Sten said, "And?"

"Dad, please, silence."

"I'm sorry."

Asa said, "Those times, a dragon would strike out at the knights. I've been taught that Gird-metal armor protects me, but the firsthand accounts of being struck are remarkable. Engineers say Gird-metal acts *weird* and it is that *weirdness* that protects against powerful blows that should be instantly fatal. I don't understand it. In training, I received blows to show how well I'm protected — the armor makes a purple flash — but I would never want to be struck as hard as those accounts describe."

She hesitated again as she wrapped her arms around herself.

"As soon as the dragon was clear, it would flee. No people were ever harmed in those battles. Dragons were, occasionally, but none were killed until the advent of crossbows."

Sten was eager for her to get to the point but refrained from drumming his fingers on the table.

"I found only one reference to a person being harmed: General Patrick, except he was a Colonel then."

Sten said, "The knight who fought the Dragon Paladin?"

Patrick was Knight General in command of the Dragon-Slayer Academy. Sten had never met him, but he did see him once, six years ago, when he came through town on his tour explaining and promoting the Paladins' Peace.

Everyone knew Patrick was now friends with the dragon who had almost killed him. The two of them led the Arbitration Committee created by the Paladins' Peace to arbitrate disputes, and they were the ultimate promoters of the peace they had created. However, regardless of his association with that dragon, hints inadvertently dropped by Asa about things not talked about outside the Dragon-Slayer Academy indicated Patrick had made changes to the organization based on lessons learned when the dragons had attacked at the end of the Dragon War. If war ever came again, the dragon-slayer knights were ready to do what needed to be done.

Asa said, "I've seen the deep dents caused by the dragon's teeth, the deep gashes from the dragon's talons, and the crush marks from the dragon's tail in his armor, but no one ever talks about anything more than that." Asa moved forward on her chair, leaned in, and spoke in a hushed tone. "What he wrote about the incident in his report has more details: his armor failed. The seals on his left rerebrace and pauldron separated exposing his shoulder and arm. The dragon slashed him with her talons and he bled profusely. But, by then he had slashed one of the dragon's wings and her neck and her arm and had hit the dragon in the chest with a crossbow bolt. They were both wounded — maybe even mortally wounded — except, for some reason, they helped each other, they saved each other. That led them to forging the Paladins' Peace."

"Wow." Anitra was wide-eyed. "Is it a secret?"

"No one talks about it, but it's not a secret. It's right there in the records for anyone to read, although I wonder if anyone ever has."

"It sounds like something everyone would talk about," said Anitra. "Why don't they?"

"General Patrick wrote that he managed to reassemble his armor so when he returned home, no one knew he was wounded, and he kept his arm and shoulder covered when he was out in public to keep people from seeing the wounds. He didn't talk about it, kept his wounds hidden, and no one noticed."

Sten said, "Did the information you found lead you to a conclusion?"

"No," said Asa. "I still believe dragons are monsters."

"But, you didn't find any evidence to contradict my conclusion."

"I can't accept the idea that dragons have never harmed anyone. I just can't."

"That leaves us at an impasse. I'll accept that we disagree, but it doesn't change what I must do. Are you willing to attend tonight's community meeting with Anitra and me? I must report on what's happened with keeping Dragon away from the village."

"I'll go."

ᢍᢍᢍ

That evening, the meeting hall wasn't quite at capacity, but the crowd was as noisy as usual. Sten sat with Asa, Anitra, Sochi, and Ned and Ted in their accustomed seats. Marita and the Village Council, including Sasha, came onto the stage.

Marita banged her gavel and said, "I call this community meeting for the Village of Splain to order. First order of business is the Master Builder's report regarding progress with our dragon problem. Master Sten, you have the floor."

Sten had steeled himself for being the center of attention, but he still felt nervous. He stepped onto the stage eschewing the lectern so he could address the Council and the crowd and spoke using his voice of authority. "Thank you, Mayor Marita. Working with Dragon has been interesting. He's a hard worker, diligent, pays attention to details, takes pride in his work, and he can be trained to do many useful tasks that will free work-teams to work on other priority projects.

"We did have a few difficult moments as we learned about our differences and how to work together, but those issues have been resolved.

"Tomorrow, I will work with him on roofing Miss Lisa and Mister Oliver's house. Since it's their house, Miss Lisa and Mister Oliver have committed to helping and I hope a few members of Foreman Douglas's work-team will also be willing to work with Dragon.

"Dragon is remarkable. Therefore, my efforts to work with him will continue."

Murmurs flowed through the room as people whispered to each other. Sten wanted to say more, but he couldn't outcompete the hum of the crowd. Marita banged her gavel to restore order.

Sten said, "One more thing. I read the historical accounts contained in the old journals looking for information about dragons and the kinds of threats they pose. I learned something astonishing: Everything we've been told our entire lives about dragons is a fallacy.

Dragons have never harmed anyone. Dragons aren't monsters; in fact, dragons are friendly."

That was the end of the meeting. No amount of gavel banging could quiet the crowd. Asa locked eyes with Sten and mouthed *Now you've done it*. Asa, Anitra, Ned and Ted, and he snuck out and went to their homes.

Once home, Asa said, "I'm going with you tomorrow."

"Please, no, you're not," Sten said. "And, I'm not taking the sword either. I understand how you feel, but I trust Dragon and I must show him that trust. He will not harm me or anyone, and I want him to know we won't harm him and for him to feel safe."

She glared, but he knew she would do as he asked.

Anitra said, "When will I get to see the dragon?"

"I don't know. I still don't know where this will lead. For now, I'm still coping one day at a time."

∞∞∞∞

The brightening sky and fading stars heralded the morning's arrival. Walking toward the stables, Sten breathed deeply of the fresh air and felt good about the day's prospects.

From around the corner of a building, spreading out in his path, stepped four figures shrouded in the gray light.

"Mister Viren, Mister Nellis, Mister Sato, Miss Nyxie, good morning." Sten stopped when they didn't make room for him to pass.

Viren said, "You shouldn't be doing what you're doing."

"What is that?"

"Wasting time with that dragon."

"I've been given the task of dealing with him. I'm doing my job, unlike some people I know."

"We're going to put an end to that."

"How?"

Sten hadn't noticed the cudgel before Viren pointed it at him. Nellis and Sato also held cudgels.

"By making it a bad day." Viren stepped forward.

Sten stepped back. "Are you sure you want to mess with me?"

Viren sneered. "What can you do about it?"

"I admit, I'm easy going, and avoid conflict, but it's common knowledge my spouse is a dragon-slayer knight."

"So?"

"What isn't common knowledge is Sergeant Asa needed a sparring partner and Knight Ned and Knight Ted aren't always available. She taught me to spar with her. Are you sure you want to test my training?"

With narrowed eyes and in total silence, Viren raised his cudgel and lunged.

Sten said, "Oh, bother." He knocked Viren's arm aside with a swing of his pack and with his other hand performed a simple palm strike to Viren's face sending the man staggering backward into his companions.

"Who's next?"

Sato came at him. Sten performed a side kick into Sato's chest that knocked the wind out of him and sent him flying several paces before he landed on his back.

"You haven't seen the last of us," said Viren as he used his hand to hold back the blood leaking from his nose.

"Maybe this should be the last time I see you. Your welcome in Splain, Mister Viren, has waned." As the group backed away, Sten said, "Miss Nyxie, why are you hanging out with those thugs? You're not like them."

Nyxie hesitated then said, "Master Sten, I —"

Viren interrupted her. "Nyxie, please, come on."

She followed Viren and the others. The group moved down a side street with two of them staggering. Sten was glad they hadn't all attacked at once. He had not had much practice handling multiple opponents simultaneously.

Abaccus nickered when Sten entered the stable.

"It's good to see you too, Abaccus." He gave the horse a horse treat. "It's already been an eventful day. Let's go have some more adventure."

Chapter 29

<Kedekitley>

Roofing a Structure

<Kedekitley> circled to survey the site for threats. Human was waiting. Standing with Human were two other humans who were new to <Kedekitley>. Two dragon-spans away, next to a new structure erected since his last visit, stood the six humans who had been there that time. Inside the structure to the west were three horses, only one of which he recognized; the other two were new to him. Behind the grove of trees to the north, again set the same wagon and two horses as last time. The armored human was not present. Seeing nothing threatening, <Kedekitley> committed.

Landing and approaching Human, <Kedekitley> said, "I will not violate the Paladins' Peace."

The two humans standing with Human backed away two steps.

Human said, "Dragon, I'm glad you came."

"Hello, Human. Where is the armored human?"

"I don't need Asa's protection, or that sword. Dragons don't harm people."

That statement bolstered <Kedekitley's> feelings of safety, but he maintained his vigilance regardless.

"What task do you wish for me to perform to help the humans?"

"We will finish roofing the house. All that remains is installing the shingles. This is *Miss Lisa* and *Mister Oliver.* They have promised to help." Human turned toward the two humans and said, "Right?" stretching out the word.

Without taking their wide-eyed gazes off <Kedekitley>, the two humans, in unison, nodded three times.

"Right." Human made a despairing sound. "I tell you what, let me be the go-between. Talk to me and I'll handle Dragon so you don't have to." He turned to <Kedekitley> and said, "I'm still hoping to get some members of the assigned work-team to help." He motioned toward the other six humans. "They have promised not to run off, even if they end up not helping."

The horse <Kedekitley> had seen before came striding up.

Human said, "Abaccus, did you unlatch the stall door?"

The horse nuzzled Human and walked over to <Kedekitley>. He held out his hand, but the horse shied back.

Human gathered stalks of grass and handed them to <Kedekitley>. "Give this to him."

<Kedekitley> held out the grass. The horse came over and took the grass from his hand.

He said, "Horses consume grass?"

"They do." Human patted the horse on the neck.

Lisa said, "Your horse isn't afraid of the dragon?"

"Why should he be? Dragons are friendly. I'm not surprised Abaccus isn't afraid of him, even though he was initially shy."

The horse found more grass and commenced consuming it.

After glancing at Oliver, Lisa said, "We're ready to get to work, with the dragon."

<Kedekitley> followed Human and the other two humans to the new structure. The six other humans pointed and talked amongst themselves. They looked as if they might bolt.

"These are the shingles." Human tapped one of twenty stacks of flat tree slices. "These are made from frively trees. They're great for shingles because the wood's durable and resists burning. Since you're tall enough when you stand on your hind legs, you can lift the shingles up to us from ground level."

"How would you transport the shingles onto the roof if I were not here?" <Kedekitley> picked up a shingle to judge its mass.

"We would have carried them up the ladder a few at a time."

"Your solution to the problem of transporting the shingles onto the roof is not sophisticated. I will design a proper solution to the problem."

"We already have a solution: shingle hoists. But, none were available for this project. We should make more of them. For now, we're going to do it the old-fashion way so we can finish the house. Your help is just what we need to make the process easier. Are you ready?"

"I am ready."

Human and the other two humans fastened belts that held tools around their waists, placed clear coverings over their eyes, and climbed a ladder onto the roof.

"Please, start handing them up."

<Kedekitley> handed up a shingle that the humans nailed into place. He handed up another, and another. The process was boring, yet he was helping the humans. That's what he wanted, was it not? He had not expected the help he provided to be this simple and boring, though.

Two humans from the group of six came to the structure, climbed onto the roof, and began nailing shingles. This required <Kedekitley> to work more quickly. When the remaining four humans joined the effort, Human climbed down and helped <Kedekitley> by handing him shingles from the stacks to hand up to the roof.

At midday, the humans stopped working for what Human called a *midday meal break*. The humans washed their hands and sat to consume what <Kedekitley> assumed was grass using utensils to scoop the human food into their mouths. Not caring to watch, he gazed at the sky hoping to see <Arizesyley> fly over on her patrol.

When she did, she circled twice. <Kedekitley> longed to join her, but instead he resigned himself to sticking to the tedious task of helping the humans, and to admiring her beauty from a distance until she was out of sight.

When the humans finished consuming the human food, the humans each visited a small structure similar to the small structure at the road-repair site, washed their hands, and returned to work.

When the last shingle was in place, the humans climbed down and congratulated themselves by shaking hands and patting each other on the back.

Human said, "Dragon, thank you for your help."

"You are welcome, Human. What task do you wish for me to perform next to help the humans?"

"I'm working on a design for a big and challenging project. Your help would make the work a lot easier. North of the village, the Lurean Road fords a creek. We want to construct a bridge there. Can you meet me at the creek tomorrow morning to talk about the project and what I'll need you to do?"

"Tomorrow, I will be at the location you specified." <Kedekitley> took flight feeling good about his progress at making friends with the humans.

Chapter 30

Sten

Replace Fallacy with Truth

Sten didn't have to pick up his hat. Everyone else did. Oliver climbed to the roof to retrieve his.

Loosening his hat's chinstrap, Sten said, "What do you think? Dragon can be useful, can't he?"

Douglas said, "He's still a dragon."

"He is a dragon. But, dragons don't harm people, they never have, and we can train them to do many jobs, jobs more challenging than just handing up shingles."

Lisa stepped forward. "I, for one, liked him, once I got over the shock. He was big and scary."

"And, intimidating," said Sten. "That was my reaction the first time I faced him, but you get used to him. He's actually quite friendly. It helps if you take to heart that dragons don't harm people."

Oliver said, "I'm willing to work with him here on the farm, when the opportunity presents itself."

Douglas said to his work-team, "Are you willing to work with the dragon again?" The other five work-team members nodded. "There you have it, Master Sten. We'll work with him."

"Wonderful. Please, spread the word about how well things went today and how you're willing to work with Dragon again. If we're going to use him, we need to build a consensus that it's safe to work with him."

∞∞∞∞∞∞

Asa and Anitra had the evening meal ready when Sten arrived home.

"I made the buttery rolls," said Anitra as she pushed the breadbasket toward Sten.

He took a bite of one, nodded, and said, "They're as good as always."

While Asa's rolls had a smooth dome shape, Anitra's were always bumpy and spiky. The rolls tasted perfect, but not adhering to her mother's preference for a flawless shape was one of Anitra's methods of rebelling.

Anitra often challenged conventions and tested authorities like her parents and teachers, but not in a bad way. She was always questing, always seeking, always trying to expand beyond any limits placed upon her, but seldom did she misbehave.

Asa said, "What happened with the dragon?"

"I was hoping you'd ask."

"As if you weren't going to tell us if we didn't ask." Asa picked up a roll and began picking off the bumps and spikes to eat first.

"The job went well. We finished roofing the house. And, more importantly, the entire work-team worked with Dragon."

Asa sighed.

"In fact, the work-team members said they are willing to work with him again and will tell everyone how wonderful he is."

Asa gave a deeper sigh.

"Tomorrow, I'm meeting with him at the Connela Creek ford to talk about constructing the bridge I've been designing. I'll ask him about lifting and manipulating the beams to help with construction. If he can do that, imagine how much easier it'll be to construct the bridge."

"Dad, when will I get to see the dragon?" Having watched how her mother ate a roll, Anitra picked up a roll and began plucking the center out from the bottom to eat first, saving the bumps and spikes for last.

"I don't know. Things are going well, but I'm still not comfortable with letting you go near him."

Asa pointed her spoon at him. "You're admitting that regardless of what you say, you're afraid of the monster."

"He's not a monster. And, yes, I still feel fear. What do you expect? I was raised to fear dragons. But, my efforts to replace fallacy with truth will drive out what was drilled into me as a child."

Staring into her bowl as she stirred her stew, Asa said, "I can't. I won't."

Chapter 31

<Kedekitley>

Insufferable Genius

<Kedekitley> landed. <Arizesyley> stood in the foyer watching.

He went to her and performed his greeting hug. "<I love you and missed you. What did you find?>".

"<I also love you and missed you. I found nothing. I saw you interacting with the humans. Did the humans damage you?>"

"<The humans were friendly. I helped the humans install shingles on the roof of a structure.>"

"<You installed shingles?>"

"<I helped the humans by handing the shingles to the humans on the roof. The humans performed the task of installing the shingles. At the beginning, the task was tedious, and boring, but when eight humans began installing the shingles, supplying the shingles as quickly as the humans were installing the shingles became a challenge. I offered to design a solution to the problem of lifting the shingles to the roof, but my human friend did not accept my offer.>"

"<Have the humans only asked you to perform physical labor? Do the humans not know you are a genius at designing solutions to problems?>"

<Kedekitley> smiled. "<You believe I am a genius?>"

"<Everyone knows you are a genius.>" <Arizesyley> huffed and said, "<Sometimes, you are an insufferable genius.>"

"<Thank you for the the sarcasm, and the complement even though the premise for the complement is not true.>" He rubbed his head on hers then said, "<Tomorrow, I will meet with my human friend to discuss what my human friend called a *big project*. My human friend wants to construct a bridge. That task should be

more interesting and challenging than the tasks I have performed thus far.>"

"<I remind you the Council said dragons are not to interact with the humans.>"

"<And, I remind you the Council said no to eradicating the humans.>" After staring into her ruby red eyes, he said, "<Let us soak in the hot spring.>"

She grinned and said, "<That idea is a good idea. You *are* a genius.>" She turned and left the weyr.

He followed.

Chapter 32

Sten

Mathematics Error

"I want to go see the dragon." Dressed in her favorite green trousers and shirt, a spring green Sten thought was too garish, Anitra stood at the door.

"You can't, not today. You need to go to school. The school's on my way. I'll walk with you."

Anitra's "Okay" oozed disappointment.

As they approached the school on the north end of the village, Sten said, "We're planning to remodel the school and add more classrooms. Maybe, when the time comes, Dragon can help with that."

"Can I see him then?"

"We'll have to wait and see."

"I'm tired of waiting."

Sten watched Anitra enter the school. The day the dragons attacked, the school had been left untouched. The building had been full of children and teachers cowering under their desks. When the dragons couldn't scare the occupants out, the dragons skipped damaging the building. They had avoided a few other buildings as well when people refused to run, the library being one of them. In hindsight, if people had stayed in the buildings, the dragons might not have damaged any of them. Sten now understood why: The dragons didn't want to harm anyone.

A fifth of an hour walk farther north brought Sten to Connela Creek. He moseyed along the road following its long switchback down the slope as traffic kept passing him until he reached the bottom. At the ford, the gorge spanned 50 paces. During the low-water phase of the dry season, down its middle, the creek spread 40 paces wide and was shallow enough to wade across.

He watched the wagons and horses ford the creek and head up the switchback on the other side. The descent, the fording, and the climb out of the gorge slowed traffic. Moreover, during the high-water phase of the wet season, the creek could run so deep and fast it stopped traffic until the water level dropped. The solution to those problems was a bridge. The traffic on this stretch of the Lurean Road had increased enough, and was forecast to continue increasing, for this project to be pushed to near the top of the priority list.

Sten walked downstream to the 15 paces wide narrow point where solid rock bluffs 30 paces high stood sentry on either side of the creek. During low-water, before and after the Connela Creek Narrows the creek averaged 15 paces wide. The narrows constricted the flow into an eight paces wide channel that deepened and hastened the water. During high-water, the slack water upstream of the narrows left sand that became beaches on either side when low-water season came.

Sten sat on a large, flat boulder on the beach, listened to the murmur of the creek, and watched the brilliant blue sky as he counted the cotton fluff stuffing clouds that appeared over the south rim of the gorge, marched across the gap, and disappeared over the north rim. It was a wonderful day to watch the sky in anticipation of seeing a dragon.

Dragon arrived, circled twice, and hovered with his wings beating a rapid figure eight as he studied the ground. Sten thought Dragon's wings changed shape, but he decided it was his imagination and the way the wings were sweeping.

A large and powerful predator overhead invoked primal fear, but Sten pushed that aside so he could marvel at how magnificent Dragon looked with his primary wings spread wide and his tail wings fanned out like that of a hawk. Except for his size, the neck sticking out in front, and the tail sticking out behind, his silhouette did look like a hawk.

The gorge was about as wide as Dragon's wingspan, which meant he ran the risk of hitting the walls. He turned to align his wings lengthwise with the creek, which gave him more room off the ends of his wings, reduced the sweep of his wings to not hit the walls, and settled to land on his hind legs as softly as a mote of dust. Sten held onto his hat and used his arm to shield his face from the kicked up sand.

Closing his wings and dropping to all fours, Dragon said, "I will not violate the Paladins' Peace."

Sten lowered his arm and said. "Dragon, I'm glad you came."

"Hello, Human. What task do you wish for me to perform to help the humans?"

"It would have been easier to land if you had landed farther upstream where the gorge is wider."

Dragon twisted his neck to look behind him and said, "What you say is correct. I will consider that option next time."

Sten noticed Dragon's accent had shifted — he was sounding less archaic.

When Dragon turned back, he looked behind Sten prompting Sten to look over his shoulder. Sten didn't see anything, so he turned to Dragon and said, "As for the task. I'm planning to construct a bridge to span the creek from there to there." He pointed to the rock bluffs overhead. "Your help lifting the beams into place will make the job a lot easier. Let me show you the design." Sten pulled the design document from his pack and spread it on the flat boulder.

Dragon approached.

Sten fervently believed Dragon would not harm him, but the massive creature approaching still instinctively sent his pulse racing even as he felt empowered by his belief.

Sten said, "It'll be a truss arch bridge. We'll build falseworks to support the bridge as we assemble it from precut beams. Once all the beams are in place, we'll remove the falseworks and have a finished bridge."

The silence stretched as Dragon stared at the design, tilting his head to one side then the other before he furrowed his brow and said, "Of what material will the beams be made?"

"They're cut from posimly trees. They have excellent tensile and compressive strength and exceptional durability. We use them for many construction projects."

"Do you mean the tall trees with twisting longitudinal fibers?"

"Twisting grain describes it. The frively trees we use to make shingles are similar but have a straight grain."

Dragon sat, lifted his head, and proclaimed, "The structure will fail catastrophically." He looked behind Sten again.

Sten said, "What makes you think that?" and then checked over his shoulder assuming someone or something was approaching.

Dragon made a jaunty tilt of his head. "I am skilled and experienced at designing and constructing structures. I am familiar with the properties of the construction material you will use. And, the structure you designed is similar to the structure I designed for the Pavilion at the Conclave Grounds, except instead of a road, my structure has shingles on top."

"If you say so." Sten tapped the paper. "I know what I'm doing; more so than what a dragon would know. I calculated all the vector mechanics accounting for the compression and tension forces involved. It will be a sturdy and safe bridge."

Dragon pointed to the left side of the diagram. "This beam," he pointed to the same mirrored beam on the right side, "or this beam, whichever is weaker, will fail the first time a heavy load comes onto the structure."

"No, it won't. See these notes?" Sten tapped the numbers scrawled in the margins. "They show there's plenty of safety margin."

Dragon shook his head. "The structure will fail catastrophically."

"No, it won't. I'll prove it." Sten retrieved his slide rule from his pack and did the math. "See the numbers match."

"What is that device?"

"It's a slide rule for doing math. See, I'll do it again." He repeated the calculations and froze before saying, "Oh, bother. I put the decimal point in the wrong place. One should always double-check one's decimal points. You're right. The bridge would have failed. People would have died. How did you know?"

"I told you. I am skilled and experienced at designing and constructing structures. I made assumptions, which I do not like to do, but my mathematical calculations indicated the structure would fail catastrophically."

"How did you do the math?"

"I thought the mathematical calculations."

Sten's thoughts stumbled. "You did that math in your head?"

"I am a dragon. What did you expect?"

"I didn't expect that."

Dragon again looked past Sten.

Sten again looked over his shoulder and said, "What do you keep looking at?"

"Behind that bush is a human child."

On the downstream side of the cliff where an eddy formed when the water ran high was a deposit of sediment in which grew a dozen bleagger bushes. Sure enough, through the glossy dark green leaves of one of the bushes, Sten could see garish spring green.

"Oh, bother." To Dragon, he said, "Please, wait here." He strolled to the bush, which was almost as tall as he was and an arm span wide and said, "Anitra?"

Anitra stepped out. "Hello, Dad."

"Why are you here?"

"I wanted to see the dragon." She stepped to the side so she could see past Sten. Her eyes were wide. "He's amazing." Then she laughed.

"Yes, he is, even more so than I had thought." Sten turned to see Dragon standing on his hind legs, his fists on his hips with elbows akimbo, his chin held high, and his wings spread in a horaltic pose as if he were a heroic statue. Sten added, "And, silly," before turning back to Anitra to say, "How'd you sneak past me?"

"I didn't follow the road. I used the trail." She pointed at a trace on the slope farther down the creek. "It's a lot shorter than the road."

"You need to get back to school."

"But, Dad."

"Please, go. And, tell Professor Hutchmen to give you extra homework to make up for the class time you missed."

"But, Dad."

"Please, go."

With a pout and her chin lowered, Anitra hiked up the trail and out of sight.

Dragon approached from behind Sten and said, "You agreed with the human child that I am amazing."

"I also said you're silly."

"I am also a genius. <Arizesyley> told me so."

"If you say so."

Sten walked to the boulder, picked up his bridge design, and stared at it.

Dragon said, "Are you not well?"

"I'm fine. I can't believe I made a mistake. I'm embarrassed. I don't make mistakes. But, there's been so many interruptions and ... things happening." Sten glanced at Dragon. "Not that I'm making excuses or blaming anyone other than myself. I'll have to rework the design." He took a sharp breath as he had an idea. "Would you be willing to review the new design to ensure I didn't make any other mistakes?"

"I am willing to review the bridge design. Except for the error, I am impressed. I did not know the humans were sophisticated enough to create such designs."

"Thank you, I think. Meet me in the wagon yard the day after the day after tomorrow and I'll give you a copy of the new design to review."

Dragon snorted. "Do you mean in three days?"

"Yes, on the third day."

"In three days I will be at the location you specified." Dragon spread his wings, paused looking past Sten, and said, "A horse is approaching."

Sten turned. "Abaccus."

Abaccus went to Dragon and nuzzled his hand.

Dragon said, "I like the horse."

"He likes you too." Sten patted Abaccus and said to Dragon, "I'll see you in three days."

"Our meeting today was enjoyable, Human."

"I agree, and I learned something that has changed the world even more than it had already changed."

Sten clutched the bridge design to his chest as Dragon left in a gust of wind.

"What do you think, Abaccus? Should I teach Dragon to move farther away before he takes flight? Please, give me a ride home."

Chapter 33

<Kedekitley>

Human Said I Am Amazing

When <Arizesyley> arrived at their weyr, <Kedekitley> hurried to her, hugged her, and said, "<I love you and missed you. What did you find?>"

"<I also love you and missed you. I found nothing.>"

<Kedekitley> began pronking like a four-year-old dragonet.

"<What have the humans done to you now?>"

He stopped bouncing and said, "<I thought you would never ask.>"

<Arizesyley> sighed. "<As if you were not going to tell me if I did not ask.>"

"<My human friend said I am amazing.>" He cocked his head.

"<You are amazing.>"

"<I told my human friend you said I am a genius.>"

"<When I said you are a genius, you denied being a genius. Now you claim to be a genius?>"

"<Telling my human friend you said I am a genius was appropriate.>"

"<What prompted the human to say you are amazing?>"

"<My human friend made an error.>"

<Arizesyley> tilted her head. "<All right then. The human made an error saying you are amazing?>"

<Kedekitley> sighed and dipped his head. "<My human friend was correct saying I am amazing. My human friend made an error in his bridge design.>"

"<I still do not have any idea what you are talking about. You are performing poorly at presenting the information.>"

"<My human friend made a design for a bridge. I analyzed the design, performed mathematical calculations, and found an error.>"

<Arizesyley> tilted her head again. "<All right then. The humans design things? Are the humans' designs like your designs?>"

He nodded. "<My human friend's bridge design was similar to my designs. I was surprised to learn the humans are sophisticated enough to create designs comparable to my designs.>"

"<I am also surprised. What was the error?>"

"<A mathematical calculation was in error by two orders of magnitude.>"

"<The humans can perform the mathematical calculations required to design a bridge? Again, I am surprised.>"

"<I too was surprised.>" He held his hands as if they contained an object. "<My human friend used a tool to perform the mathematical calculations. My human friend is not sophisticated enough to do the mathematical calculations by thinking as I can.>"

"<You are special, Kedekitley.>" She rubbed her head on his. "<No other dragon can think mathematical calculations as you can. Why would you expect the humans to be able to think mathematical calculations?>"

"<I did not know the humans could perform any kind of mathematical calculations, but my human friend demonstrated remarkable sophistication and skill performing complex mathematical calculations using the mathematical calculations tool. However, the error was obvious. My human friend should have recognized the error. My human friend's confidence that his mathematical calculations were error free kept him from recognizing the error.>"

<Arizesyley> smiled. "<You know about letting your confidence keep you from recognizing an error, do you not?>"

<Kedekitley> frowned. "<I made an error one time.>"

"<The structure collapsed.>"

"<The error taught me to always review my mathematical calculations to ensure the mathematical calculations are error free. The mathematical calculations tool my human friend used would be useful. I should ask my human friend for a mathematical calculations tool to add to my tools collection. Other dragons might also benefit from using a mathematical calculations tool.>" He paused before saying, "<I am off topic.>"

"<What was your intended topic?>"

"<My human friend now understands I have useful skills for designing solutions to problems.>"

"<Does the human's new understanding mean the human will no longer ask you to perform physical labor?>"

"<My human friend might still want me to perform physical labor. I am superior to the humans when it comes to performing physical labor. However, I hope my human friend will ask me to do more tasks that require thinking.>"

"<I remind you the Council said dragons are not to interact with the humans.>"

He pulled <Arizesyley> into his arms. "<And, I remind you the Council said no to eradicating the humans. I am becoming more inclined to believe the humans will not attack again.>"

"<I do not accept that the humans will not attack again. I will continue flying my patrols.>"

Chapter 34

Sten

Double-check One's Decimal Points

When Sten arrived home, Asa rushed to him, hugged him, and said, "You're safe."

"Of course I'm safe."

"I was afraid the monster would harm you."

"He's not a monster."

Asa kept hugging.

Sten hugged back and said, "I'm sorry I made you worry, but it makes me feel good that you do. When Dragon first began showing up and you confronted him, I worried about you too. But, we don't need to worry. Dragon is friendly. He would never harm anyone." After a pause, he said, "Has Anitra come home?"

"She's in her room. She said she had extra homework to do."

"I'm going to check on her then I'll give you a report about today's events."

∞∞∞∞

Sten knocked on Anitra's door.

From behind the door came a gasping squeak, a thump, a rustling, another lighter thump, and then, "Come in."

Sten opened the door. Anitra sat in her chair crooked relative to the desk.

"Oh, it's you. Hi, Dad."

"Are you okay?"

"I'm fine. I was working on my extra homework."

On the desk lay her journal and several homework papers. Shoved to the side were scissors, scraps of undyed cotton cloth, loose pieces of cotton fluff stuffing, and a needle and thread. On the bed lay a blanket sloppy and awry with a couple of lumps under it.

Looking at the papers, Sten said, "Your homework looks finished."

Anitra turned her chair toward the desk, "I'm almost done. I must review my work one more time. One should always double-check one's decimal points."

Sten smiled and said, "That is a good lesson. I hope you learned it well."

"I learned a lot today."

Sten scowled. "I expect you not to sneak off again."

"I'm sorry, Dad." She dipped her chin. "I won't do it again, I promise."

"Very well. I'll leave you to your ... work." He glanced at the blanket on the bed, ruffled her hair, and left the room, closing the door behind him.

∞∞∞∞

Waiting at the table, Asa patted Sten's place and said, "Please, tell me what happened today."

He sat and said, "Dragon is more than I thought he was."

"In what way?"

"He's smart."

Asa crossed her arms on the table. "You mean he's deceptive and is fooling you?"

"No, he's smart, as in educated. He looked at my bridge design and found a math error, an error that would have caused a failure of the bridge, an error that would have killed people. He found the error by doing the math in his head."

"Dragons can't do math."

"That's what I thought. But, like in so many ways, I underestimated him. He's remarkable."

"I can't accept that."

"Regardless, I have to rework my design, thanks to him — which is a good thing." Sten took Asa's hand in his. "Don't you see? I've come to realize he and I aren't that different." Then he thought about how

Dragon had made his heroic pose when Anitra said he was amazing. "Except, he might be sillier than I am." He paused and added, "I should also mention Anitra."

"What about Anitra?"

He smiled and said, "Few things are worse, or more rewarding, than having a precocious child."

Asa's brow creased. "What did she do this time?"

"She was there."

"You let Anitra go with you?"

"No. After I dropped her off at school, she snuck down to the creek and hid behind a bush while I was talking with Dragon. Dragon noticed her and pointed her out to me."

"I'm going to have a word with her."

"The issue was handled. Professor Hutchmen gave her extra homework for skipping part of school and I've spoken to her about it. She promised she wouldn't do it again."

Asa sighed. "Precocious, indeed."

∞∞∞∞

Sten worked the remainder of the day, the next day, and into the next day on an updated bridge design paying special attention to his work, especially decimal points, to avoid embarrassing himself again. To have copies of the design and its accompanying notes to give to Dragon, Sten asked Ned and Ted to replicate the documents using their colloid replication machine. On the morning of the third day, Sten went to the wagon yard.

Chapter 35

<Kedekitley>

Full of Surprises

Human had been sitting in the middle of the open space, but he now stood and watched <Kedekitley> circling. <Kedekitley> detected numerous humans hiding around the periphery of the open space, but he saw no armored humans.

Decision made, he folded his wings, dropped toward the ground, spread his wings again at the last moment, made a gentle four-point landing, and said, "I will not violate the Paladins' Peace."

"Dragon, I'm glad you came." With none of the hesitancy he had shown before, Human stepped closer. "I have my revised bridge design, and I want to explain the numbers and symbols so you can interpret it."

"Proceed."

Human handed him a plant fiber cord and said, "This is one of those precise measurements I mentioned. This is the length of a pace." Then he handed him a metal cylinder with a knob on top that Human held as a handle. "This is another precise measurement. It's a bronze calibration weight with the mass of one sten." <Kedekitley> took the two items. "This is the bridge design and notes." Human displayed and explained the design pages and a set of notes about the symbols, the human numbering system, and the human measurement system. He then said, "I'm assuming you have your own way of doing the math, so I won't explain how I do it." He handed <Kedekitley> the design and notes documents.

"I understand what you have taught me." <Kedekitley> returned the notes documents.

"Those notes are to help you interpret what I've written." Human pushed the documents back. "You should take those with you."

"I learned what you taught me."

"If you say so, but I'd feel better if you'd take those in case you need to reference them."

<Kedekitley> huffed. "I will take them with me." He lifted his left wing and stretched open his pouch.

Human gasped and said, "What in the world?"

"What is the problem?"

"Dragons have pockets?"

<Kedekitley> placed the documents inside his pouch. "Dragons have pouches, one on each side, that allow us to carry our eggs until they are close to hatching and to carry our hatchlings until they become dragonets and are large enough to fly on their own. The pouches are also useful for carrying other items."

"May I look at it, and touch it?"

"You may look at and touch my pouch."

Human pulled the pouch open and said, "It's not a pouch. It's a pocket." After the examination, Human said, "Amazing. You're full of surprises."

"Thank you."

"You're welcome. Do you have any questions?"

"I have no questions."

"I have tasks I've been putting off that I must complete. So, can you meet me here again in five days, if that's enough time for you to review the bridge design?"

"Five days is adequate for reviewing the bridge design."

"Okay. We're set."

"I will return in five days."

<Kedekitley> took flight feeling good about everything.

Chapter 36

Sten

What's Happening to You

"Dragons have pockets."

Asa pulled back in Sten's arms in the midst of their greeting hug. "What are you blabbering about?"

"Dragons have pockets on their sides under their wings. And, I got to touch him. He looks like he's covered in scales, but he's not. His hide just has a pattern etched into it. He feels supple or pliable or — well, he feels warm and comfy."

"Sten, what's happening to you?"

"I'm learning more about Dragon. He's amazing."

Asa turned away. "You got people around the village talking about that dragon as if dragons are friendly."

"Dragons are friendly."

"You've only met one."

"I've met two, sort of, but I don't think the one that destroyed the carriage represented a typical dragon, and that was a different circumstance — they were at war. It's true Dragon's the only dragon I've gotten to know, but he's friendly, and amazing."

Asa sighed. "I don't know what to do about this."

Sten took her hand. "There's nothing to do. I'm keeping Dragon away from the village, and making use of his skills to get work done. Things are going well."

Chapter 37

<Kedekitley>

The Orphaned Human Child

When <Arizesyley> entered the weyr, <Kedekitley> bounced to her to give her his greeting hug. "<I love you and missed you. What did you find?>"

"<I also love you and missed you. I found nothing.>"

"<The humans are not preparing to attack.>"

"<Give the humans the opportunity and the humans will attack.>" <Arizesyley> huffed then said, "<What are you working on?>"

Taking her to his drafting table, <Kedekitley> said, "<This is the design my human friend created for the bridge he wants me to help construct. The design is excellent, and sophisticated. The humans appear to be more sophisticated than we believe them to be. I am analyzing the design to ensure there are no mathematical calculation errors.>"

"<The Council said dragons are not to interact with the humans, and now you are validating the humans' mathematical calculations?>"

She scowled at him and thus began again their discussion about making friends with the humans versus eradicating the humans and how either way they both thought the Council's edicts were wrong.

When the discussion concluded, <Arizesyley> walked toward the weyr entrance. "<I am flying another patrol.>" At the foyer, she looked back and said, "<I love you. You are the best dragon. I am glad you are my life-mate.>"

Even though he wished she had stayed with him, he understood she felt frustrated and sought to suppress the feeling by flying another patrol. To ease his angst, <Kedekitley> immersed himself in mathematical calculations.

∞∞∞∞

<Arizesyley> returned. <Kedekitley> bounded to her, embraced her as he always did, and said, "<I love you and missed you. What did you find?>" He sniffed. "<Why are you emitting the scent of the humans?>"

<Arizesyley> pulled something out of her pouch and set it down.

<Kedekitley> reeled back. "<Where did you acquire a human child?>"

The human child ducked behind <Arizesyley's> leg and peeked at <Kedekitley> with eyes the green color of plant leaves. Tangles of hair a color almost as dark as burnt plants swathed her head and dangled to her shoulders. Her skin was almost the same color as the dust that covered her except for an irregular spot of red on her left cheek that flowed down the left side of her neck to where it disappeared under her clothing and reappeared where her left arm protruded from her clothing.

<Arizesyley> said, "<The human child was orphaned.>" In the human language, she said to the human child, "Do not be afraid. This dragon is my life-mate. He is a good dragon. Sometimes, he is too good. He helps the humans by validating their mathematical calculations." She glowered at <Kedekitley> with creased brow.

<Kedekitley> continued speaking in the dragon language. "<Why did you bring her to our weyr?>"

"<Her? How do you know the human child's gender?>" She moved to look at the human child, but the human child moved to stay behind her.

"<I was taught to identify a human's gender using ultrasound and scent signatures that contain gender specific data points. If you are not correct, the human will correct you. Regardless, you need to return the human child to the humans.>"

The human child moved to stay behind <Arizesyley> every time she moved keeping <Arizesyley> between her and him.

"<The human child's parents were murdered by the humans. I could not leave the human child alone and in danger of not surviving. Dragons nurture food animals, although, the human child is not a food animal. The human child is a sophont.>"

"<Your instincts activated; so, even though you want to eradicate the humans, you brought the human child to our weyr?>" <Kedekitley>

tried to get another look at the human child, but the human child continued moving to stay hidden behind <Arizesyley>. He began to think the brief look he had when <Arizesyley> first set her down would be the only look he ever had of her. "<You need to return the human child to the nearest human town to where you found the human child. I will go with you.>"

<Arizesyley> paused, looking at nothing in particular. Finally, she said, "<You are correct. It is best that I return the human child to the humans. I can do the task on my own. I am brave, and I will be vigilant. You stay here.>" She put the human child back into her pouch. As she left, she said, "<That the humans murder other humans as well as dragons is more evidence the humans are monsters and need to be eradicated.>"

As he watched her leave, <Kedekitley> tried not to worry, after all <Arizesyley> was capable. He returned to performing mathematical calculations.

∞∞∞∞

<Kedekitley> rose to rush to <Arizesyley> as she came into the weyr, but froze when he saw she was clutching the human child to her chest. She set the human child down.

<Kedekitley> said, "<You did not return the human child.>"

The human child curled up in the corner and cried.

"<You are damaged.>" <Kedekitley> rushed to <Arizesyley> to examine her cuts, scrapes, and gouges.

"<I am not damaged.>"

"<You have gashes.>"

"<I am well. The gashes are superficial.>"

"<Did the humans do this to you?>" He wrapped his arms and tail around her and laid his head against her neck. "<I am sorry I told you to go to the human town. I should have accompanied you. I should have gone in your place. You being damaged is my fault. I did not expect the humans to attack you.>"

<Arizesyley> wrapped her tail around him. "<The incident is not your fault. I was being brave and doing what we thought was best for the human child.>"

Glancing to the human child, he said, "<Is the human child damaged?>"

"<I scanned the human child with my ultrasound. I detected no damage.>"

The human child cried out, "Why, why, why did you take me there?"

"I was returning you to the humans."

"The Cultists want to kill me."

<Kedekitley> said, "<What happened?>"

"<The humans attempted to murder the human child. I told you the humans are monsters and must be eradicated.>" To the human child <Arizesyley> said, "I am sorry, human child. I did not understand the humans wanted to damage you." She freed herself from <Kedekitley>, went to the human child, hooked an arm around her, and said, "I promise to never let the humans damage you, ever."

<Kedekitley> crouched next to <Arizesyley> and the human child and said, "<What will you do?>"

"<I will keep the human child.>"

"<You know nothing about the humans. How do you think we can care for the human child?>"

"<Did you say *we*?>"

"<If you keep the human child, I too keep the human child.>"

"<You are the best dragon, but me choosing to keep my human child makes my human child my responsibility.>" <Arizesyley> brushed her human child's hair to dislodge pieces of plant.

"<I accept you wanting to be responsible for your human child, but I will assist you.>"

"<Thank you. Since you know about the humans, you can tell me what to do.>" Then, <Arizesyley> clasped <Kedekitley's> hands and, in a panicky tone, said, "<What should I do?>"

"<Based on what I have observed, you must first show your human child where to make a toilet for when she needs to reduce her mass and where to find clean water for drinking.>"

"<That is a beginning. While I do that, construct a nest for my human child.>" <Arizesyley> took her human child and left the weyr.

<Kedekitley> paused as he pondered the problem of this unexpected turn of events, decided the solution to the problem was simply to except the situation, and then he turned his thoughts to constructing a nest.

Nest construction was easy, when one had the necessary materials. The problem he had to solve was that he had no nest constructing materials and it was too late in the day to collect materials. The solution: pilfer materials from the existing nest. He pulled several tree boughs from the rim of the nest, weaved the boughs into a wreath on the floor, and removed some of the nest bed plants from the existing nest to distribute inside the wreath.

When <Arizesyley> and her human child returned, <Kedekitley> showed <Arizesyley> the temporary nest in the corner. "<I did not have the materials for constructing another nest. Instead, I removed some of the materials from our nest to construct a place for your human child to sleep. Tomorrow, I will gather the materials needed to construct a proper nest.>"

<Arizesyley> said, "<Thank you,>" and then to her human child, she said, "You will sleep here."

After she placed her human child in the temporary nest, <Arizesyley> joined <Kedekitley> in their nest.

<Arizesyley> said, "<Did you notice the red highlight on my human child's cheek, neck, and arm? I did not know the humans had highlights as dragons do.>"

"<I had noticed the highlight. No other human I have seen has had dragon-like highlights.>"

"<The highlight means my human child is special.>"

∞∞∞∞

Not long into the night, <Kedekitley> heard <Arizesyley's> human child moving about and crying.

<Arizesyley> said, "<My human child's body temperature is below what I thought was the normal body temperature for my human child.>"

"<Your human child must be cold.>"

"<You did not tell me the humans become cold.>"

"<The clothing the humans wear is supposed to keep the humans warm. That is what Xenkerdecley told me. Why else would the humans wear clothing?>"

<Arizesyley> nudged <Kedekitley> with her snout. "<You do not know much about the humans, do you?>"

He nudged her back. "<I know some things about the humans.>"

To her human child, <Arizesyley> said, "I am sorry, human child. I did not know you would become cold. Come to our nest. I will keep you warm."

Her human child whimpered and said, "I can't see you."

"<That is something else I should mention,>" <Kedekitley> said. "<Besides having limited visual acuity, the humans see poorly when light intensity is low.>"

"<That information is useful to know. Is there more information I need to know?>"

"<There is probably more information. I will tell you when I think of more information.>"

"Come toward my voice. You will encounter nothing between where you are and where I am." <Arizesyley's> human child took careful steps as she came toward the nest. "You are progressing well." A moment later <Arizesyley> said, "One more step and you will touch the nest. Climb in."

<Arizesyley's> human child climbed into the nest. <Arizesyley> wrapped an arm around her and drew her close, but her human child continued crying.

<Arizesyley> said, "Why are you still crying?"

"Mommy and Daddy are dead." <Arizesyley's> human child's breaths were uneven. "They told me to run and hide. They said they would stop the Cultists." She stopped speaking for a moment then said, "The Cultists killed them. My fault, my fault, my fault."

<Arizesyley> remained silent, her human child still sobbing, before she said, "I know how you feel."

"How can you know how I feel?"

"Because ... my parents were also murdered by the humans."

<Arizesyley's> human child gasped and stopped her crying. "What happened?"

"The humans with Gird-metal armor and Gird-metal murder weapon swords attacked the weyr where my parents and I lived. The humans had new murder weapon crossbows that shot Gird-metal bolts." <Arizesyley> paused, taking several breaths. "My parents told me to run and hide. They said they would stop the humans. The humans murdered my parents." <Arizesyley> began crying. Between her sobs, she said, "It is not your fault the humans murdered your parents anymore than it is my fault the humans murdered my parents. It is not our fault. We should not blame ourselves."

<Kedekitley> had never heard <Arizesyley> speak of the loss of her parents in such stark terms. His heart ached for her. Together <Arizesyley> and her human child cried. Tears came to <Kedekitley's> eyes as he breathed deeply to keep himself from crying.

As he did every time <Arizesyley> cried in the night, <Kedekitley> comforted her by covering her with his wing. This night, he also covered her human child.

∞∞∞∞

Morning had just arrived when <Arizesyley's> human child said, "I'm hungry."

"<That is something else I should mention,>" <Kedekitley> said. "<The humans consume human food several times per day. I will acquire human food for your human child.>" He rubbed his head on <Arizesyley> and trotted out of the weyr.

Stopping on the flight deck outside the weyr, he looked around. Where to find the grass the humans used as human food? He'd never considered such a thing before. He needed a special type of grass. Grass covered the meadow outside the weyr, but the grass was too short to be the human food grass humans preferred. <Xenkerdecley> had described the human food grass as being tall. <Kedekitley> also thought the grass needed to be soft and moist.

He flew north toward a cirque that held a small lake and a meadow that might contain the correct type of grass to be human food grass. Landing in the middle of the meadow, he analyzed the grass and decided the grass was ideal. The grass had the same luminous color as

<Arizesyley's> magnificent green highlights and a delightful aroma that reminded him of growing up with his nest filled with similar grass. Maybe he should add grass to <Arizesyley's> and his nest. Then he thought better of it — <Arizesyley's> human child would consume the nest. He used a talon as a scythe to cut a bundle of human food grass and returned to the weyr.

He delivered the human food grass to <Arizesyley>. She scrunched her face and said, "<Thank you. This looks ... delicious.>" She forced a smile to cover her grimace, turned to her human child, handed her the grass, and said, "This human food is for you."

Her human child accepted the grass, stared at the stalks with an odd crease in her brow, and said, "It's ... grass."

<Arizesyley> nodded. <Kedekitley> nodded along with her.

"People don't eat grass."

The surprise caused <Kedekitley> to gape.

<Arizesyley's> shoulders slumped and she cocked her head before saying, "All right then. Are you certain the humans do not consume grass? My parents taught me the humans consume grass."

"I'm sure people don't eat grass."

<Arizesyley> turned to <Kedekitley> and said, "<If the humans do not consume grass, what human food do the humans consume?>"

"<I did not pay attention to the human food my human friend consumed,>" said <Kedekitley>. "<I assumed the human food was grass.>"

"<That is not helpful.>"

<Kedekitley> looked at the weyr's ceiling as he sought a solution to the problem. He could design only one solution. "<We must ask the humans what human food to feed your human child.>"

<Arizesyley> frantically shook her head. "<The humans want to murder my human child. The humans are monsters and must be eradicated.>"

"<What else can we do besides ask the humans? We can visit my human friend's human town. The humans in my human friend's human town have been good to me. Although, the first time I visited, the humans appeared frightened, but the humans did not attack me. I believe the

humans will help us. I will accompany you and stand by your side to protect you, but I do not believe the humans in my human friend's human town will attack us.>"

<Arizesyley> frowned and opened her mouth to speak, but hesitated when she glanced toward her human child who was staring at them, feet apart, fists on hips with elbows akimbo, brows pinched, and the corners of her lips turned down. <Kedekitley> had seen Human make a similar facial expression when Human became angry with the other humans at the structure construction site. He knew something was about to happen.

Turning to <Kedekitley>, <Arizesyley> said, "<How many of the humans do you know?>"

"<I only interact with my human friend. My human friend interacts with the other humans.>"

<Arizesyley> snorted, narrowed her eyes, and said, "<You know one human you believe is a good human, and based on that you believe the other humans are also good humans? I do not trust the humans and I do not want to go to the human town.>"

<Kedekitley> motioned toward <Arizesyley's> human child. "<Your human child needs to consume human food. We need information about human food and how to care for your human child. I cannot design a another solution to the problem.>"

"Please, stop, stop, stop. Don't talk about me when I can't understand you." <Arizesyley's> human child's outburst silenced both of them and left <Kedekitley> startled even though he had expected something to happen. "What were you saying about me?"

<Arizesyley> said, "My life-mate and I will go to the human town to ask the humans what human food to feed you."

"No, no, no. Please, don't leave me."

"I will take you with me."

<Arizesyley's> human child backed into the corner. "No, no, no, they'll kill me."

"We will go to the human town where my life-mate's human friend lives. My life-mate says the humans in his human friend's human town are good humans."

"No, no, no."

Lowering her head to be level with her human child, <Arizesyley> said, "I trust my life-mate's judgment that the humans in his human friend's human town are good humans. We need information the humans can provide."

Her human child crossed her arms, creased her brow, forced the corners of her lips down, but remained silent as she shook her head.

<Kedekitley> looked from one to the other as <Arizesyley> and her human child argued. What would they do if her human child refused to go to the human town? It would be wrong to force her human child to go to the human town. <Arizesyley> wanted to be the one to go to the human town instead of letting <Kedekitley> go alone because she felt responsible for her human child. He couldn't design a solution to the problem.

"Come with me," <Arizesyley> said. "I promise to protect you. I will not allow you to be damaged."

<Arizesyley's> human child provided the solution to the problem when she softened her expression and said, "Okay, okay, okay, I'll go. But, I'll be angry with you if they try to kill me again."

"I will keep you safe." <Arizesyley> stretched open a pouch and said, "Climb into my pouch."

Before climbing in, <Arizesyley's> human child said, "It's a pocket."

Chapter 38

Sten

Two Dragons in the Plaza

Sten and everyone else in the meeting were startled to their feet by the loud clanging from the bell tower on top of the building. The bell tolled the rapid, panicked pattern that indicated a dragon attack.

Over the din, Sten said, "Oh, bother. We'll reschedule this meeting." He put on his hat, ran out of the administration building, stopped a woman charging past, and said, "Please, report."

"Two dragons in the plaza. Everyone's afraid more may be coming. The knights are on their way. Excuse me, I have places to be."

"Thank you," said Sten, but the woman had already run away. The bell went silent as Sten dashed toward where he needed to be.

People who had not run away were taking positions at the corners of buildings to watch the excitement in the plaza. Sten pushed past them. In the plaza, Dragon and a new dragon were facing Asa and Ned and Ted.

Sten kept running as he yelled, "Please, stop."

Dragon appeared calm with his wings closed, but the new dragon had her wings out and up and ready for flight.

He reached Asa, paused to catch a breath, and said, "I'll handle this."

From the tilt of her helmeted head, Sten knew the expression she wore beneath. To Ned and Ted, she said, "Please, stand down, but stay here and stay ready." The three knights, in unison, sheathed their swords then Ned began checking fasteners on his armor.

Sten approached Dragon and said, "Dragon, it's good to see you, but ... what's going on? We're not scheduled to meet again for four more days, and you're not supposed to land in the plaza."

Dragon said, "Human, I am pleased to see you. My life-mate and I need information."

After studying the new dragon — she had striking yellow zigzag highlights and acted as if she was concealing something — Sten said, "Information? About what?"

"We need information about how to care for my human child," said the new dragon with an accent not quite as strong as Dragon had had when Sten first talked to him. The dragon pulled a child out of her pocket and set her down. The child ducked behind the new dragon's leg and peeked out at Sten.

Sten gasped and said, "Where did you get her?"

Sasha, Sochi, and Anitra came running from the bakery that fronted the plaza. Several people came out from behind the buildings to gather around to get a better view. The new dragon tensed her wings and moved closer to Dragon. The child stayed close to her.

Sasha said, "Please, come here child, we'll help you."

From behind the new dragon, the child said, "No, no, no."

The new dragon picked up the child, brought her wings around to conceal her, and said, "I am responsible for my human child. I will not allow my human child to be damaged."

Dragon said, "I too will not allow my life-mate's human child to be damaged."

Sten opened his mouth to speak but Sochi interrupted before he could.

Sochi said, "We won't harm her."

From under the new dragon's mantled wings, the child said, "No, no, no. Please, don't give me to them. They'll kill me."

The new dragon said, "We need information about how to care for my human child."

Sasha said, "What kind of information?"

"What human food should I feed my human child?"

"I'm hungry," said the child from under the new dragon's wings.

Sochi turned to Anitra and said, "Anitra, please, fetch a box of cinnamon breadsticks."

"Yes, Grandpa." Anitra ran to the bakery.

Sasha said, "Why does she think we'll kill her?"

"The humans attempted to murder my human child. The humans are monsters. I now keep my human child safe, but I need information about how to care for my human child."

Sochi said, "Who tried to kill her?"

The child said, "Cultists."

Sten wanted to say something, but he didn't know what to say. When he had come running, he had believed he would be handling the dragons. However, Sasha and Sochi had taken that duty leaving him feeling useless.

Anitra returned with a box and handed it to Sochi.

"Thank you, Anitra. Here child, we have food for you."

The child said, "No, no, no."

When Sochi stepped forward, the new dragon stepped back, tightened her wings, laid back her ears, bared her teeth, and growled a low rumble that Sten could feel in his sinuses. He had heard Dragon growl once, but that had been a growl of frustration. Even though the new dragon intended to appear formidable, Sten didn't think she meant any harm. This growl simply meant *back off*.

Sochi, moved back a step, held out a placating hand and said, "It's okay. I won't harm her."

Sochi's words did not appear to calm the new dragon. She glanced at Dragon who simply sat in a relaxed pose, apparently intending it to be a subtle message to the new dragon to stay calm.

"Anitra, you're less threatening." Sochi handed Anitra the box. "Please, take them to her."

Asa said, "No," and moved forward.

The new dragon tensed and appeared ready to leap skyward.

As if he could stop the dragon-slayer knight, Sten held Asa, her armor cold against his arms, and said, "It's okay. They won't harm Anitra."

Asa stopped, but rocked from foot to foot, hand on the hilt of her sheathed long sword, every muscle tense and ready for action.

Anitra went halfway toward the new dragon, sat in the grass, and said, "Please, let me give her one of these. They're good."

Anitra had wanted so badly to see dragons. She was getting a good look now. Sten kept telling himself dragons were friendly and not a threat, and he believed it or he wouldn't have let Anitra do what she was doing.

The new dragon bobbed her head, paused, glanced at Dragon, who continued to display a calm demeanor, opened her wings, and set the child down. The child tried to hide behind the new dragon again, but the new dragon pushed the child out in front and said, "Let the human child give you the human food."

"These are cinnamon breadsticks. They're good." Anitra removed a breadstick from the box, took a bite, and said, "Yum."

Looking at the new dragon, the child said, "Please, come with me."

The child sat opposite Anitra with the box between them. The new dragon, towering over the children at many times their height, sat behind the child and looped her tail around herself, but she kept her wings partially spread.

Anitra said, "They're made of a special kind of bread that's rolled up with butter and sugar and cinnamon inside." She showed the layers in the one she had bitten. "And, they're covered with sugar and cinnamon. See, the white stuff is sugar and the brown stuff is cinnamon." After taking another bite, she picked up a second breadstick, and held it out to the child.

The child took the breadstick, bit into it, and smiled.

Anitra said, "What's your name?"

Between bites, the child said, "*Naia.*"

The new dragon said, "You have a human name?"

"Yes. It's *Naia.*"

"Why did you not tell me you have a human name?"

"You never asked."

"My name is *Anitra,*" said Anitra. Pointing behind her, she said, "That's my grandma, *Sasha,* and grandpa, *Sochi.* They're bakers. That dragon-slayer knight," she pointed, "is my mom. Her name is *Asa.* When she's not being a Knight Sergeant, she's a tailor." She pointed at Sten. "That's my dad. He's Grandma and Grandpa's child. His name is *Sten.* He builds things."

Dragon gaped at Sten and said, "You have a human name?"

Sten smiled. "Yes. It's *Sten.*"

"I always call you *Human.* You never corrected me."

"*Human* works."

"A *sten* is the human measurement for mass."

Sten laughed and said, "It's a different sten. A *sten* is the measurement for mass, but *Sten* is also my name."

After a sigh, <Kedekitley> said, "The human language is terrible. I do not understand how the humans communicate without confusion."

"We manage ... most of the time."

Asa said, "I've heard you call this one *Dragon*. What do you call the other one?"

"Calling Dragon *Dragon* works well with him calling me *Human*, but," he pointed toward the new dragon, "I don't know her."

"You don't know that dragon and you let Anitra approach her?"

"She's a good dragon."

"How do you know?"

"First off, dragons don't harm people. Furthermore, she's Dragon's mate. Dragon wouldn't have a mate that wasn't as good as he is. So, I know she'd never want to harm anyone."

Dragon gave the new dragon a wink. Sten wondered what it meant. Was it some sort of secret joke between them?

Sasha said, "What's your name?"

The new dragon held her head up in a show of pride and said, "I am <*Arizesyley*>."

Sten said, "People can't make some of the music-like and growly noises of the dragon language, so we can't say their actual names. That's why you have to give them a name."

Naia said, "Her name is *Cinnamon*."

Sochi said, "Why *Cinnamon*?"

Naia held up another breadstick and compared it to the new dragon's arm. "Because — well, except for her beautiful red, green, blue, and yellow colors — she's the color of cinnamon; therefore, her name is *Cinnamon*." She pointed at Dragon. "His name is *Spice*."

Sten said, "His name is *Dragon*."

Naia's adamant response was, "No, no, no, his name is *Spice*. Cinnamon and Spice and Naia are nice." She laughed then ate the breadstick.

"Maybe we should ask them if it's okay to call them *Cinnamon* and *Spice*," said Sten. "I think that would be the polite thing to do."

The two dragons exchanged glances then Cinnamon said, "Calling me *Cinnamon* and calling <Kedekitley> *Spice* is acceptable."

Sten stepped closer to Dragon and said in a whisper, "I'll keep calling you *Dragon* because it's more awe-inspiring."

Dragon said, "I will keep calling you *Human* because the name is descriptive."

Cinnamon said, "May we have more of the human food to take with us?"

Sasha said, "Please, leave Naia with Sochi and me. We'll care for her."

"No, no, no." Naia tried to hide behind Cinnamon again.

Cinnamon picked up Naia and said, "I promised my human child — Naia — that I will keep Naia safe from the humans. I will care for Naia. May we have more of the human food?"

"She needs more than cinnamon breadsticks. In fact, the breadsticks should only be an occasional treat. She needs a balanced diet with," using her fingers, Sasha counted off each item as she went, "fruits and vegetables, and meat and fish, dairy products, beans and nuts, and things like bread and noodles and cereal made with grain." Then she waved a hand. "And, she's filthy and needs to be washed. And, she needs new clothes; what she's wearing are in tatters. And, she needs boots."

Cinnamon made small circles with her wings and her tail twitched.

Sasha made calming motions with her hands. "Please, don't leave. I understand you won't give her up, and apparently, she doesn't want to leave you. We'll gather supplies you can take with you."

Sasha pointed and beckoned. Three people from the crowd came to her and Sochi. Sten hesitated as Asa made hand signals to Ned and Ted, who stood straighter and placed their hands on the hilts of their swords, before she followed him to the huddle and removed her helmet.

Asa whispered, "Knight Ned and Knight Ted and I are ready to rescue the child."

After glancing at the dragons, Sasha used even quieter tones to say, "Please, no."

"We can handle the dragons."

"Please, not so loud. We'll give them what they want."

Before Asa could speak again, Sasha shushed her and said, "Please, trust me."

Sten said, "I agree with Councilmember Sasha. We give them what they want. They won't harm Naia. They want to care for her."

Continuing with her almost inaudible whisper, Sasha said, "We'll make it so they'll need to return in a few days.

"Apprentice Serath, please, go to the warehouse and fill a box with enough food to last about three days. Fruits, and vegetables like peas, corn, and potatoes, and some rattidash root. Toss in some spices too. And, dried meat, cheese, and bread.

"Inn Keeper Tintasen, please, fetch a box of household items like cooking pots, plates, bowls, cups, utensils, canteens, a blanket and pillow, personal care items, pails, towels, soap, fire starters, and anything else you can think of for someone who would be camping.

"Merchant Yacha, please, fetch one of your child-sized washing tubs."

Sasha turned to Anitra who was trying to squeeze into the group and said, "Anitra, the clothes you recently outgrew should fit Naia. Would you like to give her some trousers and shirts, and boots, and a coat?"

"Yes, Grandma." Anitra extracted herself from between Sasha and Sten and ran off.

Turning to the huddle, Sasha said, "Please, take whomever else you need from the crowd to help you. Are there any questions?" When no one spoke, she said, "You're dismissed."

As the group broke and people ran off in different directions, Sten pulled a man from the crowd and said, "Skipper Bekka, please, fetch a cargo net from the docks."

Sasha turned to Cinnamon and said, "We're gathering supplies. Please, be patient."

Asa put on her helmet and returned to Ned and Ted making hand signals again as she approached them. Ned and Ted removed their hands from their swords and resumed an at ease stance. Sten knew dragon-slayer knights had a hand signaling language — although, Asa had never taught him anything about the hand signals — he could guess what she had said to them, and he was glad she had them stand down.

Sten turned to the dragons and noticed Dragon resettling his wings and returning to a sitting position. Dragon's wings had been tightly closed when Sten entered the group huddle, and he had been sitting. He must have stood while Sten wasn't looking, but he now resumed his relaxed pose. Cinnamon glanced at Dragon who made a gesture with his head that prompted Cinnamon to set Naia on the ground. Sten firmly believed dragons didn't harm people, but that might not hold true if they had to defend themselves from attack. Asa had said the only time dragons actually fought was when they were trapped or they were protecting other dragons as they fled. Had Dragon been ready to do just that?

"What's wrong with Naia's skin?" said Sasha. "I thought it was dirt, but it's not all dirt."

"No, no, no." Naia grasped at Cinnamon. "They want to kill me."

Cinnamon picked up and cradled Naia and again mantled her wings. "I will not allow Naia to be damaged."

From under Cinnamon's wings, Naia said, "My splotch is why the Cultists want to kill me."

"It's only a birthmark," said Sasha.

"The Cultists say it makes me a beast child."

"It doesn't make you a beast. Many people have birthmarks. I have one, although it's not as awesome as yours. It's on my — well," Sasha blushed, "it's located where I can't show it off."

Sten smiled at his mother's discomfiture then to Dragon he said, "Dragon, we really are willing to take Naia and care for her."

Naia said, "No, no, no. Please, don't give me to them."

Dragon said, "<Arizesyley> — Cinnamon — promised to care for Naia and to protect Naia. I will assist Cinnamon. The humans do not need to worry about Naia. Naia will be safe and well cared for."

"I know, and I trust you, but still —"

Tintasen and a helper arrived with two boxes. Bekka came with a net.

Sasha opened the two boxes. "These boxes contain all sorts of things like a blanket and pillow, teeth cleaner, hair brush, pails, towels, soap, cooking pots, plates, bowls, cups, eating utensils, fire starters, and canteens." Then she said, "And, here comes the washing tub."

Yacha, carrying a large, tin tub approached. Behind him came Anitra pulling her dark blue wagon whose wheels squeaked with every turn. Sten hadn't gotten around to fixing the squeaking problem, but he did have a solution in mind that involved applying lubricant.

"Are you hiding Naia again?" said Anitra. "Please, put her down so I can show her what I brought."

Cinnamon set Naia down, but Naia held on to the dragon's hand.

Anitra opened the box that rode in the wagon and said, "I brought all sorts of clothes, and a coat, and boots and socks, and books."

"Books?" Naia pulled Cinnamon with her as she went to the wagon and picked up one of the books.

Anitra said, "Do you know how to read?"

"Of course I know how to read. Mommy and Daddy —" Naia hesitated, clutched the locket hanging around her neck, swallowed hard, and said, "Mommy and Daddy taught me well."

"I have something special for you."

"All of these things are special."

"This is even more special."

From under the coat, Anitra pulled out a stuffed animal and handed it to Naia.

Naia said, "It's a dragon."

"A dragon?" cried out Asa as she flailed her arms. "I told you not to make a dragon."

"Oh, Mom. " To Naia, Anitra said, "Mom taught me how to make stuffed animals. She's shaped like Dad's dragon. When I made her, he had been the only dragon I'd seen."

Cinnamon said, "No dragon is that color."

"I only had cotton fabric and no dyes to color it."

Naia tried to hand the stuffed dragon back to Anitra. "No, no, no, I can't take your dragon."

Anitra refused to take the stuffed dragon. "It's okay. I made two of them."

"You made two of them?" Asa tried to step forward, but Sten held onto her.

"Oh, Mom." Anitra rolled her eyes and pulled a second, identical stuffed dragon from under the coat. "They're siblings. You keep one and I'll keep one."

Naia grinned, hugged the stuffed dragon, and said, "Thank you, thank you, thank you. I'll call her *Sugar*."

Asa gave up her half-hearted struggles in Sten's arms. Sten knew that if she had wanted to get away from him, there was nothing he could have done to stop his dragon-slayer knight spouse. Her outburst had been her way of expressing her opinion.

Serath returned with her box.

Sasha opened the box and said, "This box has food — fruits and vegetables, dried meat and fish, peas, corn, cheese, and bread. It's not a lot, but it'll last a few days. You'll have to return when you need more."

Cinnamon tilted her head and said, "All right then." She paused before continuing, "I am overwhelmed. I did not know caring for Naia would be complicated. I do not know where to begin. What is the purpose of that container?"

Sasha said, "It's a washing tub. You use it to wash laundry and to wash Naia."

Cinnamon tilted her head again. "All right then." After taking a breath, she said, "I do not know how to wash Naia."

"I'm not a baby." Naia's outburst froze everyone. "I can wash myself. I can dress myself. I can prepare food. I can read and write. I'm almost grown-up. I know how to use all these things. Mommy and Daddy taught me well." She again clutched the locket hanging around her neck.

Dragon said, "With so many containers, multiple trips will be required to transport the supplies."

"I have a solution to that problem," said Sten as Sochi and he spread the net. "This is a *cargo net*. We can load everything into it for you to carry in one trip."

Sten and the others placed the boxes into the net.

Cinnamon said, "I am responsible for Naia. I will carry the supplies."

Dragon stepped between her and the net. "I will carry the supplies while you carry Naia."

Cinnamon and Dragon stared at each other in an irresistible force meets an immoveable object sort of way. Sten moved back wondering how this would play out between these two immense and powerful creatures.

Finally, Cinnamon said, "You carry the supplies."

"Please, put the wagon in too." Anitra pulled the squeaking wagon to the net.

Naia said, "You're giving me your wagon?"

"I think you'll need it."

"Thank you, thank you, thank you."

Anitra held Naia's hand. "Dad has his dragon friend, but I've never met anyone who lives with dragons. Please, visit and tell me what it's like."

"That's a good point," said Sasha. "You need to return with Naia occasionally, and not just to fetch more supplies. You can't raise her to be a dragon. She needs to socialize with people so she knows how to be a person. She needs people friends. She needs to attend school."

Sochi said, "Please, remember, we're always here, ready and willing to help with anything you need."

Sten returned to Dragon's side. "Dragon, we're still scheduled to meet in four days. You can tell me then how things are going."

"I told Cinnamon the humans in this human town are good humans," said Dragon. "Thank you for your help. I have enjoyed seeing you again, Human." He took hold of the closed end of the cargo net and prepared to take flight.

Cinnamon put Naia, who still held the stuffed dragon, into a pocket and said, "I am tempted to believe what — Spice — said about the humans in this human town being good humans. Thank you for your help."

The two dragons took flight.

Sten had forgotten to use his chinstrap. His hat landed halfway to the bakery.

Marita brought Sten his hat where he stood with Sasha, Sochi, and Asa, and said, "We need to have a community meeting this evening. Please, be there, all of you."

Sasha said, "We'll be there, Mayor Marita."

Chapter 39

<Kedekitley>

Settling In

Naia refused help moving the supply boxes into the weyr saying she was *almost grown up and could do it herself.* She used the little blue wagon to carry the supply boxes. <Kedekitley> and <Arizesyley> winced with every agonizing squeak of the wagon's wheels.

<Kedekitley> shuddered at an especially loud wheel squeal and said, "<After what happened to you when you attempted to return your human child to the humans, I had worried I was wrong about good humans.>"

After rubbing her ear, <Arizesyley> said, "<I still believe the humans are monsters.>"

"<Some of the humans are good humans and some of the humans are bad humans. I am reassured the humans in my human friend's human town are good humans as good as my human friend.>"

"<The humans in your human friend's human town acted as if they were good humans, but I still believe the humans must be eradicated.>"

Naia said, "Done, done, done. Now I want to try out the tub."

<Arizesyley> tilted her head. "All right then." She exhaled and took another breath. "I do not know what to do with the washing tub."

"We fill it with hot water."

<Arizesyley> tilted her head to the other side. "All right then."

<Kedekitley> loved how cute <Arizesyley> looked when she was puzzled.

Naia sighed. "I can make a fire to heat water."

"We could use water from the hot spring. The hot spring water is already hot."

"You have a hot spring?"

"I will take you to the hot spring."

"We should take the tub, a pail, a towel, soap, brush, new clothes, and socks, and the boots." After putting the items in the wagon, Naia picked up the wagon's handle and said, "Please, show me, show me, show me."

"Wait." <Kedekitley> went to his tools collection to retrieve a container of friction reducing fluid. He applied the fluid to the wagon's wheel bearings, and said, "Now move the wagon." When Naia rolled the wagon, it didn't squeak. <Kedekitley> preened. "The problem is solved."

<Arizesyley> hooked her tail around him, rubbed her head on him, and said, "You are the best dragon."

He lifted his chin. "Thank you. While you learn how to use the washing tub, I will solve the problem of constructing a proper nest for Naia."

∞∞∞∞

<Kedekitley> watched <Arizesyley> lead Naia down the hot spring path, then gathered the cargo net and took flight.

First stop: tree boughs suitable for the nest's foundation. Second stop: tree boughs suitable for the nest's floor. Third stop: tree boughs suitable for the ring around the nest. Fourth stop: nest bed plants to make the nest soft. Fifth stop: pleasant aroma, yellow, five-pointed flowers. And, a sixth stop, one <Kedekitley> hadn't made in years when constructing or refreshing a nest: grass.

The cargo net was a wonderful solution to the problem of carrying many items. Dragons had a similar solution to the problem and it pleased him the humans were sophisticated enough to have the same idea. The risk with the solution was overloading the net, which could lead to a situation in which the mass in the net added to the mass of the dragon would result in a total mass that exceeded takeoff mass. While dragons were powerful fliers, the amount of their additional mass carrying capacity was limited.

In the weyr, he assembled the foundation, constructed a floor on that, enclosed the floor with a wreath of tree boughs, distributed the nest bed plants in the center, added the yellow, five-pointed flowers, and covered the new nest bed with grass. Lastly, he added the remaining grass to his and <Arizesyley's> nest.

He admired his work. He had always imagined someday he would construct a nest for his and <Arizesyley's> egg and hatchling, and a new nest for when the hatchling became a dragonet, and then, when the dragonet became a young-dragon, teach the young-dragon how to build their own nest. He had never imagined constructing a nest for a human child. What dragon would have?

∞∞∞

When <Arizesyley> and Naia entered the weyr, <Kedekitley> smiled, held his head high and proud, and said, "The problem is solved. Look at what I constructed."

Naia climbed in and bounced. "It's a nest, and it's my size, and it's soft, and it smells like honeystar flowers and fresh grass."

He gave the edge of the nest a pat of pride. "The nest is larger than you are. I constructed the nest to still fit when you become an adult-sized human."

<Arizesyley> said, "Do not consume the grass."

Naia scowled. "I told you, people don't eat grass."

"That is why I decided to add grass." He waved a few grass stalks. "Grass is a nice nest bed material and I now know Naia will not consume the grass."

<Arizesyley> hooked her tail around him, rubbed her head on him, and said, "You are the best dragon."

He puffed up with delight and said, "Thank you."

Naia retrieved the blanket and pillow from the supply boxes and put them in the nest.

<Kedekitley> said, "I placed your nest next to Cinnamon's and my nest. If you wish, the nest can be moved."

"This spot is perfect, perfect, perfect." Naia laid the cloth dragon on the pillow allowing the dragon's tail to drape onto the blanket. "Thank you, thank you, thank you."

<Arizesyley> felt the grass <Kedekitley> had placed into her and his nest. "<You added grass to our nest.>"

"<The grass reminds me of my nests while growing up. I wanted to try grass again, and to find out how you like grass.>"

345

"<The grass has a nice aroma. I am willing to learn how well grass works for sleeping.>"

"<You will like the grass, I am sure.>" He rubbed his head on her.

<Arizesyley> said, "<Fly a patrol for me. Because of today's activities, I have not had an opportunity to fly a patrol. I am concerned I will miss signs the humans are preparing to attack. I need evidence to present to the Council, but I must stay with my human child to keep my human child safe.>" Naia glared at <Arizesyley> who said to her, "I am not talking about you."

"<I will fly a patrol.>" <Kedekitley> loosened his wings and flexed his tail.

"<Thank you. Do you know where to patrol and what to look for?>"

"<Of course I know where to patrol and what to look for. I have flown patrols with you before.>" He loped out of the weyr to the flight deck and leaped into the sky.

∞∞∞∞

<Arizesyley> had changed her patrol route recently, but <Kedekitley> didn't know the details of those changes. He understood the value of using unpredictable patrol routes so the humans would never know when she would fly over if they even realized she was flying over. He decided he could patrol any route he wanted as long as he achieved the mission objective of spotting suspicious human activity, if any.

He flew south along the foothills, across the Lesser River, over multiple human towns, going as far south as it takes a human to travel in several days. Then he turned north flying close to the Great River that dominated the valley, passing over more human towns, past the armored humans' training place, over Human's human town, going as far north as it takes a human to travel in several days. He returned along the foothills and back to the weyr.

∞∞∞∞

At the weyr, he went to <Arizesyley>, who stood ready to accept his embrace, hugged her, and said, "<I love you and missed you.>"

<Arizesyley> snuggled in his hug before she said, "<I also love you

and missed you. What did you find?>"

"<I found nothing. However, the humans in my human friend's human town were gathering in their meeting structure. That activity is not suspicious. The humans are not preparing to attack.>"

"<Give the humans the opportunity and the humans will attack.>"

Naia came running. "Anitra gave me pajamas. I haven't had real pajamas since I outgrew my old ones. Anitra was so nice. I want to see her again."

<Arizesyley> said, "When I take you to the human town for more human food, you will see the human child Anitra. Now, you, Spice, and I must sleep."

"I'll get ready for bed." Naia paused before saying, "Please, come with me."

"Why do I need to come with you?"

"I don't want to go outside alone. Please, come with me to visit the necessary, wash my hands, and clean my teeth."

<Kedekitley> smiled and said, "<You keep saying you are responsible for your human child.>"

<Arizesyley> sighed and followed Naia outside.

<Kedekitley> examined the human food the humans had provided. The human food had been sorted into collections. The items the humans consider human food were strange, but indeed grass was not among the human food items.

He climbed into the nest, inhaled the aroma of the grass, and reminisced about when he was a hatchling, a dragonet, and a young-dragon living with his parents on the east side of the mountain range, a time when life was simpler, a time when he could never have imagined having a life-mate as marvelous as <Arizesyley>, a time when he could never have imagined having the humans in his life.

When <Arizesyley> and Naia returned, Naia went to her supplies. <Arizesyley> joined <Kedekitley> in their nest. After walking two circles and making little marching steps, she lay down to cuddle against him.

<Kedekitley> said, "<Did you learn how to use the washing tub to wash your human child?>"

"<My human child washed herself.>"

"<Why is the human food divided into collections?>"

"<My human child divided the human food into the collections. She called it a *meal plan.*>"

"<Did you help your human child?>"

"<My human child did not require my help. My human child is sophisticated.>"

<Kedekitley> agreed. <Arizesyley's> human child was sophisticated. The more he learned about the humans, the more impressed he became. The humans were more sophisticated than what he had been raised to believe.

Dressed in the clothing she had called *pajamas*, Naia sat on one of her supply boxes clutching the object she wore around her neck.

<Arizesyley> said, "Naia, are you well?"

"I'm fine." She came to the nest and said, "May I sleep with you again?"

"You have your own nest now."

"I know, I know, I know, but I want to be with you. Please."

<Arizesyley> hesitated before saying, "You may sleep with me."

"Thank you, thank you, thank you."

Naia prepared a sleeping place next to <Arizesyley> using the blanket and pillow, climbed in, snuggled with the cloth dragon, and nestled against the real dragon.

Naia said, "I love you, Mother."

"I am not your mother."

"You're not *Mommy*, but you take care of me. That makes you *Mother*. Spice is *Father*. You and Father are all I have. Thank you, thank you, thank you for taking care of me." After a pause and a scratch at the back of her neck, Naia said "Goodnight, Mother."

After her own pause, <Arizesyley> made a cooing sound, sighed, and said, "Goodnight, Naia."

For the first night in many nights, <Arizesyley> didn't cry.

<Kedekitley> pondered that Naia considered him her father. A strange concept, yet he understood Naia's meaning. Naia's meaning pleased him.

Chapter 40

Sten

Did You Not See What Was Happening

A capacity crowd again filled the meeting hall. Sochi, Anitra, Sten, Asa, and Ned and Ted sat in their accustomed seats. Sten looked for Viren and his hangers-on, but didn't see them. Rumor said they had left the village. Good riddance as far as he was concerned.

Marita and the Village Council, including Sasha, came onto the stage.

Marita banged her gavel and said, "I call this community meeting for the Village of Splain to order. Let's start with this." She turned to Sasha. "Councilmember Sasha, why did you let those dragons take that child?"

The mob murmured.

Asa stood. "Yes, why? Knight Ned and Knight Ted and I were ready to rescue the child."

Sten jumped to his feet. "Naia's safe."

The murmurs increased to a rumble.

Marita banged her gavel.

"I'm sorry, Mayor Marita." Sten sat.

Asa stayed standing.

"Please, order." Marita rapped her gavel again. When the crowd quieted, she said, "Please, finish what you were saying, Master Sten."

Sten stood and said, "Thank you, Mayor Marita. I keep telling everyone dragons don't harm people. Those two just want to take care of Naia, and need our help to do so."

Asa said, "How can you guarantee they won't harm her?"

"Nothing's absolute, so I can't guarantee it, but I found no evidence that dragons have ever harmed people, and I've learned enough about Dragon, or Spice, or whatever you want to call him, to trust him. And, by extension, I trust his mate."

The crowd again broke into rowdy noise.

Marita banged her gavel, but she was ignored.

Sasha stood and yelled, "Please, silence."

The room went quiet and everyone focused on Sasha.

Sten was impressed with the acoustics of the stage. The walls and ceiling were angled to focus the sound into the audience, which made this venue excellent for plays and concerts. However, the room itself needed something to dampen the noise made by the audience. Then again, his mother's voice was forceful. She would have been heard no matter what the acoustics. He had experienced his mother's forceful voice on several occasions while growing up.

Marita said, "The floor is yours, Councilmember Sasha."

Sasha said, "Thank you, Mayor Marita," and turned to look at Asa. "Did you not see what was happening?" Sasha then moved her gaze to the audience and continued, "The child, Naia, was terrified of us and she wasn't going to be willingly taken from that dragon. And, that dragon, Cinnamon, she was like a mother miser cat. You weren't getting between her and her kit. Moreover, she was terrified of us as well, and even more so of you, Sergeant Asa." She pointed at Asa. "Her wings were open and her muscles tense. She was ready at any provocation to take the child and flee, and then you would have never seen the dragon or the child ever again.

"And, the other dragon, Spice. He looked calm placidly sitting there, calm because he had grown to trust and respect Master Sten. His calm and constant reassurance to his mate was all that kept Cinnamon from taking the child and fleeing. But, did you look into his eyes? The fierceness I saw there was frightening." She pointed at Asa again. "And, when you said you were ready to take the child, I think he heard you. He narrowed his eyes, loosened his wings, flexed his fingers, and stood in preparation for a fight. If you had moved against them, he would have fought with everything he had to give Cinnamon and Naia a chance to escape, and he would have done a lot of damage and harmed a lot of people.

"And, there's the Paladins' Peace. By attacking the dragons, we would have broken the Paladins' Peace. That would have brought the wrath of all the dragons down on us.

"Take the child from the dragons? No. Our best option was to give the dragons what they wanted. We have established a friendly relationship with them, but we only gave them enough food for a few days. They want what's best for Naia; so, they'll return for more food and more guidance on how to care for her, thus giving us more opportunities to work with them to ensure we do what's best for Naia."

Sasha paused to look over the crowd before saying, "Are there any questions?" When no one spoke, she said, "You're dismissed."

Marita cleared her throat.

"Sorry, Mayor Marita. I return the floor to you." Sasha sat.

Marita said, "Thank you, Councilmember Sasha. Are there any questions or further comments?" When no one spoke, she said, "This meeting is adjourned," and banged her gavel.

The crowd filtered away.

Sten smiled and said to Asa, "My mom's awesome."

Asa said, "And, I'm a failure."

Chapter 41

<Kedekitley>

Stone Ring and Cooking Pot

<Kedekitley> enjoyed morning flights. The wind had a crisp newness and the sun warming the ground created rising columns of air on which he could soar without expending effort. On these kinds of days, he enjoyed the falling game when he would use updrafts to gain as much altitude as he could then close his wings to fall waiting to flare his wings at the last moment to arrest his fall. He would start the process over again by finding another updraft to carry him to high altitude. When he flew with <Arizesyley>, they would make a contest of the game by seeing who could create the most aerodynamic profile to reduce drag and thus fall faster than the other, or else to create a profile with the most drag to fall slower than the other.

He missed <Arizesyley>. He was away from her because he was flying another patrol for her, and paying attention to the humans and their activities took precedence over any games. The sooner he was finished, the sooner he could return to the weyr to be with her, but he didn't want to return to the weyr quicker by being remiss in his duty to observe the humans.

When he arrived at the weyr, <Kedekitley> dropped from the sky, backwinged, and landed next to <Arizesyley> where she lay, wings spread wide, in the sun soaked meadow outside the weyr. Naia sat in the shade under <Arizesyley's> wing reading a book. The gust of wind from his landing turned several of the book's pages.

"Hey, hey, hey."

<Kedekitley> said, "Oops. I am sorry, Naia."

Naia scowled, made a point of turning the pages back one at a time while glaring at him with narrowed eyes, then resumed reading. He had become confident in his ability to understand human expressions; so, he knew what Naia's expression and actions meant: He should be more aware of the air movements he caused when taking flight and landing.

<Arizesyley> lying on the ground meant he couldn't hug her; so, he lay on the ground, spread his wings wide across the grass like she had hers, laid his head near hers, and said, "<I love you and missed you.>"

<Arizesyley> said, "<I also love you and missed you. What did you find?>"

"<I found nothing. The humans are behaving as the humans normally behave. What have you been doing?>"

"<I have been watching over my human child. She reduced her mass, washed her hands, and consumed human food. Next, she picked up rocks on the weyr floor, and straightened the contents of the supply boxes. She called the activity *chores*. Now she is reading. Did you know the humans teach the human children reading, writing, mathematics, and science?>"

"<My human friend is sophisticated enough to know those subjects. I am not surprised to learn the humans teach the subjects to the human children.>"

They lay silent, listening to the wind stirring leaves in the trees and to Naia turning book pages. He stared into <Arizesyley's> beautiful eyes and basked in contentment.

She smiled and said, "<My human child said she can tell you love me because she sees a glimmer in your eyes when you look at me. My human child is correct. When you look at me, your eyes sparkle.>"

<Kedekitley> struggled for how to respond to such an unexpected statement before saying, "<I understand statistics and probability. Science and mathematics guide me in my endeavors. I consider myself rational. Therefore, I do not believe in luck. However, that *you* love *me* is the luckiest thing that has ever happened to me.>"

<Arizesyley's> subtle smile bloomed even greater. "<That is the most outlandishly sweet and sentimental thing you have ever said to me. You are the best dragon.>"

The mood was lost when Naia closed her book and said, "I'm hungry."

<Kedekitley> decided to recapture the mood another time, but for now, he laughed and said, "<I told you the humans consume human food several times per day.>"

<Arizesyley> raised her head and motioned with her snout toward the weyr. "Retrieve human food from a human food collection."

Naia said, "Please, go with me."

"You and I are not in danger. We are safe. The weyr is safe. Be brave. Go inside, retrieve human food, and consume the human food here."

Naia looked at the weyr, took a deep breath, and said, "Okay, okay, okay, but, please, don't go away."

"I will be here. I will watch for danger. I will keep you safe, and Father will keep me safe."

Taking her book with her, Naia darted to the weyr.

<Kedekitley> said, "<Are you troubled?>"

"<I am experiencing unexplained emotions.>"

"<What emotions?>"

"<Fear, anxiety, sadness, happiness, excitement. I am familiar with and often experience those emotions, but today the emotions occur when I know of no reason to be experiencing the emotions.>"

Naia dashed back from the weyr, the folded blanket cradled in her arms. "I was brave. Mommy and Daddy would be proud of me."

Naia spread the blanket in the shade of a tree close to <Arizesyley>. Wrapped in the blanket were human food containers and the cloth dragon. She placed the cloth dragon, opening and spreading its wings wide, on one side of the blanket, and set the human food containers between the cloth dragon and her.

Naia said, "I'll have a picnic. I have meat, cheese, bread, jancy berries, and a canteen of water."

<Arizesyley> folded her wings.

"No, no, no, where are you going?"

"I am going nowhere." <Arizesyley> rolled over onto her back and spread her wings again.

Naia laughed.

To <Kedekitley>, <Arizesyley> said, "<I have heard my human child make that sound before. What does the sound mean?>"

"<That sound is how the humans laugh.>"

"<The humans laugh?>"

"<Your human child must think something is humorous.>"

"Naia, what is it you think is humorous?"

"You."

"Why do you think I am humorous?"

"Your feet are sticking up in the air." Naia laughed again.

"My ventral surface needs sun-time."

<Kedekitley> folded his wings, said, "That idea is a good idea," as he too rolled over and reopened his wings.

Naia laughed more and said, "Now both of you look funny." She rolled the cloth dragon over so its feet stuck up in the air.

<Kedekitley> wanted to laugh too if <Arizesyley> and he looked as funny as the cloth dragon.

<Arizesyley> huffed and said, "Consume your human food."

After consuming the human food, Naia rewrapped the containers and cloth dragon in the blanket, took a deep breath, and rushed to the weyr. It wasn't long before she ran back, her hair streaming behind her as if it was struggling to keep up.

Naia said, "See? I was brave."

"You performed the task well." <Arizesyley> righted herself.

"No, no, no, where are you going?"

"I have had enough sun-time. I will sit in the shade now."

<Kedekitley> righted himself. "I will join you."

Naia stayed close to <Arizesyley> as she settled in the shade. <Kedekitley> lay next to her, pressed against her, entwined his tail with hers, and reveled in his happiness.

<Arizesyley> said to Naia, "What will you do now?"

"I don't know. I'll think of something. Please, don't go away."

"Father and I will stay here."

Always staying within sight, Naia explored the meadow and especially the weyr's cliff face.

<Kedekitley> said, "<Your human child appears fearful of being away from you.>"

"<I am my human child's protector; although, I am also feeling fear.>"

"<What do you fear?>"

"<I fear the humans surprising us, I think. If the humans were eradicated, we would no longer need to fear the humans surprising us and murdering us.>"

"<The journey would be long and difficult for the humans to come here.>"

"<That knowledge does not mitigate the feeling. I am paying attention to my senses. I will detect the humans approaching, unless the humans are wearing Gird-metal armor.>"

With a haughty cock of his head, <Kedekitley> said, "<I have a solution to that problem. I noticed when the humans are around, other creatures move away. I focus my senses on those other creatures. If the creatures move away, I seek the cause of the creatures' departure. The problem is solved.>"

"<That idea is a good idea.>" She rubbed her head on him. "<You are the best dragon.>"

"<Thank you.>"

Naia returned and said, "I want to build a hearth."

"All right then," said <Arizesyley> with a tilt of her head. "What is a *hearth*?"

"A place where I can build a fire so I can cook. I picked the perfect spot." She pointed to the bare stone ground at the far right side of the cliff face. "There. It'll be out of the way, yet easy to use. May I?"

"You may construct a hearth. I will provide assistance."

"I don't need help, but thank you, thank you, thank you for offering to help."

Naia went to the weyr.

<Arizesyley> said, "<My human child moved out of sight of me without appearing to fret.>"

"<Maybe having something on which to focus her attention keeps your human child from thinking about her fears. Or, maybe your human child is feeling more confident.>"

"<Those are possible explanations. I am also feeling less fearful and more confident.>"

Naia came out of the weyr pulling the wagon. She took the wagon to an outcrop of gray slate where broken blocks of rock each almost as wide as her lower arm was long lay scattered about. She loaded the wagon, pulled the wagon to where she intended to construct her hearth, and began constructing, returning to the rock pile when she needed more.

When the tenseness in <Arizesyley's> tail relaxed and she closed her eyes, <Kedekitley> also closed his eyes to drowse.

∞∞∞

<Kedekitley> leaped to his feet at the same moment as <Arizesyley>.

<Arizesyley> said, "<Where is my human child? Wait.>" She paused. "<My human child is there.>" She rushed toward the trees. <Kedekitley> followed.

Naia burst from the edge of the forest to meet her.

<Arizesyley> swept her up in her arms, mantled her wings around her, and said, "You are safe. Did you see the humans?"

Naia said, "I saw no one. I suddenly felt afraid, so I ran."

<Kedekitley> said, "<I will find the intruders.>"

"<Be vigilant. I cannot detect the humans. The humans must be wearing Gird-metal armor.>"

He used his dragon stealth to move among the trees. That someone as large as him, relative to the creatures of the forest, could move so quietly always amazed him. According to his parents, stealth was a dragon trait that helped make dragons the superior species in the universe. He believed them. Being stealthy was fun, and it was useful when hunting food animals.

His mental map showed no disruption to the normal distribution of creatures among the trees, except for the area where Naia had been. He made a loop around the perimeter of the meadow and found no evidence of anything unusual. He then took flight searching farther away from the weyr, especially above and below the cliff where the humans would have left their horses. The weyr was at the back of a small, hanging cirque that would be difficult for the humans to reach and impossible for horses.

357

When he returned to <Arizesyley> and Naia, he said, "<I found no evidence of the humans. I believe your human child going among the trees is what caused the creatures to move away.>"

<Arizesyley> set Naia down and said, "<That is a reasonable explanation.>"

Naia cleared her throat and said, "Language, language, language."

<Arizesyley> said, "I am sorry, Naia. Father and I were monitoring the creatures in the forest. The creatures moving away would indicate the humans were approaching. You going among the trees caused the creatures to move away. That means there was no danger. I will provide assistance to search for sticks, if you tell me what *sticks* are."

"No, no, no, I don't need help, but you can come with me."

<Kedekitley> tagged along as <Arizesyley> went with Naia to meander amongst the trees investigating downed tree pieces, which he assumed is what she meant by *sticks*. She collected three sticks as long as two of her steps, one stick three times longer, and two long segments of vine before carrying everything to the hearth.

<Arizesyley> said, "You constructed an impressive structure."

Naia had constructed a ring of stones as wide as she was tall and as tall as she was wide.

<Kedekitley> walked around the circle of stones. "I agree with Mother, the structure is impressive. The stone blocks are fitted together well."

Naia grasped the object hanging around her neck. "Mommy and Daddy would be proud of me. It's perfect, perfect, perfect for all the kinds of fires I plan to make, from big to small. Now, I'll make a cooking crane."

<Arizesyley> tilted her head and said, "All right then."

<Kedekitley> didn't know what a *cooking crane* was either, although he did understand the concept of a *crane*. He began imagining what Naia could possible mean.

Naia said, "I'll show you."

He was excited to be shown; so, he quit trying to imagine the crane.

She used a vine to tie together at one end the three same-sized sticks, set them with the not-tied ends spread apart on the ground, braced those ends with rocks, and placed the longer stick horizontally across the top.

"This is a *cooking crane*. I hook the cooking pot on the end of this stick and swing it over the fire to cook the food."

The cooking crane was a marvelous solution to the problem of holding a cooking pot over a fire. Naia was indeed sophisticated. Now <Kedekitley> just needed to know what a *cooking pot* was.

<Arizesyley> again said, "All right then."

"When I start cooking, you'll understand. Now I need firewood. Please, come with me."

<Kedekitley> again went with <Arizesyley> and Naia. She left the wagon at the edge of the trees, walked among the trees gathering sticks of all sizes — long, short, thick, thin — and loaded each armful into the wagon. She unloaded the full wagon next to the hearth and returned to the forest to collect more sticks.

After observing the kinds of sticks Naia collected, <Kedekitley> collected a few to add to the wagon.

Naia caught him. "No, no, no." She removed his sticks from the wagon and held them in her arms.

<Kedekitley> dipped his head. "I am sorry, Naia. I wanted to help."

"I can do it myself. I'm almost grown-up and don't need help, but thank you, thank you, thank you for offering to help." She put his sticks back in the wagon, which made him smile, and clutched the object hanging around her neck. "Mommy and Daddy would be proud of me."

<Arizesyley> said, "Father and I are also proud of you."

"Yes, Mother and I are proud of you," <Kedekitley> said. "You are remarkable."

Naia smiled in the same manner <Kedekitley> had seen Human smile. Unlike a dragon's subtle smile, a human's smile filled the human's face.

"Thank you, thank you, thank you, Mother and Father."

Naia created a significant collection of sticks then said, "That's enough firewood for now. I'll rest before moving to the next step." She sat, leaned against <Arizesyley>, and panted. "Daddy liked to say a fire warms you twice."

After resting, Naia constructed a structure of sticks in the middle of the hearth and used one of the fire starters the humans had provided to set the structure on fire. As the fire caught, she added more sticks to increase the fire's size.

"While that burns down into a good cooking fire, I'll prepare what I'll cook."

She placed various animal flesh pieces and plant pieces into a container, which must have been what Naia meant by *cooking pot*, that had a wire loop on top. Then she added water and powders whose aromas indicated were also made from plants. With the container's wire loop hooked over the end of the cooking crane's horizontal stick, she swung the container over the fire, and used a rock to hold a length of vine tied to the other end of the stick to keep the container suspended.

"That needs to cook for a while. Do dragons cook?"

<Arizesyley> said, "Dragons never cook."

"Do dragons build fires?"

"Father and I have not needed to construct a fire, but the Conclave always has a fire. The fire provides a warm, welcoming place to gather and talk with other dragons."

"What's the *Conclave*?"

"The *Conclave* is a gathering where dragons socialize, teach special subjects to hatchlings, dragonets, young-dragons, and sometimes older dragons, and have discussions and make decisions about policies and plans." She turned to <Kedekitley>. "<With the disruption caused by caring for my human child, I forgot about the Conclave in two days. I want to speak to the Council about my eradicate-the-humans solution to the humans-murdering-dragons problem. I cannot leave my human child. I cannot take my human child with me. What will I do?>"

<Kedekitley> said, "<I want to speak to the Council about my make-friends-with-the-humans solution to the humans-murdering-dragons problem, but I should stay with you.>" He paused to think. "<I am not able to design a solution to the problem. You and I may not be able to attend the Conclave.>"

Naia said, "Language, language, language."

"I am sorry, Naia. Father and I were talking about the Conclave. How is the human food cooking progressing?"

Naia used the cooking crane's horizontal stick to move the human food cooking container away from the fire and prepared to use a tool that <Kedekitley> recognized as being like one of the tools Human used when consuming human food.

<Arizesyley> said, "What is that tool called?"

"This is a *spoon*. And, this is a *bowl*. I'll use the bowl after the food is cooked."

She used the spoon to dip a small amount of the human food, blew on it, and sipped. "Not bad, but it needs to cook longer." She moved the human food cooking container back over the fire.

<Kedekitley> marveled at Naia's amazing cooking device as they sat watching the fire and watching the human food in the human food cooking container bubble.

Then Naia sampled the human food again. "Now it's done, done, done." She used the spoon to fill the bowl with the human food, dipped a small amount of the human food out of the bowl with the spoon, blew on it, and consumed it. "That's good, good, good. Mommy and Daddy would be proud of me." She held out a spoonful of the human food. "Would you like some?"

<Kedekitley> grimaced, but <Arizesyley> politely said, "Thank you for offering, but we only consume food animals."

Naia said, "You'll never know what you're missing," then she continued consuming the human food.

<Arizesyley> said to <Kedekitley>, "<I thought caring for my human child would be complicated, but my human child cares for herself. My human child does not need me for anything.>" A narrowed-eye look from Naia prompted <Arizesyley> to say, "Consume your human food and ignore us talking."

<Kedekitley> said, "<Your human child's knowledge and skills are impressive. I did not know the human children were sophisticated.>"

"<You believe you know everything about the humans.>"

"<I never said I know *everything* about the humans.>"

Naia emptied the remaining human food from the human food cooking container into the bowl, finished consuming the human food, and said, "I'll do the dishes now. Please, come with me."

She used the wagon to carry a pail, a towel, and soap, and led <Arizesyley>, with <Kedekitley> following, to the hot spring to use hot water to clean what she'd used to cook and consume her human food. After returning to the weyr, she put everything away, and led <Arizesyley> and <Kedekitley> back to the fire.

"After our evening meal, Mommy and Daddy and I would sit and watch the fire." She held the object hanging around her neck. "Sometimes we'd talk. Sometimes we'd tell stories. Sometimes we sat quietly. I feel like sitting quietly tonight."

Naia sat between <Arizesyley's> arms and leaned against her. As the fire burned out, Naia fell asleep.

<Kedekitley> thought Naia was cute sleeping while leaning against <Arizesyley>. The humans were remarkable. He was more convinced than ever that his make-friends-with-the-humans solution was the correct solution to the humans-murdering-dragons problem.

<Arizesyley> said, "<My human child has disrupted and changed my life.>" She paused as she smoothed Naia's hair. "<I like this new life.>"

He went with <Arizesyley> as she carried Naia into the weyr and climbed into their nest. He joined her in the nest as she laid Naia and the cloth dragon next to her and covered them with the blanket.

<Arizesyley> said, "Goodnight, Naia."

Naia was wonderful, and she made <Arizesyley> happy. That made <Kedekitley> happy.

Chapter 42

Sten

Too Much Was Happening

Asa sat at the table, her face buried in her hands. She had said nothing since coming home from the community meeting. Sten was concerned for her. Too much was happening that challenged her beliefs. Too much was happening that was changing the world around her. He felt guilty for causing it.

Sten said, "Asa, are you okay?"

She dropped her hands and said, "I'm okay. I'm just a failure and don't deserve to be a Knight Sergeant."

"That's not true."

"I failed to recognize the situation with the dragons. Your mother saw it. I should have seen it too. I could have caused a disaster. I would have caused a disaster if it weren't for your mother." She held out her hand. "Anitra, may I see your stuffed dragon?"

"Yes, Mom." Anitra handed Asa the stuffed dragon. "I'm sorry I made the dragons even though you told me not to."

"That's okay. I shouldn't restrict what you make. You should make whatever you want." Asa studied the shape and stitching of the stuffed dragon. "I like the fasteners on the primary wings and the tail wings that keep the wings closed like a real dragon yet unhook to let the wings open all the way. The shape and proportions are perfect. You only saw a dragon once before you made this?"

"Yes, Mom. I promise."

Asa handed the dragon back. "It's well made. It's better than what I could have done. What do you call her?"

Anitra fastened the wings closed. "Since Naia calls hers *Sugar*, I'm calling mine *Candy*. That way they both have sweet names."

Sten and Asa laughed. Anitra smiled at their reactions.

Sten nodded and said, "Those are good names for dragons."

Asa closed her eyes and bent her head. "Dragons aren't sweet."

"They are once you get to know them."

Anitra said, "I liked Cinnamon and Spice. They're friendly and helpful, and they're trying hard to take care of Naia. And, I liked Naia. I want to see her again."

"As your grandma said," said Sten. "We only gave them enough food for a few days, so they should return for more, we hope. You'll get to see Naia then."

Asa said, "You really think they'll return?"

"Dragon has been helping me and he seems to enjoy it. He wouldn't abandon me. What's your opinion about how they were treating Naia?"

Asa paused before saying, "I'm surprised dragons would protect a child. I could never have imagined it if I hadn't seen it. And, how did those dragons end up with her anyway? And, Naia was so afraid of us. What could have happened to cause that? And, who are the Cultists she said wanted to kill her? There are so many questions."

"You know my mom. I expect her to probe for answers the next time the dragons visit. She's skilled at getting information out of people."

"Dragons aren't people."

"Dragons aren't so different from us. We might as well consider them people and treat them with the respect that comes with that."

Asa sighed and rested her chin in the palm of her hand.

Sten said, "I know I'm the reason that the dragons and what I've been doing has caused you stress, and I'm sorry for that, but I need you to do something for me."

"What?"

"Even if I cause you more stress, remember I love you."

"I know you love me." She took his hands. "I noticed it the first time I met you, and it still happens. When you look at me, your pupils dilate, and it's as if there are little sparks in there."

Sten laughed.

Asa sat straight, her hands still in his. "That wasn't supposed to be funny."

"It's not that it's funny." He pulled her closer. "When you look at me, your pupils do the same thing."

Anitra said, "Are you finished making googly eyes at each other? What is it you want Mom to do?"

"The next time the dragons come, the bell will not ring and I want you there, but not in your armor. And, I don't want Knight Ned and Knight Ted to show up in armor either."

Asa pulled her hands from his and buried her face again. The silence stretched until she said, "That's not a good idea."

"It's a must, though. We need Cinnamon and Dragon to be comfortable and to trust us. A dragon-slayer knight is intimidating. But, for you to be there, without armor, shows our good intentions."

She leaned her forehead on her clinched fists and exhaled heavily. "You've been talking up dragons, and you got that work-team to say wonderful things about your dragon friend, and now most of the village seems to have changed their opinions about dragons. They even gathered around when the dragons came with Naia." She lifted her head, furrowed her brow, and looked at Sten, "I'll not wear my armor, but I want Knight Ned and Knight Ted to stand by in armor. I'll have them hide so the dragons won't see them, but if things go bad, they'll respond."

"That's acceptable, as long as they're not seen. From what you've said and what I've witnessed, Dragon can't detect Gird-metal armored knights without actually seeing them, and I assume it's the same for Cinnamon. But, I know if Knight Ned and Knight Ted are visible at all, at any time, Dragon will notice them. He's done it before."

Anitra wiggled in her chair.

Sten said to her, "Are you okay?"

She said, "This is exciting. I'll get to see the dragons again."

"Don't forget about Naia."

"I'll get to see Naia again too."

Chapter 43

<Kedekitley>

Sleepover Invitation

Another morning flying a patrol for <Arizesyley> while she stayed with Naia. <Kedekitley> tried hard to discover the humans preparing to attack — that was his task and he would do his task to the best of his ability — but it turned out to be another routine day.

He returned to the weyr, hugged <Arizesyley>, and said, "<I love you and missed you.>"

"<I also love you and missed you. What did you find?>"

"<I found nothing.>"

Naia said, "Are you asking Father if we can go visit Anitra?"

"Naia wants to visit the human child Anitra in the human town."

<Kedekitley> bounced. "We can visit the human town. I can visit Human again."

Naia leaped into <Arizesyley's> pouch, peeked out, and said, "Please, go, go, go."

∞∞∞∞∞

<Kedekitley> followed as <Arizesyley> glided into the human town's central open space. The humans scattered, but they only went far enough to give <Arizesyley> and him room to land.

<Arizesyley> closed her wings and said, "<The humans moved out of the way, but the humans did not run away.>" She set Naia down.

"<The human behavior indicates the humans do not fear us.>" <Kedekitley> closed his wings and moved closer to <Arizesyley> as more of the humans gathered around staying a couple of dragon-spans away. "<Nevertheless, the humans are still reluctant to come close. Also, the bell did not ring, which is another indication that the humans do not fear us.>"

"<Do you think the armored humans will confront us?>"

"<I assume the armored humans will respond. The armored humans always respond.>"

"<I do not like the armored humans.>"

Sasha and Sochi pressed through the gathered humans to come close, which didn't surprise <Kedekitley>, but he was surprised when a hoard of the human children rushed past the human adults who tried but failed to stop them.

<Kedekitley> said, "<The human adults may be reluctant to come close, but the same does not apply to the human children.>"

<Arizesyley> picked up Naia, brought her wings around to cover her, and said, "I will protect you."

The human children stopped in front of <Arizesyley>. Anitra said, "Please, stop hiding Naia."

Naia said, "It's all right, Mother. You may put me down."

<Arizesyley> began to move, but checked herself by straightening and tightening her wings. Then she uncovered Naia and set her down in front of the human children.

One of the human children pointed at <Arizesyley> and said, "She has yellow lightning bolts on her wings."

Another human child said, "I like the green and blue stripes on her neck and tail, and the red edges on her wings."

A third human child pointed at <Kedekitley> and said, "That dragon has red marks that look like flames. May we touch you?"

<Kedekitley> straightened his shoulders to help show off his red highlights, and nodded to <Arizesyley> who then said, "The human children may touch us."

A gasp came from the gathered human adults as the human children, making *oohing* and *aahing* sounds, swarmed <Arizesyley> and him.

Human and Asa joined Sasha and Sochi.

<Arizesyley> said, "<That human female is the lead armored human without her Gird-metal armor. I recognize her sensory signature from when she removed her head cover during our previous encounter.>"

"<That is more evidence the humans do not fear us.>"

"<All right then. The human behavior is not expected.>"

Human said, "Dragon, it's good to see you, but ... what's going on?"

"Human, I am pleased to see you. The human children are touching Cinnamon and me."

"I see that." To Naia, he said, "Do you need more food?"

"No, no, no, I don't need more food yet. I just wanted to visit Anitra."

Sasha waved her hands at the human adults and said, "Please, go back to whatever you were doing." She made the same hand motions at the human children. "Please, that's enough touching. Anitra, please, take Naia and the children to the playfield and continue your game."

"Yes, Grandma. Please, everyone come with me." Anitra herded the human children as if they were a collection of food animals she wanted to move in a particular direction. "Please, you too, Naia."

Naia looked at <Arizesyley> who rocked from foot to foot. Then she stopped rocking, took a breath, and said, "Be brave. Go with the human child Anitra, but stay where I can see you."

Naia followed Anitra and the other human children.

Sasha said, "Please, come sit in the shade of the plantus tree and we'll talk while we watch the children."

<Kedekitley> followed as Sasha led the group under the tall tree with wide branches that grew next to the structure. Under the tree, Sasha, Sochi, Asa, and Human sat on benches, the two couples each holding hands. <Kedekitley> reclined alongside <Arizesyley> in the grass. She nestled against him and entwined her tail with his, but she kept watching the human children and Naia. <Kedekitley> watched as well. The human children were running around kicking a ball.

<Arizesyley> said, "What is the game the human children play?"

Sochi said, "It's called *calcephera*."

<Arizesyley> tilted her head. "All right then. What is *calcephera*?"

"The children are split into two teams. That's why half of the children wear blue vests and the other half wear red. Anitra gave Naia a blue vest like hers. There's a net at each end of the field. One team defends one net. The other team defends the other net. The objective of the game is to kick the ball into the other team's net while keeping the other team from kicking the ball into your net. Anitra's explaining the rules to Naia."

<Kedekitley> said, "Dragons have a similar game, except dragons do not kick the ball with our feet. Dragons use our tails to hit the ball." As he said this, he tried to demonstrate with his tail, but it was entwined with <Arizesyley's> tail.

"It sounds like a fun game," said Human. "I'd like to see it someday."

Sasha leaned forward. "Did I hear Naia call you *Mother*?"

"Naia calls me *Mother* and Spice she calls *Father*, but Naia says we are not *Mommy* and *Daddy*. *Mommy* and *Daddy* were Naia's human parents."

"What can you tell us about Naia?"

"Naia is wonderful," said <Arizesyley>. Her wings vibrated and <Kedekitley> felt her tail try to flick even though it was entwined with his. She again glanced toward the human children. <Kedekitley> followed her gaze as she said, "I expected caring for Naia would be complicated, but Naia cares for herself. I did not know the humans could be skilled, talented, and sophisticated."

Sasha laughed. "Well, in my experience, most people aren't."

Human said, "Naia strikes me as being precocious."

Asa bumped her shoulder into his. "You say that about all the children."

"I do not. I only say it about Anitra, and now Naia."

"It sounds like Naia's one of the exceptions, not the rule," said Sasha. "But, what I mean is where did you find her?"

<Arizesyley> said, "I found Naia under a rock."

Sasha's brow creased. "Under a rock?"

"Naia was hiding."

"Hiding from what?"

"Naia was hiding from the humans she calls *Cultists*."

Sasha said, "That still doesn't tell me what happened."

<Arizesyley> drew a breath and said, "Naia said the human Cultists stole human food and supplies from Naia's home. Then the human Cultists burned Naia's home, called Naia a beast child, and attempted to murder Naia. Naia and her parents ran. Naia's parents told Naia to hide. The human Cultists murdered Naia's parents, but the human Cultists could not find Naia. Naia was hiding under a rock. I found Naia hiding under a rock."

"That's horrible."

"Me finding Naia hiding under a rock is not horrible."

"Not that." Sasha sighed. "The Cultists murdering her parents is horrible."

"I returned Naia to the nearest human town to where I found Naia," <Arizesyley> said. "The human town turned out to be where the human Cultists lived. The human Cultists attempted to murder Naia. In response, I took Naia to our weyr. I told Naia I would protect her from the humans. Now, I care for Naia."

"When did this happen?"

"Today is the fourth day since I found Naia."

"It's only been four days?" Sasha glanced toward the playfield. "She must still be terribly traumatized."

Naia ran around on the field amidst the other human children while occasionally kicking the ball. <Kedekitley> could hear Naia's laughter. He was glad Naia was having fun. And, Naia having fun relaxed <Arizesyley>.

<Arizesyley> said, "I can feel that playing the calcephera game with the human children is making Naia happy. Feeling Naia is happy also makes me happy. Is feeling that a human child is happy normal?"

Sasha said, "It's obvious she's happy right now, but I'm concerned about her trauma. The murder of her parents surely caused emotional damage. Does she have outbursts of anger?"

<Arizesyley> shook her head. "Naia has had moments of frustration, but Naia is never angry."

<Kedekitley> agreed with that assessment. Naia had expressed frustration and she had had moments when she was annoyed, but none of that was anger. Naia was normally calm.

Everyone became quiet as they watched Naia running and laughing and acting joyful.

Then Sasha took a breath and said, "I'm worried she's suppressing her anger inside her, and the hatred of those people who murdered her parents, and the fear of those people. Occasionally, she probably feels overcome by despair. And, she feels vulnerable. That's why she's latched onto you as her protector; what better protector can she have than the dragon who rescued her? That's why she's anxious when she's separated from you. Hypervigilance is something else I've noticed; she's always looking for signs of danger and betrayal. Her self-esteem has been damaged too; that's why she keeps trying to prove her abilities and worth. And, she probably blames herself for what happened. It's good she has you. You provide her security and comfort."

"Naia does not need me," said <Arizesyley>. "Naia does everything for herself and wants no help. Naia says she is almost grown-up."

"She may think she's almost grown-up, but she has a long way to go. Children need a loving and nurturing environment and caregivers who provide affection and guidance. She needs you, and it's obvious you want what's best for her. That's what it means to be a mother."

<Kedekitley> could tell from <Arizesyley's> shift in posture that she was upset. She said, "How do I repair Naia's emotional damage?"

"We don't want her dwelling on her loss and becoming depressed and withdrawn. Being preoccupied with painful memories can turn one's own mind into one's worst enemy. I'm glad to see her playing with the other children. She needs to stay engaged. Socializing with family and friends is good for her. You and Spice are her family. We and the children are her friends."

Naia kicked the ball into one of the nets. The human children screamed.

<Arizesyley> leaped to her feet. <Kedekitley> stood but then ducked as <Arizesyley> extended her wings and bunched her legs preparing to leap as she said, "The human children are attacking Naia."

"Please, wait." Sasha stood and made up and down motions with her hands. "It's okay. The children are celebrating. Naia kicked the winning goal."

The hoard of human children with Naia and Anitra in the lead came running to the human adults.

Naia said, "Mother, Father, did you see? I won the game."

"Father and I saw you win the game." <Arizesyley> picked up Naia and rubbed her head on her. "You performed the task well."

Anitra said, "Dad, may we have cake to celebrate?"

"It's meal time." Human stood. "If it's okay with Grandma and Grandpa, after eating, you and the children may have cake."

Asa examined Anitra's hands, looked at the other human children, and said, "If all of you wash your hands first."

"Please, come on everyone." Anitra led the human children around the side of the structure.

Asa said, "Please, you too, Naia."

Naia's smile filled her face as she looked at <Arizesyley>.

"Go with the human children. I will be near. Call out if you need me. My dragon hearing enables me to hear you." She set Naia down.

Naia ran after the human children.

"Dragons are too large to fit through the door, but you should be able to stick your heads in to watch." Sochi waved in the direction the human children had gone. "The banquet room's backdoor is around back. Please, follow the children."

∞∞∞∞

<Arizesyley> beat <Kedekitley> to the door and stuck her head in. He moved from side to side trying to see past her.

He nudged her and said. "<Your horns are wonderful, but I want to see the human children and your horns are in my way.>"

A poke from her tail made him jump. She said, "<Wait your turn.>"

From inside the structure, he heard Sasha say, "Spice, please, come to the window. I'll open it for you."

The window opened. <Kedekitley> rushed over and stuck his head through. He thought he had a better view, so he wrinkled his nose at <Arizesyley>. She wrinkled her nose at him.

Many of the human children were already sitting on benches at a long table. The other human children were washing their hands. Naia sat next to Anitra. Every human child was talking. Aromas of animal and plant origins filled the air.

Sochi said, "Please, everyone calm down. Food's being served."

The human children stilled and became quiet.

In front of each of the human children, the human adults placed a bowl containing pieces of animal flesh and plants and a container of liquid, but no human child touched the human food until Sochi said, "Everyone's served. You may eat now."

The human children began consuming the human food and the talking resumed.

Sasha said, "Please, no talking with your mouths full."

To <Kedekitley>, <Arizesyley> said, "<Have you seen this human behavior before?>"

He shook his head. "<This human behavior is new to me. I have always been told the humans are not sophisticated. Yet, consider the things the humans accomplish. Our belief that the humans are not sophisticated is wrong. We must accept how sophisticated the humans are so their future actions do not surprise us.>"

Sasha approached <Arizesyley> and said, "Anitra asked her mother and father if Naia can do a sleepover. Asa and Sten said yes, if you're okay with it."

"All right then." <Kedekitley> heard the clack of <Arizesyley's> horns hitting the doorframe as she tried to tilt her head. Then she said, "What is a *sleepover*?"

"Naia would spend the night here with Anitra."

Naia stopped talking with the human children and turned toward <Arizesyley> who looked at Naia and forced a smile. Naia returned to talking with the human children. To <Kedekitley>, the interaction appeared strange as if something had passed between them.

"I know what you're thinking." Sasha glanced toward Naia. "But, it would be good for her to spend time with Anitra. They'd play games, and talk, and eat, and sleep, if Naia is willing to be away from you for the night."

"Would a sleepover with the human child Anitra help repair Naia's emotional damage?"

"I believe it would help. You'd bring her back tomorrow morning. She'd spend the day and night. Late on the next day, you'd return to take her home."

<Arizesyley> turned to <Kedekitley>. "<What course of action should I take?>"

"<You are responsible for your human child. You must decide on the course of action you should take.>"

Naia and Anitra approached <Arizesyley>.

Naia said, "Mother, Anitra asked me to do a sleepover tomorrow night."

Several expressions flashed across <Arizesyley's> face. She said, "Come outside, Naia, and we will discuss the sleepover invitation."

<Arizesyley> led Naia away from the structure, settled in the grass, wrapped her tail around her feet, and mantled her wings over herself and Naia. <Kedekitley> poked his head in where her wings met.

<Arizesyley> said, "You look well, Naia."

Naia said, "Your eyes are the color of embers glowing in a fire."

<Kedekitley> said, "This activity is not solving the problem. The situation needs to be analyzed and summarized, the problem defined, and a solution designed."

Naia smiled and said, "Father is smart."

<Arizesyley> smiled. "Father is a genius and the best dragon."

<Kedekitley> huffed and said, "May I continue? The situation is Naia has been invited to do a sleepover with the human child Anitra. That will require returning with Naia tomorrow morning and leaving Naia with the humans while Mother and I leave. Naia will stay here all day, sleep here that night, and stay here until Mother and I return to retrieve her late the next day. The problem is Naia and Mother fear the humans and neither Naia nor Mother want to be separated from the other. What is the solution to the problem?"

Naia said, "I like the people of Splain."

"All right then," said <Arizesyley>. "What is *Splain*?"

"Anitra told me the village is called *Splain*. I fear Cultists. I don't think any Cultists live in Splain. The people here are nice."

When <Arizesyley> said nothing, <Kedekitley> said to her, "Do you trust the humans in the human town Splain?"

<Arizesyley> hesitated, looking at her hands as she wrung them, before saying, "The humans have acted as good humans. The humans have provided help. I thought I would always fear the humans, but the humans in the human town Splain make me feel comfortable."

<Kedekitley> said to Naia, "Would you be comfortable being separated from Mother while participating in the sleepover with the human child Anitra?"

Naia said, "Yes, but I don't want to live here. I want to live with you."

"You will always be a part of our family." <Arizesyley> hooked the tip of her tail over Naia's hand. <Kedekitley> added his tail's tip to the handholding. <Arizesyley> went on, "You will always live with us. Nevertheless, there is no reason you cannot visit with your human friends. Participating in the sleepover with the human child Anitra will be good for you."

Naia said, "I'd like to do the sleepover."

<Arizesyley> said to <Kedekitley>, "<Will the humans protect my human child?>"

"<You know how I feel about my human friend. That feeling also applies to my human friend's family. I believe the humans will protect your human child. Nevertheless, you must make your own choice.>"

Naia said, "Language, language, language."

<Arizesyley> rubbed her head on Naia. "I accept the choice for you to do the sleepover with the human child Anitra."

"Thank you, thank you, thank you."

<Kedekitley> said, "The problem is solved," and pulled his head out from under <Arizesyley's> wings.

From under her wings, he heard <Arizesyley> say, "I will miss being with you, but you and I will be brave."

"Yes, yes, yes, Mother. We'll both be brave, brave, brave."

<Arizesyley> separated her wings and folded them closed.

Naia ran to Anitra where she stood with the human adults and said, "Mother and Father said I can do the sleepover."

<Arizesyley> said to the human adults, "You humans will protect Naia using the same diligence I use to protect Naia."

"We will," said Sasha. "I'll give her a pack to carry what she wants to bring with her tomorrow. And, please, give me a moment to make a sandwich for her to take with her for her evening meal tonight."

∞∞∞∞

At their weyr, <Kedekitley> joined <Arizesyley> watching over Naia as she spent the remainder of the day preparing for the sleepover by washing her clothes and herself, and placing into the pack clean clothes and her personal care tools. When evening approached, Naia opened the box Sasha had given her filling the air with the aroma of scorched animal flesh, plants, and fermentation.

"Wow. Look at this. It's the fanciest sandwich I've ever seen." She took a bite. "Umgoof."

<Arizesyley> said, "No talking with your mouth full."

Naia swallowed and said, "It's good."

As Naia continued consuming the human food, <Arizesyley> laid her head down.

<Kedekitley> said, "<Are you troubled?>"

"<After what I learned about my human child's emotional damage, I realized I have the same emotional damage. Did you know I have emotional damage?>"

"<I have always known about your experience with the humans and how that experience influences your beliefs and actions, but I have never thought of you as having emotional damage.>"

"<You have always been good to me, and good for me. You are the best dragon.>"

He entwined his tail with hers and rubbed his head on her. "<Will you be all right?>"

"<I am well. My human child's excitement about the sleepover is making me feel better.>"

Naia's eagerness to prepare for the sleepover had prompted her to place her teeth cleaning tool, pajamas, and the cloth dragon in the pack. She retrieved them.

After preparing herself for the night, Naia said, "I'll sleep in my nest tonight." She climbed into her nest with her blanket, pillow, and the cloth dragon.

<Arizesyley> said, "Goodnight, Naia."

After a period of silence disturbed only by the normal sounds of the night, Naia said, "Mother?"

"Yes, Naia?"

"May I sleep with you?"

"Climb into our nest."

Naia climbed into the nest, spread her blanket, placed her pillow, hugged the cloth dragon, and nestled against <Arizesyley>. "Thank you, thank you, thank you, Mother."

"I will always be here for you, Naia."

<Kedekitley> added, "I too will always be here for you, Naia."

"Thank you, thank you, thank you, Father. I love you both."

Chapter 44

Sten

Return for the Sleepover

"I told you my mom would get information out of Cinnamon," said Sten as Asa, Anitra, and he came into the house.

"Who are the Cultists Cinnamon and Naia mentioned?" Asa set the three sandwich boxes she carried on the table. "I haven't heard of any group like that. They sound like people who need to be dealt with."

"Mom will talk to Naia about it. She'll get some details that should help us figure out who they are."

"Is that wise? The child is still traumatized. Wouldn't interrogating her cause more trauma?"

Sten cocked an eyebrow at Asa.

Asa said, "Okay, I admit, Sasha knows how to deal with people. She'll glean information from Naia without further traumatizing her."

Sten turned to Anitra. "And, you need to help by letting your grandma have time with Naia. The more we learn, the better we can help Naia."

"I understand, Dad. I'll give Grandma plenty of time with Naia."

"Once we have information, we can contact the other villages to see if they know anything. Now, how about those sandwiches." He eyed the sandwich boxes, rubbed his hands together, looked at his hands, and then said, "Maybe we should wash first."

After cleaning up, they sat at the table, the sandwich boxes distributed according to the names on the boxes.

"I'm pleased things are going well with the dragons. I knew I was right about them." Sten fondled his sandwich box. "From what I read in the journals, people wouldn't have survived the First Days without the dragons' help. Imagine how wonderful it would be today if our ancestors had kept a relationship with them instead of driving them away."

"They must have had their reasons." Asa popped open her box. "Wow, look at that."

"I couldn't find anything in the journals that explained why they drove the dragons away, but it appears to have been instigated by one person, but then there were many followers. I imagine when it was clear their help wasn't wanted anymore, the dragons left. I should ask Dragon if he knows the story from his side." Sten popped open his box. "Wow, indeed. I didn't expect anything less from my mom, though."

Anitra had already removed her sandwich from its box. "It's my favorite."

"My mom knows us well and what each of us likes best." Sten took a bite of his sandwich.

Anitra took a bite of hers and said, "Umgoof."

Asa swallowed so she could say, "Please, no talking with your mouth full." When Sten prepared to speak, she glared at him and said, "Please, you too."

He chose to stay silent and continue eating.

"You think dragons are like people," Asa said. "Well, there are bad people, and those Cultists are an example. I bet there are bad dragons too. Maybe that's why our ancestors drove them away. Don't be fooled into thinking dragons are homogeneous and they're all like your friend." She paused looking at her sandwich, and then looked at Sten. "And, one more thing. That dragon thinks you're typical of people. You're not. You're smarter, kinder, and better looking than most." Sten smiled, which caused Asa to pause, a smile coming to her lips. "Make sure he knows that." She took a bite of her sandwich.

Sten said, "Cinnamon mentioned the Cultists and how they tried to murder Naia. She and Dragon know not all people are good."

The next opportunity Asa had to speak, she said, "This sandwich is superb. Why can't I make sandwiches like this?"

"Mom can teach you."

"She tried. I still can't do it. Didn't she teach you when you were growing up?"

"Mom and Dad taught me everything about the bakery. I can make everything they make as well as they can."

"Your sandwiches are never this good."

"I can make everything, except for my mom's sandwiches. Her intuition about the flavors, textures, and proper proportions of all the potential combinations of breads, meats, cheeses, vegetables, and spiced condiments allows her to create infinite medleys of awesomeness."

Asa tilted her head toward Anitra. "Anitra's sandwiches are almost as good as Sasha's. After a few more lessons, she'll be making sandwiches just as good."

Sten nodded. "Then, if Anitra's willing, we'll be having sandwiches more often."

Anitra smiled but kept eating.

Everyone concentrated on their sandwiches.

Sten stared into Asa's eyes as he ate. She stared back.

Anitra paused her eating to say, "Are you two making googly eyes again? Naia says Cinnamon and Spice make googly eyes at each other too."

Sten said, "What else did Naia say about the dragons?"

"They love each other. They're nice and kind. They're smart. Their nest is huge, big enough for both of them to be in it together. She says she's been sleeping inside the nest next to Cinnamon."

"Doesn't she have her own place to sleep?"

"Spice made a nest for her. She said it's soft and comfortable. But, she gets afraid at night. There are sounds and she has bad thoughts and dreams. She said she feels safer sleeping in the nest next to Cinnamon."

"I hope that's not a problem during the sleepover. By the way, it was a great idea you had about doing a sleepover. It'll be good for Naia."

Now that they were finished with their sandwiches, Sten said to Asa, "How are you feeling about the dragons?"

Asa took a deep breath, looked at her hands as she wrung them, and said, "I have mixed feelings and it causes me great consternation, but I like them. They're not like how I thought dragons were supposed to be, not like I was raised to believe them to be, and not like what I was taught at the Dragon-Slayer Academy. They're not malicious. I don't know what to do with that knowledge. And, they're concerned for Naia. They love Naia and want what's best for her. And, Naia loves them and is devoted to having them as her parents. There's no way we could separate her from them without causing even more trauma. But, if Naia ever wants to live with people, I'm willing to take her in."

Sten held her hand. "I'm willing to take her in too, but I'm betting she'll never want to leave Cinnamon and Dragon. What about tomorrow?"

"I'll go with you and Anitra to meet them. And, I'll not have Knight Ned and Knight Ted standby. Speaking of tomorrow, morning is a long span of time. What time in the morning are they supposed to arrive?"

"Dragon always arrives at about the same time, so I assume it will be at about that time."

"I guess that narrows it down about as much as it can be."

Anitra said, "I'm excited. Naia and I will have so much fun."

∞∞∞∞

Morning found Sten at his mother and father's place waiting with Sasha, Sochi, and Asa. Anitra waited outside in front of the baked goods display window. She mostly sat, but when her excitement overwhelmed her, she paced with frenetic energy.

Sten said, "Anitra said that Naia said she has problems at night with bad thoughts and dreams, and being with Cinnamon is what helps her sleep. Will that be an issue with her spending the night?"

"I don't think so," said Sasha. "Cinnamon helps her sleep by providing a sense of safety, and love. If we give her the same feelings, she should be fine. We need to help her feel empowered to defeat those fears on her own. We'll watch her and see where it leads."

"They're here." Anitra ran into the plaza.

"Anitra, please, stop." Sten, followed by the others, jumped up to chase after her. "Don't get in the way of them landing."

The dragons landed with a gust of wind that ruffled everyone's hair and clothing. Naia climbed out of Cinnamon's pocket and retrieved her pack from Cinnamon's other pocket.

Cinnamon brought her head close to Naia and said, "Behave appropriately, be brave, and have fun."

Naia hugged the dragon's snout. "I know this is hard for you, Mother. Please, you be brave too. We will both be brave until you and Father return tomorrow."

To Sasha, Cinnamon said, "For me to trust the humans is difficult, but I trust you humans to care for Naia until Spice and I return."

"We'll take good care of her," said Sasha. "We won't let you down."

"We'll see you tomorrow," said Sten as he herded everyone toward the bakery to give the dragons room to take flight.

Cinnamon hesitated with her brow drawn and making what might have been a frown — dragon expressions were hard to read without practice — but she finally turned and took flight with Dragon at her side. Sten watched the wall of wind roll across the grass before it hit him.

After recovering from the wind gust, Sasha took Naia's pack and said, "What will you two do first?"

"If it's okay with Naia," said Anitra, "I'll show her the school, and the library, and the shops, and my home, and my room, and my stuffed animals." She turned to Naia. "Is that okay, Naia?"

Naia nodded and said, "I would love to see those things."

Sasha patted the children on their shoulders and said, "Please, return for the midday meal."

"We will, Grandma."

Anitra was already describing how much fun school was as she and Naia ran off.

Chapter 45

<Kedekitley>

Feeling Anxious

They hadn't gone far when <Arizesyley> spiraled down and landed on a treeless knoll. <Kedekitley> followed to land beside her. She walked in circles flicking her tail.

He moved farther away to keep from being stepped on and said, "<Are you not well?>"

"<I do not know what is wrong. I am feeling anxious.>" She reversed her circling. "<I often feel anxious, but not like this.>" She stopped, fidgeted, and looked in the direction of the human town where it was hidden by tree-covered hills. "<I need my human child.>"

<Kedekitley> had never seen <Arizesyley> like this before. "<Should we return to the human town?>"

She nodded and said, "<Yes,>" then shook her head and said, "<No, I do not want to return to the human town. My presence would disrupt my human child's sleepover. The sleepover is good for my human child. We should continue to our weyr.>"

Maybe he could get her mind off Naia. "<We can attend the Conclave.>"

"<You are correct. The Conclave begins today. I keep forgetting about the Conclave. I must speak to the Council about my eradicate-the-humans solution.>"

He stepped closer to her. "<You promised your human child that you would protect her. How can you still want to eradicate the humans?>"

"<Eradicating the humans is the only solution that ensures the humans never again murder dragons.>"

"<What will you do about your human child and the good humans who are helping you?>"

As soon as he said it, he regretted having said it. <Arizesyley> was in distress over Naia already. All he was doing was adding to that distress.

She stopped fidgeting, stared at him, and then said, "<I do not have a solution to that problem. Let us go to the Conclave.>" She took flight.

<Kedekitley> quickly followed as she headed deep into the mountains toward the Conclave Grounds.

They made stops to reduce their mass, to drink from a riotous creek, and to hunt food animals. <Kedekitley> caught his food animal immediately, but he was concerned about <Arizesyley>. Because of her agitated state, she kept spooking the food animals before she was close enough to capture one. She required multiple attempts.

Upon landing on the flight deck at the Conclave Grounds, <Arizesyley> jumped from foot to foot.

<Kedekitley> said, "<Are you still troubled?>"

She crossed and uncrossed her arms a couple of times seeming not to know what to do with them. "<I must return to my human child. I will not disrupt my human child's sleepover. I will hide where the humans will not see me.>"

"<What about speaking to the Council?>"

"<Will you speak for me? You know everything I want to say.>"

<Kedekitley> couldn't keep surprise from his voice. "<I have my own solution to propose, and it is the opposite of your solution.>"

"<You are a genius. You will find a way to speak for both of us.>" She made her pleading eyes.

After gazing into those pleading eyes, <Kedekitley> said, "<I will speak for both of us. I have no idea how, but I will design a solution to the problem of presenting both of our solutions.>"

"<Thank you. I will see you when you return tomorrow.>" She prepared to take flight.

<Kedekitley> said, "<I love you and will miss you. Stay safe.>"

"<I will stay safe. I love you and will miss you too. You are the best dragon.>"

<Arizesyley> flew away dodging to avoid collisions as she forced her way upstream against the flow of arriving dragons leaving <Kedekitley> standing on the flight deck feeling powerless to help.

Chapter 46

Sten

Separation Anxiety

Sten returned to his parent's home and bakery from a meeting with his project supervisors where he had received project status updates. Two of the supervisors had asked about getting help on their projects from Dragon. That pleased Sten, except he had been imagining using Dragon on the projects he supervised, and he was looking forward to it. He didn't know how to deal with the jealousy he felt that other people were expecting him to share Dragon. However, having to share him was inevitable. Or, was it? The solution to the problem was more dragons so he wouldn't have to share his.

Anitra and Naia were in the banquet room. Sasha was talking to Naia. Anitra came to Sten and led him into the kitchen.

"Dad, Grandma is talking to Naia about how she's feeling."

"Is something wrong?"

"After Cinnamon left, Naia said she was feeling bad, that she was missing Cinnamon a lot, but she was brave, her mommy and daddy would be proud of her, and her mother and father will be proud of her too. So, I took her on the tour of the village as I said I would. When we stopped at home, Mom even showed her some of her tailoring work."

"How'd it go?"

"Naia likes the things I like. She's smart too. I have never felt like any of the other children were like me. Naia is. I never imagined there was anyone else in the world like me."

Sten patted her on the shoulder. "It's nice to find someone with whom you can share interests and have meaningful conversations."

"I told her she's a part of my family. I told her to call you *Uncle Sten*, Mom is *Aunt Asa*, and Grandma and Grandpa are *Grandma* and *Grandpa*."

"That's a good idea. We do feel like she's a part of our family and we want her to feel that way too."

Anitra peeked into the other room before turning back to Sten. "I understand how she feels because I miss you and Mom when you're not with me. But, Naia is missing Cinnamon even more than that."

"She's had some bad experiences. Spending time with you, and with us, should help her."

Sasha came into the kitchen. "Anitra, please, keep Naia company while I fetch fixings for making sandwiches."

"Yes, Grandma." Anitra returned to the banquet room.

Sochi arrived and joined Sten in time to hear Sasha say, "Being away from Cinnamon is causing Naia to suffer a bad case of separation anxiety, but she seems to be handling it well. She's motivated to prove how brave and almost grown-up she is. That's helping her cope.

"We're making sandwiches, fancy sandwiches as Naia calls them. I'll teach her some of my methods, and give Anitra another lesson at the same time. That'll help get Naia's mind off Cinnamon for a while. Please, help me gather the fixings."

Sten and Sochi helped Sasha carry bread, meat, cheese, vegetables, and condiments into the banquet room. It was always fun to make sandwiches with his mother, and Sten was sure he too would learn more about how to make really good sandwiches.

Chapter 47

<Kedekitley>

The Conclave

<Kedekitley> watched <Arizesyley> disappear over the next mountain ridge. He was already missing her. Since becoming life-mates, they had always attended the Conclave together. Now he felt lost and alone even among a thunder of dragons.

Naia was causing her distress. But, why, and how? Maybe the other dragons who interacted with the humans would understand what was happening. He needed to talk with them before this evening's Council meeting.

He followed the paved path through the mountain pass from the flight deck where arriving dragons landed to where he could see into the huge ancient glacial cirque and hanging valley that held the Conclave Grounds. Dragons swept around him as he stopped to admire the view of the summits that enclosed the basin on three sides. From the ice and snow on those peaks, melt water cascaded into several streams that meandered across the broad flat valley. Crossing those streams were numerous bridges that knitted the entire valley together. The streams joined into a single flow in time to spill over the hanging valley's southern rim creating a dramatic waterfall that could only be seen if one flew out of the valley and looked back.

A multitude of magnificent dragons covered the valley floor with those milling about causing chaotic swirls of motion around those who stood in static clusters having conversations. Tingles wriggled across <Kedekitley's> hide at the sight of so many dragons. Dragons were solitary creatures and being around others caused everyone angst. Exceptions to the angst were life-mate couples and life-mates with their one-at-a-time hatchling, dragonet, or young-dragon, and to a lesser extent, short visits with family and friends, and working on projects with other dragons.

Then there was the Conclave that caused boundless angst. But, dragons needed to congregate, to socialize, to meet others, to craft community plans and policies, to settle disputes, and to teach special subjects to hatchlings, dragonets, young-dragons, and sometimes older dragons. Dragons enjoyed these opportunities to gather and for the length of the Conclave tolerated the angst. Even though the thunder of dragons in attendance was not all of the dragons in the world — most dragons only attended occasionally — there were always far too many for his comfort.

<Kedekitley> had met <Arizesyley> at a Conclave. He had been feeling overwhelmed by all the dragons and had sought a place to be away from them, but where he could still watch. As he had approached a large, flat boulder overlooking the valley he saw another dragon approaching from the other side. They had stared at each other each hoping the other would go elsewhere. When it became obvious they were an irresistible force meeting an immoveable object, they had agreed to share the boulder as long as each stuck to their end.

They had sat in silence for a long time. Then, down in the valley, a dragon jumped off a bridge into one of the streams, floated downstream, and went over the waterfall. A moment later, the dragon soared into view heading away from the Conclave. <Kedekitley> and <Arizesyley> had laughed and <Kedekitley> had said, "That's an excellent method to escape the crowds." That broke the awkward tension between them. They had been together ever since.

One last thing he admired before continuing along the path into the valley occupied the northern end of the valley: the Pavilion he had designed and helped construct. He puffed up with pride at its splendor and then swaggered into the mayhem below.

∞∞∞∞

<Kedekitley> kept space around him as he drifted in the current of moving dragons swirling through a sea of dragons. Some of the dragons aimlessly ambled about while others appeared to have deliberate destinations. He identified many. Some he knew casually and some

because of having worked with them on projects, but none of them were who he was looking for.

As he searched, he made his way to the scheduling table and asked for a speaking slot at that evening's Council meeting. He suspected the scheduler had anticipated his request and had been holding onto the slot when he was assigned the first slot of the evening. That was satisfactory because it would allow him to be finished quickly instead of having to endure the anxiety of having to wait his turn.

A few dragons approached him to enquire if he would be doing his presentation about his make-friends-with-the-humans solution. These dragons were excited by the prospect and offered him their support, which reassured him, but made him wonder if <Arizesyley> had been there if other dragons would have approached her to express their support for her eradicate-the-humans solution.

As he searched, <Kedekitley> sensed his parents. They were standing near the fire pit, which had already been prepared but wouldn't be lit until after the evening's Council meeting.

"<Mother. Father.>"

In unison, his parents responded, "<Kedekitley.>"

They embraced him in a tangle of necks, tails, arms, and wings, an embrace that came with no angst whatever as memories of his growing up years filled his heart with love and warmth.

They separated and Mother said, "<Where is Arizesyley? Is she well?>"

"<Arizesyley is well. She is observing the humans.>"

Father said, "<Is Arizesyley still concerned about the humans?>"

"<Arizesyley's desire to eradicate the humans has not diminished. She is collecting useful information about the humans' activities.>"

"<What about your desire to be friends with the humans? How is that pursuit progressing?>"

They looked at him with narrowed eyes. Did they know something? Only <Arizesyley> knew he'd been interacting with the humans and she wouldn't have divulged the information.

"<It is not about *me* being friends with the humans. It is about *all dragons* being friends with the humans. I am still proposing

make-friends-with-the-humans as the solution to the humans-murdering-dragons problem and I will again promote that solution this evening.>"

With scrutiny still in her eyes, Mother said, "<Is Arizesyley coming to the Conclave to again promote her eradicate-the-humans solution?>"

"<I will speak for both of us.>"

Mother's and Father's eyes widened.

Father said, "<Those two solutions are contradictory. How will you combine them?>"

"<I am designing a solution to that problem.>"

Mother scrutinized him again and said, "<What else have you been doing?>"

He pursed his lips before saying, "<I have been analyzing a design searching for mathematical calculation errors.>"

Father looked toward the north and grinned. "<I see your Pavilion has not collapsed, yet.>"

<Kedekitley> turned to look and again puffed up with pride. If the dragons packed together, the Pavilion was large enough to cover everyone attending the Conclave. That feature would be useful when it rained, except that dragons wouldn't want to pack together.

"<Do not tease Kedekitley.>" Mother poked Father with her tail. "<Kedekitley only made an error one time. Everything he has designed since has been perfect.>"

Father wrapped an arm around <Kedekitley>, squeezed, and said, "<I know that fact. I am proud of Kedekitley. He is a genius.>"

<Kedekitley> did not like being called a genius because he knew he wasn't, but he had learned to accept the complement because arguing against the assertion never changed anyone's mind.

"<Thank you, Father. What has been happening in the east?>"

"<A few dragonets are about to enter their Emancipation Cycle, so we are constructing more weyr structures for them to live in. You are lucky to have so many caves in the western region of the mountains.>"

"<I was reminiscing about my nests when growing up and remembered the grass,>" <Kedekitley> said. "<I added grass to Arizesyley's and my nest. Arizesyley liked the grass.>"

Mother nodded. "<Grass is a pleasing nesting material. That reminds me, because you turned out so well, your Father and I are planning for a new egg to see if we can create another genius.>"

"<I will have a sibling?>"

"<Yes, genius, the hatchling will be your sibling.>"

"<That is exciting news.>"

Father moved his head closer and said, "<What are Arizesyley's and your thoughts about caring for a child?>"

<Kedekitley> froze wondering why Father had used the word *child*. He finally said, "<Caring for a child is complicated?>"

"<We know that fact,>" said Mother. "<The question is when will Arizesyley and you have an egg?>"

<Kedekitley> relaxed. His father must have meant a hatchling. He said, "<We have not yet made plans for an egg.>" After another delay fretting over what his parents might know, he said, "<I must continue searching for Improecley. I want to speak with her.>"

"<Improecley was near the Pavilion.>" Father motioned in that direction.

"<Thank you.>"

Mother and Father embraced him again before he went toward the Pavilion.

∞∞∞∞

As <Kedekitley> approached, <Improecley> saw him, finished her conversation with another dragon, came to him, and for privacy led him farther away from the others.

"<Kedekitley, I am pleased to see you. Will you be doing your presentation about your make-friends-with-the-humans solution at this evening's Council meeting?>"

"<I will be doing a presentation that combines Arizesyley's and my solutions to the humans-murdering-dragons problem.>"

<Improecley> stared at him wide-eyed. "<Those two solutions are contradictory. How will you combine them?>"

"<I am designing a solution to that problem. May I ask about your human friend?>"

<Kedekitley> realized how inappropriate his question sounded once it left his mind and entered the world. He had spoken with <Improecley> several times about making friends with the humans, but he had never pried into her personal relationship with the humans. She didn't seem to mind, though.

An odd look came to her face, her wings vibrated, and the tip of her tail flicked. She said, "<Patrick is wonderful. Patrick is smart and talented. Did you know Patrick is the Knight Champion? The humans say Patrick is the Human Paladin. Of course, the humans say I am the Dragon Paladin, but that is ridiculous. I am not a paladin. And, one more thing. Patrick is cute.>" <Kedekitley> stepped back startled by <Improecley's> sudden animation. Normally, she was impassive. "<What would you like to ask about Patrick?>"

<Kedekitley> stepped closer again and said, "<Does being away from your human friend cause you distress?>"

<Improecley> slumped, her vibrancy gone. "<Yes, being away from Patrick is difficult. However, we cannot always be together. We each have responsibilities that require us to be apart. The first time was the most difficult, but since then I have learned to live with the discomfort. The feeling is not as painful once I learned what to expect and accepted the discomfort. We meet on a regular schedule to discuss any issues that might have arisen between dragons and the humans. I always look forward to those meetings. Have you experienced the discomfort of separation?>"

"<Why would I have experienced the discomfort of separation?>"

"<Has Arizesyley experienced the discomfort of separation?>"

<Kedekitley> was stunned into silence. Did everyone know <Arizesyley's> and his secret?

<Improecley> saved him from having to respond when her thoughts drifted back to her human friend. "<Patrick said, when we fought, I was furious; so, Patrick calls me *Fury*. I was absolutely furious when we fought, and so was Patrick. However, when Patrick damaged me and had the opportunity to murder me, Patrick hesitated, which gave me the opportunity to strike. A section of Patrick's Gird-metal armor failed and I damaged Patrick.>" She paused, held up her right hand, and from the tips of her fingers, extended her blade-like talons. Turning her hand as she

stared at the sleek cutting edges, she said, "<I could have murdered Patrick.>" She inhaled sharply, withdrew her talons, curled her finger, and brought her hand close to her chest. "<I could not murder Patrick any more than Patrick could murder me.>"

"<What happened?>"

Staring at the highest of the snowcapped peaks, and with a catch in her voice, she said, "<The world changed.>" She turned to <Kedekitley> and said, "<I support interacting with the humans. I will argue in support of your make-friends-with-the-humans solution in the Council discussions after tonight's Council meeting. Your presentation is important. Perform the task well.>"

He thanked her for her time, bowed his head in an acknowledgment of respect, and went looking for the next dragon he wanted to speak with.

∞∞∞∞

Around the edges of the valley were hundreds of spacious arcades that provided cover for small groups of dragons in stormy weather, sleeping places for the night, and training areas during the day. In one of the arcades, <Kedekitley> found <Emidonley> sitting in the middle of a mathematics class full of young-dragons of an age early in their Emancipation Cycles.

<Kedekitley> remembered his Emancipation Cycle. He was 12 years old when he transitioned from being a dragonet to being a young-dragon and began spending occasional nights in his own weyr apart from his parents. As time progressed, he spent more and more time on his own until age 17 when he transitioned from being a young-dragon to being a fully emancipated, solitary adult dragon. Through the years of his Emancipation Cycle his parents continued to care for him, provided him education, and took him to Conclaves for more education such as the class on advanced mathematics <Emidonley> now attended.

The class concluded. As the young-dragons scattered, <Kedekitley> called out to <Emidonley> who came to him.

With excitement in her voice, she said, "<Oh. Are you *Kedekitley*?>"

"<I am *Kedekitley*.>"

"<The teacher spoke about you. You designed the Pavilion, and you are skilled at performing mathematical calculations, and you only made an error one time, which caused a structure to collapse, but you learned from that error. The teacher said if I work hard and practice performing mathematical calculations, and learn from my errors, I too can be perfect.>" She looked at him with wide eyes. "<I want to be like you. You are a genius and you want to be friends with the humans.>"

Shaking his head, <Kedekitley> said, "<I am not a suitable choice for a role model.>" He felt embarrassed, but she had given him an opportunity to guide the conversation elsewhere. "<Speaking of being friends with the humans, may I ask about your human friend?>"

<Emidonley's> wings vibrated and the tip of her tail flicked. "<Luke is wonderful. Luke is friendly and kind and caring and smart and talented and funny and cute. Luke calls me *Ladyhawk* because he said I am a *lady*, which is a female, and the first time he saw me he thought I was a *hawk*, which is a bird. Calling me *Ladyhawk* demonstrates how sophisticated Luke is. What would you like to ask about Luke?>"

"<Does being away from your human friend cause you distress?>"

She sighed and said, "<Yes, I miss being with Luke. The first time we separated, the separation caused painful discomfort. I do not understand why I felt as I did, but since that first time, I have learned to expect and accept the discomfort. With practice, the feeling is not as painful and I know the discomfort will cease when I next visit Luke.>"

"<How often do you visit your human friend?>"

"<Attached to his inn structure in the human town Darmok, Luke, his father, and my mother and father constructed a weyr structure for me. I live in the weyr structure on my Emancipation Cycle Days. Currently, my Emancipation Cycle Day is every 18th day, but I visit more often than that.>"

"<You live in the human town on your Emancipation Cycle Days?>" <Kedekitley> couldn't keep the astonishment out of his voice.

<Emidonley> nodded vigorously. "<The humans in the human town Darmok are good humans. After <Mettagovley> hatched, the bad humans moved away.>"

<Kedekitley> had heard the story about two Gird-metal armored humans protecting a hatchling and the hatchling's parents from a group of bad humans. When he first heard the story, he had been skeptical, but had since come to believe the story to be true. That the bad humans had left the human town was information new to him.

<Emidonley> continued by saying, "<When I visit Luke, he teaches me what he is learning in the human children's school. Did you know the humans teach the human children reading, writing, mathematics, and science?>"

"<I have heard the humans are sophisticated enough to teach the human children those subjects. I am told Mettagovley also lives near the human town.>"

"<Mettagovley and his parents live in a weyr in a hill above Mettagovley's human friend's farm that is on the edge of the human town Darmok.>"

"<Is Mettagovley attending the Conclave?>" He looked around.

"<Mettagovley is in the cognitive development class.>" She pointed.

A group of dragonets sat in an arc with their necks and tails straight and their snouts pointing at a teacher. They were being still and quiet as they concentrated on the teacher's instruction. <Kedekitley> didn't remember much from when he was a four-year-old dragonet that included being still and quiet. Then the class concluded. The dragonets erupted in disarray and scattered in every direction, some running, some taking flight. *That* was how <Kedekitley> remembered being at that age.

One of the dragonets flew straight at <Emidonley> and him for four wing beats before crashing and sliding, his tail flopping over his back. He jumped to his feet and ran the rest of the distance with his wings still flapping. He closed his wings and ran around <Emidonley> saying, "<Emidonley, Emidonley, like Emidonley,>" before he skidded to a stop, looked up at <Kedekitley>, and said, <Who is this?>

<Emidonley> said, "<This is *Kedekitley*.>"

<Mettagovley> bounced in circles around <Kedekitley> saying, "<Kedekitley, Kedekitley, like Kedekitley.>"

<Kedekitley> pulled in his feet and wrapped his tail around himself to keep them from being stomped. The dragonet was a typical four-year-old:

volatile, rambunctious, and charged with energy. The next year would see significant change as <Mettagovley> became more mature, calm, and focused.

<Kedekitley> said, "<I heard you have a human friend.>"

<Mettagovley> stopped bouncing, his wings vibrated, and the tip of his tail flicked. "<Jake is wonderful.>" He spun while pronking and said, "<Jake, Jake, like Jake.>" He stopped and looked at <Kedekitley> again. "<Jake calls me *Squawk* because that was the first thing I said to him. Jake and I will be heroes.>" His eyes turned sad. "<I miss Jake.>" Then he perked up and began bouncing. "<I will be with Jake again when I return to my weyr.>"

<Emidonley> said, "<Because Mettagovley's weyr is close to Jake's house, Mettagovley gets to spend a lot of time with Jake.>"

"<Jake, Jake,>" said <Mettagovley> while spinning again.

Just as <Improecley> loved her human friend, so did <Emidonley> and <Mettagovley> love their human friends. And, the distress of being separated from their human friends was manageable, even for a four-year-old dragonet. The knowledge comforted <Kedekitley>. <Arizesyley's> distress could be managed. However, he too had a human friend. Why did he not feel the same distress? Is there something different about him? He would have to worry about that problem another time.

He thanked <Emidonley> and <Mettagovley> for their answers to his question, said his goodbyes, and went in search for the next dragon he wanted to speak with.

∞∞∞∞

<Kedekitley> spread his wings to catch the sunlight as he sat on the slope overlooking the valley. He feared everyone in the thunder of dragons knew that <Arizesyley> and he had been interacting with the humans. However, he also believed other dragons in that thunder were also secretly interacting with the humans. That was why some dragons were excited about his solution.

Yet, he had an obligation to <Arizesyley>. How could he convince the Council to accept his make-friends-with-the-humans solution and yet still argue for <Arizesyley's> eradicate-the-humans solution?

He saw <Xenkerdecley> sitting on the slope near the pavilion watching the activity below. He made his way over to him.

∞∞∞∞

"<Kedekitley, I am pleased to see you. Will you be doing your presentation about your make-friends-with-the-humans solution, and will Arizesyley be doing her presentation about her eradicate-the-humans solution?>"

"<Arizesyley is observing the humans. I will speak for both of us.>"

<Xenkerdecley's> jaw dropped. "<Those two solutions are contradictory. How will you combine them?>"

"<I am designing a solution to that problem.>"

"<I would say good luck but I know you do not believe in luck.>"

"<*Hard work and perseverance achieves more than luck ever will.*>"

<Xenkerdecley> rolled his eyes. "<Where did you hear that nonsense?>"

"<I learned that *wisdom* from you.>"

<Xenkerdecley> smiled. "<I am glad you listened to me. Did the information I provided regarding the humans help you with interacting with the humans?>"

"<How is it everyone knows about Arizesyley and me interacting with the humans?>"

<Xenkerdecley's> jaw dropped again. "<You and Arizesyley have been interacting with the humans? No one knows you and Arizesyley have been interacting with the humans.>"

"<My parents, Improecley, and you made comments that made me believe everyone must know our secret.>"

"<Your guilty conscience made you believe everyone knows your secret. The other members of the Council, except for Improecley, will be irritated if they find out <Arizesyley> and you have been interacting with the humans. They are already displeased with Improecley, and with Emidonley and Mettagovley and their parents.>"

"<Kedekitley's> shoulders slumped. "<No one knew our secret and I divulged it?>" He wiped his face with his hand.

"<Your secret is safe with me, but the secret is distressing you.>"

"<I have learned much about the humans and that knowledge is a heavy burden.>"

<Xenkerdecley> wiggled into a more comfortable position and said, "<Share with me the knowledge you have gained.>"

<Kedekitley> told the story about his human friend, about <Arizesyley> and her human child, and about the good humans in one human town and the bad humans in the other human town. <Xenkerdecley,> in his wisdom, asked questions and led <Kedekitley> through an analysis of his problem. When their discussion was complete, <Kedekitley> knew what to do for his presentation.

"<Thank you for helping me.>"

<Xenkerdecley> took <Kedekitley's> hand. "<From the first time you came to me as a dragonet asking questions about mathematics, I knew you would achieve great things, but I did not know those great things would include changing the world. I support interacting with the humans. In the Council discussions after tonight's Council meeting, I will argue in support of your make-friends-with-the-humans solution.>"

After hugging <Xenkerdecley,> his friend, his mentor, a dragon who caused him no angst whatever to be near, <Kedekitley> went to prepare for his presentation.

Chapter 48

Sten

Abducted

The bread, meat, cheese, vegetables, and condiments were arranged on the banquet room table. Sten handed Sasha a jar of condiment as she prepared to begin her how-to-make-great-sandwiches lesson when a hay wagon pulled up outside.

Sten went to the window. "Oh, bother. What are they doing?"

The door exploded inward as a battering ram crashed through. Behind the shivers of timber rushed in a group of brawny men.

The reflexes Asa had taught Sten triggered. He struck the first two men neither of whom would get up again anytime soon.

Using the jar in her hand, Sasha hit a man with too much nose on his face shattering the jar and smearing the fragrant, yellow paste across that nose. As he spun from the impact, she kicked him in the back toppling him face first into a bench breaking the bench and reshaping the man's nose.

With a punch to the gut followed by an uppercut, Sochi drove a man into a wall. The man crumbled to the floor and the wall's plaster collapsed on him.

Anitra used the cutting board to kneecap a man. When he cried out and bent to grab his knee, she brought the board down on his bald head splitting the board and dropping the now unconscious man to the floor.

With an angry scream, Naia stabbed one of the men in the buttocks with the bread knife causing the man to imitate her scream.

Behind the mayhem of the brutes came Viren's friends, Nellis and Sato, followed by Viren himself. Nyxie tugged on his arm, arguing with him. Viren slapped her and yelled, "Get out there and watch the wagon."

Nyxie staggered, hand to face, eyes wide. She turned, ran out the door, and past the window heading away from the wagon.

The table flipping was the last thing Sten saw before more men dragged him to the floor, gagged him, placed a hood over his head, and bound his hands and feet.

Many arms picked him up, restrained him, carried him, and tossed him. From the smell and scratchy feeling, hay had cushioned his landing. Four thumps, groans, and muffled expressions of indignation indicated Sasha, Sochi, Anitra, and Naia had joined him. He struggled against the weight of men holding him down as the movement of a wagon began.

∞∞∞∞

Filled with a rage he had never experienced before, Sten lost track of time as he strained against his bindings and the weight of the men, all to no avail. After a while, the wagon stopped. He was again manhandled, dropped on the ground, and a cuff placed around his ankle. When he kicked, he found his foot anchored.

The stifled bellows of the others joined his attempted shouts of derogatory names, but after a while, he lay still, exhausted. The others also became quiet. Things stayed that way for a while.

A series of moans came from Naia, he thought — the children sounded similar with gags in their mouths. Whatever she was trying to say was full of excitement, but then she calmed, mumbled a few moans, and became quiet again.

"Still no sign?"

Sten didn't recognize the voice.

A second voice accompanied by the sound of boots on cobblestones said, "Nothing yet. Your followers aren't very smart, are they?"

"No need to be rude, Mister Travis."

"They were only supposed to snatch the dragon's pet, but we can still make this work."

"I'm expecting you to make my followers look like heroes."

"Mark my words," said the one called *Mister Travis*. "My people have the weapon needed to make it look like your followers killed a dragon that was breaking the Paladins' Peace. That'll bring you more followers."

"And, we'll finally kill the beast child, and you'll get your Dragon War back."

"Don't just kill the child. Please, kill the others too. Make sure it looks like the dragon did it."

The boots on cobbles walked away.

Followers? Kill the beast child? Were these the Cultists Naia and Cinnamon spoke of? And, who is Travis and why was he trying to restart the Dragon War? Sten began pulling at his bindings again. He had to get free and stop the madness. He wished Dragon was there to help him. He needed Dragon. Where was Dragon?

Horns sounded.

The voice that must have been the Cultists' leader said, "That's not the signal for the dragon's coming. What's happening?"

Footsteps ran up and someone with panic in their voice said, "It's the people from Splain, a lot of them, on horseback and in wagons. The three dragon-slayer knights are with them on their warhorses. The mob looks angry."

Using his own panicked voice, the Cultists' leader said, "Please, kill the hostages. Then you might want to run." That was followed by the sound of boots running away.

A heart-stopping roar echoed from everywhere. There came a gust of wind, a ground trembling thump, and what little light Sten could see through the hood vanished.

Naia said, "Mmm."

A dragon's voice said, "Stay down and under my wings."

Sten's ankle cuff and bindings fell off. He pulled the hood off his head and the gag from his mouth. Over him was a dragon, wings mantled to cover the others and him. Yellow zigzags decorated the dragon's wings. It was Cinnamon, and she was in danger. Already, arrows were bouncing off her hide making drumming sounds, but Travis's people had a worse weapon.

Naia pulled off her hood and gag and said, "Now what, Mother?"

"I do not know."

"Don't you have a plan?"

"I could not design a solution to the problem."

An object ripped through Cinnamon's wing and lodged in her hip causing her to gasp.

Naia yelped in pain, clutched her own hip, and cried out, "Mother, Mother, Mother."

Cinnamon took a stuttering breath and said, "I am well."

"No, no, no, you're not."

Sten said, "It's a crossbow bolt."

Another bolt tore through her wing over Sten's head and penetrated the dragon's ribs near her wing shoulder joint. Cinnamon gasped again and Naia screamed, clutching her own ribs. An instant later, with rage contorting her face, Naia forced her way out from under the protection of Cinnamon's wings.

Anitra followed her.

Cinnamon pulled her head out from under her wings and yelled, "Naia, stop."

"Oh, bother." Sten pushed his way out, shouted, "Naia, Anitra, please, stop."

Sochi followed him.

Most of the Cultists were running away, but a few held their ground. Sten prepared himself for a fight and pursued Naia and Anitra.

From under Cinnamon's wings, Sasha said, "Please, don't move. Those bolts might cause more damage if you move. Sten and Sochi will protect the children."

Naia charged at the man holding the crossbow. Another man was handing him a bolt for the weapon. Naia shrieked a feral cry and hurled herself into the man's knees sweeping his feet out from under him. He tumbled into the other man causing the bolt to clatter to the ground. The empty crossbow hit the ground and released with a *thwack*.

Naia picked up the bolt and beat the man who had been holding the crossbow. With each bash on the man's head and torso, she screamed a word. "Please. Stop. Hurting. Mother. Stop. Stop. Stop."

The other man got to his feet and came at Naia. She swung the bolt. The needle sharp point sliced across the man's belly causing him to choke out a cry, wrap his arms around his middle, and fall to the ground.

The thug with too much nose, a nose that was now misshapen, and who had scabby gashes across his face, charged Sten. Sten's roundhouse kick to the man's head instantly incapacitated the man.

Sochi said, "Were did you learn that?"

"Asa's been training me, but it's our secret."

From behind Naia, a woman with a sword came charging at her. Sten was still too many steps away to save Naia. Anitra picked up a spear and swung the butt end at the woman catching her in the face. The sword tumbled free and a few teeth came out of the woman's mouth as the woman made a half summersault before hitting the ground.

Anitra's follow-through brought up the steel-bladed end of the spear. She lunged at a man charging at her from behind the woman. Her reach was too short for a full stab, but she caught enough of the man's chest to cause him to scream, turn, and run, blood saturating his shirt.

Sten had had concerns about Asa teaching Anitra dragon-slayer fighting skills, and those moves were some of those skills. Sten's opinion had now changed. He was proud of his precious and precocious child and glad Asa had taught her how to fight.

Ready to fight, Sten and Sochi stopped next to the two children. The two men and the woman Naia and Anitra had left sprawled and bleeding on the ground moaned, but everyone else had run away.

The mob from Splain, armed with every sharp edged implement used by every craft in the village, and a few farming tools, surged over everything. Asa in full Gird-metal armor and riding Maximus also in Gird-metal armor and followed by Sayneigh who carried Asa's equipment approached. Abaccus, saddled and ready, also followed.

Sten said, "How did you find us?"

"Miss Nyxie came and got me, but you were already gone. I convinced her to tell me where they took you. Then she ran off. I have no idea where she went." She turned to the people following her and barked, "Please, round up the hooligans. Don't let them get away."

Naia said, "Mother saved us, but now she's hurt." She ran toward Cinnamon.

Sten, Sochi, and Anitra followed Naia, but Asa being on horseback arrived first. Cinnamon laid back her ears, bared her teeth, and made a growl far scarier than the previous time Sten had heard her growl. This growl was a promise of violence.

Asa dismounted, removed her helmet, and said, "It's all right. It's me. I'm here to help you." She turned to a Splain villager who carried a fire poker like a sword and yelled, "You, please, fetch Doctor Dan."

Maximus and Sayneigh stayed back, but Abaccus trotted to Cinnamon and nuzzled her.

"It's okay, Abaccus." Sten patted the horse on the neck. "Someone, please, take care of Abaccus, Maximus, and Sayneigh."

A hostler gathered the reins. "Sorry, Master Sten. We brought a string of extra horses. Abaccus untied himself. I'll take care of them."

Sten gave Abaccus another pat as the hostler led the horses to the side.

Dan rushed up and stared. "I doctor people and animals. I don't know anything about dragons."

Asa pushed him. "They can't be that different."

Dan stumbled forward. "They're a lot different."

Cinnamon turned her head and spat on herself where the crossbow bolt protruded from her ribs and then turned back to Naia.

Naia stroked Cinnamon's snout and through her tears said, "It's okay, it's okay, it's okay, Mother."

Cinnamon said, "I must rest."

"Yes, yes, yes, Mother. Please, rest."

"You do not understand. Rest is a special state dragons enter that concentrates our metabolic energy on damage repair. Rest is similar to sleep, but different. I might look dead, but I will be fine. I do not know how long I will be in rest. Do not worry about me."

More tears streamed down Naia's face. "Okay, okay, okay, Mother. I'll watch over you. I'll keep you safe."

"I know you will. I trust you, and the good humans." Cinnamon nuzzled Naia and said, "I love you, Naia."

As Cinnamon's eyes closed, Naia keened.

Tears swarmed in Sten's eyes. He said, "Naia."

"No, no, no. It's like sleep, only different. You heard what Mother said."

"You should come with me."

"No, no, no. I won't leave her."

Sten didn't know what to do. "Naia, please, come on."

She pushed him away. "I can feel Mother. Mother's still here."

"What do you mean *you can feel her?*"

"I don't know. For days, I've felt Mother, here." She tapped her chest with her fist. "Sometimes I feel how she feels. Sometimes I feel pictures, sometimes words. Sometimes I feel ideas. I can still feel her. She's in a lonely place, a place of white light."

"It's your imagination."

"No, no, no. It's real. Mother's still here. She's just resting. You heard what she said. I have to stay with her. I have to protect her." She wiped at her tears and sniffled.

Dan held a mirror to one of the dragon's nostrils. He said, "It's slow and shallow, but she's breathing." He used a stethoscope from his medical bag to listen to her chest. "Please, silence. Everyone be quiet." He listened for a long time. "Slow but steady. And, when I say slow, I mean really slow."

Sten said, "So, what do we do?"

"I know nothing about dragons — no one does — but whatever this rest thing is, we still have to help her. Why did she spit on herself?"

Asa stepped forward. "Dragon spit stops bleeding, kills germs, and relieves pain. General Patrick said the Dragon Paladin spitting on him is what saved his life."

"Disgusting," said Dan. "I wouldn't think that was very sanitary." He began pulling items out of his medical bag. "Apprentice Serath, I need you."

Serath came out of the crowd. "I'm here, Doctor Dan."

"Please, fetch all the medical kits you can. Have the medics keep what they need for their patients, but fetch everything else here." Serath ran off. Dan continued, "We'll remove the bolts. But, I can't operate on a dragon, their hide's too tough, so all we can do is try to stop the bleeding and hope for the best."

When Serath returned with an armload of medical kits, Dan sorted through the bandages and containers of salves. He said, "This salve is a mixture of antiseptic, analgesic, and coagulant. It does everything dragon spit supposedly does, but it's more sanitary. The dragon's orangey-red blood looks odd, but I'm hoping this salve works on it."

Sten placed his hand on Naia's shoulder and said, "Let's move out of the way."

"No, no, no. I'm not leaving Mother." She wrapped her arms around Cinnamon's neck.

"She won't be in the way, Master Sten," said Dan. "Apprentice Serath and I need your help with the bandages."

Douglas and his work-team, who had become comfortable with dragons after roofing Lisa and Oliver's house, held Cinnamon's wing as Sochi and Sasha pulled the bolt out of her hip. Sten handed Dan and Serath the salve and bandages as they treated the wound.

"That wasn't too bad," said Dan as he cleaned his hands. "I'm worried about the one in the chest, though. It might have penetrated something vital."

Blood initially surged from the second wound as the bolt was pulled out. Dan pressed cloth pads against the wound until the bleeding slowed. He tried to clean the spittle off, but gave up when he couldn't and simply applied salve and bandages over it.

Dan nodded his satisfaction. "The bandages will need to be replaced frequently. Other than that, it's wait and see. Let's do something about the holes in her wing."

As he examined the wing damage, Dan paused and said, "These wing sails aren't membranes; they're sheets of muscle. And, look at these cartilage rods running parallel between the support bones that run from the wing's leading edge spar bone to the wing's trailing edge."

Sten looked closer. "What does it mean?"

"By contracting and relaxing the wing sail muscles to bend the rods along with positioning the wing bones — look at the muscles attached to the wing bones and look at how the bones all have multiple articulation joints — dragons can reshape their wings."

"I had noticed Dragon's — ah, Spice's wings appeared to change depending on his aerial maneuvers. I thought it was my imagination. That must give dragons a lot of control and versatility in flight."

Dan ran his hand over the wing. "And, look at this row of triangle-shaped wedges that stick out just behind the wing's leading edge. They must be important for flight; why else would they have them? I really want to learn more about dragons."

After doing their best using surgical tape to bind the edges of the holes in the wing sail together, every cut, scrape, and gouge in the dragon's hide caused by arrows and spears was bandaged even though those injuries looked superficial.

Sten picked up a splintered arrow whose head had snapped off. "Look at this. It broke as if it had hit an iron plate, yet dragon hide feels supple to the touch. There's much to learn about dragons."

Naia wanted no company as she kept her watchful vigil over Cinnamon ensuring no one and no thing disturbed her, except for when bandage changes were needed. She only left the dragon's side to visit the necessary. At those times, she asked Anitra to stand guard. She trusted Anitra more than anyone else to help protect Cinnamon. Anitra took the role seriously, guarding the dragon with a vicious glare and holding the spear she still carried from the battle.

When Sten came to Naia to give her a bowl of food, Naia said, "No, no, no. I don't want any."

Sten knelt and held out the bowl. "It's called *cawl*. It's made with meat, and potatoes, and all sorts of vegetables. It even has rattidash root in it. It's delicious. Inn Keeper Tintasen made it. It's one of the dishes he serves at his inn. He likes putting rattidash root in everything."

"No, no, no. I'm not hungry."

"What will Cinnamon say when she wakes up and learns you haven't been eating?"

After staring at the bowl, pondering, Naia said, "Okay, okay, okay, I'll eat it. I want Mother to be proud of me."

She took the bowl and spoon and began eating as if she were a ravenous child. Sten wondered when she had last eaten since being abducted interrupted sandwich making.

Next to the dragon, Sasha and Sochi prepared a sleeping pallet for Naia. She sat on the pallet, but instead of lying down, she leaned against Cinnamon with her arms draped around the dragon's neck.

After Sten arranged for a heavy cargo wagon that Dan requested be brought from Splain, he had a moment to think. They were in the Village of Tanagra. It wasn't far from Splain, but it was off the main road and trade route. It was a small village that had been damaged at the end of the Dragon War. The people had drifted away until it was left empty. The Cultists were squatters. In the surrounding hills there had been several farms, but Sten didn't know if any were still active. He wondered if one of those farms had been Naia's.

From a vacant house, Sten borrowed an old, overstuffed settee for Asa. Next to the settee, he prepared a sleeping pallet for Anitra. Asa made it her duty to ensure the blanket she draped over Naia stayed on her during the night. When she finally sat down on the settee, he sat with her, holding her hand, and fell asleep. Part way through the night, he woke when Asa, asleep, tipped into him, her armor cold on his skin. He took his turn watching over Naia and Cinnamon as the two moons, Echna and Mina, journeyed westward across the sky.

Chapter 49

<Kedekitley>

Dragon Council Presentation

When <Kedekitley> stepped onto the Pavilion's testimony platform, the Council to his left and the audience to his right, everyone's attention focused on him.

He presented the facts. The human population was increasing and spreading. The humans continued to train more armored humans. And, while the humans had not yet violated the Paladins' Peace, there was a risk the humans would return to their murderous ways. The problem needed a solution.

Murmurs of agreement from the audience bolstered his confidence, so he continued.

Solution: Eradicate the humans. A large number of the humans could quickly be eradicated, but as the humans' numbers diminished, the task would become more difficult until it became almost impossible to find the few remaining humans.

The risks: Not knowing how far the humans had spread beyond the valley of the Great River. Eradicating the local humans would cause any humans outside the valley to conclude dragons had become an existential threat. Those humans would act to protect themselves by attempting to eradicate dragons thus throwing dragons into a new perpetual war with the humans. Moreover, the humans were more sophisticated and inventive than we believe them to be. The humans would invent weapons even more lethal than those the humans currently have. In fact, the humans may already have new weapons that the humans keep hidden.

<Kedekitley> felt encouraged by the audience's increased murmurs, but <Improecley> broke eye contact by turning as if she were examining the roof of the pavilion. <Improecley's> human friend would know about

the new weapons. Could her human friend hide that knowledge from her? After pondering that, which allowed the audience time to become quiet again, he proceeded.

Another solution: Make friends with the humans by teaching the humans that dragons were worthy of keeping around, worthy of being a part of their lives. Being friends with the humans would incentivize the humans to not murder dragons. Dragons would become a normal, safe, and even desirable part of the humans' lives.

The risks: Two categories of the humans existed — good humans and bad humans. The bad humans will always want to damage or murder dragons. However, irrefutable evidence indicated the good humans would endeavor to protect dragons. Having good humans as friends will reduce the risk presented by bad humans because the good humans will oppose the bad humans. Nevertheless, the risk from bad humans will remain.

<Kedekitley> waited for the new murmurs to subside before he went on. The facts presented, the problem defined, and solutions proposed he made a call to action.

He stood tall, held out his left hand, and said, "<Eradicate.>" He held out his right hand. "<Or, make friends.>" Referencing each hand in turn, he said, "<The humans can be violent and murderous. The humans can be helpful and protective.>" He cupped his hands together as if he were presenting the future to the Council and the audience. "<Eradicate or make friends. Each solution requires effort on the part of dragons. Each solution has its rewards and risks. If no action is taken, however, eventually the humans will abandon the Paladins' Peace, and,>" he punched the fist of one hand into the palm of the other, "<the humans will return to their murderous ways. Safety is not found in ignoring the humans. Dragons must be proactive in dealing with the humans. Eradicate or make friends. Dragons must choose.>"

More presentations followed, but <Kedekitley> didn't listen. The energy he had expended had left him mentally and physically exhausted. He settled and waited on the rock overlooking the gathering where he and <Arizesyley> had first met. The Council would discuss, deliberate, and decide, and by midday the next day, would announce their decision.

Chapter 50

Sten

The Dragon Awakens

In the morning, Sten wasn't surprised when Abaccus sauntered up carrying his lead rope.

"Untied yourself again, did you? I'm sure it's more interesting here than with the other horses." Sten removed the lead rope. "Just stay out of the way."

Tintasen provided the morning meal for everyone remaining on site. Without arguing, Naia ate the eggs and biscuits after first eating the rattidash root served with them. Afterwards, she settled down leaning against Cinnamon again. She kept tracing a finger over one of the yellow zigzags on the dragon's neck.

Sten, Asa, and Anitra sat on the settee waiting for something to happen. Sten worried nothing would. How to help Naia deal with her loss if Cinnamon never woke was a problem he didn't want to have to solve.

All three of them jumped when Naia moved to Cinnamon's face. Sten came closer to see what she was doing.

"Mother, Mother, Mother, are you awake?" Naia peered closer. "I can feel you're waking up."

The dragon's eyes fluttered open. Reflected in the eye closest to Naia, Sten could see Naia's smiling face.

Naia straightened and said, "Doctor Dan, Doctor Dan, Doctor Dan, Mother's awake."

A crowd instantly gathered. Asa and Anitra stood at the leading edge.

Cinnamon said, "Naia, are you well?"

"I'm fine, Mother."

"Have you consumed human food? The humans consume human food several times per day."

"I've had plenty to eat."

Dan pushed past the crowd. "Please, stand back. Give her room to breathe." When Cinnamon lifted her head and wiggled, Dan waggled his hands and said, "Please, don't be moving about. We managed to remove the crossbow bolts and control the bleeding, but we don't want your wounds to start bleeding again."

The dragon turned her head to look at herself, including lifting her wing to look at the bandages under it, which caused Naia to flinch.

Dan said, "Please, don't be moving."

Naia said, "Doctor Dan has been taking good care of you."

"I did my best, but I have no experience doctoring dragons."

"Thank you for helping me." Cinnamon turned to Naia. "Naia, have you slept?"

Sasha and Sochi stepped forward. Sasha said, "We've been caring for Naia. She fell asleep with her arms wrapped around you and slept all night."

"I kept having dreams I was floating in a white emptiness," said Naia. "It was strange, and lonely."

Dan checked the dragon's bandages and said, "I want to move you to Splain. It'll be easier to care for you there."

Cinnamon tilted her head and said, "All right then." She turned to Sasha. "Is this human," she nodded toward Dan, "one of the humans you said are not sophisticated?"

Sasha made a puzzled look. "Why do you ask that?"

"The human told me not to move about, but now the human says I am to move. The contradiction does not sound sophisticated."

Dan said, "When you first woke, I didn't want you to make any drastic movements. We'll be careful when we move you to Splain."

Sten pointed toward a wagon that set next to the crowd. "We brought our strongest wagon. It'll hold your weight. We have a double team of horses to pull it. Can you climb onto the wagon?"

Cinnamon stood. "I can climb onto the wagon."

When she attempted to close her damaged wing, Naia said, "It hurts, it hurts, it hurts."

"I am well."

"No, no, no. You're not well. Your wing, chest, and hip hurt. I can feel it."

Dan said, "Moving your wing is flexing muscles we don't want flexed. With your permission, I will bind your wings to hold them in place so you don't accidently flex them."

The dragon froze, staring at Dan.

Sten said, "Please, do what Doctor Dan says."

"Yes, yes, yes, Mother. Doctor Dan is helping you."

Cinnamon looked at Naia and smiled the same subtle dragon smile Sten had learned to recognize from Dragon. "Yes, Naia." Turning to Dan, she said, "You may bind my wings."

To Serath, Dan said, "Apprentice Serath, please, fetch a long rope." Turning to Cinnamon, he said, "You may close your right wing on your own, but let us do all the work of closing your left wing. Please, do not tense any muscles as we do it." Sten moved out of the way as Dan motioned forth Douglas and his work-team to help again, "As we fold her wing closed, I'll check on how it's pulling on the wounds and bandages." Anitra rushed forward to help by lifting the tip of Cinnamon's wing.

The wing folding went well. Serath returned with a rope that was looped under Cinnamon's body and wrapped around her five times before being tied off leaving both of her wings bound.

"That should work for now," Dan said. "Let's try the wagon again."

As Cinnamon went to the wagon, Naia flinched, wrapped her arms around herself, and said, "Mother, Mother, Mother."

Cinnamon turned to her. "Yes, Naia. My damage still hurts a small amount. I am sorry you feel the pain too."

When she climbed on, the wagon listed and creaked. She fit after she wrapped her tail around her and bent her neck so she curled into a knot.

Sten said, "You're not as heavy as I thought. The springs barely compressed."

"Dragon anatomy has minimal mass," said Cinnamon. "Too much mass makes flight difficult."

Naia climbed onto the wagon.

"Naia." Sten put his hands on his hips. "It's not safe to ride up there."

Cinnamon wrapped her arms around Naia as Naia said, "You're making Mother ride up here, and other people are riding in wagons."

"The other wagons have sideboards. This one doesn't. That's why we're strapping Cinnamon down."

"You are strapping me down?" The dragon sounded indignant.

"With your permission. The straps will keep you from bouncing off if we hit a bump."

"Please, let them strap you down, Mother. Cargo is always strapped down."

"I am cargo am I?"

Sten said, "You're a passenger, but we don't want you to fall off."

Cinnamon again made a subtle smile. "You may strap me down."

When the cargo straps were in place, Sten said, "Naia, time to get down."

"No, no, no. I'll ride here. I'm snug in Mother's arms."

Cinnamon tightened her grip on Naia and narrowed her eyes at Sten. "Naia is safe with me."

Remembering Sasha's example of a miser cat and her kit, Sten said, "Okay, but keep a secure hold on her."

Abaccus gave a snort as he sauntered up with Maximus, Sayneigh, and Sunshine following. The horses each carried their own lead rope. Sten was concerned that by untying the others, Abaccus was teaching them bad habits. Regardless, he chuckled and patted his horse. "I see you're raring to go. Thank you for fetching the others." He handed the lead ropes for Maximus and Sayneigh to Asa and Sunshine's lead rope to Anitra and said, "I told you. Abaccus is remarkable."

More than enough horsepower was available to pull the lighter than expected wagon as Cinnamon and Naia rode to the Village of Splain with Sten, Asa, and Anitra riding beside them.

Chapter 51

<Kedekitley>

Dragon Council Rejection

As the mountain peaks caught the first rays of morning, the ice and snow glowed a ruddy hue that tinted the valley where dragons were already milling about mixing and matching. <Kedekitley> again reminisced about meeting <Arizesyley> on this rock. The Conclave was a common place to meet a potential life-mate. Where else do solitary dragons ever congregate? He missed his life-mate and hoped she was well and with Naia.

Soon the sun ventured over the peaks and poured its light into the valley. Sitting on his flat rock perch, he spread his wings to bask in the sunlight as he patiently waited for the Council to announce the results of their deliberations.

When the Council appeared, a wave of motion swept across the thunder of dragons as they turned to face the pavilion. The Speaker for the Council stepped onto the testimony platform.

Her first announcement was that <Kedekitley's> solutions were rejected and the edict that dragons are not to interact with the humans remained in effect.

Many dragons in the valley expressed loud opinions about the decision, but <Kedekitley> didn't listen. He dropped flat to the rock and hid under his mantled wings. After taking several deep breaths, and growling, he said, "<I do not want to be here.>" Without the courtesy of using the flight deck to take flight, he spread his wings, rudely launched himself into the air over the thunder of dragons, veered south out of the valley, banked hard to the right, and headed west toward his weyr and <Arizesyley>, Naia, and Human.

Chapter 52

Sten

His Life Had Changed

The people that still accompanied the wagon split off to do whatever they needed to do as the wagon stopped in the plaza. Hostlers took Abaccus, Maximus, Sayneigh, and Sunshine. Anitra went with Asa to put away her armor and clean up. Sochi and Sasha went to check on the damage that Asa said had been done to the bakery's backdoor and wall. Dan, Serath, and Douglas and his work-team stayed.

Sten said, "We'll put you here in the plaza while we prepare a shelter for you to stay in while you heal."

Naia climbed down, the straps were removed, Cinnamon stepped off, and the wagon was taken away. Dan and Serath removed the ropes holding her wings, Douglas's team again held the wing as Dan and Serath examined and replaced the bandages, and then Dan instructed the team to place the wing on the ground in a relaxed position as Cinnamon lay down. At that point, Naia appeared to be relieved.

"Things are looking good," said Dan. "We'll leave your wing open like this for now. Please, don't be moving about."

Cinnamon said, "I will not move about."

"I need to check on my other patients, but I'll check on you again later."

Dan, Serath, and Douglas and his work-team left.

Yacha approached with his largest tub.

Sten said, "Do you wish for water to drink?"

Cinnamon nodded. "Yes, I would appreciate water to drink."

"I didn't have an opportunity to ask you about it before; so, when I sent word ahead, I guessed about how to give you water. I hope this method isn't offensive."

Yacha set the tub down.

Cinnamon said, "The container is a washing tub."

"It's not a washing tub. It's a watering trough. I'll fill it with water for you to drink."

Cinnamon made her subtle smile. "That idea is a good idea. You are a genius like Spice."

Sten smiled, shook his head, and said, "I doubt that." A small, wagon-mounted water tank arrived. "This is *potable water*." He took a cup from the cupboard on the side of the wagon, drew some water, drank it, and said, "See? It's good for drinking. I'll fill the watering trough for you."

Once the watering trough was full, Cinnamon lowered her head, puckered her lips and drew in water.

Naia laughed.

Cinnamon lifted her head, water dripping from her snout, and said, "Naia, what is it you think is humorous?"

"You."

"Why do you think I am humorous this time?"

"You make slurping noises when you drink."

Cinnamon huffed. "You often think ordinary things are humorous." She put her snout back in the water and resumed slurping.

Naia continued giggling.

When Cinnamon finished drinking, Sten moved the watering trough and said, "How about food? Do you need food? We can fetch food for you."

"I do not need food."

"That's good. I have no idea what or how to feed a dragon. If there's nothing else you need for now, I'm going home for a short while, but I'll be back."

"I am comfortable and satisfied. Thank you, and all of the good humans, for helping me."

Sten headed toward home, but stopped when Naia came after him.

"Uncle Sten," Naia whispered. "Anitra told me you can make pictures."

Sten whispered in return. "I like to think I'm reasonably talented at art."

"Will you make a picture of Mother and Father for my locket to replace this baby picture?" She opened the locket she wore around her neck and showed it to him.

"I can do that. It's not large. It wouldn't take me long."

"Thank you, thank you, thank you." She handed him the locket and ran back to Cinnamon.

On his way home, Sten passed numerous families headed toward the dragon, many carrying bouquets of flowers.

At home, Anitra, at Asa's insistence, had placed her spear in the armory. She wasn't allowed to carry it around the village no matter how much she wanted to show it off. Then they told Sten they would see him back at the dragon and left as they discussed how to get Naia to leave Cinnamon long enough to bathe. Sten cleaned himself then sat at his desk to work on the picture for Naia's locket. He already had the image in mind.

He made a sketch, inked it onto the best Gration Marshes art paper he had, and began coloring. First, he did Cinnamon and her yellow zigzag highlights. Then, he did Dragon and his red flame highlights. After lacquering the finished picture to protect it, he set it aside to cure and pondered the image of Dragon. He missed Dragon.

In his journal, he added details about how these events with the dragons had changed his life. Nothing would ever be the same again. He ended the journal entry with *There is no friend who is a better friend than a dragon friend.*

Staring out the window, motion in the sky caught his attention: a dragon's silhouette like that of a hawk. Dragon was arriving. He placed the cured picture into the locket and headed toward the plaza.

Chapter 53

\<Kedekitley\>

The World Has Changed

\<Kedekitley\> couldn't sense anyone as he landed and entered the weyr. From the looks and scent of the place, no one had been there since \<Arizesyley\>, Naia, and he had left the previous day. That was to be expected. The sleepover should still be in progress. He headed toward the human town. \<Arizesyley\> and Naia must be there. Human would be there too.

He circled the human town. Something was wrong. Many of the humans had gathered in the human town's central open space. In the middle of the space lay \<Arizesyley\>. On her head and around her neck were flowers. Her left wing lay spread on the grass and it had bandages that concealed damage.

He dropped hard to the ground, roared, and lunged causing the humans to scurry away.

\<Arizesyley\> said, "\<Kedekitley, what are you doing?\>"

"\<The humans have damaged you.\>" He lunged at the humans again to encourage them to move farther away.

"\<Stop that behavior.\>"

Naia stood from where she had been nestled in \<Arizesyley's\> arms, stepped toward \<Kedekitley\>, and said, "Please, stop, stop, stop, Father. Stop scaring people."

\<Kedekitley\> looked at Naia then at \<Arizesyley\>, confused.

"\<I agree with my human child. Stop trying to scare the humans,\>" \<Arizesyley\> said. "\<Do not make me have to get up to reprimand you. My wing, chest, and hip hurt, and the human doctor told me not to move about.\>"

"\<You are damaged.\>"

"<The good humans of the human town Splain did not damage me. The good humans of the human town Splain treated my damage and are caring for me.>"

"<How were you damaged?>"

"<The human Cultists damaged me. The human Cultists are some of the bad humans.>"

He began examining her.

She squirmed. "<Stop scanning me with your ultrasound. You put a strange modulation on the sound that makes the sound tickle.>"

"<I must determine the extent of the damage. The modulation improves resolution and precision. You should learn how to make the modulation.>"

She pushed him with her snout. "<I am well.>"

"<You are damaged.>"

"<I am ... slightly damaged.>"

"<The damage to your hip is severe enough, but the damage to your chest is serious. The damage to your chest was almost fatal.>" <Kedekitley> moved to lay on <Arizesyley's> right side, hooked his tail around hers, and placed his neck and head against hers.

"<I will be well soon.>"

Naia said, "Language, language, language. Mother, Father, what are you saying?"

"Father is upset I am damaged." <Arizesyley> reached out to draw Naia into an embrace.

"It's okay, it's okay, it's okay, Father. Doctor Dan is taking good care of Mother."

<Kedekitley> said, "What happened?"

"The Cultists abducted us. Mother was brave. She saved us, but she got hurt doing it."

"Naia was brave and performed the task well." <Arizesyley> nuzzled Naia. "Naia stopped the human Cultists who were using a murder weapon crossbow and Gird-metal bolts to damage me. Naia damaged the human Cultists."

Sochi, Sasha, Asa, and Anitra approached.

Sochi said, "It was more than the Cultists. There were others, led by a man called *Mister Travis*, who want to restart the Dragon War. Naia took down two and Anitra took down another and wounded another all by themselves."

Anitra held up her chin, grinned, and said, "You should see my new spear."

Naia said, "We were protecting Mother. Mommy and Daddy would be proud of me."

"I am also proud of you." <Arizesyley> rubbed her head on Naia.

The humans who had retreated from <Kedekitley> returned to stand close.

<Kedekitley> said, "You said *the Cultists abducted us.* Who are *us?*"

"Me, and Anitra, and Grandpa Sochi, and Grandma Sasha, and Uncle Sten."

"The human Cultists took Human? Was Human damaged? Where is Human?" <Kedekitley> stood, looked around, and called out, "Human, where are you?"

"Dragon, I'm here." Human was running toward him.

<Kedekitley> galloped to meet him, scooped him up, and began turning him around as he scanned him with his ultrasound. "Human, are you damaged?" He then hooked his tail around him and rubbed his head on him.

Human wrapped his arms around <Kedekitley> and said, "I'm fine. I'm glad you're back." Human reached behind himself to scratch the back of his neck. "I missed you, Dragon. When I was in the thick of the fight, I needed you and I was afraid I'd never see you again." Human laid his cheek against <Kedekitley> and squeezed with his arms.

<Kedekitley> made a cooing sound as he felt warmth radiate from his core, from his heart, a warmth that filled him with joy.

They clutched each other for several moments more before Human said, "I need to give this to Naia." In his hand, Human held the object Naia normally wore around her neck. "Please, put me down, and come with me."

<Kedekitley> set Human down and followed as he went to Naia.

"Here's your locket, Naia. The picture you wanted turned out well."

Naia took the locket, opened it, smiled her exaggerated human smile, and said, "It's perfect. Thank you, thank you, thank you, Uncle Sten."

<Arizesyley> said, "All right then. What is a *locket*?"

The humans gathered closer to see Naia's locket.

"A *locket* is a small case for holding a keepsake." Naia held up the open locket with her hand covering the left side and showed it around. "See, this picture is of Mommy and Daddy. The other side had a picture of me when I was a baby, but I'm almost grown-up now. Uncle Sten made a new picture to put there." She uncovered the left side. "It's a picture of you, Mother, and you, Father."

A shimmer came to <Arizesyley's> eyes and she sighed. She picked up Naia, gave her a tail hug, rubbed her head on her, and said, "Naia, I love you."

To <Kedekitley>, <Arizesyley> said, "<The world has changed. I will keep the humans.>"

<Kedekitley> settled in the grass facing <Arizesyley>. Human sat on his arm and leaned against him.

"<I agree.>" <Kedekitley> hooked his tail over Human's hand. "<I had not understood how you knew your human child's feelings, and I had not understood the cause of your distress when away from your human child. From Improecley, Emidonley, and Mettagovley I learned that something happens when a dragon has a human friend. It has now happened to me. A connection forms. I can feel my human friend's happiness.>"

"<All right then. What is the cause?>"

"<I do not know the cause. This effect is something we need to study.>"

"<What happened at the Conclave? Did you do both of our presentations?>"

<Kedekitley> nodded. "<I designed a solution to the problem of combining our two solutions.>"

"<You do not sound enthusiastic.>"

He dipped his head. "<I failed.>"

"<That is good. I do not want to eradicate the humans now, at least not the good humans.>"

"<The Council also rejected making friends with the humans. The edict that dragons are not to interact with the humans remains.>"

"<That is not good.>"

"<Change begins with the actions of a few.>" <Kedekitley> paused to smile. "<I believe many dragons are already making friends with the humans in secret as we have and many more are ready to try. The Council cannot stop the process. Friendships with the humans are inevitable.>"

Naia said, "Language, language, language."

Human said, "We can tell you and Cinnamon are talking about something important. We feel left out."

<Kedekitley> nuzzled Human and said, "Cinnamon and my conversation was simple. The world has changed."

Thank You for Reading

Thank you for reading *The Dragon Universe Utopia Origins*. Please consider leaving a review on your site of choice. Reviews are important to every author's career.

Acknowledgement

Thank you Don and Melinda for your years of advice, critique, and patience as I practiced the skills of fiction writing.

About the Author

Lester D. Crawford writes speculative fiction. He enjoys creating science fiction and fantasy stories for all ages, stories that explore the relationships between contrasting characters and the struggles that bring them together, stories that use themes of love, loyalty, friendship, kindness, acceptance, family of origin, and family of choice.

He always wanted to be a story teller, to create science and science fiction and fantasy books and movies. However, he could not find that path.

The path our life takes is best described by chaos theory with chaotic regions, times of steady state, and areas with strange attracters. Unpredictable opportunities create many possible outcomes as we make our life choices.

Each of us is the product of those unpredictable opportunities. Even if we feel we are in control as we pursue our goals, that chance, accidents, and coincidences do not occur, and the journey feels well managed, we are still at the mercy of happenstance. When opportunities arise and we choose a path, the path not taken might have been the path we should have taken.

After years of experimenting with various opportunities, which eventually led to a career in information technology, Lester finally found the right path — the path that led to writing his stories.

Writing is a powerful tool. Writing enhances intelligence and critical-thinking skills for both writer and reader. Writing spreads knowledge today, and across generations. Writing forms bonds that can make the world a better place. Writing is magic.

Lester's stories bring him joy. He hopes his stories also bring you joy.

Thank you for your support.

www.LesterDCrawford.com
www.TheDragonUniverse.com
www.Dracotation.com

This rock is my rock.

www.ingramcontent.com/pod-product-compliance
Lightning Source LLC
Chambersburg PA
CBHW030910300726
48970CB00001B/91